Handsome, r

TYCOON
BACHELORS

Three sensual stories, bursting with
passion written by a bestselling author
you cannot afford to miss!

We're proud to present

MILLS & BOON

Spotlight

*a chance to buy collections of bestselling novels
by favourite authors every month – they're
back by popular demand!*

April 2008

The Barones: Rita, Emily & Alex

Featuring

Taming the Beastly MD by Elizabeth Bevarly
Where There's Smoke… by Barbara McCauley
Beauty and the Blue Angel by Maureen Child

Tycoon Bachelors by Anne Marie Winston

Featuring

Billionaire Bachelors: Ryan
Billionaire Bachelors: Stone
Billionaire Bachelors: Garrett

May 2008

The Barones: Joe, Daniel & Karen

Featuring

Cinderella's Millionaire by Katherine Garbera
The Librarian's Passionate Knight by Cindy Gerard
Expecting the Sheikh's Baby by Kristi Gold

Protecting Her

Featuring

Night Watch by Suzanne Brockmann
Downright Dangerous by Beverly Barton

TYCOON BACHELORS

ANNE MARIE WINSTON

Billionaire Bachelors: Ryan
Billionaire Bachelors: Stone
Billionaire Bachelors: Garrett

MILLS & BOON

Pure reading pleasure

*This collection is first published in Great Britain 2008.
Harlequin Mills & Boon Limited,
Eton House, 18-24 Paradise Road, Richmond, Surrey TW9 1SR*

TYCOON BACHELORS © Harlequin Books S.A. 2008.

The publisher acknowledges the copyright holders of the
individual works, which have already been published in the UK
in single, separate volumes, as follows:

Billionaire Bachelors: Ryan © Anne Marie Rodgers 2002
Billionaire Bachelors: Stone © Anne Marie Rodgers 2002
Billionaire Bachelors: Garrett © Anne Marie Rodgers 2002

ISBN: 978 0 263 86099 3

064-0408

*Printed and bound in Spain
by Litografia Rosés S.A., Barcelona*

Billionaire Bachelors: Ryan

ANNE MARIE WINSTON

MILLS & BOON
100 YEARS
of pure reading pleasure

100 Reasons to Celebrate

We invite you to join us in celebrating
Mills & Boon's centenary. Gerald Mills and
Charles Boon founded Mills & Boon Limited
in 1908 and opened offices in London's Covent
Garden. Since then, Mills & Boon has become
a hallmark for romantic fiction, recognised
around the world.

We're proud of our 100 years of publishing
excellence, which wouldn't have been achieved
without the loyalty and enthusiasm of our
authors and readers.

Thank you!

Each month throughout the year there will
be something new and exciting to mark the
centenary, so watch for your favourite authors,
captivating new stories, special limited
edition collections…and more!

ANNE MARIE WINSTON

RITA® Award finalist and bestselling author Anne Marie Winston loves babies she can give back when they cry, animals in all shapes and sizes and just about anything that blooms. When she's not writing, she's chauffeuring children to various activities, trying *not* to eat chocolate or reading anything she can find. She will dance at the slightest provocation and weeds her gardens when she can't see the sun for the weeds any more. You can learn more about Anne Marie's novels by visiting her website at www.annemariewinston.com.

For Mary Anne Trent

'Truly great friends are hard to find, difficult
to leave, and impossible to forget.'
—G Randolf

One

"Boston financial wizard Ryan Shaughnessy comes in sixth on our list of the Northeast's most desirable bachelors. Shaughnessy, 32, a self-made multimillionaire with diverse business interests, holds the patent on Securi-Lock, a decade-old technological innovation that has taken the world of home security in a new and vital direction. Widowed two years ago and childless, Shaughnessy makes his home in the exclusive Brookline community of Boston's Back Bay. He stands six-foot-three and weighs in at 205 pounds. If you want to capture the interest of this eminently available hunk, you should take up swimming, rowing and jogging."

Ryan Shaughnessy glared at his lunch date with ill-concealed poor humor. "Put that thing away."

Jessie Reilly was still chortling as she dropped the magazine back into her bag. "I'm impressed," she said, and the sparkle dancing in her eyes made him narrow his own. They'd grown up together and he knew that look. It usually meant trouble for him. "I mean, who'd ever have thought that skinny kid next door would grow up to be an 'eminently available hunk'?"

Ryan forgot to be annoyed as her amused gaze met his. Jessie looked as good as she always did to him, in a slim-fitting charcoal suit and high black boots to protect her feet from January's icy weather, and he felt the familiar little shock of attraction in his solar plexus when her wide smile lit her face. "If I'd known you were bringing that rag," he told her, "I might have skipped lunch." *Right. Like you'd ever miss an opportunity to spend time with Jessie.*

Jessie had been his neighbor during his childhood, his first hopeless adolescent love and his good friend forever. She joined him here on the third Wednesday of every month for lunch. As she shook her dark hair back from her face, it gleamed with coppery highlights. He was aware that more than one man in the room watched her as she relaxed at the table he'd reserved by the fireplace in the Ritz-Carlton Hotel's bar.

"I'm glad you didn't skip out on me," she told him. "I've been thinking about you, wondering how you're doing." Her eyes were a smoky green-gray in the winter light streaming through the windows that overlooked the Public Garden, a dark ring around the irises giving them a striking intensity. He knew she didn't just want to know generally how life was. She meant, "How are you getting along since Wendy's death?" She'd asked him the same question, casually sandwiched into their conversations, once a month for the past two years. But he didn't want to go there today, so he answered it in the general sense.

"Life's good. Business is good. How about you?"

Her eyes reproached him but she let it slide. "I'm all right. Business is...business."

Something in her tone made him glance sharply at her, and to his critical eye her expression looked troubled. "Something wrong at the gallery?"

"Not wrong, exactly." She hesitated. "I just learned this morning that my biggest rival in the area is expanding. Until now they haven't affected my business at all, but with a larger place and more inventory..." She shrugged. "It's a little worrisome."

Jessie owned a fine arts gallery a block away on Newbury Street that catered to the idle rich and those who aspired to the lifestyle. Ryan had bought gifts there in the past and he'd been impressed by both the quality and the unique selection of items she stocked. The prices...she clearly had targeted the well-to-do doctors and lawyers that blanketed the Boston population like the snow outside the windows covered the landscape. "So what are you going to do about it?"

"I don't know." Their drinks arrived, and she curled long, delicate fingers around the stem of her wineglass. "I've barely had time to think at all this morning. It was busy from the moment the doors opened until I sneaked out at lunch time." Then she shrugged her shoulders, deliberately shaking off her cares. "I'll figure something out, I'm sure."

"I'm sure you will." He toasted her with his drink. "You're one of the most resourceful people I know. Not to mention bullheaded, stubborn and tenacious."

She shot him a narrow-eyed stare. "Gee, thanks. I think." She took a sip of her drink.

The waitress approached and he ordered lobster sandwiches for each of them. They made small talk until their meals arrived, discussing the lousy—if expected—winter weather, a new artisan Jessie had discovered who hand wove silk scarves and blankets, a new idea he was kicking around.

Minutes later a shadow fell across the table. He glanced up, expecting food. Instead, a tall blonde with enormous blue eyes stood beside the table. She looked like she might be twenty-one. Maybe.

"Ryan Shaughnessy?" The voice was low, smoky, calculated to arouse.

"That's me. And this is Jessie Reilly."

Jessie started to offer her hand but the blonde merely flicked her one disinterested glance and then turned back to Ryan, giving him her hand as if she expected it to be kissed. "Hello. I'm Amalia Hunt. Of the Beacon Hill Hunts? Would you like to join me for dinner? Tonight, if you're available, or any night of your choosing."

Good God. Not again. He sighed and released her hand. "Miss Hunt. Of the Beacon Hill Hunts." It was hard to keep the sarcasm suppressed. The elite of Boston's elite were a truly unique species. Very taken with their own status and too insular to recognize that said status wasn't worth much in the real world. He sighed again. "Thank you for your kind offer, but I'm afraid I'll have to decline." He tilted his head meaningfully at Jessie.

The young woman's eyes flicked over Jessie again, probably estimating her net worth based on her wardrobe and jewelry. "My loss. But if you change your mind, here's my card." She leaned forward and tucked a business card into the breast pocket of his suit jacket, giving him a truly enjoyable view down the front of her low-cut blouse as she did so. "Bye-bye."

Jessie coughed, and he realized she was on the verge of choking with laughter. He glowered at her. Well, hell, he wasn't going to go out with Miss Beacon Hill, but he was a man, wasn't he?

The young woman drifted away, leaving dead silence in her wake.

"Don't say a word." Ryan looked across the table at Jessie. She was looking down at her linked hands again, but he knew it was only because she was trying not to burst into laughter. "Not...a...word," he repeated through his teeth.

The server appeared with their meals then, saving him for the moment.

When the man departed, Jessie said, "Well, gee, considering you used me as an excuse to brush off that poor little thing..."

"You were convenient," he said. "On the way here I got stopped by a woman with a similar proposition. I could have used you then, too."

Jessie grinned. "Such a cross to bear."

He ignored her needling as he applied himself to his meal. Lobster sandwiches were a house specialty, and they dug in.

Well, he dug in. Jess was a nibbler. She could make a meal last longer than it took a Southerner to recite the Declaration of Independence. When his sandwich was gone, he looked hopefully across at hers. She was still nibbling one section, but when she caught him eyeing the other half, she put a protective hand over it and said, "No way, José."

She knew him too well. "Never hurts to try."

When he looked back at Jessie, she was chewing her lower lip and her face looked troubled. Something was bugging her. Or she was thinking about something important. But given the way she was scrunching up her brow, he suspected a problem.

He and Jessie had grown up next door to each other in Charlestown, north of Boston across the Inner Harbor, squarely in the center of the blue-collar Irish district. That had been two decades before the first waves of young urban professionals had discovered the pretty, bow-fronted houses. His father had been a stonemason. She'd lived with her grandparents and her mother, who'd worked two jobs most of her life.

Jessie was two years younger than he. She'd been his first love. No, it had been infatuation, even if it had lasted an inordinately long time, he assured himself. And it hadn't been returned. As far as he knew, she'd never known how he felt about her when they'd been teenagers. It was probably a good thing. He treasured the friendship they still shared.

"You've got something on your mind," he said, resisting the urge to reach over and smooth the furrows from her forehead with his thumb.

It was an educated guess, but her eyes widened, and an odd look—consternation mixed with something that looked almost defiant—crossed her face. She nodded. "I do. I wanted to talk with you about a decision I'm considering."

"Why me?"

She eyed him cautiously. "Because you're my oldest friend and you probably know me better than anybody in the world and I need an honest opinion." She didn't pause for a single breath throughout the recitation.

He picked up his wine and took a sip, savoring the light, crisp taste of the vintage. "All right. What's up?"

"I'm thinking about having a baby."

He heard the words, but it was as if they hit an invisible

wall and bounced off. He shook his head slowly, trying to wrap his brain around the syllables and turn them into something sensible. *I'm thinking about having a baby.* Nope. They still didn't want to compute. Hell, he'd expected her to bring up something to do with her business. Something for which she needed his financial wisdom.

Carefully, not meeting her eyes, he said, "I wasn't aware you were...with anyone."

"I'm not."

Thank God. The reaction was immediate and instinctive, relief rushing through him so heavily he felt as if he might sag beneath its weight.

It was only that he felt protective toward her, he assured himself. Nothing more. Well, at least, nothing more than serious fondness. He'd loved her wildly, futilely, through his high school years, had pined for her during college when she'd been with someone else, had finally recognized his obsession, conquered it and married a wonderful woman. Jessie and Wendy had been friends from the day they'd met, as well. Wendy had joined them at these lunches often in what he thought of now as "the old days." It was only natural that he would still feel some attachment to Jessie. She was a large part of his past.

"Ryan?" Her voice called him back to the present. "Are you all right? I didn't mean to give you such a shock."

Slowly he shook his head to clear it. "If you're not in a relationship, then how do you propose to, ah, get started on a baby?"

"That's what a cryobank is for."

"A cryobank?" He knew what she meant but he couldn't believe what he was hearing.

Color rose in her cheeks and she didn't meet his eyes. "It's a sperm freezing and storage facility." She reached

into her satchel again as she spoke. "I've already been
through a battery of tests at a fertility center. I've had
some preliminary testing and a physical. They started me
on some special vitamins and things. I'm considered an
excellent candidate for pregnancy. All I have to do is select a donor and have the procedure done."

"The procedure?"

"Artificial insemination." She came up for air with a
folder clutched in her hand. "I've already selected some
possibilities but I wanted your opinion." She extended the
folder across the table.

Ryan stared at it, making no move to take it. "Tell me
you're not serious."

Jessie's gaze was level. She didn't speak.

"Oh, hell." He rested his elbows on the table and
speared the fingers of both hands through his hair. "You
are serious. Jess…why? Why this way? Why right now?"

"I'm going to be thirty in November, Ryan." Her voice
was quiet. All traces of the earlier humor had fled. "I
want a family. Children," she amended. "I want to be a
parent while I'm still young and energetic enough to keep
up with my kids and enjoy them." Unspoken between
them was the memory of her own childhood, one that he
knew had been lonely and joyless. He remembered her
grandparents as stuffy, disapproving old prunes who had
never forgiven their only daughter for an out-of-wedlock
pregnancy. And Jessie's mother…well, the best thing his
own mother, who rarely had a harsh word to say about
anyone, had said was, "It wouldn't kill her to cuddle that
little girl once in a while."

"Thirty is young," he said desperately. "Women are
having children well into their forties these days. Why
don't you wait just a few more years? You might feel
totally differently—"

"I didn't ask you to criticize me," she said sharply, and he could see the rising Irish temper that went with the red glints in her hair. "I've already decided to have a baby. I merely wanted your opinion on which donor I should choose. But just forget it." She started to withdraw the folder, but he grabbed it from her.

"Wait." He was stalling, trying to think of some way to talk her out of this insane idea. The thought of Jessie, *his* Jessie, going to a sperm bank, caused his chest to grow tight with repugnance. "I'll look at them."

He placed the folder in front of him, looking down over the list of information contained on the first set of stapled sheets, then scanning the second and the third. There were at least three more. "These don't provide a lot of information."

"Oh, these are just the preliminary profiles," she said. "If I like some of these, I'll request medical and personal profiles that are much more detailed. Family background, academic records, that sort of thing."

"Who fills these out?"

"There are medical evaluations and personality test, things like that," she said, "but most of the personal information comes from the…the donors." She looked past him rather than at him.

"And does anyone check to see if they're telling the truth?"

"I…well…I don't know." Her eyebrows rose. "Why would they lie?"

"Beats me. But to assume that the information these anonymous men volunteer is accurate…isn't that a pretty big risk? I read a case about a guy who knew he carried a rare genetic heart defect that often resulted in death during the young adult years—and he lied on his application. Later, he had an attack of guilt and told his genetics counselor, but when they contacted the sperm bank, his sperm already had produced successful pregnancies for several women. It was a big bioethical mess.''

Jessie rubbed her temples with her hands. "That has to be a pretty isolated incident, though, don't you think?"

"You'll be living with the results for the rest of your life," he said impatiently. "What if the guy just neglected to mention that diabetes runs rampant in his family? Or schizophrenia? Or that he's got other hereditary diseases or conditions in his genetic makeup that could affect your child?"

"They screen the donations for genetic problems and diseases," she said. "All the donors have complete physicals and genetic work-ups. I have some literature on it."

"But they couldn't possibly check for everything," he pointed out. "And are there background checks to see if these men are telling the truth about themselves?"

"I...I don't know. I doubt it." Jessie looked shell-shocked. "But they're supposed to fill in everything they know."

"And maybe they do." He made a deliberate effort to soften his censorious tone. "Probably 99 percent of these men are honest and trustworthy. Hell, maybe they all are. But you have to assume that there could be some false-hoods, for your own protection."

Jessie sighed deeply. "Darn it, Ryan. I should have known I'd be more confused than I already am after I'd talked with you."

"Thank you," he said.

"It *wasn't* a compliment." But she smiled. Reaching across the table, she took the folder from him and replaced it in her satchel, then shook her head. Her eyes were troubled. "I was planning to do this the next time I ovulate, but I can see this is going to require a lot more thought than I'd anticipated.''

He couldn't dredge up an appropriate response to that, so he merely murmured, ''Good.''

The rest of the meal went quickly. She declined coffee, telling him she had to get back to relieve one of her sales staff, and they parted outside the Ritz. As he bent to kiss her cheek and she tilted her face up to his, the sweet scent of her filled him with an unexpectedly sharp longing, and he nearly closed his arms about her before he could catch himself. Unaware of his mental turmoil, Jessie backed away a step and waggled her fingers at him with an impish grin. ''Same time, same place next month, big boy.''

He managed a wave and stood for a long moment as she turned and walked down Arlington Street. Finally he turned and moved off in the other direction, taking a right on Beacon Street past the Public Garden and the Commons, heading back to his office on State Street in the financial district.

As he paced off the steps, his mind churned. What had happened back there? It was just that he missed having a woman in his life, he assured himself. Since his wife's death in a traffic accident, he'd led a lonely life. Being half of a couple had suited him. It had felt comfortable. He hated going home to the costly mansion in Brookline now, hated the silence after the day staff had left in the evening. He hated attending cocktail parties and charity events and having eager mothers thrusting their oh-so-eligible daughters in his path. The bottom line was that he simply hated being single.

And then there was the thought of children, which he'd put out of his mind years ago. Until Jessie's bright idea had dredged it up again.

Children. A stab of longing pierced him. He'd wanted

kids with Wendy, always assumed they'd start a family someday…but it hadn't been quite that simple. And now she was gone.

So marry Jessie. She wants a baby…you want a family.

The idea was so shocking that he stopped dead in the middle of the sidewalk on Tremont Street, causing a woman walking past to glance at him oddly.

Marry Jessie. The thought made his heart race alarmingly. Wryly, he acknowledged that some things never changed. Part of him was still that adolescent boy with the crush on his lissome young neighbor.

Marry Jessie. She was as different from his deceased wife as two women could be. Wendy had been blond and blue-eyed, petite and yet buxom. She'd been quietly charming, almost passive, rarely arguing with him. She'd been content to make a home for them; she'd felt no need to prove herself in a career. She'd been musical and elegant. Each night when he'd come home there'd been drinks in the drawing room.

Jessie…Jessie wasn't any of those things. Except elegant. With those long legs and the graceful way she carried herself, she was most definitely that. His mouth curved at the mere notion of Jess sitting home waiting for any man. She was volatile, determined to succeed at her business. If she disagreed with him, she said so in no uncertain terms. She had a tin ear, although she got offended if anyone suggested that perhaps she shouldn't sing.

For the first time, the striking differences made him pause. Could he have chosen Wendy, in part, *because* she was so completely unlike Jess?

It was an unnerving thought. He'd told himself he was over Jessie, that she'd been an adolescent fantasy. He'd married another woman and forgotten her. But in the back of his mind, he had to admit that it was possible he'd been comparing other women to her for the past ten years or more. And he *was* over her, he assured himself. Just because he couldn't stop thinking about her now didn't mean anything except that he was still as physically attracted to her as he'd always been.

So where did that leave him? Was it ridiculous to think that he could make a life with her now, a life that included the children he'd always wanted?

He'd reached his building, walking most of the way on automatic pilot while he'd thought of her, and as he stepped out of the elevator and walked down the hall to his office, a new determination hardened within him. The moment he'd hung up his coat and taken his messages from his office assistant, he went into his inner office and closed the door. Then he reached for the phone.

What did he have to lose?

After lunch Jessie was answering a customer's questions about a line of glazed pottery she carried when the telephone rang. Excusing herself, she moved to the phone. "The Reilly Gallery. May I help you?"

"Jess."

A small shock of surprise ran through her. "Ryan?" Normally she didn't see or hear from him from one month to the next unless they crossed paths at some social function. "Did I forget something?"

"No." There was an odd quality to his voice, as if he were unsure of something. "I wondered if…I'm calling to ask you to have dinner with me."

Dinner. With Ryan. "Why?"

He chuckled, and abruptly he sounded like the adult she'd come to know, self-confident and calm. "I had some other thoughts about your, um, selection process that I wanted to discuss with you.''

"Oh.'' Well, that was good, wasn't it? After what he'd said at lunch, she'd been in a blue funk thinking about the risks. "When and where?''

"How's tomorrow night? I'll pick you up. Seven all right?''

"Tomorrow evening works for me. And seven is fine.'' What she really wanted to say was that tomorrow night was *soon*. But she didn't have any reason to delay, and she didn't even know why she instinctively wanted to do so.

When she hung up the phone, her assistant had taken over with the customer she'd been helping, so she headed into her small office. On her desk was a loan application she'd picked up from her bank on the way back to the gallery after lunch. Ryan's question, "What are you going to do about it?'' had occupied her thoughts during the walk, and she'd realized she had little choice. If she wanted to compete, she was going to have to expand. And to expand, she'd either have to get a loan, or use the money she'd set aside for the artificial insemination. And using that fund wasn't something she was prepared to do.

Thoughtfully she stared at the application. Although she regularly paid on the loan she'd taken out when she started her store, she had a line of credit that was running a little higher than it should right now. It was a temporary thing, based largely on the inventory she'd recently ordered in anticipation of the spring and summer tourist season. But she suspected she'd have to pay it down before she could get a loan. And then there were the sales figures…it would take a few days to pull all that together.

Another loan. Or, if she rolled her current one into it, a larger loan. The mere thought made her nervous. She'd

worked hard to get to where she was now. She could pay
her bills, live comfortably and save for a leisurely retirement someday. To her, loans meant that someone else
would own what she'd worked so hard to build, and with
that came the implied threat of loss. Her business was her
independence; she *couldn't* lose it. Still, she shouldn't
have any trouble meeting her financial obligations even if
they increased. It would simply mean cutting her personal
spending and watching her pennies at the gallery. But she
wasn't at all sure she was going to look like a good bet
to Mr. Brockhiser, the lender at Boston Savings with
whom she would be dealing.

The rest of the afternoon was insane, and it wasn't until
Jessie closed the door to her apartment that evening that
she thought about Ryan again. Thoughtfully she put away
her coat, boots, scarf and gloves. Her home was only four
blocks from her shop, and like many Bostonians, she preferred to hoof it as much as possible rather than fight the
notoriously clogged roadways.

She was afraid Ryan might be right about the sperm
donations. How *did* she know that what she saw on those
profiles was accurate? The screening process had sounded
so complete when she first read through it. But the bottom
line was that this was, at best, a game of chance.

When she'd first gone to discuss the procedure at the
fertility center, they'd asked her if she had a donor lined
up or if she planned to select one from a cryobank's stock.
She'd never even considered asking any of her friends to
donate *sperm,* for heaven's sake! She'd thought it would
be far too embarrassing. Not to mention the fact that
something within her warned her against using a friend
for such a purpose. What if the guy wanted rights to her
child at some later date? Probably an irrational fear, but...
And what about the fact that most of the decent men she

knew were already married, some with children of their own? She couldn't, and shouldn't, generalize, but she knew it would bother *her* if an acquaintance asked the man she loved to donate sperm for another woman's child. Oh, she'd read about people who'd done it, but it just wasn't an approach she felt comfortable using.

So that left bachelors. Jessie shuddered. Most of the single men she knew were single for a reason. She'd dated a number of them and hadn't been impressed by one yet. How could she possibly ask a guy she didn't even like? Okay, so that meant she could really narrow down the list, she thought as she pulled a bag of premixed tossed salad from her refrigerator and poured some into a bowl. There was a chicken breast left over from the ones she'd baked last night for herself and her assistant manager, Penny, and as she carried the food and a glass of Napa Valley Zinfandel to the small table in her kitchen alcove, she grabbed a pen and paper to start a list.

Let's see. She swirled the wine and inhaled, appreciating the fruity odors before she took a first, experimental drink. There was Edmund Lloyd. He wasn't so bad, except for that little stutter he sometimes couldn't get past. Was that a hereditary trait? She put a little question mark by Edmund's name. She'd have to see what she could find out about stuttering on the Internet.

She thought some more. What about Charles Bakler? He was a dear. But…not the brightest crayon in the box. And she wanted her baby to be intelligent. She put a frowning face beside Charles's name.

Okay. Surely she could come up with more desirable single men that that! What about Ryan? *No.* She dismissed the idea almost as quickly as it popped into her head. She could never ask Ryan. Not an option. But still…to be fair, she should list him. So she did. She didn't write anything at all beside his name.

Geoff Vertler. A possibility, except he was a pretty hearty partier, and she wouldn't want to inadvertently give her baby a predisposition to alcoholism.

Laying down the pencil, Jessie exhaled a frustrated sigh. This was stupid! She didn't even know as much about these men as she did about the candidates she'd chosen from the sperm bank. *If* what they'd written was true.

You know almost everything about Ryan, said that sneaky little voice in her head. Oh, Lord. She took a big slug of her wine. He really would be the logical choice. The one man she'd known nearly her entire life. He was smart, he was kind, he didn't have any horrible health secrets hidden in his family history. He was well coordinated, she knew, since he'd played soccer in high school and college, and he could even sing. Physically, he was...perfect. If she had a son who looked exactly like Ryan, she'd be thrilled.

But how could she ask him? Shaking her head, she pushed away from the table and rose. No way. She just couldn't.

But as she rinsed her dishes and put them in the dishwasher, a thought struck her. She was having dinner with him tomorrow night. And he'd said he had some other ideas to share with her. What if he was planning to offer to be the donor for her baby? She put a hand to her mouth—that had to be it! Why else would he want to have dinner? They normally had their monthly luncheon and went their separate ways.

Jessie danced down the hallway to her bedroom. It was perfect! She'd never have been able to approach him about it, but if he offered...just perfect. And she didn't have to worry about offending his wife since he didn't have one.

The thought doused her good humor, and she slowly tugged off her clothes and donned the oversize T-shirt in which she slept. It was purely an accident that Ryan didn't have a wife anymore. An awful, unexpected accident.

Climbing into bed, she set her alarm and snapped off the bedside lamp. But sleep eluded her.

She'd been at the University of Alabama getting her degree when Ryan had met Wendy, and she hadn't come home for the wedding. And by the time she'd come back to Boston, they had married, and Ryan already had begun to make history and money with the invention that had founded his fortune.

Wendy. She could still remember the ridiculous stab of jealousy she'd felt the first time Ryan had introduced them. Wendy had been petite and curvy, with big, arresting blue eyes and pretty cornsilk hair. She'd clung shyly to Ryan's hand, and Jessie had been jolted by the fierce feeling of possessiveness that had shot through her. Ryan had been *her* friend; for years and years the first person to whom she ran when things went wrong was the boy next door. Two years older, quiet and intelligent, he'd helped her survive what she now realized was an emotionally abusive childhood. They'd had a special bond. And though it had dimmed when she'd begun going steady with the captain of the high school football team and nearly died when she'd followed Chip south to Alabama, Ryan still had been *hers* in some indefinable way.

Jessie had chided herself for being childish and resolved to be pleasant to Wendy Shaughnessy, and to her surprise it hadn't been a chore. If there was a sweeter person alive, someone would have to prove it to Jessie.

Wendy had become a dear friend. In fact, it was she who had suggested the monthly luncheon tradition.

Who would have thought they'd be carrying on without her after only six short years?

And who, she asked herself wryly just before she finally fell asleep, ever would have imagined that Ryan would father Jessie's child? But she was sure that's what he was going to suggest. She could hardly wait for tomorrow evening!

Two

He took her to L'Espalier, a converted town house that had become one of Back Bay's premiere restaurants. It was only a few blocks from her home, but Jessie had never been there before. Partly because it was quite pricey, but also because L'Espalier was one of those places people went to celebrate life's milestones.

Over a truly superb vegetarian meal, though, Ryan showed no signs of getting around to the reason he'd asked her there. Much as they had yesterday, he kept the conversation impersonal, telling her about various causes for which he'd recently been solicited, asking her opinion on which ones would be the best to support. Maybe he'd changed his mind. Her heart sank. Could she force herself to ask him?

When she declined dessert, he asked for the check, and before she knew it, they were back on Marlborough Street, heading for her apartment. They both were silent as they walked along the sidewalk. Each of them had their gloved hands in their pockets, and walked carefully through the darkened streets; there were icy patches in unexpected places left over from a storm the week before.

Twice she opened her mouth and closed it without speaking. How to bring up the topic? Maybe he felt as embarrassed as she did. Maybe she should just go ahead and ask him. But she couldn't. Her vocal cords simply froze at the thought of asking Ryan to donate sperm. At the same time she was all too aware of his tall, broad-shouldered figure. She'd never looked at him as anything but a dear friend in the most platonic sense, but the whole notion of creating a child raised the specter of sexual intimacy, and try as she might, she couldn't rid herself of a new fascination with him. She would not, she reminded herself for at least the fiftieth time, engage in prurient thoughts about this man who'd been such a dear friend.

Right.

He had grown into an extraordinarily attractive man. His dark hair was thick and glossy and his eyes were a striking blue, made even more vivid when he had a tan through the summer months. As a child and a teenager he'd been tall but scrawny and awkward. Once he'd begun weight training, his arms had become muscular and strong. Apparently, he'd kept up some sort of fitness routine, because his shoulders now were almost bulky, and his upper arms filled out the sleeves of his suit jackets.

Stop it! Jessie told herself. Again. Ryan was her friend, not a potential lover. She ignored the quickening of her pulse.

In a few more moments they were back at her apartment building. In the hallway outside her door, she turned to him. But before she could speak, he said, ''May I come in? I asked you out tonight for a purpose and I've been trying to get around to it all evening.'' He smiled wryly. ''Trying to work up my courage.''

Relief washed through her. ''Of course. I've been wondering about it. How about if I make us some coffee?''

''Sounds good.'' He followed her as she unlocked her door and stepped into the small foyer.

Jessie took his coat and waved him into the living room while she hung up their outerwear and went into the kitchen to start some coffee. She put a paper doily on a small plate, then got some grapes from the bowl on her counter and arranged them on the tray with a handful of peanut butter cookies she'd gotten from the deli down the street on her way home earlier. Pulling out a tray, she set the plate on it along with creamer, sugar and spoons. She was pretty sure he drank his coffee black.

In another moment her little coffeemaker had finished, and she poured two cups. Walking into the living room, she set the tray on the table before the sofa and took a seat. Ryan had been standing at the window, looking out into the dark night. But when he heard her, he turned and came over to stand near her. ''Sit down,'' she invited, patting the cushion beside her.

''Thanks.'' He did so, then picked up his cup and took a drink, grimacing at the heat. She noted with satisfaction that she'd been right—he drank it black. ''Your apartment's nice,'' he said. ''I've never seen where you live before.''

''I don't do the hostess thing,'' she said. ''It's too small for parties. But given the price of real estate in Back Bay right now, I'm lucky to have it at all.''

There was a small, awkward silence between them.

Finally, Ryan stirred and turned toward her. ''Jessie, we've been friends for a long time. I know you want children.'' He took a deep breath. ''And so do I. Will you marry me?''

What? She couldn't have heard him right. But she knew she had, and her voice showed her agitation when she spoke. ''No! Ryan, that's not what I want—I mean, you don't really want to marry me, either. When you called, I thought…I thought…''

''You thought what?'' His voice was flat and distant as he stared into his coffee cup.

She felt a blush creeping up her neck into her cheeks. ''Well, I thought you were going to offer to be a…a donor.''

''You what?'' His mouth dropped open much as hers had a moment before, and his gaze shot to hers.

''I thought about what you said all day.'' She rushed on, wanting only to get this over with. ''You're right about anonymous men being risky. So I decided it would be better to ask someone I know to be a donor. But most of my friends are married, and I didn't really feel comfortable…so I made a list of bachelors—''

''And my name was at the top of your list?'' His voice sounded incredulous and his distaste was clear.

''Well, yes.'' She looked away from the cool blue eyes. ''I've known you practically forever and I know your family.'' She shrugged. ''It seemed like a logical idea.'' She could see from the dark frown that drew his brows into a single thick line that he was about to refuse so she kept on. ''Please, Ry? I'm serious about this baby. It would really, really mean a lot to me.''

But he shook his head. ''I don't think so, Jess.''

''But why?'' She was pleading and she knew it.

''I wouldn't be—I'm not comfortable with the idea that a child of mine would be raised never knowing me, never knowing I'm its father.'' He shook his head again, decisively, and her heart sank. "It would bother me not to be involved in my child's life."

"This is exactly the reaction I was afraid most of my married friends would have." She made an effort to soften her tone. "But I didn't expect it from you."

"I didn't expect it from me, either, but then I never expected *you* to ask me to do something like this." He looked down into his coffee cup again, hesitated, then shook his head. "I couldn't do it, Jess. It wouldn't be my child, legally, but I'd feel connected, responsible. I'd want to hold it, to play with it, to watch it grow up and be involved in its life. I can't imagine knowing I had a child somewhere in the world and not being a father to it." He spread his hands. "I want kids of my own. I want to give a child memories as wonderful as the ones I have of my own parents."

She was stunned by the passion in his voice. Her throat felt thick as she remembered the two people who had raised Ryan and his brother, the two people who had opened their arms and their hearts and included her in their charmed circle anytime she entered their home.

She cleared her throat. "I never even knew you wanted children." She spread her hands. "You were married to Wendy for six years—"

"Wendy couldn't conceive." His voice was harsh now and abrupt. He stood so suddenly he knocked against the table, and the coffee sloshed in the cups. Stalking over to the window, he shoved his jacket back and put his hands on his hips. "We wanted them. Badly. But we tried for three years with no luck and then spent another one finding out what the problem was. We tried in-vitro fertilization twice but no luck. And then she died."

She eyed the rigid line of his shoulders, and her heart squeezed painfully. She'd been thinking selfishly and was sick at heart that she'd inadvertently caused him sadness. Softly she said, "I'm sorry to bring up something painful to you. If I'd known, I never would have—"

"It's not exactly something you want to share with the world." His voice was curt.

Hurt pierced her heart. She wasn't "the world." She'd thought she was his oldest friend. But apparently, in his mind, that old bond didn't mean the same thing it still meant to her. She felt the hot sting of tears at the backs of her eyes and she strove to breathe deeply, to stay calm.

At the window Ryan turned, and she quickly dropped her head. As she did so, one fat tear plopped down onto her hands, tightly clenched in her lap. Smoothing it away with her thumb, she kept her head bent as he resumed his seat beside her.

"Jess?" His voice was quiet. "I don't want to argue with you. You mean too much to me."

"You mean a lot to me, too," she said. And then her voice broke and she turned at the same instant he did, moving into the arms he held wide.

Jessie had danced with Ryan before, hugged him occasionally, brushed quick friendly kisses on his cheek. But she'd never known she'd find such comfort in his embrace. Even when his parents had died, they hadn't shared a closeness like this. He'd had Wendy to comfort him then. Now his arms were hard and muscled beneath the fabric of his jacket, his shoulder a wide plane just right for her head. When she felt him press a kiss into her hair, she smiled. "I have a great idea," she said.

"What's that?" His voice rumbled up from beneath her ear.

"Let's forget this whole stupid conversation. Just pretend it never existed."

He was quiet for a moment. "If that's what you want."

She frowned, drawing back and looking him in the eye. "Isn't that what you want?"

He shrugged, hesitated. Finally he said, "I still think marriage would be a good plan, if you want to know the truth. We both want the same thing, Jess. I think we could be happy together."

She sighed. "We're never going to go back to the way we were, are we?" she asked sadly.

Soberly he shook his head. "Doubt it."

Fear shot through her at the cool, measured tone. The last thing she wanted was to lose him altogether. Reluctantly she said, "All right." She folded her hands in her lap. "Explain exactly why you think we should get married." *Get married…get married…* The words echoed in her head. Was she really having *this* conversation with *this* man?

"Okay." He stood and began to walk the length of her living room, such as it was. "Selfish reasons first. Number one—I've got ridiculous numbers of women throwing themselves at me ever since that stupid article came out. You saw how it is today. Marriage would kill all that."

"One of them might make a good wife." But she hoped not.

He shook his head. "Any woman who would come on to a man like that is *not* a woman I'd want to date, much less marry."

"Maybe not." She shouldn't feel so relieved by his terse words. After all, she didn't want to marry him. Did she? Of course not. Ryan deserved to find another woman like Wendy, a woman who would adore him and whom he could adore in return. It wouldn't be fair at all to trap him into marriage to her simply because they shared a history and a common goal.

You both could do a lot worse, pointed out a small devil's voice inside her head.

That might be true, but what if it didn't work out? A tremor ran through her at the mere idea. She didn't think she could bear losing Ryan, as she surely would if they married and it was a disaster. He'd been the rock that anchored her stormy childhood, and he still was her dearest friend in all the world. She couldn't—*wouldn't*—do anything to jeopardize that.

"Number two." Unaware of her mental deliberations, he held up two fingers of his right hand. "I liked being married. I liked coming home to someone, sharing meals, sharing conversation. Wendy and I were friends. We could talk about anything." He looked at her. "You and I have that, too."

Jessie nodded. But she was very aware that there was one thing he hadn't mentioned sharing in a marriage: a bed. A tingle of awareness shot through her, shocking her with its intensity.

"Number three," he went on. "I want children. Of my own. Running through my house making noise, breaking windows with baseballs—"

"They might be girls," she said automatically, still preoccupied by the strange feelings rioting through her.

But Ryan didn't respond. He stopped pacing, his back to her, and she could see the tension in the rigid set of his shoulders and the way his head drooped. Sensing pain in his silence, she rose and went to him, wrapping her arms around him from behind as far as they would go.

The butterflies that had been plaguing her returned the moment she touched him. He felt bulky and muscular, warm beneath her hands, and his strong back, against which she pressed herself, was as unyielding as steel. He smelled of some expensive cologne and the clean scent of drycleaned wool. Then he turned, dislodging her hold. Placing his hands on her shoulders, he bent his head and kissed her temple.

Her breath caught in her throat and she stepped back, giving him room. As she lifted her gaze to face him, he said, "So what are your objections?"

She shook her head. "When you get hold of an idea, you don't let go, do you?"

He grinned. "Just noticing?"

She smiled, then crossed her arms and lifted a finger to tap her lips. "Objections. Hmm." She spread her hands, loath to put all the things running through her head into words. "I don't know. I haven't even given marriage a thought since I was too young to know better."

"With what's-his-name."

"His name was Chip and you know it. You never liked him, did you?"

Ryan shrugged. "Maybe I just didn't think he was good enough for you."

She laughed. "You were right. And thank God I figured it out before I married him!" Then she sobered. "Actually, he was a great guy. Just not for me. I realized that I liked the things I got from him—security, adoration, the illusion of belonging—a lot more than I liked *him*. And marriage wouldn't have been fair to him." She fell silent.

"Back to your objections," he prompted.

"I don't *know*," she protested. "I suppose I always assumed that when I married it would be for the usual reasons."

"The usual reasons?"

"You know. Love," she said, throwing her arms wide. "And passion."

As soon as the words were out, she saw his face change. Though he hadn't moved, she suddenly felt as if all the air in the room were supercharged. A strange, wild flame leaped, deep in his blue eyes, and his gaze dropped to her mouth, igniting a quivering spark in her abdomen that made her catch her breath in shock. "Passion, I can promise you," he said, his voice soft and low.

Jessie was stunned. This was *Ryan,* for heaven's sake! Her friend.

But the feelings coursing through her weren't those of friendship. She felt as though an invisible cord inexorably tugged her toward him. She could almost feel his strong arms around her again. Her body ached to feel him pressed against her, and her lips practically tingled beneath his intent gaze.

Good Lord. How had she not noticed how incredibly sexy he was for all these years? Or had she? Had she simply refused to acknowledge the deep pull of attraction between them? After all, he'd been married.

"Ryan?" Her voice sounded like a stranger's.

He took a step toward her, and she instinctively put out a hand to hold him off. But he took it and tugged her toward him. "Don't you think we should explore what we could have between us?" Pulling her into his arms, he folded her firmly against him. Her hands splayed wide over his biceps. She intended to push him away, but her limbs felt weak and shaky, and when he didn't release her, she simply stood in his embrace, feeling the erotic electricity that flowed from him to her. She was shockingly aware of his hard body against hers, of the checked power in his close hold.

Jessie's teeth were practically chattering with nerves. "I…I don't know. I never thought about you—about me and you—as anything more than friends." She felt tears fill her eyes yet again. "You're the best friend I have in the whole world, and I don't want to screw things up and lose you. I *need* you to be my friend, Ry.''

Silence fell. Ryan didn't move. He didn't release her, nor did he tighten his arms. She kept her head down, knowing that if she raised her face to his right now this whole discussion would be moot, and their relationship would change forever. And despite the words of caution she'd just uttered, she couldn't stop herself from wondering what it would be like with Ryan. Would he be slow and gentle or as hot and wild as the sensations ripping through her right now? She saw again in her mind the light in his eyes and heard his deep, rough voice: *Passion I can promise you.*

His hands were on her back, and as he shifted them slightly, rubbing gentle patterns over her sensitive flesh, she shuddered. Had she ever wanted to cast rational thought to the winds so badly? Her body warred with her mind for another long moment. But finally she heaved a deep sigh and pushed back from his embrace. This time he let her go.

''No,'' she said, trying to invest her tone with a firmness she didn't feel. ''This wouldn't be right.'' She turned away, hugging her arms tightly about herself. ''I'm sorry.'' She knew the words were inadequate, but her throat felt as if someone were squeezing it with a vise.

Behind her she heard his footsteps as he went to the closet and took out his coat. Fabric rustled as he donned his outerwear, then he walked to her, stepping into her line of vision and lifting her chin with one finger. Jessie had been standing with her eyes closed, but she forced herself to open them and gaze into his blue ones.

And the moment she did, she knew that nothing would be as it had been before. Awareness leaped and crackled between them like well-fed flames.

"All right," he said. "Friends it is. But the offer of marriage still stands. Think about it."

She nodded, unable to trust her voice.

He dropped his hand from her face, stepped away. "Good night."

Jessie didn't sleep well that night. Or any night for the rest of the week. On Saturday she threw away the preliminary profiles of the donors. Although she didn't believe the process carried the risks that Ryan thought it did, it seemed impersonal and distasteful to her now.

On Sunday she walked through the Public Gardens. A young couple passed her, their faces alive with laughter as their toddler, awkward and stiff in layers of bulky winter clothing, ran in circles until she was dizzy. As the father scooped the pink-cheeked child into his arms, the baby squealed with laughter, and Jessie felt her heart contract with pain.

Why shouldn't she have that joy? Just because she hadn't been lucky enough to find someone with whom she could share her life—

Ah, but you had someone, her inner self reminded her. *And you gave him away.*

Chip. She'd been courted by a star member of the football team during her first year of high school. At the time, she hadn't given the guy behind the persona a serious thought. He'd been popular; every girl in the school had envied her. At fifteen, that was what it all had been about. In her naïveté, she'd never really thought about the fact that they had next to nothing in common. To her he'd represented safety. Security. Someone who loved her unconditionally, darn near worshipped her, for heaven's sake. In her whole life there had never been anyone like that. Ryan had been her lifeline during her childhood, but he'd distanced himself when she began dating Chip, and she'd rarely seen him after he'd left for college. Looking back, she almost felt as if he'd abandoned her. Was it any wonder she had followed Chip south to school?

It wasn't until she'd gotten to college that she'd begun to grow and change, to realize that the world was a big place and her choices were limitless. And as she had, she'd realized that she could never make a life with Chip.

She'd been fond of him, but she hadn't loved him. To marry him would have been unfair to them both. She'd used him as a crutch for a very long time, and she prayed that he'd found some sweet girl and was married, that they were happily raising half a dozen little football players and cheerleaders.

And that thought brought her back to her present problem. She could have married and had children with Chip. But…something had stopped her. She hadn't known at the time exactly why he wasn't right. She'd just known he wasn't.

And after she'd settled down in Boston and gotten her shop established, she hadn't found the right man, either.

Will you marry me?

Ryan's words echoed over and over again in her head. Was it possible she'd been tempted to blurt out, "Yes!" for one ridiculous, impetuous instant?

Familiarity, she decided. Ryan had known her forever. He knew all her warts and quirks. They had a number of interests in common. Living with Ryan would be comfortable in many ways.

But as she remembered the breathless, shocking awareness that had swamped her when he'd taken her in his arms, the word *comfortable* wasn't the one that seemed to apply.

That line of thought was dangerous. Her mind shied

away from any examination of exactly what had happened last night. Instead she focused on his refusal to help her in her quest for motherhood. She should have realized, would have, if she'd thought about it longer, that Ryan Shaughnessy would have difficulty with the concept of a biological child to which he had no rights or attachment.

Ryan's family had been a close and loving one. She should know. Hadn't she sought refuge in Mrs. Shaughnessy's plump arms more than once? Mr. Shaughnessy had been warm and boisterous, including her in the games of pitch-and-catch with Ryan and his older brother, tossing her high in the air just to hear her scream. And on the occasions when she'd eaten at the Shaughnessy house, the teasing camaraderie and open love in their home had never failed to amaze her.

Her family had been very different. Her mother, as far as Jessie could tell, felt that raising a child was little more than a duty. Her grandparents regarded her as a trial, a punishment sent by God for some unfathomable crime. They had failed as parents when their only daughter had gotten herself pregnant and, even worse, refused to marry—or even name—the father of her baby.

Unless they'd been a lot different during her mother's childhood, Jessie thought it likely that her mother had succumbed to the first man ever to say a kind word to her. A mistake Jessie herself very nearly had made with Chip, although he'd been quite different from the man who'd apparently seduced and waltzed away from her mother.

No, thank goodness she'd gotten smart. She wasn't *ever* going to believe that a man was her ticket to fulfillment. She knew better.

And where did that leave her? Alone, childless, aching for her life to mean something to somebody. Which was why, if she was honest with herself, she felt so strongly about having a child of her own.

She thought again of her fears, weighed them against the certainty of years passing her by. Could she marry Ryan? Perhaps he was right about their friendship being a good basis for the marriage. But...what if she didn't conceive? What would happen then? She had friends who had infertility problems, and the uncertainties put a strain on even the most devoted couple. What would happen to a couple like Ryan and her if something like that happened?

And then it struck her. What if they compromised? What if she agreed to marry Ryan if, and only if, he gave her a baby? She hadn't thought that her baby needed a father. After all, she'd survived without one. What her baby needed was love, and that she knew she could give it. But she also knew Ryan. He'd said marriage, and she knew he'd never go for anything less.

And the thought of giving her child a warm, loving, *complete* family was very seductive. Maybe they could even have more than one child. Then it struck her—additional children would be conceived far more conventionally if this all came to pass. She'd be tacitly agreeing to a lasting sexual arrangement with Ryan. And in good conscience, she couldn't pretend that would be a problem.

The real problem might be keeping her hands *off* him.

She shivered suddenly, though she was walking down Marlborough Street now at a brisk pace. Her mind racing, she considered the idea from all angles. As she reached the steps of her building, she nodded once, sharply, then went inside and headed straight for the phone.

When Ryan's deep voice said, "Hello?" though, for a moment her throat seized up, and she couldn't speak.

"Jessie? Is that you?" His voice was sharp enough to startle her into speech again.

"How did you know?" she asked.

"Caller I.D."

"Oh."

Silence.

"Jess? Did you call me for a reason or did you just want to breathe heavily into the phone?"

"I want to talk to you again. About this baby stuff."

On the other end of the phone, he sighed. "I don't believe there's any point in talking it to death."

"I had an idea," she said. "Could you meet me for dinner?"

"Three meals in two days. All my adoring fans are going to start to worry."

"Maybe they should."

"Jess—"

"Come on, Ryan. Live dangerously. The East Coast Grill? Seven o'clock?"

"Wow. All the way over in Cambridge? I didn't know you strayed that far from home."

"Very funny. Will you do it?"

"All right," he said. "But only because I know you'll bug me to death until I listen to you. I'm telling you right up front that there is no way I am going to change my mind."

"I understand," she said. "All I ask is that you listen."

When she arrived in a taxi at 7:05 he already was waiting. To her eternal amusement he was seated at the bar with a woman on each side of him apparently vying for his attention.

Jessie walked up behind them and put her hands over his eyes. "Guess who?"

"Hey, there." He swiveled around on his stool to face her. "You're early."

The women who'd been speaking to him were eyeing her with something less than friendliness. An imp of mischief seized her, and she placed her hands on either side of Ryan's face, leaning forward and giving him a quick peck on the lips. "Miss me?"

"Always." She hadn't counted on his quick reflexes. His hands came up before she could draw away. One shackled her wrist, the other cradled the back of her head as he returned a second, much more leisurely kiss. His lips were warm and firm, molding her own as her heart thudded, and she nearly sank into the promise inherent in the lingering caress before she remembered who she was kissing and why. When he let her go, she drew back, flustered.

He rose and settled a hand at her waist, turning to smile at the women as Jessie blinked and forced herself to focus. "It was nice meeting you."

As he seated her and moved around the small table, she sent him an easy grin, determined not to let him see she'd been shaken by that kiss. "Was I helpful?"

"Infinitely." He shrugged out of his leather jacket. "I was being accosted."

"Well," she said, "it's not every day a girl gets to meet an eminently available hunk."

"If I hear that phrase out of you one more time," he said, leaning forward with mock menace, "your derriere is going to meet my eminently available hand."

She smiled brilliantly. "Ooooh, sounds like fun. Promise?"

His eyes narrowed, and that quickly the playful moment metamorphosed into something entirely different, something dark and dangerous with undercurrents of an intensity that caught her breath in her throat.

"Okay. You folks want to order drinks?" The arrival of the server broke through the stillness between them.

She sat quietly as Ryan ordered their drinks. What was happening to her? And to the comfortable, familiar relationship she'd had with Ryan?

"So," he said when the waitress had returned with their drinks and taken their dinner orders, "what new wrinkle in your mind was so urgent that you had to see me again tonight?"

"I was thinking about what you said." She spoke slowly, cautiously.

"I've said a lot of things to you," he said, unhelpful. "Want to be a tad more specific?"

"About marriage." The words fell between them, their ripples widening, breaking up the smooth surface of the conversation.

His eyes grew more intense, bluer; she felt like a mouse caught in the cat's corner. "What about it?"

"Well, I was thinking." She stopped, swallowed. "If you were to donate—and I did get pregnant—we could maybe get married once the baby was born. I mean, it would be stupid of us to marry assuming we were going to be parents. A lot of things can happen during pregnancy and I wouldn't want to trap you into anything if it didn't—"

"Stop." He held up a hand, palm out. "You're babbling."

"Sorry. I'm nervous." She fell silent, biting her lip. "I just thought—"

His eyebrows rose. "You've been doing quite a lot of thinking lately." He picked up his wineglass and gently swirled the Merlot they were drinking, tilting the glass and absently studying the color of the wine. "Let me see if I understand what you're proposing. I donate sperm. You, hopefully, get pregnant. If the pregnancy goes to term and we have a child, we marry."

She nodded, too embarrassed to look him in the eye but relieved that he'd grasped the idea. "Exactly."

"No." He sat back in his chair, crossing one long leg over the other.

"No?" Startled, she leaned forward and glared at him. "Why not? I thought you would be happy. This way we both get what we want."

"It makes me uncomfortable," he said. "Where's the guarantee that you'll keep your end of the bargain once you get what you want?"

She was stung by the implication that he didn't trust her. "That's not a very nice thing to say. Have I ever given you reason to distrust my word?"

He shrugged. "No. But this is a life-changing discussion we're having here, not a promise to water my plants while I'm out of town."

She had to admit he had a point. But she was still annoyed. "So call a lawyer if I'm so sneaky. I'll sign a contract."

Ryan was silent. His eyes regarded her intently until she was the first to look away. Finally he sighed. "Okay, here's another compromise. You get pregnant. If everything goes all right for the first couple of months..."

"The first trimester," she said, showing off her knowledge.

"Right. If everything goes well through the first trimester, we marry then. I don't want my child born out of wedlock."

She sighed. "You are an amazingly old-fashioned fuddy-duddy."

His broad shoulders rose and fell again. "An eminently available fuddy-duddy, though. There are lots of women who would leap at the chance to marry me and have my babies."

It would have been the perfect opportunity to say, *Fine. Let one of them have you.* But her tongue wouldn't wrap itself around the words. Something inside her recoiled from the idea of another woman bearing his children. And hadn't she decided he'd be a perfect biological father for her own? A perfect father in many ways? A perfect husband— She cut off that thought before it took root.

"It's not just being old-fashioned," he said suddenly. "I'm helping you out. You can return the favor. If I'm married, there won't be any more of those annoying articles."

He had a point. And the reminder that this would be something of an exchange of favors made her feel better. It was nice that she wasn't the only one getting something out of the arrangement. "All right." She spoke slowly, cautiously. "I guess we could get married if the early part of the pregnancy goes well."

He nodded once. "It's a deal, then."

The waiter returned with their dinners. Ryan had the barbecue that had been one of the Grill's outstanding specialties for years. She'd ordered the Grilled Sausage from Hell. Though it was wonderful, she could only manage to eat about half of it, so Ryan polished off the rest as well as his own meal.

"So what happens next?" he asked as their plates were removed.

"I'm monitoring my cycle. I'll use an ovulation kit to determine when we go. I'm pretty regular so it'll probably be the middle of next week."

"Stop." He held up a hand. "I know the rest. We

talked about artificial insemination when Wendy and I were going through this, but ultimately we learned her fallopian tubes were blocked."

She nodded. The same sense of shock and hurt that she'd felt when he'd first told her about Wendy's and his infertility treatments rolled through her again. "I cannot believe you never told me about that."

He looked away. "Like I said, it was a very personal thing."

And none of her business. She read between the lines. "I'm sorry," she said. "I don't mean to be nosy." She hesitated. "I guess it bothers me a little that there are these big parts of your life about which I know nothing. We shared just about everything growing up, didn't we?"

"Not by a long shot." His answer was quick and sharp. "After you started dating Mr. Football Star, there was a whole lot we didn't share."

She was stunned by the vehemence in his tone. The Ryan she recalled from high school had been absorbed in academics and weight lifting. He'd rarely sought her out and often had little to say when she'd made time for him. Was it possible she'd hurt him somehow? Offended him without realizing it? She wanted to ask him, but she wasn't sure either of them was ready to open such a can of worms. "Maybe we should just agree to start from this moment," she said carefully. "If this works out, we could be sharing a family in less than a year."

He nodded without looking at her. But after a moment he reached across the table and took her hand. "Good idea," he said quietly. His palm engulfed hers and his thumb rubbed across the back of her knuckles gently, creating a warmth that sizzled up her arm into her bloodstream. A heavy pool of heat settled low in her abdomen and she shifted slightly in her seat. "I have a good feeling

about this," he told her. "We're going to be good together...in lots of ways."

The heat in her belly expanded, and her breathing grew
short as her imagination shot vivid mental pictures of one
way they could be good together across her mental screen.
"I, ah, you're probably right." Hastily she pulled her
hand from his. "Well, I have to work tomorrow so we'd
better call it a night."

But as they parted outside the Grill, the impact of exactly how much her life was going to change as a result
of this night hit her squarely in the face. She turned to
Ryan, holding out both hands. "Thank you."

He smiled, his dimples carving deep grooves in his
cheeks as he took her hands and squeezed them lightly.
"Thank *you*, Jess. I'll call you tomorrow."

"All right." And as she hopped into her compact car
for the short drive home, she found that she was practically jittering with excitement and happiness. But if she
was honest with herself, it wasn't entirely the prospect of
finally realizing her desire to have a baby that was at the
heart of it.

She was going to marry Ryan if things went well. And
though she never would have suspected it, she found the
idea held immense appeal.

Three

———

She called him the following morning to tell him that the fertility center had confirmed that next week would be the best time for her to conceive if he wanted to "do it" right away. As he punched the off button on his office speaker phone, he knew a moment's relief that she still wanted to go through with the plan. He'd been afraid she would change her mind and go for an anonymous donor.

Ryan could have told her what he really wanted to do right away, but he had the feeling that might just send Jessie running for the hills. He wondered what was going through her mind at the thought of marriage to him. Had it even struck her yet that this would be permanent, a real marriage in every way? They hadn't talked at all about where they would live. About how many children they wanted or about whether or not she wanted to continue working.

About sex.

He was pretty sure she'd never thought about sex, about lovemaking, in connection with him before. In high school he'd been merely her pal, the guy next door. She'd begun dating the football player when she was a freshman, and they'd seen less of each other from that time on. Not that she had noticed.

No, he'd been the only one to suffer. He'd left for college at the end of the following year, but he'd kept tabs on her during his infrequent visits home, each time hoping against hope that she was free. Looking back, he didn't know if he'd have had the nerve to ask her out even if she had been, but it had been a moot point. Two years later she'd graduated and promptly headed south to Alabama.

That was when he'd let reality seep in around the edges of his dreams of a life with Jessie. And with reality had come Wendy. If Wendy had lived, he'd have remained faithful. His feelings for Jessie never would have gone anywhere outside his own mind.

But Wendy was gone. And Jessie had come to him with a proposition most sane men would have laughed at. Not him. Not with her.

How did she feel about him? Was there any hope that she wanted him as much as he wanted her? His euphoria faded. For the first time he fully appreciated the situation he was in. For years Jessie had been out of reach, and he'd resigned himself to a life without her. Suddenly he was faced with the possibility of sharing the rest of his life with her. But still, sweet as that thought was, it wasn't enough. It was a frustrating feeling for a man who controlled a significant financial empire, a man who'd met most challenges with success in the past decade.

The memory of her appalled reaction when he first mentioned marriage still stung. And last night, she'd almost hyperventilated when he'd obliquely mentioned sex. There definitely had been times when he'd have sworn there was attraction between them—was it just his longing that made it so?

No, he was pretty sure she felt something for him. To-night, when he'd been holding her hand, she'd looked dazed and distinctly...aroused, just as she had earlier when he'd kissed her and her mouth had softened and clung to his. He'd found himself cursing the public place and the table between them. And when he'd nearly kissed her in her apartment that night, she'd trembled in his arms, and he'd felt the battle she was fighting with herself. She'd wanted him then. She'd wanted to lift her face to his and let the attraction roaring between them take over...but she'd backed off. *This wouldn't be right.* Why not? What was she hiding from him? Or was she hiding from herself?

After lunch, working on impulse, he picked up the phone in his office again and dialed the number of her store. After two rings, her brisk, business-like voice said, "The Reilly Gallery. May I help you?"

"I'm beyond help," he said. Something within him seemed to calm and settle at the sound of her voice. He was, indeed, beyond help.

She laughed, and her voice softened. "Hi."

"Hi, yourself. Having a busy afternoon?"

"Not especially."

"Good. I wanted to ask you where you want to live." She was silent for a long time. "Live?"

"Yeah. House, furniture, place to hang your hat. Home, dwelling, abode. Cottage, castle, condo—"

"Enough! I know what you meant. I guess I just fig-ured..."

"Figured what?"

"Well, why don't we wait until we find out if there's going to be any need to get married before we start making plans?"

He wanted to tell her he had a need to marry her regardless of whether or not she got pregnant. But he could tell from the skittish tone of her voice that that probably wasn't the smartest thing he could say right now. So instead, he said, "Would you like to come to dinner on Saturday evening?"

"Come to dinner?" she echoed.

"At my home," he clarified. "I know you've been there a time or two, but this way you can look around the whole place and take your time thinking about what we should do about housing when and if we marry."

"I guess that's a good idea." Although she didn't sound sure.

"Great. I'll pick you up at seven."

"Oh, no. I can—"

"I'll pick you up," he repeated. "Seven on Saturday. See you then."

After he hung up, he swiveled his leather executive chair toward the window. His suite of offices was on the top floor of the towering building he'd purchased from one of the Russell heirs nine years ago. Looking out the window, he had a perfect view of the harbor and the bay beyond it, with boats of all shapes and sizes looking like toys around the wharves. To the north, Christopher Columbus Park along the waterfront was conspicuously pristine beneath its mantle of white snow as the Atlantic Avenue traffic flowed past it.

He was a wealthy man. The view before him proved it—his office was in the heart of Boston's financial district—and yet he still felt like the tongue-tied kid from the Irish enclave whenever he talked to Jessie. The next few months were going to be difficult, he sensed. It was his nature to push forward, to maneuver and outflank until he'd gotten what he was after. But if he continued to try to press Jessie, he was sure to fail.

Spinning his chair around again, he looked over his calendar. Before this…arrangement had come about with Jess, he'd been considering some travel to make his presence known at several of his other enterprises around the country. But now he thought he'd better reschedule. At least push his plans back until after they found out whether or not the artificial insemination worked.

She was ready when he arrived on Saturday evening and he drove her out to Brookline where his home was located. It was a straight drive out through the prestigious lower blocks of Commonwealth Avenue to the five-bedroom Georgian Revival mansion he and Wendy had purchased back when they still had dreams of filling it with a large family.

Although they parked in the garage behind the house, he had to drive around the block to get to it, and Jessie craned her neck as they passed the stately entrance on Commonwealth with its gracious bow front. It was easily the largest town home in the area.

"Did I ever tell you how much I admired your taste in a home?" she asked.

"No, but thank you." He hoped she liked it. He'd gotten sort of attached to the place. If she didn't, he'd buy something else that she liked better, though. He'd rather have Jessie than the house any day. *And a family,* he added silently, hastily. A family was the reason he wanted her so badly.

"Exactly how old is this house?"

"It was built in 1866." And he'd better stop thinking so much or he was going to be insane.

"Amazing."

She slanted him a smile as he helped her from the Mercedes and they walked through the winter gardens to the back entrance.

"This garden is nice in the spring and summer," he said. "I found a landscaper who does an outstanding job. He also takes care of the terrace on the roof."

"The terrace on the roof." She smiled. "Did you ever imagine, when you were a kid, that one day you'd own a Victorian mansion in the Back Bay?"

He shook his head. "My dreams ran more along the lines of getting the girl and finding a job. It's funny how this just…happened."

"It did not just happen. You made it happen."

He shrugged. "Maybe. But there was a certain amount of luck involved. I had the right idea at the right time and was lucky enough to get backing from a financier who had a weak moment." He showed her into the less formal family room, then held up a finger as he moved away. "Just let me find out what time Finn plans to serve the meal."

After a quick conference with the man who'd been with them since before Wendy's death, he reentered the family room.

Jessie was standing with her back to him at the bay windows that overlooked the back gardens. She turned and smiled when he came in, and the force of her smile smote him heavily in his vulnerable heart. "I know what you're doing," she said as he opened a bottle of Chenin Blanc and poured two glasses.

He raised an eyebrow as he crossed to her, handing her her drink. "You do?"

"You're trying to make me fall for your house so I'll agree to live here."

He swirled his wine and inhaled, enjoying the rich bouquet. "Is it working?"

"Probably. I had thought I'd like to stay close to the shop, but this really isn't that far and it's so lovely." She took an experimental sip of her own drink, then regarded him with concern in her eyes. "But..." She hesitated.

He waited.

"If it bothers you to stay here—I mean, you lived here with Wendy—"

"It's all right." He spoke quietly.

There was a short silence, then he spoke again. "Have you thought about whether or not you want to continue working after the baby's born?"

Her gaze flew to his, then bounced away. "I feel superstitious talking about this. You, of all people, know that it's not always easy to get pregnant."

"But I have a good feeling about it." And he did. Strangely, his experiences with Wendy didn't feature in his thoughts these days.

She looked at him, worrying her lower lip.

That small motion drove him crazy, for more reasons than one. "Stop that." He reached out and touched her bottom lip with his finger, gently tracing over the line of her lip just below where she had caught it between her teeth. "Your lips are too pretty to be damaged."

Instantly she released the lip. "Uh, thank you." Her voice was strangely husky.

"Here. I have something to show you." He turned away as if the intimate moment were nothing out of the ordinary. Jessie took a seat at his side as he settled himself on the couch.

"What is it?" she asked as he removed the lid of a large, square box.

"Photos." He reached into the tissue and extracted a worn black photo album. "I had a lot of Mom's and Dad's things put in storage, and recently I've been going through them. I found this last week. There are a few of you in here."

"Of me?" Her eyes grew big. "I can count on one hand the number of photos I have of myself other than school photos. Could I have copies made?"

He nodded. "Sure. Want to take a peek?"

She plopped herself down beside him, her arm brushing his. "Does a fish like water?"

Together they opened the old book. He hadn't gone through it all before. He hadn't had a surfeit of time, and if he were honest with himself, it was difficult. He'd had a good childhood, but his parents were gone now. His father had keeled over from a massive heart attack his last year in college, and his mother had died four years ago. His brother, Vinson, lived several hours away now, and those happy days when they'd run up and down the old streets of Charlestown with Jessie hot on their heels, shouting in her high treble voice, "Wait fo' me, guys!" were but a memory.

"Oh, look!" She pointed at a picture in the far corner. "There's the Big Brown Bomb."

The Bomb. He chuckled. He'd forgotten about the wood-paneled station wagon they'd once had. His father would pile a whole bunch of the neighborhood kids into it and take them for bouncing jaunts out into the Massachusetts countryside for the sheer pleasure of hearing the kids yell every time he gassed it over a bump in the road. "Remember the time Willy Evert threw up down the back of Dad's neck?"

She was holding her sides, laughing hard now. "I'll never forget it. Your dad nearly ran off the road trying to get out of his shirt."

Grinning fondly, they paged through the rest of the album, reminiscing over many of their shared antics. On the last page was a picture of the two of them on the day he started seventh grade. He was holding Jessie's hand, grinning at the camera. At his side, Jessie wasn't grinning, though. Instead, she wore a distinct pout.

He pointed to the photo. "What a face! What were you thinking that day?"

Her eyes narrowed as she thought back over the past. "I was upset," she said finally. "You were going to junior high school, and I still had two years of elementary school left. You had walked me to school every day of my life until then. It was the first time I'd ever had to be away from you, and I remember thinking I wasn't going to be able to stand it." She traced a light finger over his grin. "You, on the other hand, look thrilled to be moving on."

"I couldn't have been too thrilled," he said honestly. "I hated it when we were separated."

There was a small, gentle silence. It should have been awkward, he thought, but it wasn't.

"Oh, Ryan." She sighed. "We used to be so close. What happened to us?"

"You abandoned me for a jock." He'd meant the words to come out lightly, but as he saw her face change, he realized he hadn't been entirely successful. He forced himself to smile. "And I made millions and found a woman who would have me."

"Dinner's ready." Finn, his household assistant, breezed into the room. "When do I get an introduction to this ravishing beauty, Ryan?"

Jessie smiled and put out a hand. She didn't seem at all fazed by the neon-pink streak that marched through Finn's blond hair, or the leather pants that looked as if they'd been painted on his skinny butt. As Finn shook her hand firmly, she asked, "Why? Are you going to take me away from him?"

"Oh, no, darling." Finn batted his eyelashes outrageously. "I just want to borrow some of your clothing if it's all as exquisite as this outfit." He ran a long, elegant finger down the sleeve of her silk blouse.

As she laughed, Finn tapped the face of his watch and made an expressive face at Ryan. "Five minutes or less. You know how peeved I get when you wait until the lettuce is soggy."

As he turned and marched back out of the room, Jessie caught Ryan's eye. "Where on earth did you find him?"

He shrugged, grinning. "Finn's unique, isn't he? His aunt was our housekeeper until four years ago, when she had to retire because of knee problems. Finn filled the housekeeping position temporarily and gradually I found out he's an excellent chef, as well as a slick hand on a computer. He does laundry and oversees the yard work— the all-purpose manservant, you could say. I don't know what I'd do without him." He sobered. "He was a rock when Wendy was killed. His partner died of AIDS complications just before I hired him, so he knew what I was going through."

"I like him," she said.

He nodded. "So do I. However, he'll become highly unlikable in a hurry if we don't get started on his dinner."

"We wouldn't want that."

She preceded him into the dining room, where Finn had set their places at right angles at one end of the dining table. There was a gas fire merrily blazing in the fireplace.

Fresh cymbidium orchids in a clear glass bowl with cracked crystal marbles graced the center of the table and silver candlesticks held white tapers that matched the flowers.

"This is lovely," she said. "You shouldn't have gone to so much trouble."

He couldn't help it, he had to laugh. "I didn't," he confessed. "All I did was give a few directions. Finn's the one with the vision."

"You know what I mean," she said.

He shrugged. "I wanted to make it special."

Her eyes were very dark and green. "Why?"

"We're about to begin a new chapter in both of our lives."

Her gaze was on the table now. "Yes. We are." She was silent until after their meals had been served.

After Finn left the room, he cleared his throat. "How long after the procedure will it be before you know whether it worked?"

"They'll be monitoring me with bloodwork every three days to see if something the nurse called my Beta count is rising. I gather it's a hormone. It should rise steadily, and when it's over two thousand they begin to relax. After six or seven weeks, the fertility center will send me back to my regular obstetrician for the rest of the pregnancy, barring any complications. Which I don't expect, of course."

"Okay." He made a production out of cutting the excellent marinated sirloin that Finn had set before him. "Let's do it."

And do it they did. He rose early the next Thursday morning and went to the fertility center, where a very efficient nurse handed him a specimen collection cup and ushered him into a room where apparently, legions of men just like him produced "specimens." The room contained what the nurse primly referred to as "visual aids," men's magazines and a video machine with a couple of porn flicks to choose from.

As he unzipped his pants, he knew a moment's nervous concern, probably shared by every other guy who'd ever stood in there alone, expected to perform on command. What if he couldn't...he'd never had any problem remotely resembling it before, but this was a lot of pressure...it didn't bear thinking about.

In the end, though, all he had to do was think of Jessie, and his body responded as it always did to thoughts of her. Did she truly understand how things would be between them when they married? Though he'd happily give her a room of her own, he intended that they would share a bed every night. He thought of the sound of her husky voice whispering into his ear, the way her green eyes sparkled when she teased him, the clean, fresh scent of her hair and the way it felt like cool silk beneath his fingers, the feel of her soft flesh as he pulled her against him and drew her under him the way he'd dreamed of doing for years. Soon it would be *her* hands on him, exploring, stroking, guiding him to the hidden, humid center of her body....

As he repeated the same thing the following day, he mentally crossed his fingers as he washed his hands and his breathing slowed and calmed. If this clinical, somewhat humiliating process worked, he thought, tucking his shirt back into his pants and shrugging into his jacket, soon he'd be marrying Jessie.

She hadn't wanted him to stick around during her procedure, but he called her that evening. "Everything go okay today?"

"It went fine. Now all we have to do is wait."

"Do you have any restrictions?"

"No," she said. "They had me lie still for about ten minutes afterward, and that was it."

"That was it? Ten minutes? Hardly seems like enough time for my little swimmers to start fighting their way upstream."

She laughed, as he'd intended, and the constraint in her tone eased. "They have a powerful incentive, though."

The days dragged as she waited until she could ascertain whether she'd achieved her goal. Several evenings later she picked up a folder she'd brought home from the gallery and made herself go through the invoices, recording information on her laptop computer as she prepared the accounts payable. Working in the evenings kept her from pacing around the condo wondering if she was pregnant.

But halfway through the pile, she found a misfiled sheet of paper. It was short and to the point, and she could have recited it with her eyes closed. It was from the bank to which she'd applied for a loan. "We regret to inform you that your application for the following loan has been declined."

Suppressing the very unladylike words that clamored to be said, she set the sheet aside. She'd been sure she would qualify for that loan, and to learn that she'd been denied had been a setback she hadn't anticipated. When she'd called, Mr. Brockhiser had told her that their loan committee wasn't comfortable with her debt-to-income ratio. End of discussion. Still, there were other banks in Boston. She'd already applied to another one; perhaps they'd look more favorably on her.

Just then someone knocked on the door. She leaped for

it, knowing it was Ryan. He'd offered to drop by with dinner.

"Hi." He carried a bag from the deli down the street.

"Here." She handed him a small envelope, at which he stared.

"What's this?"

"A key." She avoided his questioning gaze. "I thought you might like to have a key to my place...since we're...you know."

He laughed. "Yeah. Whatever we are." He pocketed the key. "Thanks." Then he walked to the table and set out the sandwiches and cookies he'd bought. "Dinner arrives."

"Thanks." She indicated the sandwiches. "Which one do you want?"

"Either. I know you like seafood salad but if you don't want that one, I'll take it and you can have the turkey."

She reached for the seafood salad sandwich. "You're a prince."

"So they tell me." He took a bite of his own sandwich, then said, "We need drinks," and vanished in the direction of her kitchen. When he returned with two glasses of water, he said, "So how long do you have to wait now to find out if this worked?"

"About ten more days. My Beta count is rising but it's too early to tell."

He nodded, but she could see the excitement lurking in his eyes. He was as impatient as she was. "Would you like to go down to Chinatown this weekend? They celebrate the Chinese New Year."

"That sounds like fun. I've always wanted to do that."

"You never have? You'll love it," he predicted. "There's a parade, and they have dances with dragons and lions, and firecrackers. And we can have dinner at the New Shanghai.''

"I've heard it's fabulous."

"It is. Wendy used to love it. She always had the sliced lamb with scallions."

Wendy. Again. Was it disloyal to wish her former friend wasn't included in every conversation they had?

Probably. And selfish, too. But still…if they were going to marry, *she* would be his wife soon. Would he continue to talk about Wendy then?

She forced herself to smile at him. "Sounds fabulous," she said. "I'll put Saturday night on my calendar."

The week passed surprisingly quickly, and before she knew it, their date was upon her. Dressing snugly to combat the chilly winter weather, she was just digging her gloves out of her dress coat pockets when the doorbell rang.

She walked to get it, puzzled. "Why didn't you just come in?" she asked when she opened the door to find Ryan standing there. "I gave you a key, remember?"

"I know." He shrugged. "It just seemed a little… presumptuous to walk in."

She reached up and patted his cheek. "That's thoughtful. But feel free to walk in anytime."

He took her wrist, holding it against his cheek when she would have dropped her hand. "Anytime?"

The look in his eyes was surprisingly intimate, and immediately her mind flashed back to his words from the night they'd discussed marriage. *Passion, I can promise you.* She cleared her throat as a jolt of pure sexual electricity shot through her. "Sure. Any friend of mine is welcome anytime," she said, trying to emphasize the friendship they'd agreed on. She wasn't sure she was very successful, though, since it came out as a croak.

He lifted her wrist to his mouth, and her eyelids fluttered closed as she felt his hot breath sear her tender flesh. Then his lips were on her, lightly pressing a kiss to the sensitive spot at the base of her hand, and she shivered as a knot of quivering nerves drew taut in her abdomen.

"What are you doing?" she managed.

He looked at her over the hand he still had pressed to his mouth, and his blue eyes were full of a triumphant mischief. "Seeing how you taste. Why?"

"I—nothing." She yanked her hand back, too flustered to pretend the caress hadn't scrambled her brain cells. Her skin tingled all over. "I thought we agreed to...to...to be friends."

"That was friendly." His tone was innocent.

She flung her bag over her shoulder and marched toward the door, unnerved by the sexual vibrations zinging around her small condo. "Hah."

"It wasn't *un*friendly," he pointed out.

"No, it certainly wasn't," she grumbled under her breath. Darn him! How were they supposed to keep their friendship the way it had been when he did sneaky things like that?

He didn't say anything else, but he whistled as they rode down to Chinatown, and when she glanced over at him, a small smile played around the corners of his lips.

The Chinese New Year's parade and celebration was noisy and bright and exuberant, and by the time the last float had gone by and the last firecracker had exploded in a shower of brilliant color, Jessie forgot she'd been annoyed with him earlier. From where they'd parked they walked down Hudson Street to New Shanghai and were seated moments after Ryan identified himself.

The room in which they sat was pretty and airy, its white linens giving it a more formal look than most of the local Chinese eateries. Ryan ordered the evening's special, a plate of baby eels glazed in a hot pepper and orange sauce, while Jessie stuck to a more mundane vegetarian entree.

"Uck! How can you *eat* those?" she said when the waiter departed.

He grinned. "Easily. Watch."

She grimaced again as he swallowed a spicy bite. "Gross. You always were a more adventurous eater than I was."

He laughed. "I'm a more adventurous eater than most of the known world. Mom always said I'd eat anything that wasn't nailed down."

The words brought a wave of unexpected nostalgia sweeping through her so strongly that tears stung the backs of her eyes. "How did you bear losing them?" she blurted out. "If they'd been my parents, I'd still be devastated."

Ryan's eyes grew shadowed, and for one brief moment she caught a glimpse of the grief that would always be with him. "We had a wonderful life together," he said quietly, "and I don't think they had any regrets. I miss them every day and, yeah, I wish they'd lived longer, but the memories are so good…" He trailed off, then spoke again after a moment of reflection. "What do you remember best about them?"

"That's easy." She sensed his unspoken need to gather memories of his family. In fact, she shared it. It was one of the most seductive things about their relationship, in some way, that they shared so much history. "Your mom was such a good cook. I remember she could hardly wait for the Michigan cherries to come in each summer. As soon as she got some, she'd bake pies and cobbler. She let me help, and it's still one of the few things I truly love to do in the kitchen.''

He was smiling now, his gaze faraway. "I'd forgotten about the cherries. That woman did love cherries." He reached across the table and squeezed her hand, then lightly linked their fingers and held the connection. "Thank you."

"You're welcome. Hmm. What do I remember best about your dad?'' she mused. "I remember how he would toss me up in the air and catch me again, and the smell of his pipe when he sat on the porch with your mother on summer nights while we caught fireflies. I remember how, after he'd been fooling around in the car engine he'd come after us with greasy hands, pretending to be a monster.'' She shook her head. "I used to wish he was *my* father, because I thought there wasn't a more wonderful dad in the world than Mr. Shaughnessy."

Ryan had been chuckling, but his laughter faded at her last words. "Jess—''

"Do you know,'' she said, "I have more vivid memories of *your* family than I do my own? That's sad.''

"It *is* sad,'' he said, "but look what you've become. I've always been amazed that your childhood didn't squelch your drive and determination. And it's another reason why I think we should marry. We share memories. We *know* how to make a child feel loved, how to give it security and a warm family atmosphere.''

She nodded. "You're right. I never realized where I got my ideas about being a mother, but you and I both know they didn't come from my mother." She thought bitterly of the way her mother had simply faded out of the picture when Jessie's grandmother had caught Jessie in some, usually minor, misdeed. If there had ever been a time when her mother had intervened while her grandmother was administering a "whipping" with the yard-stick, she couldn't remember it. "I'll never, *ever* hit my kids," she said suddenly, fiercely.

"I know." His fingers squeezed hers again, gently. "You're going to be a great mother. *We* are going to be great parents."

His words echoed in her head, driving home the enormity of the decision they had made in a way nothing had before. *We.* It was going to take some getting used to, thinking of herself as half of a pair.

She was pregnant!

At the end of the third week, the longest weeks of her life, another blood test confirmed her Beta count had risen sufficiently to make pregnancy a real possibility. And her period was eight days late. She was *never* late. Jessie wanted to dance around the room, but she was afraid to bounce her uterus around like that. Although the doctor had assured her this should be as normal a pregnancy as any other from this point forward, she figured there was no sense in taking chances.

A baby. She felt her eyes misting. She hadn't realized exactly how much she'd wanted this. It was hard to take in. She couldn't wait to tell Ryan!

She walked out of the clinic to her car, but as she climbed in and reached for her cell phone, she realized her hands were shaking. Carefully she dialed his office number, and when an automated voice picked up, she punched the sequence for his private line.

"Hello?" His deep voice made her heart leap.

"Hi, there."

He laughed, and she could imagine him relaxing, spinning his chair around to look out the plate glass window over the Boston cityscape. He would have the sleeves of his shirt rolled up and the knot in his tie probably had been loosened an hour or so after he got into his office.

"Well, hello." His voice warmed when he recognized her voice. "What are you up to today?"

"Guess." She worked hard to keep her voice level.

"Uh…" Apparently she'd interrupted him in the middle of some deep thought, because he didn't get it. "Give me a hint."

"I had a doctor's appointment today."

"Jess!" She had his full attention now. His voice rose as he said, "Are we going to be parents?"

"I'm almost positive." She didn't bother to hide her delight. "My counts are rising, and all the signs are positive."

"God, Jess…" He sounded a little dazed. "That's *great*."

"I know. I can hardly believe it! Oh, Ryan, I'm so excited."

"I know the feeling." His voice became jubilant. Then he grew quiet. "I wish I was there to celebrate with you."

I wish you were, too. Sternly she reminded herself that this wasn't a normal arrangement. She had no reason to expect him to be glued to her side. "It's okay," she forced herself to say calmly. "We'll celebrate tonight."

"We should go out for dinner," he said. "Do something special." There was a loaded pause. "Does this mean we can get married now?"

She was silent. Part of her wanted to shout, "Yes!" and she had to suppress the urge. His words reminded her of the reason they'd discussed marriage in the first place. Quietly she said, "In twelve weeks, remember?"

"Right." His voice was a little subdued now, too. "I guess I'll see you tonight."

They said goodbye, and she slowly replaced the handset

on the base, wondering why she felt so let down. She was pregnant. She should be thrilled.

And she was, she assured herself stoutly. It was just that…in the past two weeks things had changed between Ryan and her. They'd grown closer in a different way, a warmer, more affectionate way. It had been all too easy to forget that they were together because they each wanted a child. Too easy, she thought, to pretend that they were a normal couple falling in love.

They'd gone out several more times after the Chinatown trip, and though he hadn't kissed her, Ryan had held her hand, wrapped one hard arm around her back and touched her frequently. So frequently that she'd spent half their time together listing all the reasons it would be inappropriate for her to throw herself into his arms and beg him to kiss her.

He made it all too easy to pretend that love was a part of what was growing between them, with his solicitous attentions, the warm light in his eyes when he looked at her and the interest he displayed in every word she said.

Later that afternoon a large bouquet of pink and blue flowers were delivered to the shop. A small teddy bear on a stick was stuck into the middle of the arrangement, and two baby balloons danced gaily above the blossoms. Fortunately she was alone because Penny would have had a million questions and Jessie probably would have wound up telling her what was going on.

She couldn't keep herself from smiling as she detached the card and took it out of the small envelope. In bold block letters, Ryan had written: *Thank you for making my dream come true.*

She stared at the card. It would be easy to misinterpret those words, she thought as her heart beat faster. But he hadn't meant them in a romantic way. She was indeed making his dream come true: by giving him the child for which he'd always longed. And the sentiment on that card only acknowledged her part in that.

"Thank you for the flowers," she said when he arrived to take her to dinner that evening. She indicated the sizable bouquet in the middle of her small dining table.

He grinned. "I thought it was appropriate." Then he came toward her, gathering her into his arms and hugging her hard, lifting her feet clear of the floor. "This is going to be so great!"

She nodded, struggling free of his arms as her pulse raced. He used every opportunity to touch her, it seemed, and though he acted completely unaffected and innocent, she was sure he was doing it on purpose. It just wasn't fair of him to touch her like that, she thought. In the circle of his arms it was too easy to forget their arrangement.

Four

Three weeks passed.

One morning Jessie sat in her office with the door closed and a scowl on her face as she reviewed the contents of her latest rejection by the venerated monetary institutions of Massachusetts. Her loan application had been denied by the second bank with a speed that was less than flattering; a third bank informed her that they weren't taking on any new business loans for at least the next six months. Glumly she licked the flap of the envelope that held yet another application. Sooner or later she'd get lucky.

She'd better.

In the past few days she had investigated other avenues, but the interest rates at loan companies were staggering, and she knew better than to even consider it. In the meantime, her competitor had held a grand opening of their new, expanded store and she actually had customers who had the nerve to exclaim to her how wonderful it was. Grr-r-r-r.

And to top it off, she thought, as she hit the print button on her computer that would start payroll checks, she felt lousy. She'd been too queasy to eat breakfast every day for the past week. By midmorning, she was able to keep down a few dry crackers, and she was guzzling diet, caffeine-free soda which seemed to calm her stomach a little, but she was picking at lunch and dinner. Nothing appealed to her.

And she was tired. In the mornings she dragged herself around the store. Every day it was a fight not to simply lay her head on her desk and take a short snooze in early afternoon.

Ryan had been away for much of the past week on an extended business trip to the Northwest and he expected to be gone for at least another ten days. Though he called nearly every evening, she hadn't told him how she was feeling. It probably would pass by the time he returned.

Jessie finished the last of her decaf tea and set her mug in the dishwasher, then wound her scarf around her neck as she prepared to brave the icy morning. It was ridiculous for her to be missing Ryan. In the past she'd seen him exactly once a month. Once or twice a year there'd been a chance meeting at an art gallery opening, a charity event, a Pops or Boston Symphony Orchestra opening night. She'd nearly always had a date, and he'd been with Wendy. Their contact had been a casual moment of conversation at intermission or a wave across a ballroom.

No, she shouldn't be missing him. Wouldn't be, either, under normal circumstances, she assured herself. But nothing was normal right now.

As she walked briskly down the street to the gallery, hoping to settle her stomach, she prayed for a better day today. She hadn't dared to put anything more than tea in it this morning. Yesterday her queasiness hadn't been confined to breakfast but had lasted nearly the whole day. She had barely been able to tolerate the odor of her assistant's Reuben sandwich at lunch, and dinner, at which she'd met two other women who owned small local specialty shops, had been a disaster. She'd wound up in the bathroom on the verge of losing what little she'd been able to put in it.

She'd pleaded the flu to her friends and staggered homeward. Once she was in a horizontal position, she'd felt much better. But she could hardly spend her workday horizontal. As she arrived and began the process of opening the store, she took slow, deep breaths. She had too much to do to worry about a little morning sickness.

By lunchtime, though, she was barely holding on. Penny, her assistant manager, kept fluttering back and forth between the shop and the storeroom, where Jessie was sitting on a packing crate with her head resting against her coat, which was hung on the wall beside her.

"Gawd, Jess, you look *awful!* Maybe you should just go on home and rest. If this is the flu, I don't want it."

Jessie made a face at her. "Thanks, Pen. I can always count on you to know just the right thing to say."

Unrepentant, Penny giggled. "Sorry. But I'm *serious!* Nobody wants to feel like you obviously feel."

"You're right. I'd better just go home." She latched on to the excuse gratefully. She didn't want to tell anyone about this pregnancy until she was sure it was a go. "Why don't you see if Melissa can come in today and tomorrow?"

Penny nodded and scurried off to call Melissa. Then, before Jessie could catch her, she'd hailed a cab.

"It's only a few blocks," Jessie told her.

"A few blocks too many when you feel like that," Penny countered, giving the cabby a generous tip to make up for the short trip.

At home, she slept for several hours. *Good grief, Charlie Brown,* she admonished herself. She'd read about the difficulties that many women encountered during the early weeks of pregnancy. She'd thought she was prepared, but this unrelenting nausea was worse than anything she'd ever experienced.

Much to her dismay, the next week was no better. She went to work, but several times she actually had had to lie down on the floor in the stockroom. Even water made her poor stomach rebel.

Penny was worried sick. She alternated between tender solicitude and keeping a cautious distance until finally Jessie snapped, "For heaven's sake, Penny, it's not contagious. I'm just pregnant."

That, of course, had precipitated not only a shocked moment of silence but a million questions and oodles of sage advice—from a twenty-one-year-old whose closest encounter with pregnancy was once a year in the ob-gyn's office when she went for her annual female exam.

"Please," Jessie said as she crawled into yet another cab to go home scant hours after arriving at the gallery, "don't say anything to anybody, Pen. I don't want anyone to know just yet."

Penny nodded. "I understand. Now you just go home and rest. Don't worry about a *thing*. I'll schedule extra help for next week and make sure all our shipments come in."

She stepped back and closed the cab door after giving the cabby quick directions, and Jessie closed her eyes, hoping she could make it home without retching.

At home she lay down on the bed without even removing her clothes and fell asleep.

The next day was even worse. She could keep the nausea at bay only if she lay perfectly still. Even turning from one side to the other, made her head spin and her stomach lurch. Blindly she reached for the phone she'd set on the bedside table.

Her fumbling fingers knocked it to the floor.

Well, cuss. She had to call Penny and let her know she'd be late today. Carefully she turned her head just enough to see the clock on the nightstand. Eight-thirty. She was normally at the gallery by now, but Penny still wouldn't be there. She'd just close her eyes for a few minutes and try to call around nine....

The next time she surfaced, she forgot to be cautious. The moment she sat up and swung her feet to the floor she felt her stomach rebel. Cold sweat broke out all over her body as she quickly lay back down and took slow, deep breaths until she thought the danger was past.

She reached out a hand for the phone, but when her groping fingers encountered nothing but the clock, the lamp and the novel she'd been reading, she remembered she'd knocked it to the floor.

The floor. Okay, that wasn't so bad. Surely she could get the phone off the floor. She inched herself to the edge of the bed on her back, then reached down and flailed around. Her fingers just brushed the carpet. No phone.

Gingerly she began to move her head in small increments until she was looking sideways. Then, equally slowly, she rolled herself slightly to the side so that she could see the floor.

There it was! Half-hidden beneath the bed, but well within her grasp. Holding her breath, she made one quick lunge. Her fingers closed over the handset and she flopped onto her back on her pillow as another wave of nausea rolled through her. Success. With trembling fingers, she lifted it and punched the button she'd programmed for the shop, then lay listening to the ring as she willed herself to breathe and relax.

"The Reilly Gallery, Penny speaking. May I help you?"

"Hi, Pen."

"Jessie! I was *worried* when I got here and you weren't already around. If I hadn't heard from you by lunch, I was planning to come over and check on you. How are you feeling?"

She tried to chuckle, but even to her ears, it sounded a little weak. "Pretty rocky. Can you hold down the fort without me for a while?"

"Abso*lute*ly." Penny must've been a cheerleader in high school. Everything she said sounded like a pep talk. "Don't even *think* about coming in here today. Just rest and take it easy. Have you called the doctor?"

"No." She hated admitting that things weren't going well. But now she began to worry. What if there was something wrong?

The minute she punched the off button from speaking with Penny, she called the doctor's office. A cheery nurse fielded her call.

"Nausea is fairly common in the first trimester, Ms. Reilly."

"But this is...really bad."

"Perhaps you have a touch of the flu, as well. Have you been exposed?"

Of course she'd been exposed. She worked in retail, for heaven's sake. But all she said was, "Probably. Still, this doesn't seem like flu. I have no fever, and when I lie very still I feel all right. It's just when I move that I start to feel sick.''

"Morning sickness affects everyone differently," the nurse said confidently. "Once your hormone levels settle down, I'm betting you'll be feeling fine again."

"This isn't just a little morning sickness, though," she said anxiously.

"Sometimes it occurs in the evening. With a few unlucky ladies, it lasts all day. But it should begin to subside around twelve to fourteen weeks."

Twelve to fourteen weeks! She was only working on her seventh. Quickly she did some mental math. Forty or so more days of this? No way. She'd be dead. When she said as much to the nurse, the perky voice laughed brightly.

"That's what they all say. But it'll pass. You wait and see." The woman went on to give her several suggestions for things that might settle her stomach. "If none of this works and you still are vomiting in a few days, call us again and we'll bring you in for an exam."

Days of this? The thought was too horrible to contemplate. She *had* to get over this! She couldn't afford to spend one day, much less twelve weeks or more, lying in bed watching the light shadows change on the ceiling.

This was ridiculous. She had to get something into her stomach. That probably was why she felt so awful. She always felt sick if she skipped a meal or waited too long to eat. She could control this. It was simply mind over matter.

But first...maybe she'd take a little nap. She had intended to try to go in to work but Penny's idea might be better. Rest, relax, try to eat right. Surely she'd feel better tomorrow.

But tomorrow came and the tomorrow after that and

yet a third one, and she still could barely manage to get around her apartment. By now she was counting days until she could call the doctor. The nurse had said a few days. Was three days a few? A week?

She wanted Ryan. It was irrational, she knew. They had made each other no pledges, merely contracted a marriage for some very tangible reasons. But still, she wanted him to hold her, to make her feel better.

But Ryan was away. And though he called her frequently, she didn't tell him how bad she felt. She didn't really know why. Was she afraid he would rush right home...or was she afraid he wouldn't?

She slept a lot. Penny came by each afternoon with updates on the gallery and got instructions. Jessie tried to eat, but even chicken broth and dry crackers wouldn't stay down. Trying to eat became such an ordeal that she simply didn't. Even sipping ice water was a risky proposition. By the following Monday, she was too tired and lethargic to dress. She called the doctor's office on the dot of 9:00 a.m. and got an afternoon appointment. How she intended to actually get there was anybody's guess, she thought, but she was going if she had to call for an ambulance and go in on a stretcher.

Ryan checked his watch at noon on Monday. He'd just climbed off a plane from Chicago and could hardly wait to see Jessie. He walked quickly to the bank of phones in the airport, wanting to hear her voice. She'd be at the shop.

But she wasn't.

"I'm sorry, Ms. Reilly is unavailable today. May I help you?"

"Tell her it's Ryan."

"I can't, sir. She's not in the gallery. Is this something

I could help you with? Or perhaps I could give her a message?"

"When will she be back?" She probably was out to lunch.

The woman on the other end of the line hesitated. "I can't say, sir."

There was a hint of something…worrisome in her tone. Alarm rushed through him. "What's wrong? Is she sick?"

"I—are you, uh, her significant other?"

He massaged the bridge of his nose. "I guess that's as good a description as any."

"Oh, good." Relief colored the youthful voice. "She's at home. If you want to talk to her, why don't you go by and see her?"

"Why isn't she in the shop?"

"I can't say, sir."

"All right, forget it. I'll go see her myself."

"Oh, good. That would be, like, *really* a good thing."

As he drove through the manic Boston traffic to Marlborough Street, he was aware of how tense he was. He purposely hadn't let her know he was coming home a few days early, so it was no one's fault but his own if she had lost the baby and he didn't know it.

Lost the baby. He knew that these early days of a pregnancy, whether a "high-tech" one or one conceived the old-fashioned way, could be tricky. He was conscious of a sick feeling in the pit of his stomach as he snagged a hard-to-get parking space in front of her Victorian brownstone and raced up to her apartment.

He rang the doorbell and waited. And waited…and waited. Impatiently he rapped on the door and rang the bell again. Finally, he opened it with the key she'd given him.

"Ryan!" Jessie stared at him.

He stared back. Clinging to the doorframe, she looked like absolute living hell. Dark circles ringed her eyes, and her bouncy dark hair lay flat and lifeless. There were hollows in her cheeks, and the sweatsuit she wore hung on her, clearly showing that she'd lost weight. "Did you lose the baby?" he demanded, anguish welling within him.

"No." Her voice was hoarse but her eyes went wide with shock. She made the smallest negative movement of her head. "I...I—excuse me." And she turned and bolted back down the hallway to her bathroom.

Too startled to catch her, he stared after her for a moment. She'd said she hadn't lost the baby. Then what...? And then he heard an unmistakable sound. Closing the front door, he quickly walked down the hall to the bathroom. The door had been pushed nearly closed, but it hadn't latched.

"Jess, I'm coming in."

"Don't!" But her voice lacked force, and he ignored her, shoving open the door and entering.

She half lay on the floor beside the toilet bowl. Her eyes were closed, and her face was white.

Without speaking, he flushed the toilet, then soaked a washcloth in cool water, wrung it out and knelt beside her. Gently he began wiping her face. "Is this morning sickness?"

She tried to smile. "No. It's more like every day, all day sickness."

He was appalled. "How long?"

"Over a week. First it was just mild nausea but it's gotten worse. It's a little better if I'm lying down."

"Okay." He set the washcloth aside and slipped his arms beneath her shoulderblades and knees, lifting her into his arms. She groaned and closed her eyes, but he wasn't worried. There couldn't possibly be much in her stomach to bring up. Leaving the bathroom, he walked down the hall to the bedroom and lay her on the wreckage of her bed. "Why didn't you tell me?"

She made a feeble motion with her hand, and her voice was fretful. "I didn't want to worry you."

Panic rose again. This couldn't be good for the baby. "Where's your phone?"

"Why?"

"I want to call the doctor," he said patiently. "This isn't normal."

"I already called," she said. "I have an appointment at three-thirty."

"I'll take you."

"All right. That would be…good." Her passivity was frightening, simply because it was so unlike her. He glanced at his watch. It was just after two. No sense in waiting until three-thirty.

"Can I bring you anything?" he asked.

"A settled stomach."

He chuckled because she expected him to. "Sorry, that's on back order." He tugged the mess of covers she'd twisted to the foot of the bed, straightened the sheet beneath her as best he could, then gently covered her with the sheets and blankets. Her eyes were closed; she appeared to be dozing.

Reaching for the phone he called the doctor's number. A woman with a cheery voice answered and tried to put him off, but he insisted. "I'm bringing her right in or taking her to the hospital. Your choice."

"All right," she said. "I guess we'll try to work her in early."

"No," he said. "Don't try. Do it. We'll be there in fifteen minutes."

The doctor's office wasn't far. Going back into the bedroom, he shook out a large quilt. Pulling back Jessie's blankets, he wrapped her in the quilt despite her feeble struggles and carried her down to the car. As a precaution he brought along the plastic wastebasket she indicated beside the bed.

At the doctor's office he carried her straight up to the desk and demanded that they find a place where he could lay her down. After taking one quick look at Jessie, a nurse showed them into an examining room with a vinyl exam table. "Lay her here," she said. "I'll get the doctor as soon as I can."

Once the doctor came in, things began to move.

"She's going to need to be admitted to the hospital for a few days," the doctor told him. "She's dehydrated. We'll put her on an IV to get some fluids into her, and I'll give her something for the nausea, as well."

"It won't hurt the baby?"

The doctor shook his head. "No. The biggest danger to the baby right now is the dehydration."

Six hours later she claimed she was beginning to feel better. She actually lifted her head from the pillow in the private room he'd secured and looked around.

"The hospital," she said in disgust. "I don't have time for this."

"You don't have a choice." Ryan straightened from the windowsill where he'd been reading the paper while she napped.

Her eyes were wide and sad. "This isn't how I envisioned spending my pregnancy," she said. "What am I going to do about the gallery?"

"Don't you have an assistant who could handle things temporarily?"

"Yes, but she's young and not very experienced." She

was clearly fretting. "I can't afford to have anything happen to my shop."

"All right," he soothed. "I'll go by and see how things are doing tomorrow. If there are any problems, I'll make sure they get straightened out."

"What do you know about running a gallery?" she asked in a mournful tone.

"Nothing." His made his voice cheery so she'd smile. "But I'll figure it out. I do know a few things about money, you know."

"I know." Her lips curved the slightest bit, and her words were slurred. "I suppose if you can do for the gallery what you've done for yourself I shouldn't complain. Maybe I should send *you* in to try to get me a loan."

"You're applying for a loan? Why?"

"I want to expand. Remember I told you I had competition?"

He nodded, recalling the conversation. "Yes. Expansion is a good decision."

"Tell that to the banks," she muttered.

His nose for business smelled trouble. "You've approached a bank?"

She nodded faintly. "Approached and been sent packing. By three so far. I'm in a risky business, apparently."

He snorted. "That's ridiculous. Bank boards can be so shortsighted." He took her hand and smoothed his thumb over her knuckles as her eyes drooped. "Stop worrying. I'll make you the loan."

"No!" Her eyes flew wide open. "Under absolutely no circumstance will I borrow money from you."

"It wouldn't be a crime, you know," he said testily. "I wouldn't be where I am today if someone hadn't helped me."

"I said no. Ryan, I'm serious. I want to handle it my own way!"

"All right, all right." He put his hands against her shoulders and pressed her back in the bed as she struggled to sit up. "I'll keep my nose out of your business."

She closed her eyes then, and he didn't speak anymore. Sleep—and fluids—were the best thing for her right now. Especially if they could control the unrelenting nausea. Beneath the light hospital sheet, she looked even thinner. She hadn't been big to start with—she couldn't afford this.

Afford. The word reminded him of what she'd just said about her gallery. Didn't she realize that she wasn't going to have to worry about money as soon as they were married?

Probably not. They'd hardly spoken since they'd sealed their deal over dinner. There had been no discussions of finances, of household affairs or combining their lives. They hadn't even spoken much about the baby yet.

Leaving her a note on the rolling tray at her bedside, he left the hospital and retrieved his car. Might as well go see if there was anything at The Reilly Gallery that he needed to straighten out. The last thing he wanted was for Jessie to be worrying about her business, even if its success or failure was immaterial to her future.

It was dark outside the single window in her room when she awoke again. As she stirred, Ryan rose from the reclining visitor's chair and came to stand beside the bed.

"Hey," he said softly, putting a hand over hers where it lay at her side. "You've been sawing logs for a couple of hours now."

She turned her head, looking in vain for a clock. "What

time is it?'' Then it struck her that the nausea had subsided.

"Eight-thirty,'' he said. "They'll throw me out in thirty minutes.''

"I feel better.'' Experimentally she lifted her head and looked from side to side. Her stomach felt a little jittery, but nothing like the rolling waves of sickness in which she'd been wallowing since last week. "Could you raise the head of the bed a little?'' When they'd brought her in, they'd laid her down in a flat position, for which she'd been intensely grateful at the time.

Ryan moved a little and pushed the button, moving her into a slightly more upright position. "Too much?''

"No, just right.'' She turned her hand and clasped his. "Thank you.''

"No problem. All I did was push the button.''

"Not for that. For taking care of me.''

"That's my job,'' he said softly. "You're carrying my baby, remember?''

"I remember.'' She swallowed the small pang of disappointment at his response. Of course that's why he was concerned. She could lose the baby. "Have you talked to the doctor?''

He nodded. "He wants to keep you for at least two days, give your system a chance to recover. Then he'll evaluate and decide what to do.''

"What does that mean?'' she asked apprehensively. "I've got to get back on my feet. I have to work.''

Ryan shrugged. "You can ask him when you see him tomorrow. I'm just the messenger. Oh,'' he said, "you're scheduled for a sonogram in the morning.''

A sonogram? She knew she'd have several eventually, but when she'd called to make the appointment for her first prenatal checkup—which wasn't until next week, come to think of it—they'd told her they probably wouldn't do one until eight weeks or so. Simply the way her doctor liked to do things, the nurse said.

"Why is he going to do a sonogram now?"

Ryan hesitated. "I think he wants to be sure the baby's okay. Apparently, dehydration can be a problem."

Dear heaven. She felt tears rising. What if something had happened to the baby because she hadn't insisted on seeing a doctor last week? "Oh, Ryan," she whispered, "I'm sorry."

"Hey." He squeezed her hand. "Let's not panic yet. He assured me it was just a precaution."

"Will you come with me when they do it?"

From the way his face lit up, she could see that she'd pleased him. "Of course."

The sonogram wasn't what she'd expected. It was far, far more. When the technician slapped a cold, tingly goo on her stomach and began to run the equipment, a little thing that looked almost like a shrimp swam into view. "There he is," said the woman. "Turning backflips, lively as you please."

Ryan was holding her hand. He increased the pressure until her hand hurt, but she barely noticed for the awed delight racing through her.

Then the technician said, "Uh-oh!"

"What?" Ryan spoke at the same time Jessie did, and her feelings mirrored the apprehension in his voice.

But the lab worker was laughing as she pointed to the screen. "Look."

As they watched, something flickered on the black-and-white screen behind and to one side of the shrimp. The technician moved the sonar wand to one side and suddenly, Jessie realized what she was seeing. "There's another one!"

"Twins?" Ryan sounded shocked.

"You bet." The technician was grinning. "Two of the little guys in there doing the backstroke. Congratulations times two!"

"Twins." Jessie said, echoing Ryan. Did her face hold the same stunned expression of shock that Ryan's did? "I never dreamed there would be more than one."

"I take it you two weren't in treatment for infertility," the technician said. "We see a fair number of in-vitro moms in here with multiples." Then she pointed to the screen again. "But those siblings usually are fraternal. You know, from multiple eggs being fertilized. It looks like these two little ones share a single placenta. So you're going to have identical babies."

Later, after Jessie had been transferred back to the bed in her hospital room, they stared at each other. "Twins," she said. "I can't believe it." Her feelings were mixed. Having a child had been something she'd wanted so badly—but, she now realized, she'd wanted it on her terms. One baby, one easy pregnancy, nothing that would interfere too dramatically with her life and her work. Now here she was, stuck flat on her back in a hospital room, with a business that sorely needed her attention and not one but *two* babies growing inside her.

Two babies! The thrill that had come on the heels of the technician's words returned. If only she didn't have to worry about how she was going to manage two babies and expanding her gallery, she'd be ecstatic. Oh, Ryan's money could purchase the best in child care, she was sure. But then her babies would be taken care of by strangers. She wanted to care for them herself. In fact, she was a little shocked by the maternal possessiveness that seized her when she considered hiring help.

"I can't believe it, either." Ryan's response broke into

her chaotic thoughts. "There are no twins in my family. Are there in yours?"

The questions snapped her out of the fog she'd been in. "I don't know," she said slowly. "Nobody ever mentioned family. I don't even know if my grandparents had any relatives. My mother wasn't a twin—that I know of."

Ryan's eyes softened and she knew he was recalling her childhood. "Did they leave any personal papers or anything that might have family history?" Then he sat down beside her on the bed. "I don't suppose it matters, though. The reality is that we are going to be the parents of twins."

She gauged his expression. He didn't appear to be having any negative thoughts.

He stood up and began to walk around the small room. "When you get out of here, we'll get married. You can move in right away and then—"

"Whoa, horse," she said. "That wasn't the deal. We get married at the end of the first trimester."

Ryan looked impatient. "Why wait?"

She lifted her chin. "There are still eight weeks to go. Who knows what could happen. Hasn't this—" she waved wildly around the room "—taught you anything?"

His face was a thundercloud. "Nothing's going to happen."

"You don't know that."

He sighed, pushing back the sides of his suit jacket and stuffing his hands in his trouser pockets. "It just seems silly to wait. I hate the thought of people counting backward on their fingers to figure out which came first—the engagement or the embryo."

She almost laughed. But he was so serious. For the first time she realized how much the idea of having children out of wedlock bothered him. And it made her question the arbitrary time limit she'd set for this marriage. Was she *really* worried that something might happen to her baby? Babies, she corrected herself. No. This pregnancy might not be a laugh a minute so far but she had a good feeling about it.

So why was she really waiting? She'd accepted the idea of marriage, had even begun to look forward to creating a real family for her children. And then there were the other aspects of it—she was attracted to Ryan. She was *more* than attracted, if she could face the truth. His touch made her insides shiver. Just the memory of the way he'd said, "I can promise you passion," got her all hot and bothered and wondering exactly how it would be to share a bed with him, to run her hands over every hard, muscled inch—

"Are you ignoring me?" His voice sounded distinctly combative.

"No." She studied his face, dark brows drawn together, blue eyes glaring at her over that straight, uncompromising nose. He probably had shaved this morning, but already his jaw was shadowed with dark stubble that gave him a rakish look. "We can get married now if you like."

His expression changed to one of blank shock. "What? Why?"

She shrugged, smiling. "You're right. Nothing's going to happen. Why wait?"

He came toward her then, his eyes leaping with blue flame. "I'm not going to ask you if you're sure, because I'm afraid you'll say you're not." He sat on the edge of the bed and leaned toward her as she sat, mesmerized by the look in his eye. He cradled her cheeks in his hands, his big fingers sliding into the silk of her freshly clean hair and cupping her skull. "Thank you," he murmured as his mouth brushed over hers.

She inhaled sharply at the first intimate contact. She was reclining against her pillows but she instinctively lifted her hands to his shoulders and his lips settled onto hers as easily as if he'd done this a million times. He tested and tasted her, gently molding her lips with the warm, supple pressure of his, his tongue flicking at the corners of her mouth. She shuddered beneath the sensual onslaught, and a small moan escaped from deep in her throat. As the sound registered, he angled his head and parted her lips, sliding his tongue between her teeth to explore the moist depths of her mouth. She sank against him, forgetting everything but the magical sensations roaring through her at his touch—

"Whoops!" said a nurse's voice. "Looks like everything's fine in here!" A giggle faded as the door slowly closed, and Ryan lifted his mouth a fraction.

He was breathing heavily; she could feel her own heart pounding.

"Jess," he said in a deep, hoarse voice, "marriage is going to change our relationship. Are you ready for that?"

"Ryan," she said, equally seriously, "unless I'm mistaken, our relationship changed more in the last minute than it has in twenty-some years."

He chuckled, and his breath was hot and sweet on her face. "You don't hear me complaining." Dipping his head, he pressed one brief kiss to her lips, then gently took his hands from her face, letting her hair slip through his fingers. "I have to leave now. In the morning I'll make arrangements for a ceremony. Do you want a church? A minister? Justice of the peace? As long as we're married, I don't care how."

"I don't care, either," she said. "I know you'd like to get it done, so whatever's fastest is fine."

"If you weren't in that hospital bed, I'd be glad to show

you fast,'' he said, and she shivered at the blatant sensuality glowing in his intense gaze. Then he touched her lips with one long, blunt finger and swung out of the room, leaving her shocked at his frankness, flustered at the thought that they might be married in just a few days, and aching for him to touch her again.

Five

Just before noon the next day the door to Jessie's hospital room opened and Ryan came in. He had a large white box tied with pink and blue ribbon beneath one arm and as he came toward her, he set it on the bottom of the bed.

"Hey, there," he said. He loomed over her and caught her chin in one hand, kissing her briefly. "How are you feeling today?"

"Good." She wished he'd lingered over that kiss the way he had last night. The thought had her clearing her throat. When was she going to get used to his touch? This ridiculous meltdown of all her circuits that happened every time he put his hands on her had to stop. Concentrating on his question, she said, "They might take the IV out today. I'm actually having a soft diet for lunch."

He made a face. "Yuck."

She made a face at him. "It beats not eating anything."

"You have a point." He hitched up his suit pants and

sat on the edge of the bed, facing her. "I made some calls this morning. We could get married in two days."

"Two days!" She'd assumed there was a waiting period but apparently that wasn't so. "All right," she said cautiously. "I guess we might as well go ahead if I'm out of here by then."

He laughed. "Now that's what I call a ringing endorsement."

"It's just...I'm having a little difficulty keeping up with everything." She pleated the sheet with her fingers. "The doctor told me this morning that he wants to see how my body reacts when they take me off the antinausea drug. If I start to feel sick again, he'll prescribe something that should help, and I'll be able to go home." Then she sat up a little straighter. "What's happening at the gallery?"

"I just came from there. Penny and Melissa are working, and Penny has someone else named Jil on the schedule." He looked questioningly at her and she nodded, satisfied. Jil and Melissa were both part-timers who knew the merchandise and the artisans behind them well enough to speak with confidence. "Penny wanted me to tell you she sold four pieces of the Ramirez collection and one of the beaded crystal bags this morning and that sales have been steady."

"That's good news," she said. "Emanuel Ramirez is a Southwestern artist who designs silver jewelry. He's sent me some really stunning things."

"Where did you find him?"

"One of my friends was in Arizona and saw some of his work. She was so impressed she called me. She has a good eye and she's found successful items before, so I flew out and met Mr. Ramirez and brought back some samples to see how they'd do in Boston." She couldn't prevent the satisfied smile. "I can't keep the stuff in stock."

"You enjoy what you do." He was studying her face.

"I do. It's exciting to find new artists and new items that are unique. A lot of my clientele is tourists, of course, but I also have a growing number of people in the area who come in on a regular basis for wedding and birthday gifts. I've been thinking about looking for some distinctive baby gifts when I expand." She forced herself to ignore the little voice that said, *If you can get a loan.* "I think they would be a hit."

"Speaking of baby gifts," he said, reaching for the large box he'd brought in, "why don't you open this?"

"What is it?"

He shrugged. "I thought the first gifts our babies received should come from me."

Working the ribbon over one corner she slipped the lid off the box. Clouds of pink and blue tissue obscured whatever was inside. Carefully she lifted the tissue out of the way. Two stuffed toys, white tiger cubs with wide blue eyes, were nestled side by side in the remaining tissue. One was reclining; the other sat up. They had golden chains around their necks with faceted crystal hearts dangling from them.

She pulled them from the box and stroked the soft fur. "They're adorable," she said. "We'll keep one in each crib. They can watch over the babies for us."

He smiled indulgently. "There's something else in there."

Her senses went on red alert at the tone in his voice. Slowly, she set the stuffed animals to one side and reached back into the tissue. Her seeking fingers found a small box, and she withdrew it from the larger container. "Ryan, if this is what I think it is, you don't have to—"

"Shh." He laid his finger against her lips. "You know me well enough to know that nobody makes me do anything I don't want to, Jess. Just open it."

The little box was wrapped in glittering gold paper with a white bow. She tore away the wrapping to expose a black velvet box. Slowly, she exerted the pressure necessary to flip open the hinged lid. The ring inside was as spectacular as she'd feared.

It was composed of diamonds, one very large round-cut center stone with four small diamonds lining the band on each side. It was beautifully, classically cut and the stones caught the lights and shot shining sparks in all directions as she tilted it from side to side. "Ryan, this is incredibly lovely," she said. She intended to add that she couldn't keep it, but he forestalled her with a gentle hand over her mouth.

"Thank you, Ryan," he said. "I'll cherish it forever."

Her breath huffed out in a chuckle beneath his hand before he withdrew it. "But I can't accept it," she said seriously.

"Of course you can." His eyes were a deep sapphire today and they pinned her beneath a level stare. "You're going to be my wife, the mother of my children. Someday you can pass this ring down to one of our children." He leaned forward and took her upper arms in a light grasp. "Do you have any idea how happy you're making me?" His voice was intense, his eyes more so.

She hesitated.

"Please, Jess," he said, "don't make too much of this. You're beautiful. I want to give you beautiful things." Gently he took the ring from her and slipped it onto her finger.

"You think I'm...beautiful?" She had to clear her throat. "I thought you'd see me forever as the skinny, knock-kneed little kid who drove you crazy following you and Emily Preswick around when you were twelve and I was ten.''

He smiled. ''You were a pain in the butt that year, I'll grant you. But yes, I do think you're lovely.'' His smile faded and he brushed her cheek with surprisingly tender fingers. ''Your skin feels like silk to my touch. You have roses in your cheeks again and your eyes are sparkling. Your lips…'' His voice faded.

She shivered. He was looking at her mouth now and there was no mistaking the expression on his face. Slowly he leaned forward, cupping a hand around the back of her neck and drawing her to him as he set his lips on hers.

He wasn't tentative this time, though his mouth was gentle. Seductive. Warm and firm on hers, growing hotter and bolder, sweeping aside all her rational objections. He slipped his free hand around her back and pulled her against his chest, and her pulse leaped as her body, clad only in the silky pajama top he'd brought her from home, met the broad planes of his chest.

Her hands came up, clasping the heavy muscles of his shoulders, and he parted her lips, his tongue dipping deliciously deep, sweeping exploratory circles in her mouth until she met and answered his demand with forays of her own. His hand slid from the back of her neck to circle the base of her throat, and her pulse leaped as her breasts tightened in sensual hunger. But he didn't touch her there, didn't move his hand lower. He merely brushed his thumb against the racing pulse in her neck, over and over again, as he thrust his tongue into her in a shockingly intimate imitation of lovemaking.

Finally, he tore his mouth free, sliding it down her throat to nibble a path across her collarbone. ''Jess,'' he murmured against her skin. ''I want you.''

"I know." Her fingers were in his hair, caressing the silky strands. "This seems so odd."

"Not to me." He drew back, then stroked his palms from her shoulders to her elbows and back, slowly savoring the soft flesh with an absorbed look on his face. "What could be better than marrying your best friend, with whom you just happen to share incredibly hot sex?"

"We aren't," she reminded him.

"Yet." He sounded confident. "We will. And it will be hot enough to blister the paint off the walls."

"Could get expensive." She deliberately reached for a lighter tone.

He grinned, making his dimples deepen and her stomach contract. "Good thing I've got that covered."

She was released early in the afternoon of the following day. Minus the IV *and* the nausea, courtesy of the prescription the doctor had already started. He'd instructed her to take it easy until her twelfth week, at which time they'd start easing her off the drug and see how she felt. When she'd ask him to define "easy," she was immediately sorry. No working. No extensive walking. No stairs. Let someone wait on you for a few weeks. Her mind had reeled at the implications of all the restrictions. Then he'd said, "No sexual relations." Ryan was in the room during the doctor's visit, and she hadn't been able to look at him, though she could feel her face burning. Could he possibly be feeling as chagrined and frustrated as she?

An orderly took her down to the entrance in a wheelchair, where Ryan was waiting in the sedate silver Mercedes in which she'd ridden before.

"Guess we're going to have to get some car seats for this buggy," he said as he helped her into the car. "Or get a minivan. They make them with child seats built in now.''

She grimaced. ''The ultimate family transportation. I vote for buying car seats.''

''Mr. Shaughnessy?'' A woman came out of the hospital, holding the white box that held the two tiger cub toys he'd brought Jessie, just as Ryan lowered himself into the car. ''Don't forget this.''

Jessie's breath caught in her throat. Not at the thought of forgetting the stuffed animals, but at the arrested expression on Ryan's face. Turning, she looked at the woman walking toward them. She was short, petite and blond. Wide blue eyes were fastened on Ryan's face and she was smiling…*she was Wendy.*

Oh, not really, but the hospital attendant walking toward them with the box looked enough like Ryan's deceased wife that the likeness would be hard to miss. She glanced back at Ryan and saw that he certainly hadn't missed it. On his lean face was acute anguish, a deep, soul-searing grief burning in his blue eyes.

''I'll just pop this in the back seat,'' said the Wendy look-alike, beaming.

Ryan cleared his throat. ''Um, thank you.'' He gripped the steering wheel as the young woman placed the box in the back seat, and Jessie could see the tips of his fingers were white with pressure.

''There you go. Good luck!'' She stepped back and closed the car door, waving before hurriedly retreating into the warmth of the hospital.

It was a gray, dreary day outside, and Jessie felt gray and dreary as well. She glanced across at Ryan as he drove. His profile was somber and a muscle ticked along his jaw. She opened her mouth, then closed it again. What was she going to say? He clearly didn't want to discuss it, or he'd have brought up the topic himself.

Holy cow! Did you notice how much that girl looked like my dead wife?

No. He obviously didn't want to talk.

Insecurity hunched her shoulders deep into her coat, and she turned her face to look out the passenger-side window as her eyes brimmed with sudden tears. She didn't have huge expectations for this marriage, she assured herself. As long as they remained friendly and got along well enough to be good parents, that would be sufficient. So what if they didn't have a great, all-consuming love like Ryan had apparently felt for Wendy? Might as well keep her track record intact. She'd never known the love that most people took for granted from the ones who shared their lives. Chip had been her only experience with love, and his affection had been cloying, his tendency to set her on a pedestal and cater to her stifling rather than inspiring love in return.

When he turned on Commonwealth Avenue heading away from the Commons, she came out of her silence. "We're going the wrong way."

"No, we're not." His voice was quiet and deliberate. "No exertion, remember? The doctor said you need someone with you for a while."

"That isn't exactly what he said—"

"So you can move in a few days early. When I'm busy, Finn will look after you."

"I don't need looking after." She made an effort to relax her gritted teeth. "I just need to be a little careful. I'd prefer to stay in my own place."

Ryan shook his head. "Not an option. If I go out of town, I want to know that you're not overdoing it or lying in bed too sick to move." His right hand left the wheel and settled briefly over her stomach. "I want to see these babies alive and well in seven or so more months."

So he only wanted to be sure she was all right because of the babies. "I'll hire someone to check on me daily," she said, mentally juggling her finances, knowing she really couldn't afford it.

He simply shook his head again and kept driving toward Brookline.

"I'm not ready to move in with you," she said, trying to keep the desperation out of her voice. Why did this bother her so much? How many women would object to living in a mansion like Ryan's? With Ryan to ice the cake.

"What difference does a few days make?" he asked in a voice that dripped with reason and made her long to punch him. "We're getting married as soon as you can stay on your feet for more than five minutes without wearing out. Are you telling me you weren't planning on living with me after we're married?"

"I haven't had time to plan anything!" she yelled.

There was a small silence in the car. Ryan braked at the tail end of a traffic snarl and laid his arm along the back of her seat, turning to face her. "I want you to live with me, Jessie," he said quietly. "I don't want this to be a marriage in name only or some weird kind of commuter marriage. I want my wife and my children in my house." He raked a hand through his hair and looked out the driver's-side window. "I guess there are a few things we need to talk about, aren't there?"

She nodded tightly.

"All right." He sighed, facing forward and releasing the brake as the traffic began to move sluggishly. "Will you at least rest awhile and have dinner with me? Then, if you really want to go home, I'll take you."

He sounded so reasonable that it would have been churlish to refuse. Even if she was dying to get back to her own home. "All right."

When they arrived at his house, Ryan helped her out of the car, then bent and lifted her into his arms before she realized what was happening. She gasped and clutched at his shoulders. "You're going to give yourself a hernia."

He chuckled as he carried her through the garden. "I've carried furniture that was heavier than you, cupcake."

"Cupcake?"

"Just a figure of speech." As he went up the steps and across the flagstones of the semicircular patio, the back door opened. "I've been expecting you, Jessie," Finn called from the doorway. "Welcome. I've prepared the most scrumptious chicken consommé for you and I have a room all ready—"

She caught Ryan's warning shake of the head and Finn stopped abruptly.

"It's all right," she told Finn. Without looking at Ryan, she said, "Actually, I am more worn out than I'd expected. I think I'd like to rest before I eat. Could you take me straight to the room?"

Without a word Finn turned and led the way through the house. Ryan carried her upstairs without even breathing heavily, and she caught herself wondering exactly how much exercise he got in a day's time. His upper chest and shoulder were a hard rock wall beneath her head, and she could feel the powerful flex of muscle in his upper back as he shifted her slightly.

The room into which Finn took them was absolutely beautiful. If she'd dreamed up the perfect environment for herself, it couldn't have been better. She loved pretty, feminine things, and this was the ultimate in both. The

wallpaper was a muted pattern of pink and lavender flowers with a suggestion of soft-green leaves down to a chair
rail, beneath which was a subdued pearl and lavender
stripe. The sheer, filmy curtains over the shades echoed
the same pearly shade and a swath of fabric that matched
the flower wallpaper created a striking yet informal swag
across the top and draping down the sides. A duvet in the
same fabric was accented by silky pearl and lavender pillows as was the fabric covering a genteel lady's chair in
one corner.

The bed itself looked like mahogany, as did all the furniture in the room, including a tall cabinet whose doors
were folded back to display an up-to-date technological
bonanza of computer equipment. As Ryan set her down
on the edge of the bed, she noticed a small marble foun-
tain with gleaming pebbles in it on a table against a wall,
its small waterfall creating a pleasant, soothing sound.
When Finn touched a button on the remote control that
lay on the bedside table, a television screen unfolded from
the ceiling into a not-quite-vertical position perfect for
viewing from the bed.

"You can change the angle of the dangle, so to speak,
with these," he said, chortling as he pointed to a couple
of little, arrowed buttons. Then he set it down and walked
to the right side of the room. Sweeping open a door, he
touched a panel and illuminated the largest walk-in-closet
she'd ever seen. "Voilà. Madam's wardrobe."

"Holy cow. I could live in there," she said. Her organized heart was singing as she looked at all the cedar
shelves, vinyl zippered cupboards and hanging spaces for
a wardrobe.

To the left of the closet, a pale-pink marble bathroom
with gleaming brass accents was visible through a set of
double doors. A large, freestanding glass shower stall rose

in the middle of the room. Along one wall two wide steps led up to an enormous spa-tub with a tasteful collection of plants, candles and bath soaps ranged around its broad lip. The wall behind the tub was a thick, opaque window that let in the light without any danger of exposure to prying eyes. At one end of the tub, a television was built into the wall.

She walked slowly into the bathroom to get the full effect. His and hers sinks lined the wall opposite the tub; beside the tub, flames danced merrily in a small gas fireplace built into the wall. There was a separate, small stall with a toilet and bidet just inside her door. At the far end another set of double doors revealed a masculine suite.

"My rooms," Ryan said.

Wordlessly she turned and paced back into her bedroom. She sat carefully down on the side of the bed as both men stared at her. "What's wrong?"

"I've finally realized just how wealthy you really are," she said to Ryan. "It's a little…disconcerting."

He gave a snort of laughter. "Because I have a really cool bathroom?"

She shook her head and waved a hand to indicate the room. "It's everything." Then she hesitated, not knowing how to phrase the question burning in her brain. "Was this…?"

Ryan nodded. "Wendy's room. But Finn completely redecorated it when I told him we were getting married. New carpet, new furniture, new wallpaper and curtains—"

"The paint's not new," Finn said modestly. "I was afraid it would leave an odor and really, the paint was in fine shape. So I simply went for a look that blended with it. It wasn't difficult. There are some stunning fabrics and wallpapers out there. The furniture can be exchanged if you prefer a different style.''

''It's lovely,'' she said, smiling at Finn, hoping to mask her relief at not having to sleep in a bed that had belonged to Wendy. ''Really, really lovely.''

Finn blushed. ''We do our best.'' He turned and bustled to the door. ''I'm going to fix you a tray and bring it up. Then you can rest right here all afternoon.''

There was silence in his wake. The room seemed calmer, as if Finn stirred the very air around him. She glanced at Ryan and caught him grinning, and she couldn't prevent her own laughter from escaping. ''He's certainly…energetic.''

''He's manic,'' Ryan said. ''Give him a project and he works as hard as a squirrel on steroids. You have no idea how much fun he had with this. He did his own rooms, too. I asked him if he'd live in, and he agreed. So there will always be someone here for you when I'm not home.'' He hesitated, then walked toward her. ''Time for you to lie down. You're weaving.''

''I feel like a piece of well-cooked spaghetti,'' she complained. ''It's ridiculous.''

''You've been ill,'' he reminded her, ''*and* you're pregnant.'' He took her elbow, and she stood docilely while he pulled back the covers with the other hand. Then he bent and tugged off her fashionable boots, and when she lay down, he covered her with the duvet. ''I have some things to do. Let Finn feed you and then you can rest. I'll go by the gallery before it closes and see how everything's going.''

''Thank you.'' She laid her hand over his where it pressed into the bed beside her.

He smiled, bent and pressed a kiss to her forehead. ''No problem. Cupcake.''

She grimaced. "It's a good thing I don't have anything to throw at you."

He only laughed as he rose and walked from the room.

When Ryan got home that evening, Finn met him at the door. "She's still sleeping. I checked on her once each hour. After she ate a little soup, she crashed and burned."

Ryan nodded. "I don't think she realizes how weak she is right now." He set down the bag with the logo of a familiar department store, and Finn took his cashmere overcoat. "I'll be with her. Why don't you set dinner at that little table in my suite?"

Finn saluted with his free hand. "Aye-aye, cap'n."

He picked up the shopping bag and took the stairs two at a time, but when he got to the door to her room, he paused. The door was slightly ajar, and the new colors seemed wrong to him for a moment. He was used to seeing the cool blue-and-white scheme in which Wendy had decorated the room.

Wendy. He'd had a bad moment this afternoon when that nurse had walked toward him. Though she hadn't looked *that* much like Wendy, at first glance anyone could have been forgiven for mistaking them.

He didn't think Jessie had noticed the resemblance. She'd been very quiet on the way home, and he suspected she was fighting to stay awake. The doctor had warned them that sleepiness was a side effect of the medication she was taking.

At any rate, he'd spent the rest of the ride thinking about his life before Jessie. He'd been happy. Not delirious, but happy. Wendy had loved him totally, and his heart, bruised from years of longing for Jessie, had responded to her warmth and sweetness. And yet, if he were honest with himself, there had always been a small pocket inside him that had remained untouched. Waiting for Jessie.

He'd never in a million years have imagined this current scenario, and guilt streaked through him. Rationally he knew he hadn't wished Wendy's death. But it was hard to shake the feeling that he'd never been as good to her as she deserved.

Slowly he pushed the door wider so that he could see the bed. Jessie lay on her side, still sleeping. Her dark hair was tousled, and her face was peaceful, her lips slightly parted. One hand was tucked beneath her cheek, the other dangled over the side of the bed. Quietly he picked up a chair and set it beside her, then took her hand in his.

Her eyelids fluttered. The silvery-green gleam of her eyes appeared, and then she smiled at him, turning her hand in his and gently squeezing. "Hello."

"Hello." The moment was so sweet he thought his heart might burst. "I'm going to have to change your moniker to Sleeping Beauty."

She glanced beyond him to the window and he saw her eyes widen as she realized it was full dark outside. "What time is it? How long did I sleep?"

"About five hours," he said. "It's seven-thirty."

"Seven-thirty!" She pushed herself upright, tugging the sweater and slacks she'd worn home from the hospital into a wrinkled semblance of order.

He waited for her to protest, to demand that he take her home immediately. But all she said was, "Poor Finn. I didn't eat much of his lunch."

"It's all right," Ryan said. "He'll forgive you if you do justice to dinner. It's the same thing, by the way."

She made a face. "Tomorrow I'm allowed to eat more. You'd better warn Finn his consommé days are numbered."

He'd love to ignore the whole topic but he knew they had to talk about it. "Will you be here tomorrow?"

She hesitated, biting her lower lip. "I guess so." She looked up at him, and he couldn't resist laying his finger on the lip she was mutilating. She released it immediately and gave him a small, forlorn smile that quivered at the edges. "I don't know why I'm having such trouble with the concept of moving. I had expected to when we got married. It's just—I've had to look after myself for a long, long time. I feel odd letting someone else take over. It feels wrong, somehow."

Pity rose for the little girl who'd had to make her own school lunches, who'd often had so many chores she didn't have time to come out and play…the little girl who'd been alone long before her grandparents and her mother died, one by one, when she was in high school and college. He tended to forget the way she'd lived as a child. It would have destroyed a lesser person. But Jessie had drawn strength from somewhere inside herself and triumphed. No wonder she had trouble accepting help.

Quietly he said, "I don't want to take over, Jess. We're going to be a team. Right now we need to work out strategies to win in October." October sixteenth, the magic date. That was when the twins were due, although they'd been warned that multiples often came early.

"You're right," she said. "Accepting help will be my personal challenge." She took a deep breath. "Would it be okay with you if I stayed here tonight?"

His chest rose and fell in a deep sigh of relief. He supposed he'd better not tell her he'd been to her apartment and packed a small suitcase of things for her. "That would be more than okay," he said. "Tomorrow I'll bring you some of your things."

* * *

The next three days were quiet. He brought Jessie some clothing and her toiletries. Finn reported that she slept a great deal, though she stayed in close touch with Penny at the gallery. The doctor called on Thursday and sounded pleased when she reported that she was resting a lot and feeling much better. At night they discussed her gallery, his business dealings and read each other information from the dozens of baby books he brought home. It was extraordinarily satisfying in some ways, though he knew it was merely a lull in the action. Once Jessie began to feel better, she'd be chafing at the bit. And once the babies came…well, he couldn't even imagine it.

On Friday Ryan had appointments nonstop until three. Then he buzzed his secretary and told her to cancel everything for the rest of the day. As he'd promised Jessie, he took a pass by the gallery. Penny, the assistant manager, was young, but Jessie had chosen well and trained her even better. There was very little for him to do other than check the accounts and authorize a few payments on Jessie's behalf. Penny had even taken over the books.

When he got home, Finn didn't greet him at the door. He hung up his own coat, which was fine with him, though Finn usually insisted on doing his butler imitation, and headed through the house, wondering if Finn had gone out to the store or something. Then he heard the laughter.

He followed the sound upstairs to Jessie's room. As he neared the doorway, he heard her say, "Ha. *Q-U-E-E-N*. On a triple-word space, that's thirty and let's see, fifteen. Mark me down for forty-five points, Finn."

"You witch!" Ryan could barely understand the words because Finn was laughing so hard. He knew from experience that his employee considered himself a champion Scrabble player. "I swear those big numbers stuck to your fingers when you dipped into that bag. Rematch tomorrow.'' But humor colored his voice.

"You're on.'' Then she caught sight of Ryan lounging in the door. "Hi! Are you early? I just beat the pants off Finn.''

"You won by three points,'' Finn said testily. "And only because I couldn't get rid of that *K* I drew near the end.'' He rose and turned to Ryan. "Sorry I didn't hear you come in.''

Ryan shrugged. "Understandable. Nothing like getting beaten by a girl to make you concentrate.''

"Hey!'' Jessie shook a finger at him. "Chauvinism is uncalled for.''

Finn glared at him. "I'd like to see you do better.''

Ryan laughed. "You'd both clobber me. Numbers are my forte, not letters.''

Finn and Jessie finished putting the game pieces in the box, and Finn rose from the chair he'd set at a small table beside the bed. He replaced the chair and table in their original positions and then took the game from Jessie. "I'd better get dinner started. How does a chicken casserole sound?''

"Great.'' As he left the room, she turned to Ryan. "He's a lot of fun. I could get used to lying around in the lap of luxury all day.''

It shouldn't bother him that part of the reason Jessie was marrying him was because she knew he could provide for their children and her, he told himself. Hadn't he used his success as one of the lures when he'd been talking her into it? "Feel free to do that if it makes you happy,'' he said. " I don't care if you never work again.''

Jessie looked horrified. "You may not, but I do. I've worked hard to turn The Reilly Gallery into something unique and special. It's more to me than just a job.''

He nearly pointed out that she'd been more than happy to forget it for the past week, but his rational self reminded him that she'd been too ill to think much at all. What was the matter with him?

He was afraid he knew the answer to that. He had dreamed of Jessie for years, then given up that dream. Now suddenly the dream was tossed in his lap. Part of it, anyway. And though he anticipated the physical part of their new relationship with a need that was nearly painful, it wasn't enough. He wanted her to want him the way he wanted her. Not just physically but emotionally. He wanted her, body and soul. Heart and mind.

He wanted it all.

Six

The next day was Saturday.

Ryan knocked on the door of Jessie's room shortly after eight. She knew he'd already been up for an hour, working out in the weight room on the third floor.

"Come in," she called.

He turned the knob and pushed open the door, looping the white towel he carried around his neck. "Good morning. Shall I have Finn bring up some breakfast?"

Jessie pursed her lips. "I think I'd rather eat downstairs."

But he stepped forward before she could rise from the bed. "Uh, why don't you let Finn coddle you this morning? Save your energy."

"For what?" she asked with a wry grin. "My afternoon nap?"

"Well..." He walked to the bed and stood looking

down at her. "Actually, I thought we might go to a wedding today if it wouldn't tire you out too much."

Her eyes widened. "You mean *our* wedding? Get married today?"

He nodded. "No reason to wait, is there?"

She shrugged, shook her head. "No. There isn't." She squared her shoulders. "All right. Let's do it."

"Great." He turned and headed for the door. "I'll get Finn up here with breakfast, then he can lay out something for you to wear."

Two hours later she sat in a chair outside the office of the justice of the peace. Finn sat beside her while Ryan paced restlessly up and down the hall.

"You look lovely," Finn said. He fussed with the peek-a-boo lace across the bodice of the dressy suit she'd chosen. "That ivory suit was a wonderful choice."

She grinned at him, though her attention was still on her husband-to-be, who seemed far more nervous than he should, given the fact that *he'd* railroaded *her* into this marriage. "I never expected to wear this to my wedding when I bought it."

"Oh, dear heavens!" Finn sprang to his feet. "You don't have any flowers!" He zipped over to Ryan's side. "I'm going to get some flowers. You cannot get married without flowers."

"Get a camera, too," Ryan said. "One of those little disposable ones will do."

He caught her eye as Finn disappeared. "You heard the man. We *cannot* get married without flowers."

She chuckled. "Wanna bet?" Then she looked around. "It feels funny to be out in public again after feeling rotten for so long."

Ryan crossed to her side and took the seat Finn had vacated. He put his arm around her, hugging her close to his side. "You have no idea how relieved I am to see you feeling better."

"About as relieved as I am to be feeling better," she said. "When I scheduled this pregnancy, I didn't leave any flex time for problems like *this*. I've got to get back to work."

Ryan was silent for a moment. Then he said, "It's possible you're going to have to stick to a modified schedule for some time once you go back, you know."

"A modified schedule?" She didn't like the sound of that. Was Ryan going to be one of those husbands who wanted his wife at home? She thought he'd clearly understood her position on that the other day—

"Part-time," he said. "Until the doctor thinks you're really fit enough to handle a full schedule. Carrying two babies presents some extra difficulties sometimes."

"Once I get past this queasy stage, I'll be fine." She couldn't let herself believe otherwise. Her store *needed* her. And she needed it. She'd worked so hard to make her business what it was, to support herself, to be a success. If she didn't get back in there soon, all that would be in danger.

As she was mulling over the dark thoughts, Finn returned. He carried a bouquet of orange blossoms and made them pose for a ridiculous number of pictures on the small camera he'd bought while they waited.

Finally the doors to the justice of the peace's chamber opened. A beaming couple came out, holding hands, with several people behind them, and Jessie swallowed her nerves as Ryan took her hand and led her inside.

The ceremony didn't take long at all. Her hands shook as she placed the wedding band on Ryan's finger and accepted hers from him. His hands were cool and steady, and he put an arm around her as they spoke their vows.

When he kissed her, he kept it brief, but the telling pressure of his lips and a quick wisp of his tongue across her bottom lip turned her bones to jelly.

After the ceremony, she glanced up at him covertly. Could Ryan really be her husband now? He met her eyes and in his, she saw the warmth and reassurance she realized she'd craved. She'd been so afraid this was a mistake, so afraid Ryan would regret marrying her. So afraid he'd be thinking of Wendy today. But as they signed their names to the license, all she saw in his expression was pleasure and a confidence that steadied her. Finn snapped pictures and tossed a few handfuls of orange blossom over them as they exited the chamber. Then Ryan carried her back to the car and took her home to bed again.

Alone, as the doctor had ordered.

It was hardly the wedding day she'd hazily imagined when she'd allowed herself to consider that she might someday marry. But because it was Ryan who'd slid his ring onto her finger, it became the perfect wedding.

She went back to the doctor the following week.

As Ryan had predicted, she got edgier as she began to feel better. She'd begged him twice to take her down to the gallery "just for a quick look around," but he'd refused, telling her the doctor would let her know when she was allowed on her feet again.

She walked into the doctor's office, though Ryan had carried her out to the car, and he could feel her impatience with the restrictions.

"Well, hello," said the receptionist. "It's nice to see you in a vertical position today."

Jessie smiled. "I'm feeling much better."

When it was their turn, the doctor pronounced himself very pleased. He told her she could work three half days a week until he saw her again in two weeks, near the middle of March.

"But I feel fine now," Jessie said, clearly unhappy with the doctor's edict.

The obstetrician merely smiled. "I know. But I don't want you to overdo it. Once you've reached twelve weeks and we see how your body responds without any medication, we'll talk about working more."

As they got back into the car to go home, Jessie said glumly, "At this rate my store will be in the red by the end of the year."

"No way." He checked for traffic, then swung out onto the street. "Penny is doing a fine job. I haven't been lying to you."

"Yes, but I've already had to cancel appointments for a loan twice, and who knows when I'll be able to reschedule them?"

"You'll be back on your feet again before you know it. And I bet you'll have a loan soon thereafter."

She was silent. When he looked her way again, her lower lip was quivering.

"What's the matter?" He reviewed the conversation. What had he said? Done? The books weren't kidding when they said a woman's hormones went crazy during pregnancy.

Jessie took a deep breath and sniffed. "I feel superfluous. I'm not necessary to the gallery."

You're necessary to me. The words very nearly popped out of his mouth before he controlled the thought. "You're necessary," he said patiently. "Penny doesn't have the experience or the people skills to court your artisans. She doesn't begin to have your eye for striking displays and for what works with what. Sure, your products have continued to sell well, largely because they're unique, quality items that *you* selected." He took a breath. "You hired an efficient, organized assistant. Right now she's doing exactly what you need her to do. Soon you'll be able to do what you do best again. And once you do, that other shop will be sunk."

She didn't say anything, and her lip continued to quiver.

He didn't know what else he could say to make her feel better, so he concentrated on the traffic, feeling clumsy and awkward. He hoped he hadn't made her feel worse.

Finally she sighed. "I really hate to admit this, but I'm exhausted. I guess I'd better lie down again when we get home."

He smiled, relieved that she was recognizing her limits. "You did well today. Tomorrow you'll feel even better."

"Tomorrow," she said, "I'm going to work for a whole half day."

Three weeks later he took her to her apartment on Saturday morning. It was the first time she'd been in it since the day Ryan had taken her to the hospital. She knew he'd sent Finn over twice to clean it, and the bed had been neatly made with fresh sheets.

"Pack whatever you think you'll need for the short term," he told her. "Soon you're going to need new clothing, anyway."

She glanced down at her stomach. Although she didn't have anything to compare it to, she was pretty sure a pregnant mother of a single baby didn't look like she looked already. She was barely nine weeks and already none of her pants fit. "I'll put anything I think I can still use in one suitcase and pack the others for you to bring over when you can."

"Put a sign on anything you want to keep," he said. "The rest can either go into storage or I can arrange to have it sold."

"My lease isn't up until September," she said. "I'll put a sign on the things I want to take to your house and we'll leave the rest here. I'll have to sublet it, and it's easier if it's furnished."

"That's not a problem. I can take care of it for you."

"That's all right. I'll do it." She looked around. "I suppose there really isn't very much here that I want to take with me. I won't need furniture." She fished in her purse for her key ring and detached a key from it. "While I'm packing, you could go down to the storage room in the basement. Stacked against the left wall back toward the corner are three boxes of things I kept after my mother died."

"All right." He accepted the key, then took her by the hips and tugged her against him in one quick, unexpected move. "How about some incentive?"

Her heart skipped a beat. His body was hard and exciting against hers, throwing off a heat that nearly scorched her. Did he have any idea how much she wanted him? Tentatively she lifted her arms to his wide shoulders. "I could probably manage that."

He looked down at her, and his eyes shot a brilliant blue challenge. Suddenly she understood that look. He'd initiated the few kisses they'd shared. Now it was her turn.

Slowly she lifted herself on tiptoe. Dimly she realized she was shaking as she drew near his chiseled mouth—

And then she pressed her lips to his. His mouth was cool and firm, but it warmed, softened as she kissed him gently. His arms came around her and she slid hers up his neck into his hair. And the kiss caught fire. His mouth hardened, plundered. She gasped, and he used it to ad-

vantage, sliding his tongue deep inside her tender mouth,
bending her back over one arm as she clutched at him for
balance. He kissed her endlessly, then slid his mouth
along her jaw to her earlobe, and she jerked in shock as
she felt his teeth nibbling at the sensitive flesh. Lightning
bolts of raw sexual need shot through her; she arched her
back, pressing her lower body firmly against him. He was
taut and hard and already aroused. Deep within her, an
empty ache begged for his fulfillment.

But he was ending the moment, drawing back the
slightest bit, his mouth leaving her ear. His breath was a
hot rasp against her flesh as he lifted his mouth from her
and set her upright again, and his kiss-reddened lips
quirked at one corner.

"Whoa," he said, and his gaze was intense. "Guess
you're sorry you started that."

Somehow she found her voice. "Not sorry. Only sorry
that we can't finish it."

There was a full five seconds of silence as his eyes
narrowed. "You picked a hell of a time to admit you want
me."

She shrugged. "You picked a hell of a time to start
something."

They stared at each other a moment, then a chuckle
worked its way up through Ryan's chest, rolling out as a
rich, sustained shout of laughter. "We're a pair," he said,
releasing her and strolling to the door.

She stood in the middle of her apartment after he left,
one hand pressed against her mouth. He hadn't touched
her that way since she'd been in the hospital. Instead, he'd
kissed her on the forehead, rubbed her shoulders and casually held her hand as if she were nothing more than a
good friend.

Which she was, wasn't she? No, darn it, she was his

wife! And she wanted him to…to touch her as if she were more than just a friend.

She'd begun to wonder if he would lose interest as she grew rounder and less desirable. But that kiss! That kiss left her in no doubt that he was anticipating the day when the doctor gave her the green light to pursue normal activities.

The trouble was, making love with Ryan wasn't *normal,* for her! An involuntary shiver worked its way through her body, lingering deep in her abdomen. She wanted him, and he'd made it more than clear that he wanted her. But where did it go from there? Unhappily she walked into her bedroom and opened drawers, filling the first of her suitcases that Ryan had pulled out and laid open on the bed for her.

He was so very dear to her in so many ways. Not only did they have their childhood memories to draw them together, they had the friendship they'd established as adults. And now they had love.

Her hands stilled on the stack of sweaters she'd just set in the suitcase. No, she corrected herself, *they* didn't have love, *she* had love. Oh, God. She was a fool. Ryan had a healthy lust and affection for her, but his heart still belonged to the dead wife whom she could never replace.

And that was the problem. She wanted to give herself to him in every way there was, to show him how much she loved him with her body even if she couldn't say the words. But…she was afraid. Unbidden, the look on his face the day they'd left the hospital sneaked into her mind. Deep in her heart, she feared that Ryan would meet someone someday—someone who reminded him of Wendy and whom he could love as he'd loved his first wife.

Forcing herself to move, she resumed packing. There was absolutely nothing she could do about that. And she could hardly expect the man to forego the *normal* aspects of a marital relationship. She'd simply have to remember the circumstances under which their marriage had been arranged and protect her heart as best she could.

The sound of the opening door jolted her and she dropped the stack of socks into the suitcase in a far more haphazard manner than she usually did.

"Mission accomplished." Ryan lounged in the doorway. "The boxes are in the car. Want me to start taking down suitcases?" He indicated the ones she had closed.

She nodded. "By the time you finish, I'll have this last one ready to go."

They took the boxes home and Ryan enlisted Finn's help to carry them upstairs and unpack everything. Then he left for his office, telling her he had a few pressing things he needed to check. The trip had worn her out, and Jessie was happy to rest as Finn arranged her garments in the great big closet.

"Hey, girlfriend," he said, holding up a straight black cocktail dress. "Dynamite. I bet you look hot in this."

She grinned. "I brought it because it has no waistline and I thought if we had to go to anything formal in the next few months I might still be able to wear it."

"Ha." Finn eyed the small mound of her belly beneath the covers. "At the rate you're growing, you aren't going to be wearing anything but tents in a couple of months."

"Thanks loads. You're such a comfort."

"My pleasure."

She and Ryan's manservant, if that's what one called Finn, had reached an easy accord that delighted her. On the days she was home all day he'd begun showing her around the house, getting her acquainted slowly with the sizable rooms and their contents. He played games with her, cards and board games, which she let him win just

enough to keep him happy, and they'd taken to watching
one of the more ridiculous talk shows over the noon hour
and commenting on the guests' dramatic problems.

He was a bit like a mother hen, fussing her to rest,
fixing special meals and generally coddling her until she
had to tell him to relax. She adored him.

"Finn?" she said.

"Hmm?" He was folding sweaters and zipping them
into acrylic bags.

"Do you like children?"

He came out of the closet and sat on the edge of the
bed. "I think so. I've never really been around them very
much. I was an only child."

"So was I. What I know about babies would fit on the
head of a pin."

He grinned, his boyish face lighting up. "Hope you
learn fast."

"Me, too." She hesitated. "Are you going to stay when
there are two little terrors ripping through this place breaking vases and tracking in muddy footprints?"

He looked at her. "You're serious, aren't you?"

She nodded. "Ryan depends on you. And so do I. I
won't begin to have time to run a household of this size
with two children and my gallery."

"I'm not going anywhere." Finn's slender fingers
lightly brushed over the soft cashmere of the sweater he
still held. "Ryan's wonderful. He's kind and...tolerant.
He gave me a chance when I desperately needed one and
I'll never forget that." He looked at her, his eyes sober.
"I have a high school education. My partner was ten years
older, well-off, sophisticated...I never needed to work.
Then he got sick, and when he died, I was lost. No skills,
no one to care for...when my aunt told me Ryan was

willing to give me a try as a housekeeper, I was grateful even for the short-term offer.''

''He—*we,*'' she said, ''would be lost without *you.*'' She gathered her courage in both hands. ''I guess you must miss Wendy in your own way, as much as he does.''

Finn was stroking over the sweater again, his eyes downcast, and she couldn't read his thoughts. ''Wendy was so sweet,'' he said. ''It was a terrible, terrible thing when she…passed.''

''I knew her, too.'' She couldn't resist probing the edges of her jealousy like a child with a loose tooth. ''She seemed so perfect for Ryan.''

Finn's head came up. ''I didn't realize you knew her. Ryan has told me that you two were childhood friends but I didn't know…'' His eyes filled with tears and he reached unashamedly for a tissue on the bedside table. ''Sorry. She and I were very close.''

''I'm sure.'' Jessie waited for him to collect himself. *It's no one's fault but your own, if you feel like you're running second-best,* she told herself angrily, *even with the household help. You're the one who started this stupid conversation.*

''You look tired.'' Finn stood up, his gaze searching her face. ''I can finish hanging these things later. Why don't you take a little nappy-poo?''

His over-the-top phrasing made her smile as she suspected he'd intended. ''Good idea. I believe I will.''

But after he'd left the room, it was a long time before she fell asleep.

Ryan didn't touch her again—except for a few casual kisses on her forehead—for a long time. She went to her twelve-week checkup and the doctor announced they would begin tapering her off the medication. But to her chagrin, by the time they'd decreased the dosage to half, the nausea had returned. At fourteen weeks, the doctor upped the dosage again.

She had a second sonogram then, too. This time the babies were recognizably human, with tiny ears and features.

"That's not all we can see," the technician said. "Do you want to know what you're having?"

Jessie looked at Ryan. They already knew both would be the same sex. "What do you think?"

He was grinning. "I don't know if I can stand *not* to know, now that I know *she* knows." He indicated the technician, who was laughing. "What do you think?" he said to Jessie.

"I don't know," she wailed. "On one hand, I'd like to be surprised. On the other, we have to buy so much stuff for two babies that it would be nice to know what colors to go for. All right." She took a deep breath and said to the technician, "Tell us!"

Ryan reached for her hand and threaded her fingers through his, a different clasp than the loose hold he usually employed.

The technician smiled. "You're having girls," she said. "Think pink."

"Girls." Jessie envisioned two dainty little creatures in tulle. "Ballet. Braided hair."

"Softball and soccer," Ryan countered. "Don't be sexist." He leaned over the table and set his lips gently on hers. "Congratulations, Mama."

She returned the sweet kiss, wondering if he could feel how much she loved him. "Same to you, Daddy."

They didn't go straight home. Ryan took her shopping. "Just a short trip," he said. "Then you can go home and rest."

"I don't need to rest," she said. "Other than the fact that my body can't seem to stop feeling sick, I'm fine. Whoever figured out that lethargy goes away in the second trimester was absolutely right!"

They went straight to the infant department.

One day several weeks ago, Ryan had had a special delivery made: an enormous double stroller, two high chairs, two booster seats, two baby bathtub seats and two of several other vital items the modern world deemed necessary for rearing a baby.

But today he didn't stop to look at any equipment. Instead, he took her straight to the clothing section. "Pick out some things you like," he said. "Pink, frilly, lacy, whatever. I'm going to look for some of those teeny-tiny baseball outfits I've seen."

He came back a few minutes later, bearing not outfits, but instead, two of the tiniest Red Sox baseball caps she'd ever seen. She'd chosen several sleepers and two identical dresses, not exceptionally frilly because she couldn't stand fussy clothing. And they weren't even technically pink, but a soft shade of peach.

As they were making the purchases at the register, the clerk exclaimed over the twin clothing.

"We just found out today we're having girls," Jessie told her.

"Girls." The lady sighed happily. "I have three girls. What a delight." She efficiently folded the clothing and bagged it piece by piece. "Have you talked about names?"

"Not yet." She looked at Ryan. "We haven't even begun to toss around choices."

"You'd better get started," the clerk advised. "With my first, my husband changed his mind about the name a week before my due date. When the baby was born that night, we were still arguing about it in the delivery room!''

Jessie laughed. ''I hope we won't have that problem.''

That evening Ryan's voice over the intercom informed her that they'd be eating in the dining room.

She raised her eyebrows as she got up from the nap she'd taken, washed her face and put on one of the few blouses she owned that hung out over her unbuttoned pants. They'd eaten in her room at first, and later in the kitchen when she'd been well enough to be on her feet again. The dining room was a first.

Ryan was waiting at the foot of the steps when she came down. He smiled and offered her his arm. ''Very pretty,'' he said. ''I suppose soon you're going to need a whole new wardrobe.''

''Tents, according to Finn,'' she said.

He chuckled.

''You look nice, too.'' He was wearing a sky-blue sweater that made his eyes equally vivid, and brushed wool slacks in a camel color.

''I thought we should celebrate,'' he said. ''Hearing that we're having girls today made it more real somehow.''

''I know.''

In the dining room Finn had lit candles and closed the drapes. A low fire dozed in the gas fireplace, and silver gleamed on the table. The main course was an excellent broiled salmon steak served with couscous.

''I feel so decadent, having my meals served like this,'' she confessed as they dined.

He laughed. ''I've gotten over it.'' Then he sobered. ''Do you like to cook? If you'd rather do some of your own cooking, I can ask Finn—''

''Heavens, no!'' She grinned. ''Trust me, you do not

want me cooking for you. Why do you think I ate most of my meals out when I lived alone?''

''Ah. In that case, we'll leave the current arrangements as they are. Finn genuinely enjoys it. If he doesn't, he's a darn good liar.''

''I think he's as excited about the babies as we are.''

''Speaking of our babies…'' Ryan stood and walked to the sideboard, where he picked up a dusty-looking old book and brought it back to the table. He moved her empty plate and set it before her. ''When I was bringing in those boxes from your basement, the bottom fell out of one. As I was putting things back again, this caught my eye.''

She looked carefully at the book before it. It was a Bible, clearly quite old. She ran a finger across the cover. ''Have you looked at this?''

He nodded. ''Sorry. Simple curiosity. But I found something I think you'll agree is very interesting.''

Slowly, she opened the cover of the black Bible. It was a King James version. Inside, in an elegant penmanship she didn't recognize, was her grandmother's name before she had married Brendan Reilly. ''Was this my grandmother's?''

Ryan nodded. He turned a second page and she read the inscription in the same script.

''To Ellen Kathleen Sheehan on the occasion of her First Communion.'' She glanced at him. ''I wonder if this is my great-grandmother's writing.'' Conflicting feelings warred within her. Her memories of her grandmother were tinged with fear, respect, resentment…all tied too closely to untangle. Her grandmother's voice had been sharp, often exasperated, laced with disapproval whether she had been speaking to Jessie or to her daughter, Jessie's mother. If Ellen Sheehan Reilly had ever known a moment's affection for her bastard granddaughter, as she'd once called Jessie in a fit of cold anger, it had been buried deep. Deep enough that Jessie had never felt it. Her own children were never going to wonder why they weren't lovable. They were never going to be called bastards. They were never going to pray that their best would make their mother smile just this one time.

"You know," she said, running her finger over her grandmother's name. "I think she really hated me."

"Jessie, I—"

"No, Ryan, I really think she did. You were raised with so much love you can't imagine what it was like to share a home with that woman. She was a very strong personality. My mother and my grandfather both were quiet shadows. I can barely remember my own mother. Isn't that sad?"

Ryan picked up his chair and set it down close to her, then reached for her free hand. "I'm sorry."

She nodded. "So am I. Not just for myself, but for my grandmother. Wouldn't it have been easier just to forgive my mother? To be glad that she had a healthy grand-child?"

"Yes." His voice was certain. "It would have been. I wish I could change the past for you, Jess."

She smiled sadly at him. "So do I." With an effort she forced herself to set aside the bad memories. "Was this what you wanted to show me?"

"Not exactly." He pulled the Bible to him and leafed through it to the center section where there were pages for family genealogy—births, deaths and weddings. "Look at this."

What he'd found stunned her. There were at least three generations of her family prior to her mother's birth, all neatly chronicled in the order the events had occurred.

Names leaped out at her as she scanned the pages. Corcoran, O'Driscoll, Scally. Her own name and her mother's. Her grandmother's mother had been born in Ireland, her children in Boston. Family history, even this dry and long-dead, was something she'd always assumed she'd never have.

She blinked back tears. Then she realized he was still pointing to one specific part of the page. Carefully she read the words to herself. Ellen Kathleen Sheehan. b. 9/9/18, Boston. The date of death was blank, as was her mother's, and Jessie realized no one had been left to enter those, until now. She read the next line. Shannon Mary Sheehan. b. 9/9/18, Boston. d. 9/27/18, Boston.

Goose bumps rose. She raised shocked eyes to Ryan's. "My grandmother was a twin."

He nodded, unsmiling. "And it was another girl. Any bets they were identical?"

She sat back in her chair and reached for her water glass. "I can't believe it." She reread the entry. "Poor baby. She only lived nine days." Then she sat up straight as something else occurred to her. "Did you read *all* the other entries?"

He shook his head. "No. When I saw this, I was floored. I put the book down and walked in circles for a while." He smiled crookedly. "Someday we'll have to warn our own daughters about the twin births in their family history."

Jessie reached for the Bible again, pulling it closer and carefully reading each of the entries in the flowing, slanted handwriting. "Let's look at the other generations and see— Oh!" She stopped. "There's another set born to my great-grandmother's sister. I can't believe I never knew this." The anger within her swelled. "How could they have never shared this with me?"

"Your mother may never have known," Ryan pointed out.

"That's possible," she conceded. "Probable, in fact." She shoved the Bible away from her and blew out a breath of frustration, resting her head in her hands with her elbows on the table. "Knowing twins ran in my family might have changed a lot of things,' she said wearily.

"Like what?" Ryan stepped behind her and she felt his big hands come heavily down on her shoulders. His thumbs dug in, massaging taut muscles in her neck as he rubbed her shoulders, and she let herself relax beneath his ministrations. "I wouldn't change one single thing. In a few more months you and I are going to have two beautiful baby girls." He paused, and a note of grim humor entered his voice. "I guess it's a safe bet that we won't be naming one after your grandmother."

She snorted, unamused. "Definitely a safe bet." She rolled her head, giving him better access to the bands of tension in her neck.

The room was silent for a few moments as he continued his gentle massage. Slowly his touches became less clinical and more caressing. He slid his hands partway down her arms and back up, then into her hair.

She made a sound like a satisfied cat, somewhat startled to hear it come from her own throat. Her pulse began to beat a quick tattoo. Taking a deep breath to still her nerves, she reached up and took one of his hands, drawing it forward and pressing a kiss into his palm. "That felt wonderful," she said.

He moved to her side. Slowly, looking into her eyes, he took her elbow and helped her to her feet, then put his hands at her waist as she turned to face him. "Jess," he said, and his voice was rough velvet.

She lifted her arms to circle his neck as he slipped his hands around her and drew her close, searching out her mouth, claiming her with a sure, deep possession that shook her to her toes. She opened her mouth to him, her tongue dancing a swirling sensual pattern with his as he pulled her up against his chest, flattening her breasts against the firm, hard musculature. His thighs were hard. She made another sound deep in her throat as his thick arousal found the notch at her thighs and pressed heavily forward.

How long had she needed him without even knowing it? she wondered. Love flowed through her, tightening her arms around him as she gave herself more completely to his caresses. Her pregnancy was forgotten, the doctor's warnings unheeded as she moved her hips sinuously against his, excitement spiraling high as his body responded to her provocative motions and his hands slid down her back to palm her buttocks and pull her up tight against him.

She whimpered, squirming against him, trying to get even closer. And then he tore his mouth from hers. "Stop," he panted, his voice a fierce growl. "Do—not—move."

She stopped, too dazed to comprehend.

Ryan was breathing like a bellows, harsh gasps that moved her on his chest and sent sensation sizzling clear down to her toes. Reluctantly his arms loosened and he let her slide back to the floor. He groaned as her body slid over his and she caught her breath as his hips thrust one last time. Loosening his embrace, he took her by the arms and moved her a step away from him.

"Jess," he said.

She raised her gaze to his, her bewilderment plain. "Why not?"

He smiled, though there was a distinctly pained quality to it. "Believe me, it wasn't my first choice." His hands caressed her shoulders, his thumbs sliding along her collarbones with a light, sweet touch. "There's nothing I want more than to make love to you, but we can't. Doctor's orders, remember?"

Abruptly, she *did* remember, and her whole body sagged. "Dear Lord," she said. "What was I thinking?"

His smile widened to a wolfish grin, and his eyes glittered. "You weren't. And neither was I." Releasing her shoulders, he took her left hand, raising it between them to inspect the rings that were the symbol of his claim on her. "The day the doctor gives you a clean bill of health can't come soon enough for me. But the last thing in the world that I want to do is endanger our babies."

She nodded. Her knees were still shaking from the violence of the passion that had flared between them, but she knew he was right. And she agreed. Finally she heaved a sigh, offering him a wry grin. "You're right. I don't like it, but you're right." Then she stepped forward and raised herself on her tiptoes, pressing a gentle kiss against his stubbled jaw. "Thank you for stopping." Her voice was low. "I'm not sure I would have...thought to stop."

He groaned, taking her face between his big hands and taking her mouth in one last hard kiss before releasing her completely. "Great. Thanks for sharing *that*. I'm going to have enough trouble sleeping without knowing that if I'd kept my big mouth shut—"

She put a hand over his mouth, laughing. "But what a noble gesture. You're quite the romantic—" She stopped as his face changed. How stupid had that been? She should be the first one to remember that there had been nothing remotely romantic in their marriage agreement.

Ryan cleared his throat. "You'd better go to bed now. You've been on your feet enough today."

"Yes." She couldn't wait to escape before she gave in to the tears that were pushing behind her eyes. "I think I will."

Seven

In early May. Jessie and Ryan went on an introductory tour of the hospital for expectant parents. The tours were arranged by due date, with women who'd signed up for childbirth classes near the same time in the same tour groups.

She was the only woman in their group whose belly already led the way, and she decided it was time to acquire some maternity clothing. Ryan insisted on going along. They purchased a new wardrobe of items that were made for women who were going to wind up with roughly the same dimensions as a water buffalo.

On the way home they drove past her old apartment. She'd sublet it the month before to a young urban professional type who looked as if she would take good care of it.

They headed southwest to Brookline and home. Home. It *was* home, she realized, in a way no other residence in which she'd ever lived had been. Even her condo, which she'd made hers with art and other decor, had been just a place to live, not a place she'd ever felt attached to. At the Brookline house her whole body relaxed the moment she stepped through the door, and a sense of cozy rightness enveloped her.

Growing up, she'd never quite felt like she belonged in her grandparents' home. She'd felt tolerated. With a new flash of insight, she suspected that her mother probably had felt that way, as well. She'd give a lot to know what her mother's life had been like as a young woman, before the indiscretion that had been held against her for the rest of her parents' lives. She doubted it had been much different. She couldn't imagine her grandmother as anything other than stiff and unyielding, her grandfather quietly rigid and unaffectionate. Both of them had died during her high school years, but she'd been able to manage nothing more than a dry regret that their lives hadn't been happier.

Her mother hadn't changed appreciably after they were gone. She'd been beaten down too many times to recover, Jessie supposed. Or maybe she'd lacked the maternal instinct that even now stirred so strongly in her own breast. Jessie could hardly wait for the day when she'd hold her own babies. In any case, her mother's death during Jessie's senior year in college had been unexpected but not a life-changing trauma. Deep down Jessie had been alone for a long, long time.

Now you'll never be alone again.

The thought was quite a shock. But it was true! She was going to be a mother, a *good* mother. Her children weren't simply going to tolerate her, nor she them. And she had Ryan, as well. Even though he didn't love her, even if he didn't want to stay married to her, as she feared he wouldn't once the excitement of sharing parenthood wore off, she hoped they'd stay close, in more than a physical way.

Knowing that he was attracted to her was a sweet joy, one she could hardly wait to explore. But it wasn't enough. She longed for his love, even though she knew that was a hopeless dream.

And she was very, very good at not letting herself dream. Life had taught her to be a realist, to work hard to achieve the goals she knew were within reach with a lot of hard work. But life also had taught her how to discern when a goal was out of reach. Ryan was definitely one of those out-of-reach goals.

But they would always share these precious children and deep inside she couldn't suppress a small flicker of hope that Ryan would come to care for her a little, for the babies' sakes, of course.

Of course.

After dinner that evening Jessie went up and got ready for bed. Although she had been feeling well, and the fatigue of early pregnancy no longer dragged at her constantly, she still was exhausted and more than ready for bed.

She was already in bed, reading a book about breast-feeding twins, when Ryan knocked on the connecting door between their rooms. They shared the bath but each of them had been scrupulously polite about keeping their respective doors into the bathroom closed and knocking before they entered to be sure it was unoccupied.

"Come on in," she said. She was sitting up with the covers to her waist—or where her waist had once been—wearing one of Ryan's enormous T-shirts, which she'd found made wonderfully comfortable nightshirts.

When he walked through the connecting door, she caught her breath involuntarily. He was wearing a T-shirt and navy gym shorts, and his long, muscular legs were bare but for a dusting of dark curly hair. The shorts were a soft, stretchy fabric that clung to his lean thighs and did little to hide the raw power of his male body. In one arm he carried several books.

"Baby names," he said. "We should get started. People at the office are beginning to ask me."

"We still have a while to decide," she said mildly, but she patted the opposite side of the bed. "It can't hurt to think about it."

"There are literally thousands of names in these things," he said, indicating the books. He came around the foot of the bed and dumped the books between them, then punched several of the extra pillows into place and settled back against the headboard.

She laughed. "Well, since we know they're girls, that helps a lot. Why don't we each write down twenty or so names that really appeal to us and then we'll cross-reference our lists."

He shot her a skeptical look. "That sounds incredibly organized. Can't we just go through them and shoot some possibilities into the ether?"

"No, we cannot." She leaned over and opened the drawer of her bedside table, withdrawing a writing pad and two pens. She tore off two sheets of paper, handed him one along with a pen, and said, "There."

Ryan made a face of disgust but obediently picked up one of the books and started reading. After a few minutes he said, "Are there any ground rules?"

"Ground rules?" She laid her book facedown on her stomach. "Such as?"

"Do you want names that rhyme?"

"Uck." She made a face. "No way."

"Names that start with the same letter? Have the same number of syllables?"

"You're making this harder than it has to be," she pronounced. "I just want two names that we both like. They don't have to have anything in common but that."

He nodded and went back to his book.

An hour later, she laid down her pen. "I have a pretty good list. How about you?"

He surveyed what he'd written. "Yeah. Let's compare. You start."

"Okay. What do you think of Margarita?"

His blue eyes widened an instant before he hooted. "Like the drink? Are you kidding? She'd never live that down."

"It's Spanish," she said huffily, "and very pretty." But she struck it off her list. She'd just been testing him anyway. "Renee, Renata, Lisette, Phoebe."

"Keep Renee and Lisette. Deep six the other two."

At the end of her list, she still had six of the names she had suggested, plus an additional three that had been on both of their lists. Ryan read his list and they added five more.

"Not bad," she said, "for the first try. At least now we can roll some of these around in our heads and see how they sound after a couple of days."

Two mornings later he had showered and was dressing for work early in the morning when he heard Jessie call his name. There was an odd quality in her voice, and adrenaline rushed through him as he tore open the door to her room. Was something wrong with her?

She looked up as he entered, and the fear subsided immediately. Her face was positively glowing. Her dark hair was ruffled from sleep and she still wore the T-shirt she'd slept in. She was sitting on the side of the bed with both hands on her stomach.

"Come here, quick!" she urged him.

He hitched up the trousers he'd already donned and sat beside her. His weight pressed the mattress down and she slid against his side, so he casually put an arm around her, delighting in the soft pliancy of her body. "What?"

"Here. Feel here." She grabbed his free hand and planted it on her stomach through the shirt.

A shiver of shock ran up his spine. He flattened his hand over the firm mound of her belly, ignoring the pulse drumming in his veins. Just then, his focus on her was distracted by a slight but distinct bumping against his palm. "They're moving!"

"Mmm-hmm." She circled his wrist as far as she could and tugged his hand slightly to one side. "I think you can feel them more over here."

He could. And for several moments, they sat motionless as the tiny beings stretched and turned. But it wasn't enough for him. Reaching for the edge of her T-shirt, he said, "May I...?"

A flush touched her cheek but she nodded and he took a deep breath, fighting the nearly irresistible desire to kiss her. He tugged the T-shirt up, exposing her swollen flesh, and laid his hand possessively on her, curving it over the smooth, warm globe where his children were safely ensconced, feeling the satiny texture shift with each small movement of a baby.

A feeling of content like nothing he'd ever known before permeated his entire being. *This* was the life he'd been meant for.

Impulsively he kissed the top of her bent head. To his surprise and pleasure, she responded with a quiet murmur of pleasure, resting her head in the curve of his shoulder and cuddling against him in a sweet intimacy that made him wish for moments like it on a daily basis.

They stayed like that for a long time, feeling their babies move, until she looked up at him and said, "They seem to be settling down now. I've been feeling movement for weeks but never anything like that!"

He couldn't resist the urge. Bending low, he reverently kissed her warm, silky belly, caressing her with his hand before straightening and tugging her shirt back into place. "Sorry," he said. "But thank you for sharing that." He had to clear his throat. "It was...a thrill."

"I know." She cleared her throat, too, and her voice was soft but her eyes were steady as she said, "Ryan, you can touch me anytime."

His heartbeat doubled at the look in her eyes. "No," he said. "I can't. Not the way I want to."

She nodded, sighed. "Right." And his heart beat even faster at the acceptance implicit in the single syllable. Then her hand stroked lightly up and down his forearm, her fingers leaving a trail of fire in their wake. "But I could...touch you, if you like."

What? He realized he'd croaked the single, shocked syllable aloud. As her words arranged themselves in meaningful syllables in his brain, his entire body tightened. A distinct stirring in his groin made him shift uncomfortably.

"I said..."

"I know what you said! I just...just...ah, hell, never mind." He raised both hands and speared them through his thick dark hair in utter frustration.

"Ryan?" Her voice sounded surprisingly unsure. She waited until he looked at her. "Am I wrong about this or were you planning on consummating this marriage when it's medically allowed?''

"Jess." His voice sounded like someone was strangling him. "You know I want you. I haven't made it a secret. But we haven't even... We can't—"

She smiled gently. "I don't mind if we do things in reverse order."

Another lick of fire flashed through him and the stirring became a potential embarrassment. He exhaled heavily. "God, woman, sometimes I wonder if I'll ever know you."

She laughed and stood up, taking his hands, and he let her draw him to his feet, facing her. "Oh, you will. I can definitely promise that you will."

She was twisting everything he said, giving her words sexual overtones that he could barely resist. "I have to get to work," he said desperately.

Then she leaned into him, and as her belly pressed hard against the rigid evidence of his interest in her, she smiled. "So who's stopping you?"

"You little tease." He slipped his hands free of hers and gathered her closer, dropping his head and seeking her mouth. He tried to gentle himself, but he was so aroused and hot for her that the kiss was a wild mating of twisting, frantic tongues. He tore his mouth from hers, pressing a trail of openmouthed kisses along her jaw and down the sensitive flesh of her long, lovely neck. When he reached the neck of the shirt she wore, he caught the fabric in his teeth and tugged the overlarge neckline aside to bare one slender ivory shoulder.

"Ryan." She yanked handfuls of his T-shirt out of the way until she could run her palms up his bare back. She traced the muscles beneath his skin with shaking hands, then he felt her fingers sliding stealthily along his ribs, burrowing between them to seek out his nipples and tug tenderly until the small buds stood out for her ministrations, sending lightning jolts of arousal straight to his loins.

He groaned, dragging his mouth back up to take her lips in a deep, thrusting imitation of what he really wanted to do. She responded by sliding her hands down his belly, making the muscles contract sharply. And then, to his shock, she didn't stop, but ran one small hand deliberately down the distended fly of his jeans, caressing his swollen flesh with sweet pressure until he grabbed her wrist and held her hand away.

"Stop," he gasped.

She smiled against his lips. "Why?"

Why? He didn't have an answer for that one, his passion-fogged brain sluggish and dazed. She reached for him with her free hand, but he caught that one as well, drawing them up to press a kiss into each palm and hold them well away from his body.

"No." He realized he was panting, and he grinned despite his discomfort and the desire raging through his system that urged him to let her finish. He looked deep into her eyes, trying to make her understand. "Don't get me wrong, Jess. There's nothing I'd like more than to make love with you, but...I don't want it to be like this. I want us both there, all the way."

Her belly brushed against his body, and he swore beneath his breath. "I want a medal of honor for this, dammit."

The comment broke the tense sexual moment and she laughed, finally letting him move her a pace away. "All right." She put a hand to his cheek. "You're definitely too noble for your own good, Mr. Shaughnessy, but I appreciate the sentiment."

He kept away from her after that, knowing the limits of his own self-control, giving her chaste kisses on a daily basis but avoiding any repeat of the heated intimacy they'd shared in her bedroom.

In early June he got called to Seattle on an unavoidable business trip. It was the first time he'd left her since she'd been hospitalized, and her small, heart-shaped face looked woebegone when he told her what he was planning.

"Have you been postponing travel because of me?" she asked.

"Not exactly," he hedged. It wasn't entirely a lie. Though he'd had a few things come up, his presence wasn't essential to anything vital, and he'd sent one of his executive team in his place. "I haven't needed to be anyplace urgently."

"But you normally travel more than you have lately." It wasn't a question. She knew full well that he'd been in and out of town frequently in the past.

"I did." He took a deep breath. "But I've been thinking about changing some of that. The past few weeks were sort of a test—I sent some of my top people out in my place, and things went just fine." He put his hands on her shoulders and gently massaged. "I don't want to be a father whose work is more important than his children, so I'm going to start shifting more of the travel responsibilities to other employees. There still will be a few things I won't be able to get out of, but for the most part I'll be home."

She had a pensive look on her face, something sad and lonely lurking in her eyes. "I'll be back as soon as I can," he said. "I'm sorry I won't be here for the sixteen-week checkup."

She smiled then, though the expression he couldn't quite interpret was still buried in her green eyes. "It's all

right,'' she said. ''I'm a big girl, and Finn won't let anything happen to me. And the checkup is no big deal.
There's no sonogram scheduled.''

''I know.'' He hesitated, then took the plunge. ''Miss
me?''

To his shock, her face crumpled. ''Yes,'' she whispered. She stepped forward into the arms he held out, and
he hugged her tight to him, the bulge of their children
sandwiched between them.

''I'll be back soon,'' he said, feeling helpless when he
heard her sniff.

She nodded, stirring, and when he let her go, she
stepped back. ''Don't mind me. I'm just one big emotional wreck these days.''

But he *did* mind. He hated leaving her, though he knew
he couldn't tell her. And the way she'd clung warmed his
heart all out of proportion to the act. Telling himself it
was only that she was pregnant and feeling vulnerable
didn't do a single thing to mitigate the elation that rose
within him. He stepped forward, pulling her to him for a
gentle kiss, then grinned at her and opened the door. ''I'll
be back before you know it.''

But he wasn't. Ryan was gone for nine days. To Jessie
it seemed like an eternity.

On the second day after his departure, she had her sixteen-week checkup. Once again the doctor eased her off
the medication for nausea, and to her delight there was
no recurrence of any illness in the days afterward. But
there was something that she found even more exciting
than that. She could hardly wait until Ryan got home.

He called her every evening at eight her time, no matter
what. Although he didn't indicate that it was difficult, she

knew that it was only five o'clock his time, and she suspected it could hardly be convenient.

The night after her doctor's appointment, he had a thousand questions. "How big did you measure? So that means the babies are growing normally? Are you sure you should try going off your medication without me there?"

She answered them all patiently, pleased at his interest despite the inner voice that reminded her he was only thinking of the twins' health.

She asked about his business dealings; he wanted to know about her plans to showcase some of the new merchandise she'd recently received. She told him how much savings Finn's obsessive coupon shopping had netted him this week and they laughed about it together.

Then he said, "Weren't you expecting a decision on that loan this week?"

The question sent her spirits plummeting as low as they'd been before she'd heard his voice. "Yes," she said quietly. "No go."

"Damn! What's the matter with these people?" Frustration colored his tone, cheering her in some inexplicable way. It was nice to know he cared.

"I *really* miss you," she said before she hung up. "I'll be glad when you're home again." And she did. The house seemed too big and too quiet with only Finn and her in it. Although they still played games and kept to their regular activities, she felt the void that Ryan's absence left.

And she realized that was what had been missing from her home before. She'd tried to make it her space with furnishings and special touches, but it had still felt like little more than a place to crash when she wasn't working. And the long hours she'd worked when she was single suddenly began to look suspiciously like a way to fill up her hours so she wouldn't have to go home alone.

Ryan had changed all that. He'd shown her how it felt to have family, to know that you were going home to share your day's doings with someone who cared, someone who was sincerely interested, someone whom you loved.

What was she going to do after the babies were born? She couldn't give up her gallery. It would be an incredible act of stupidity to assume that her financial security was assured. If Ryan tired of her— The notion was so painful she could hardly give it space in her mind, but she forced herself to consider it. She knew she never would willingly give him up, nor would she ever consider breaking up the family security she was determined her children would know. But the reality of her position was that Ryan held all the cards.

So back to her first concern—what to do after the twins came.

Initially she'd assumed she would continue working full-time and hire a nanny. Now the thought was unpalatable. Could she possibly continue to run the gallery as she had been, on a part-time basis?

Cautiously she turned the idea over in her head. Now that she was married and living with Ryan, she had far fewer expenses than before. She'd have to talk to Penny and see if she wanted to continue the current arrangement. She could formally give her certain managerial responsibilities. Even if she did expand, which was looking less and less likely, she could simply hire an additional salesperson.

A feeling of satisfaction spread through her at the idea. It could work, she thought.

Despite the nightly phone calls, the days dragged. She

began sleeping in Ryan's bed simply so she could feel closer to him. The doctor had agreed that she could resume working half days five times a week, so she was out of the house more, which was good.

But when she was home, she caught herself doing ridiculous things. One evening she spent two hours in the room they'd decided would be the nursery, lying on her back envisioning how to decorate it and where to place the furniture. Another night she amused herself by making lists of the furnishings in every single room of the house from memory. Then the following night she compared her lists to the real rooms, finding to her satisfaction that she'd done a pretty decent job of recalling all the *stuff* that was packed into her new home.

On the seventh night she told him, "I think I've found a name I can live with."

"And that would be?" His voice sounded far away.

"Olivia."

"Olivia." He repeated it, rolling it around on his tongue. "I like it. It was originally on my list."

"Don't be smug," she said, smiling though he couldn't see her. "All right. That's good. One out of two."

Then he said, "I've been thinking about names, too. What do you think of Elena?"

"Elena." She did what he had done. "Very pretty. Olivia and Elena...they sound nice together."

"You realize they're probably going to wind up being called Livvie and Lanie," he warned her.

"Oh. Well, let me think about *that*."

He chuckled. "I could live with those."

They spoke for a few minutes longer. When she replaced the telephone in its cradle, she was smiling. She couldn't wait for him to get home!

But her smile faded as she slipped between the crisp

sheets of his big bed. He'd given her little indication that he was suffering as much as she was from their separation. He had probably been propositioned by half a dozen thin, elegant, *un*-pregnant women in the past week.

And though she knew Ryan would never compromise his marriage vows, she couldn't stamp out the small ember of fear that someday he'd regret marrying a woman he didn't love.

Eight

Ryan let himself in the back door as quietly as possible. *It's a good thing we don't have a dog,* he thought to himself.

He was beat. He was home two days earlier than he'd originally projected, largely because he'd been such a demanding SOB that his Seattle team had worked around the clock simply to get rid of him faster, he suspected. He didn't care; all he wanted was to be home with Jessie. He'd called from the airport to tell her he was coming home but not to wait up since he would be very late.

Leaving his suit bag in the hallway, he made his way upstairs. Finn's small apartment was on the far side of the kitchen so there was little chance of waking him. But Jessie's room was much closer to his and he doubted she'd appreciate being awakened at two in the morning.

Although he wanted to. Badly.

What would he give, he wondered, as he passed her

closed door and let himself into his own room, to be able to slide into bed with her right now? Not even for sex, although God knew he wouldn't object to that when the doctor gave her the go-ahead, but simply to be able to hold her, to fall asleep with her in his arms. The thought was enough to make him break out in a cold sweat as he stripped off his clothes. He could barely see, but there was a dim glow coming from the almost-closed bathroom door—Jessie liked the bathroom warm, he'd learned, so she often left the gas fireplace on low.

Naked, he walked across the room to the bathroom, and after a cursory glance to be sure it was empty, he took a quick shower. He shivered as the warm water sluiced over his body, half-aroused at the mere thought of Jessie's proximity, wishing the water was her hands sliding delicately over him. As he dried off and knotted the towel around his waist, he glanced at the closed door that led to her bedroom. He'd half hoped she would awaken when she heard him, that maybe she would at least come to welcome him home after she'd given him a decent interval to dress.

But after a moment's hesitation he didn't see light under her door.

Disappointed, he turned out all the lights except for the fireplace and padded across his room to the big bed against the far wall. He left the towel on the floor next to the bed and pulled back the covers to get into bed—

—and nearly jumped out of his skin when a female voice purred, "It's about time."

"Jess! In the name of—you scared me." He relaxed the combative stance he'd assumed automatically. "What are you doing?"

Her voice was still low and inviting. "Waiting for you."

His body, always quick to respond when he thought of her, went wild at the sultry tone. He nearly reached for her, but instead he forced himself to bend and snag the discarded towel, wrapping it around his waist. He couldn't touch her the way he wanted to, and he knew better than to start something he might not be able to stop. "Waiting for me to do what?" As his eyes adjusted to the dark, he could see her outline beneath the covers on the near side of the bed.

"To come to bed." She rose to her knees and faced him, and his system suffered another shock when he saw what she was wearing. Or rather, wasn't wearing. Though there was no light but in the dim glow that filtered through from the fireplace in the next room, the diaphanous material of the short gown that fluttered around her was so sheer she might as well have been wearing nothing. As she melted against him, he put his arms around her to support her, then took a deep breath as her warm, ripe figure pressed into him.

"I take it you're glad to see me." She felt so good against him. His pulse went up another notch as her belly sandwiched the ridge of his arousal between them and he nearly groaned aloud.

She buried her nose in his neck and inhaled deeply. "Oh, Ryan, I missed you so much."

"I missed you, too." He could hear the strain in his voice. "Ah, Jess, it's not that I don't appreciate the welcome, but—"

"Oh, this isn't the welcome." She lifted her head and kissed his jaw. "That comes later."

His entire body went on full alert, if it were possible to get any *fuller* than he already was. "What do you mean?"

She relaxed even more against him and he fought not

to whimper. "The doctor gave me the green light," she said.

"The green light." Did she mean what he thought, hoped—hell, *prayed*—she meant?

"All the way?" he asked hoarsely. "No...restrictions?"

She shook her head. "No. He—"

Her words ended in a small shriek as he swept her into his arms, careful of the mound of his babies in her belly. His mouth cut off her words; he thrust his tongue deep into the soft, heated recess between her lips, boldly kissing her the way he wanted to love her. Gently, but with the greatest possible speed, he lay her full-length on the mattress and sprawled beside her, still kissing her.

One arm was beneath her neck, holding her close against him, the other cupped her jaw and stroked the soft skin of her throat, seeking out the wildly beating pulse there and gently stroking a finger down to her breastbone. Their tongues tangled and teased, telegraphing need and relief and warmth. Sliding his mouth along her jaw and up, he pressed tiny kisses to her cheekbone, her temple, her forehead, her eyelids. As he graced the tip of her nose with a tiny caress, he felt her lips against his chin.

"Welcome home."

He settled his mouth over hers again, resuming the deep, consuming kisses, holding his body under strict control while he pleasured her, wanting her to be ready, no, more than ready, *desperate* for him when he finally made her his.

His hand slipped lower and lower, barely brushing over feminine bounty until he cupped the full globe of one breast in his hand. Shaping and molding, he stimulated the taut tip of her breast, making a sound of approval deep in his throat. Her arms had been restlessly tracing the swell of muscle in his shoulders and back, but she slid them up into his hair, firmly tugging his head down until she could offer him one swollen, engorged nipple.

He tested her with his tongue, flicking over the rigid peak first, then laving slow circles around the wide, dark circle of her aureola for endless moments before he drew her completely into his mouth and began to suckle. Her back arched and her heels dug into the mattress as she sucked in one swift wordless breath.

The erotic abandon in her response nearly undid his good intentions. Lifting his mouth a fraction, he muttered against her, "I want you. Are you sure this is okay?"

"Positive," she panted. Her hands still curled into his hair and she arched her back with a soft, unintelligible sound as he teased her nipple with the rough rasp of his thumb. "Ryan," she moaned. "Don't make me wait too long."

It was all the encouragement he needed. His hand spread possessively over her belly, stroking the satiny flesh and wandering down over the bulge of her warm, smooth abdomen, and he caught his breath when his fingers snagged in the soft, curling thatch of hair between her legs. She moved restlessly, shoving her hips against him. He was overwhelmed by her, by the moment, by the realization that she was going to be his after all these years. He wanted to tell her he loved her as he urged her legs apart with a shaking hand, but his tongue wouldn't form the words. She'd been so skittish when he'd first suggested marriage that he knew confessing his feelings would send her running.

And as his fingers slipped into the moist, humid crevice and he found slick, waiting heat, the last thing he wanted to do was break the mood. He drew his moistened fingers back, over the pouting bud he discovered at the top of the sweet vee of her legs, and began to rub small, gentle circles. She sucked in a breath and moaned.

"Ah," he said, "do you like that?" He still had one arm beneath her head and he leaned over her, searching out her lips again before she could answer, kissing her with the same tender care he was lavishing on her body.

His own body pulsed and throbbed against her thigh, and as she shifted beneath his hands, her hip caressed him eagerly.

She moved her arms down from his neck, stroking the furred patch of skin over his breastbone. Soon, though, her hands clutched at him helplessly as he drove her higher and higher into the heights of pleasure, and short, breathless cries escaped her throat with each soft stroke of his hand. Relentlessly he drove her on and on, his own body balanced on the knife edge of control as he brought her to the brink with his hand. Her head thrashed back and forth on his arm and she sobbed, "No, no...I want to feel you..."

"What?" He slowed his pace a fraction. "What do you want?"

Her hands moved from his hair down to grip his shoulders, then slipped farther down to tug at his waist, though she couldn't budge him. "I want you...inside me," she pleaded.

In an instant he withdrew his arm from beneath her neck and rose to his haunches, draping her legs wide over his thighs as his jutting flesh kissed the damp, satiny portal of her body. He shuddered. "I don't want to hurt you."

"You won't." She lifted her arms open to him. "Now. Please?"

He shuddered again, nearly undone at the honest need in her plaintive tone. Guiding the blunt tip of his arousal into position with a shaking hand, he slowly, slowly flexed his hips, forcing her open as he invaded her soft channel. "Jess." His voice was little more than a guttural growl as he felt the dance of satisfaction skipping up his spine. "I...I can't wait."

"Then don't." As he hovered over her and began a slow, careful thrust and retreat, she moaned and wrapped her legs around his hips. The action abruptly pulled him deeper, much deeper, and suddenly the world exploded. He leaned forward, bracing himself over her on his arms, his stroke increasing as her hips slammed up to meet his. She was crying again, sharp screams of pleasure, and he could feel himself losing control. He put a hand between them and pressed firmly down just above their joining, and her eyes flared so wide he could see them even in the dark as her body began to convulse. At the same time his frantically pumping hips surged wildly forward, jetting endless streams of release deep inside her as her hidden inner muscles gripped his hard flesh. Finally, when the last sweet shocks of pleasure had passed, they both were spent and quiet, but for the gasping sounds of their breathing.

He was careful not to let his weight crush her, and after a moment to gather himself, he pulled back from the warm haven of her body and slid to her side, gathering her in his arms. Leaning over her, he took her mouth in a sweet, lingering kiss before he lay back on the pillow beside her.

It had been everything he'd known it would be with her. And if there was any small corner of his heart she hadn't already owned, she had it now as she returned the kiss with a generosity and warmth that made him wonder once again if there was hope that she could love him someday.

* * *

Her whole body throbbed from his possession. Leisurely she turned onto her side and laid her palm over his heart. Love for this man who had shared so much of her life, and now shared everything, coursed through her and she had to bite her tongue to keep from blurting out her feelings. It was difficult to remind herself that though he cared for her and certainly had enjoyed her, he still carried Wendy in his heart. So she contented herself by saying, "I'm glad you're home."

Though it was dark, she could hear the smile in his voice. "I'm glad I'm home, too."

She laughed gently. "I'll just bet."

He stirred then, gathering her closely against him so that their babies rested between them and she was wrapped in his arms. "I hated being away from you."

"I hated you being away," she responded, touched by the vehemence in his tone. "But you didn't have to worry. I'm doing well, and Finn would have called you immediately if there'd been a problem."

He turned his head, and his whiskered chin brushed her cheek as he pressed a kiss to her temple. "It wasn't the worry," he said quietly. "I missed *you,* Jess. I can't imagine my life without you now."

She was stunned. Pleasure of an entirely different kind exploded through her at his words. And hope followed in its wake, revived. Was it possible Ryan could let go of his past and learn to love her? There had been something in his voice she'd never heard before. She was afraid to even give it a name. But she snuggled closer against him as hope rushed through her once again, and when her eyes closed, her heart was lighter than it had been in a long time.

* * *

They settled into a routine after that night, and he'd never felt happier in his entire life as the next few weeks passed. Jessie worked part-time, usually going to the gallery in the afternoons. By the time he got home in the evening, she was refreshed and interested in hearing about the things in which he currently was involved. After dinner they watched television or pored over baby books and catalogues, looking for things for the nursery they were slowly putting together. And after that…after that came the part of the day he looked forward to from the time his eyes opened in the morning.

Apparently, his satisfaction with his life showed, because people remarked on it and congratulated him on his marriage everywhere he went. One day as he was leaving after a lunch in the restaurant that occupied the old Federal Reserve Bank at the Hotel Le Meridien, a man passing through the door hailed him.

It was Mort Brockhiser, a friend as well as the vice president in charge of commercial loans at Boston Savings Bank.

"Good to see you, Ryan," Mort said, shaking his hand vigorously. He was a small, rotund man with a fringe of graying hair stretching from each temple around the back of his head, and he had a habit of smoothing his hand over the shining crown of his bald head. "Emmy and I extend our congratulations on your marriage."

"Thanks, Mort." Ryan had known Mort and his wife, Emmy, since his senior year at M.I.T., when he'd applied for the patent on Securi-Lock and Mort had backed his loan request to start production of the technology. "How's your family?"

"Fine, fine. Youngest is finishing at Harvard this year. I'm going to be throwing a 'No More Tuition' party next May." He chuckled at his own wit, then went on. "Maybe you and the wife could join Emmy and me for dinner some night. Where'd you find this lady? Emmy's dying to hear all the details.''

"We grew up together," Ryan said. No point in trying to explain anything else; it sounded too crazy. "Her maiden name was Reilly. Jessie Reilly.''

A sudden look of comprehension settled over Mort's face. "Of The Reilly Gallery?''

Ryan nodded. "One and the same.''

"She applied for a loan a few months ago," Mort said. "I visited her shop. Very nice. Would have liked to make the loan, but you know how cautious the board is these days. Her financials were a little shaky." Then his eyes narrowed thoughtfully and he chuckled. "But I guess they're not shaky anymore.''

"Jessie's very independent and an excellent saleswoman," Ryan said. "If I were you, I'd back anything she chose to try." And if he were a banker, he would. He had faith in her business acumen. And he'd become intimately acquainted with her shop and the things she stocked. She had great instincts, which was half of what it took to survive in the market.

"Hmm." Mort nodded once, then the intensity faded from his gaze. "As I said, we'll have dinner.''

Ryan nodded. "Jessie would like that, but it may have to wait awhile. We're expecting twins in October.''

Mort's eyes bulged. "Good Lord!" He had two sons of his own. "You're going to have your hands full.''

"I know." And he loved the thought of it.

The weeks passed and so did the seasons. Spring slid into summer, and Jessie grew larger and larger as their babies grew inside her. They still were able to make love, and to his delight she was endlessly inventive and far more agile than her increasing bulk indicated. And when

ANNE MARIE WINSTON 157

they lay together afterward, when she snuggled into his arms and laid her head on his chest, his heart felt as if it were going to swell and burst right out of him with the feelings he struggled to hide.

One afternoon he gave Finn the night off and came home well before Jessie was expected, to prepare a surprise for her. He'd bought roses, a stunning bouquet of red and pink ones to symbolize the love he hoped they were beginning to share, as well as the friendship they'd had for so long.

Before Finn left to visit his mother, he prepared a spinach salad and a platter of cold roast beef. Ryan had called that morning and asked him to set the glass-topped wrought-iron table for them on the terrace, and when he took the vase of roses up, he discovered Finn had done far more than simply set the table.

It was covered in a white linen cloth with snowy napkins gracing the porcelain plates. Waterford goblets for wine and water sparkled in the late-afternoon light. There were candles on the table, and two large brass candelabra with white tapers were strategically placed with an arrangement of potted palms and ferns around them. He set the vase of roses on a side table and noted the bottle of Dom chilling in the ice bucket. Good. Very good.

He took a deep breath. He'd made up his mind. Tonight he was going to do it.

Tonight, he was going to tell Jessie he loved her. That he'd loved her for what seemed like forever, that she made him happier than any man had a right to be. If he was right about the feelings growing between them, she would return the words. And his life would be complete.

Leaving the terrace, he went down to his room for a quick shower and changed into casual linen pants and a cotton shirt with a faint blue stripe. She loved him, he was nearly sure of it. If she didn't, she should be in Hollywood. She'd be a shoo-in for an Oscar.

He rummaged in his drawers for a pack of matches. The big lighter was downstairs, but he was pretty sure he'd seen matches here somewhere…they probably were in Jessie's room. Finn was always lighting good-smelling candles in there.

As he moved into her room, he thought again of the way she moved into his arms for a passionate kiss every morning before he left the house. The way she greeted him with shining eyes and another kiss in the evening. The way she moved with him when they made love, as if she knew exactly what he wanted and how to please him utterly. Last week she'd brought home a hand-blown glass paperweight in the forty shades of Ireland that she'd ordered for the store. But she'd given it to *him* because, she told him, she knew he'd like it in his office. She could have given him a piece of limestone and he'd have liked it, because she'd thought of him.

He pulled open the drawer of her bedside table. No matches.

Moving to the dresser on which sat a fat, scented candle, he opened the first drawer. Pay dirt. As he reached in for the match box he'd located, a folded piece of paper atop the dresser caught his eye.

Dining room, it was labeled in Jessie's handwriting. Slowly, he picked up the sheet of paper and unfolded it. Shock replaced incredulity as the words penetrated, and that in turn was replaced by a burgeoning pain. A leaden weight encased his heart as he read down the page:

Sideboard: Kirk-Steiff silver tea service, Kirk-Steiff cutlery for twelve, two Irish lace tablecloths, twenty-four linen dinner napkins. Breakfront: Waterford crystal goblets—champagne, water, three kinds of wine…

There were several sheets of paper. List after list of the rooms in his home and the contents of each. She'd been *casing* the place, for God's sake!

Carefully, he folded the papers exactly as they had been. He felt as if he couldn't take a deep breath as he closed the drawer and walked back through the bathroom to his room. *What an idiot you are,* he told himself bitterly. *You knew going into this that Jessie didn't marry you for love.* And now that he thought about it, he was sure his financial status had a lot to do with her decision to recruit him to father her children.

"Ryan? Where are you?"

He sucked in a deep breath. He wasn't ready to face her. Blowing it out, he met his own gaze in the mirror. No choice. "I'm up here," he called. "Bedroom."

He stayed where he was, listening as her footsteps tripped lightly up the steps and came down the hall. She entered her own room first and came through the bathroom to find him.

"Guess what?" Her voice was jubilant and her whole face was alight. She looked so beautiful and vivacious that his heart squeezed viciously into a small, tight knot.

"What?" His own voice sounded distinctly unenthusiastic to his own ears but she didn't appear to notice.

"I got a loan! The Reilly Gallery is officially going to expand." She came straight to him and threw her arms around his neck. "Oh, Ryan, I'm so happy!"

Automatically he put his hands at the sides of where her waist used to be. "That's great." He worked hard to make his voice sound more normal. Carefully he set her away from him and walked into the bathroom, going to the faucet and washing his hands to give himself something to do. "When do you plan to start?"

"Right away." She followed him, still smiling, but when he glanced at her there was a puzzled, wary look in her eyes. "I've already spoken to the owner of my building about leasing that empty space next to the gallery and knocking down a wall. He didn't seem to think there would be any problem."

"No grass growing under your feet." He forced himself to turn and smile at her. "Hungry? You can tell me all about it over dinner."

"Starving," she said, "but we might be forced to fend for ourselves. Finn's not here, and the table isn't set in either room downstairs."

"I, uh, I asked Finn to set a table for us on the terrace," he said, seeing no way to get out of it. If she'd come home just a few minutes later... "I'll go get the food and send it up in the dumbwaiter."

"Okay. Just let me change and I'll be up."

He went down to the kitchen, glad to escape for the moment. *Idiot!* he thought again. How could he have let himself think for a minute that she cared for him? Just because they'd found a great deal of physical satisfaction together didn't necessarily mean her emotions were involved.

She was faster than he'd expected, and he barely beat her up to the terrace on the roof. Wheeling the cart loaded with food over to the table, he concentrated on setting everything in place as she approached.

"This is lovely," she exclaimed. "It looks so...so romantic." Her voice dropped.

"You know Finn. I guess he got a little carried away," he said casually. "Looks nice, but the candles are overkill." Briskly he grabbed the candelabras and carried them to the far side of the terrace, then dragged the potted trees back to their original positions spaced around the fringes of the furniture. There was nothing he could do about the flowers or the wine, he supposed. He'd just have to live with those.

Jessie's face, when he dared to glance her way, wore a slightly disturbed expression. Probably relief. When she'd seen the romantic setting, he imagined she'd feared he was going to do something stupid. Something like telling her he loved her...

Stop whining, Shaughnessy, he ordered himself. *You wanted her, you wanted babies. You got both. You never expected her to love you, anyway. Not really.*

Thank God he'd seen those notes. Ignoring the throbbing ache in his heart, he held her chair. "Have a seat and tell me about your loan."

Jessie hesitated. Then, casting him a glance from beneath her lashes, she slid into the chair. As he took his own seat, he casually moved the roses off to one side.

"Are you going to open the wine?" she asked.

"Uh, I wasn't planning on it," he said. "You're not supposed to be drinking. I don't know what Finn was thinking when he set that out."

"One glass of wine would be all right."

"I don't want to take any chances with these babies." He couldn't look at her. "We'll save the real celebration for when your store's completed."

"Is something wrong?" Her voice sounded uncertain.

"Not at all." He forced himself to meet her troubled gaze. "So talk to me."

"All right." She continued to watch him. "Let's see...what do you want to know?"

"Who made you the loan?"

"Boston Savings. Can you believe it? They were polite but absolutely adamant when I made my pitch before."

Boston Savings. It couldn't be a coincidence that he'd seen Mort Brockhiser and now she'd gotten a loan from Brockhiser's bank. "Did he say what changed?" he asked neutrally.

"No. I asked him that, too. He said he'd thought all along I was a good prospect and that he was glad the board of directors had a change of heart." Her smile flashed in the evening light. "I'm too happy to care *what* was said, as long as they make me that loan!"

That was good. He decided not to tell her about his conversation with Mort. It wasn't as if he'd cosigned her note or anything like that. And, anyway, hadn't she married him for the financial benefits that came with him?

Nine

Ryan was behaving strangely.

He shooed her off to get ready for bed after dinner, telling her he would take care of the dishes. In the past they'd cleaned up together on the infrequent nights when Finn wasn't around. Jessie couldn't shake the feeling that he wanted to get rid of her, and the idea hurt her feelings. She thought they'd broken through a barrier to a new level of intimacy when they'd begun making love. Tonight Ryan was acting as if he didn't really want her around.

And what the heck was the deal with that dinner? When she'd walked out onto the terrace, her heart had leaped into her throat. The greenery and candelabra made a stunning backdrop for the roses, and the table service had gleamed in the evening sun. It had made a lovely, romantic picture, and she still wondered if Ryan hadn't asked Finn to set it up and then changed his mind for some unknown reason.

It was depressing.

She caught sight of herself in the mirror and sighed. Speaking of depressing—it was the beginning of July and she still had more than a third of this pregnancy to go. Already she looked like she'd swallowed helium balloons. How long would Ryan continue to be attracted to someone he couldn't even get his arms around?

She shucked off the oversize denim blouse and navy shorts with the stretchy front panel, then tossed them into the clothes basket along with her underwear. Donning a short silk robe, she headed into the bathroom and prepared for bed. Then she climbed into "her" side of the large bed she'd shared with Ryan for the past few weeks.

She was reading a book on infant growth when Ryan came into the room, and she set it down with a stifled yawn. "I'm glad you came up. I'm getting sleepy."

He didn't respond, though he smiled absently at her. Emptying his pockets, he stripped to his briefs and got ready for bed, then removed those and got under the covers on his side of the bed. When he turned out his light, she did the same.

She waited for him to reach for her and draw her into his arms, but tonight he merely laid one hand over the swell of her belly. "Lots of movement today?"

"Tons. But they're pretty quiet right now." She placed her hand over his. "Did something happen at the office today that upset you?"

He was silent for a long moment. "No," he said finally. "What makes you think that?"

"I don't know. You just seem…subdued." *Withdrawn.*

In the darkness she felt him shrug. "It was just one of those days, I guess." His hand began to trace small circles over her belly. "How are you feeling physically?"

She chuckled wryly, covering the hurt that sprang up

when she realized he was shutting her out. "Huge. I can't imagine getting much larger, but I know I will." She still couldn't avoid the conviction that something was wrong, but he didn't seem willing to share his problems, and she didn't know how else to let him know she wanted to be there for him. Then her attention faded from her concern as he continued to stroke her body.

The gentle circles grew larger, and his big, warm hand brushed over her breast. She sucked in a sharp breath of pleasure as sensation cut a jagged path through her. Her breasts were so sensitive right now that even his lightest touch brought heat flowing to her abdomen and made her pulse race. "Your skin is so soft," he breathed, "so smooth. I love touching you."

"I love it when you touch me, too." She shifted toward him for a kiss, resisting the impulse to blurt out *I love you.*

But he wouldn't let her turn to him. Instead, he rolled her onto her side and snuggled behind her, drawing her into the heat of his large body and cradling her head on his arm. He drew his knees up, and the rough hair along his legs brushed the backs of her thighs. The movements of his awakening flesh pressed against the soft flesh of her buttocks, and he flattened his palm against her abdomen. She squirmed as the pressure of her tightly closed legs created an erotic pleasure, then she gasped as his fingers slipped beneath her top leg and drew it up over his.

The motion pressed him forward, his hips firmly pushing at the tender cleft between her legs, and she moaned. His big hand slid up over her, cupping and stroking her breasts, his rough thumb rasping over the tender nipples until she was moving desperately against him, her pulse hammering in her throat and at the apex of her thighs. He lifted his head and caught her earlobe between his teeth, lightly scoring the tender flesh and then soothing the small sting with his tongue. He pressed a string of kisses down her neck and along the smooth plane of her shoulder. At the same time, he slipped his hand down over the mound of her belly to the hidden cove beneath, combing his fingers through the moist curls he found there.

When he lightly pressed down with one finger, she cried out at the waves of intense pleasure that burst through her, then buried her face in the pillow as one long finger slid stealthily into her humid channel. Her hips bucked and writhed, and he groaned softly into her ear, then lightly nipped at her shoulder.

She swept her hand back and down between their straining bodies, finding and freeing his swollen shaft, drawing him forward to the portal of her feminine flesh, wordlessly urging him to complete their union. Ryan spread his palm over her abdomen again, holding her in place, and she felt the blunt probe of the broad head slowing pushing into her, filling her.

He began to move, a slow steady retreat and advance, repeating the motion until she turned her face from the pillow and hissed, ''Move!''

He laughed then, deep in his throat. ''Take it easy. What's your rush?''

Reaching back her hand, she smacked him smartly on the buttocks, and he laughed again, capturing her hand and crossing it over her chest so he could shackle her wrist with his other hand. Then he replaced his hand on her abdomen, sliding his middle finger relentlessly down to trace small circles on the throbbing nub of her desire. She could feel her climax approaching, roaring down upon her to crash over her head, drowning her in spiraling ripples of sensation as her inner muscles clenched around his engorged flesh. Behind her his steely body grew taut as his own release ripped through him. He pushed himself hard against her, emptying himself in shaking, groaning pulses as she shivered and quaked around him.

Their bodies were slick with sweat as their heartbeats slowed, and after a moment Ryan reached down and tugged the tangled sheets into place without moving himself from her. He kissed her neck, but when she turned her face up to his, he merely nuzzled her temple and said, "Go to sleep, cupcake."

And as she snuggled into his arms and her eyelids drifted shut, she was disturbed. Though the distance he'd seemed to want between them earlier had vanished in the fire of their passion, she sensed something had shifted in his feelings for her.

And she was fairly sure the shift wasn't a good one.

At twenty-four weeks, a third sonogram confirmed the twins' continued health. In August her twenty-eight week check-up passed and by the beginning of September Jessie was nearly thirty-two weeks pregnant.

"I go to the doctor again tomorrow," she reminded Ryan the evening before her next appointment. Things had been good between them since the night of that weird "dinner that wasn't," although she often felt a little frustrated by his seeming determination to keep her at an emotional distance. Physically he was as passionate as he'd been since the first night they'd made love, but she sensed something…something she couldn't put her finger on, although she was sure it wasn't simply her imagination working overtime.

"I know." He smiled at her over the top of the *Wall Street Journal* he was reading. "I have it on my office calendar. I'll come home in time to drive you." He folded the paper and laid it down. "This weekend we need to get the nursery finished. I know things seem to be going really well, but if you deliver early, we have to be prepared."

"If I deliver too early," she said seriously, "they won't be coming home right away."

"Think positive." He rose and came over to the chair where she'd been sitting, reading. Putting his hands beneath her elbows he carefully helped her to her feet, then drew her into his arms, but he didn't seek out her lips as he once would have done. At the same time his big hands massaged her back, finding all the tender spots that were giving her trouble as she carried around more and more baby weight. According to the doctors, the twins were a healthy size. Good for them, not so good for her. She felt like a beached whale. It was hard to get from a sitting position to a standing one, impossible to put on her socks or tie her shoes. She was exhausted after climbing the stairs, although she rarely had to, since Ryan forbade it and carried her up and down.

She relaxed in his embrace and let him take her weight. "Umm," she said against his shoulder, "I'll give you about three days to stop doing that."

Above her head, he chuckled. "I can see we've established a pattern for life here. I'm not going to get out of this after the babies are born, am I?"

"Not a chance." She rested her head on his shoulder, pleased that he was speaking of long-term issues. "I wish the next couple of weeks would hurry and pass. I'm tired of feeling fat and ugly. I'm tired of having my back hurt and my feet swell. I'm tired of feeling tired."

He was still rubbing her back with light, soothing strokes. "I know. Soon it will be over, and you'll be your old self."

"Will that make you happy?" Since the night they'd
first made love, he'd seemed utterly enthralled with her
body, pregnant or not. But recently little things had bothered her. She tried to tell herself it was her imagination,
but there was no denying the fact that outside their bed
Ryan avoided the intimacies they'd been beginning to
share.

Now he shrugged. "I'll be happy for your sake, but I
think you're absolutely beautiful the way you are." Putting a hand beneath her chin, he tilted her face up so that
he could look deep into her eyes. "You've always been
beautiful to me, Jess. There hasn't been a day since you
were about thirteen that you didn't take my breath away."

She felt as if her heart were going to stop at the sincere
tone of his declaration. *Was he telling her he loved her?*
Or merely that she'd turned him on for years? "Why
didn't you ever say anything," she asked cautiously,
"back in high school?"

He made a rough sound of derision and let her go,
stepping a pace away. "You were with the football
player," he said quietly. "What chance would I have
had?"

"I...I don't know," she said honestly. Happiness
warred with a growing touch of...annoyance? No, not
strong enough. Anger? Too strong. Hurt was perhaps the
best word for what she was feeling. "Do you—"

"Ryan?" Finn came to the door of the den, and they
both turned toward him. "Excuse me. I have some things
you need to go through from when I cleaned closets yesterday. There's some stuff you might want."

"All right," Ryan said. He looked back at her, and his
eyes were wary. "Do you want to look through it with
me?"

She nodded, aware that an important moment had just

been lost, equally aware that there might never be another one unless she exposed her soul and took a chance that there was more between them than affection, attraction and history.

They followed Finn to the big eat-in kitchen where he had several boxes stacked near the door. "I'm going to the store," Finn said. "Just leave anything you don't want, and I'll take care of it."

A moment later, they were alone in the kitchen.

"I wonder what's in these?" Ryan said. His voice was so normal that she wondered if it bothered him at all that they hadn't finished exploring what he'd started. He ripped the tape on the top one and opened the flaps, peering into the box. "College stuff," he said. "Textbooks." He lifted it to one side and moved to the next box in the stack.

Jessie moved closer as he opened it. Then his face lit up. 'What is it?'' she asked.

He grinned at her. "Baby stuff!" he said.

"Baby stuff?" Why on earth would they have had baby things stored in a closet? She didn't remember putting anything away anywhere but the nursery.

"When we first started talking about having a family, Wendy did the nesting thing," he said. "Look through here and see if you'd like to keep anything." He lifted out a gorgeous white baby afghan crocheted in an intricate shell pattern, and there was such a tender expression on his face that she mentally cringed. "I remember when she made this. Won't Olivia or Elena look nice all bundled up in this?"

"Umm." She made a noncommittal sound, trying desperately to keep the hurt and humiliation from showing. "I, ah, just remembered something I have to tell Penny. I'll use the phone in the study."

He looked at her then, eyebrows raised. "You can use the one in here."

"No, I, ah, that's okay." She turned and fled, as fast as it was possible for a two-ton tank to flee. When she got to the study, she ducked inside and closed the door, leaning heavily against it.

Hot tears streaked down her cheeks like trails of fire. She took one trembling breath, then another. That he could so casually rave about Wendy only moments after she thought they'd been on the verge of a momentous discussion told her more clearly than any words what her role in Ryan's life was. And it wasn't that of a dearly loved wife.

She was still brooding the next day at the store when she got a telephone call from her landlord, wanting to know if she intended to lease her condo again. If she didn't, he continued, the woman to whom she'd sublet it wanted to stay there with a lease of her own.

Pleading business, she put him off to give herself time to think about it. Her first impulse had been to tell him she did want to renew the lease. She didn't need to, now that she was married and living with Ryan, but...when she confronted the little voice in her head that urged her to keep her lease, she realized why she was hesitating about letting it go.

As long as Ryan still held Wendy in his heart, their future together would always be uncertain. True, they would share children, which she was more and more certain he regarded as something that would bond them for life. The question was, could she share him with a memory? She was far less certain of that.

And then there was her other fear, one far more real than the ghost of his ex-wife. Ryan's face on the day they'd seen the nurse who resembled Wendy had burned a permanent scar in her heart. What if he found another woman like Wendy someday? Wendy had been as different from Jessie as day was from night. If he'd been drawn to a woman like Wendy once, might not there be a chance he'd be drawn to another one someday? His convictions about marriage and family might be sorely tested if he ever fell in love again. And if that happened, where did that leave her?

High and dry. Alone. As she'd been most of her life.

And because her innate caution urged her not to do anything rash, she called her landlord back and arranged a time to sign the new contract right before her appointment at the bank to sign the loan papers.

As she made her way into the bank after meeting her landlord, she was conscious of a ridiculous sense of… relief? Not exactly the correct word. But she knew she'd been right to keep her lease in place, if only because having the condo made her feel more secure, as if she still held the reins of her future.

"Mrs. Shaughnessy! Thank you for coming." Mr. Brockhiser, her loan officer, walked across the lobby as he extended a hand.

"It's my pleasure, believe me." She smiled at the man as they shook. "I was delighted to get your call. Enlarging my gallery is something to which I'm totally committed."

Brockhiser showed her into his office, then took a seat behind his desk. His eyes twinkled as he shuffled papers. "That's good, but you're certainly going to have your hands full once those babies arrive, aren't you?"

"Yes, but I—" She stopped. "How did you know I'm having more than one baby?"

"Ryan told me." The banker winked at her. "Understand you two were childhood sweethearts. My wife's dying to meet you."

"Um, we grew up together, yes." She cleared her throat. "I didn't realize you knew Ryan."

Brockhiser folded his hands atop the stack of papers. "Oh, we go way back. I knew him before he was a big success. That man has the magic touch. When he said he'd back anything you chose to do, I figured I'd go back to the loan committee with your request. You should have told me you were married to Ryan—I'd have been able to make you the loan right off the bat."

Jessie froze as the room seemed to recede, leaving her in an airless vacuum of shock. *So that's why I got the loan. Ryan guaranteed it.*

The moment was engraved in her mind with stark clarity—the banker's beaming face, the sunlight slanting across the office, the rough, tweedy fabric of the chair in which she sat. Carefully, trying to keep her voice level, she said, "Could you excuse me for a moment, Mr. Brockhiser?" She was out of the chair before he could assist her, waddling across the lobby and around the corner to the ladies' room she'd located in the bank on an earlier visit.

Behind her the banker's concerned voice asked, "Are you ill, Mrs. Shaughnessy?" But she didn't stop.

God was merciful and the ladies' room was empty. Pausing for a bare second to lock the door behind her, she sank onto the settee in the lounge area, taking deep breaths to suppress the heaving sobs that strove to burst forth.

God, she couldn't believe it. He knew, he *knew* she'd wanted to do this without his assistance. How could he have gone behind her back like that? A few tears leaked out, and as she blotted them she told herself they were tears of anger.

But deep in her heart she knew better. Ryan had given

her hope for a future she'd never dared to believe in before.

She hadn't let herself dream of love, of a lifelong marriage, because she knew it would destroy her if she let down all the carefully built walls of bitter experience. She hadn't seen that kind of love in her own life, and she was afraid—no, *terrified*—to even allow herself to think for one single second that it might exist. But Ryan had slowly excavated beneath the foundations of that fear, and even though she knew she could never be everything he longed for in a wife, she'd begun to hope that she could give him enough to last them a lifetime. She'd offered him children, her unspoken devotion, a warm happy marriage based on friendship and passion—and he'd thrown it back in her face.

He knew how she felt about accepting money from him, knew how important it was to her to be independent. And he'd ignored her feelings completely. If he loved her he'd have taken her feelings into consideration.

And that was the bottom line. She'd been kidding herself, deluding herself into imagining that they could build a life together. But they couldn't. Not *together*.

Because Ryan wasn't interested in *together*.

Ryan slammed down the phone in a rare display of temper.

Where was she? He'd called the gallery three times that morning, and Penny had told him each time that Jessie was out of the building and she didn't know where she was or when she'd return.

He'd initially called simply to invite her to have lunch with him, but when he'd realized she was out of touch, his anxiety level had rapidly grown to mammoth proportions. What was she thinking? A woman in her condition, especially with the added risk of carrying twins, should never just wander off without telling anybody where she was going.

Three weeks had passed since the day she'd walked out of the kitchen with that odd look on her face, and though he knew the moment had been a defining one in their relationship, he still hadn't figured out exactly what in hell it had defined.

She'd slept in her own room that night, pleading an upset stomach, and he hadn't had any opportunity to talk to her. The next day she'd gone for her thirty-two-week checkup, and as if the doctor were in cahoots with Jess, he'd prohibited any sexual activities until after the babies were born. She hadn't come back to his bed since. And though he'd attempted to tease her into it, she'd merely replied seriously that she wasn't sleeping well because of her bulk and the babies' movements and that she'd keep him awake. And the few times Ryan had tried to bring up that day in subtle ways, she'd managed to avoid talking about it—or even looking him straight in the eye, for that matter.

What the hell had gone wrong? Could she be upset by those baby things he'd discovered? Could she possibly be bothered by the reminders of his life with Wendy? He could hardly imagine Jess minding that. She'd loved Wendy, too. And besides, he was sure it was painfully evident that he'd never had feelings for Wendy like the all-consuming emotions that Jess roused in him. No, any suspicion that she might be jealous was only a product of his own desperate imagination.

Still, he'd tactfully put everything back in the box and set it in the closet of the nursery—only to find a few days later that Jessie had unpacked the box. The white afghan Wendy had made was draped over the back of a rocking chair, the small sweater set with its matching hat hung in the closet. So obviously he'd been off base.

His office phone rang and he realized it was his private line. Snatching up the receiver, he barked, "Yes?"

"Ryan?"

It wasn't Jessie, and his whole body sagged in disappointment. "Speaking."

"It's Mort Brockhiser. I think your wife might be ill."

It took him a moment to put the pieces together. Finally he asked, "She's at the bank?"

"Not anymore." The lender's voice conveyed his concern. "She came in to sign her loan papers, but a minute after we sat down she bolted for the ladies' room. I waited but she never came back and one of the tellers just told me he saw her leaving the bank a moment ago."

Dear Lord, let her be all right. Aloud, he said, "Thanks for calling, Mort. I'd better go home."

He called the house from his car phone but she wasn't there yet and her cell phone shifted him to voice mail so she must have it turned off at the moment. Finn promised to call him the moment she showed up. She wasn't at the shop, either, and Penny still hadn't heard from her, though she also promised to call him, concern clear in her voice.

But by the time he pulled into the garage, his car phone still hadn't rung. Finn met him at the door. The manservant was practically wringing his hands with worry. "Where could she be?" he asked.

"I don't know." He punched in the admissions department at the hospital where they'd done preadmission work, but she hadn't been admitted. Nor had the doctor's office heard from her.

Panic was an ever-present companion beating wildly at the edges of his mind but he grimly refused to allow it a toehold. Without a clear idea of where he intended to go, he decided to head back downtown. If she'd been at the bank, she could be sitting in any number of little cafés or coffee shops in the area. Though why she wouldn't call if she were ill or—his all-consuming worry—in labor was a mystery.

The phone in his car rang, and he pounced on it. "Hello?"

"Ryan, she's home." It was Finn.

"Thank God." A relief so intense he felt like sliding right down onto the rubber floor mat flooded through him. "Is she all right?"

"I...I don't know. She went straight up to her room and asked not to be disturbed."

He was already making an illegal U-turn and heading back to Brookline. "I'll be there in ten minutes."

In reality it took him less than ten.

He was out of the car before the engine had completely died and took the stairs two at a time, throwing his summer jacket at Finn on the way to her room. "Jess! Where the hell *were* you? I've been worried *sick*—"

"Stop worrying. I'm fine. The babies are fine." Her voice cut through his frantic response, cool and measured, and as her tone registered, he stopped in midstride.

"Did something happen?" he asked cautiously.

"No." Again her tone was cool.

Something was wrong, very wrong, but he couldn't imagine what it could be. He studied her for a moment. She looked fine, if a little pale.

Then he realized what she was doing. Packing. There was a half-filled suitcase on the bed and she was systematically emptying each of the drawers of her dresser. "What are you doing?"

"Packing."

Frustration began to eat at the edges of his control,

fueled by the adrenaline still rushing through his system. He hadn't meant it in a literal sense. "Why?"

She shook her head, looking down at the bag she was filling. "Because. I'm going to move out. This marriage was a mistake."

The panic gave way to a bone-deep fear. And an equally deep anger. "A mistake? What the hell is wrong with you? You've been acting weird for weeks, and then I get a call from Mort Brockhiser telling me you walked out in the middle of your appointment and he was worried you had gotten ill."

"Ah. Mr. Brockhiser. Your *good friend.*" Her voice began to heat around the edges. "Your good friend the banker mentioned today that you'd offered to back up my loan application."

"I—what?" He was taken aback. "That's not right. I *never*—"

"He told me," she said heatedly. "So don't bother denying it."

"I *am* denying it!" Ryan fell silent, his mind reviewing every scrap of his chance encounter with Brockhiser. He'd never...then his own words came floating back into his mind. What had he said? That he'd back anything she attempted? Hell, he hadn't meant it literally. "Uh, I think you—and Mort—misunderstood what I said." He strove for a calmer tone.

"It doesn't matter." She dismissed his overture with one crushing line.

"It matters to *me*. I told him if I were a banker I'd back anything you chose to try, because I believe in you," he said stiffly. "*Not* because I intended to throw money at a bad risk."

"It's not a bad risk."

"I *know* that!" he roared. "Didn't I just say so?"

Jessie sank to the edge of the bed, massaging her back and sighing. "Look, Ryan, I'm sorry if I worried you. If I misunderstood anything, I'll apologize for that, too—"

"You did."

"But this—" she gestured absently around the room "—isn't going to work."

"What isn't going to work?" He was afraid he knew what she meant, but he didn't want to hear it, didn't want to believe it.

"Our marriage."

"Why?"

"You only married me to get children!" she shouted.

"And you married me for the same reason!" he shot back, goaded beyond endurance.

There was a shocked silence in the room as the harsh words ricocheted over and over in the sullen atmosphere.

"And, of course, for my money," he added bitterly.

"For your *money?*" She sucked in a deep breath, and her voice was outraged. "If I wanted your money so badly, then why am I so upset about you horning in on my loan?"

The question hammered at his mind for a moment, but he recovered swiftly. "Oh, I guess the room-by-room lists of valuables were just for fun."

She stared at him blankly. Then her gaze sharpened. She stood and walked to her dresser, yanking open the top drawer and withdrawing the rest of the papers he'd found that day, tossing them wildly into the air, where they fluttered accusingly to the carpet. "If you're talking about these, 'just for fun' is exactly what they were. Something to keep my mind off the fact that I was going stark raving mad lying here incubating. And if you don't believe me, you can ask Finn. It was his suggestion."

Her face was paper white now, and her hands were

shaking as she turned away from him and picked up the sweater she'd discarded, tossing it in the suitcase without folding it. The small gesture was a measure of how truly upset she was, since the Jessie he knew wouldn't even toss *dirty* clothes in a basket without folding them first.

"Jess," he said quietly. Desperately. "I don't want you to go."

"I have to," she replied equally quietly.

"Where? Where will you go?" Suddenly he was fighting for his marriage, his very *life*.

"I'm staying at the Hilton over near the Hynes Convention Center for three days. Then I'll be moving back into my condo."

He was stunned. "Your condo? I thought the lease was up at the end of this month."

"I renewed it," she said tonelessly.

I renewed it. The words were meaningless for a moment. Then, as he absorbed the blow, every ounce of hope drained out of him. She hadn't just made that decision today—she'd only left the bank two hours ago. Which meant... "You never intended to stay married to me, did you?" he said, swallowing the pain that rose in intense waves to pummel his heart. "This was some temporary measure...for what? If it wasn't the money, then *why?*"

She sat down again carefully, holding her hands under the bulk of their babies as if the extra weight hurt. "I thought it would work." For the first time she looked fully at him, and there was a wealth of suffering in her eyes. "We had friendship—and I was pretty sure we would have passion, like you said—but I can't live my life like this, Ryan." She stood and walked awkwardly to the window, and her fingers were white on the sill. "It's not enough. I never expected to have a real marriage and a real family, but you made me want it all—" She shook her head blindly, then threw it back to stare at the ceiling, and he could hear tears in her voice. "I can't compete with a ghost. I'll never be Wendy. And if you ever meet someone who can give you what you had with her, I don't want to be around to watch. To be in the way. It would hurt too much."

Dear God. Was she saying what he thought—hoped, prayed—she was saying? He started forward. "Jess—"

"No." She flung out an arm, and he stopped. "Don't. We'll share the children, I promise you that. I won't move away and I won't deny you equal time. You'll be able to—"

"Jessie!" He was nearly shouting. Again. Two strides brought him to her side, his heart beating a frantic rhythm in his chest. His fingers trembled as he reached for her shoulders and gently turned her around.

She was crying. It hurt him to see her tears, but hope and happiness were rising so rapidly he couldn't focus on the pain. "Jess...are you saying..." He took a deep breath, knowing that if he were wrong, if he'd misunderstood her, his life as he knew it, *needed it to be,* would be over. He tried again. "Do you love me?"

Her eyes were deep, emerald pools, shimmering with tears that seemed to double their pace as they rolled down her face. She nodded.

She nodded! He exhaled without even realizing he'd been holding his breath. "Do you know," he said carefully, his hands sliding down from her shoulders to grip her upper arms lightly, "how long I've loved you? How many years I've wanted you?"

She stared up at him, mesmerized by the intensity of his blue eyes as he held her gaze. She swallowed. "You...you love me?"

He shook her the tiniest bit, very lightly. "I love you. I've loved you for*ever*."

She couldn't take it in. "But, you never told me—"

"You never seemed interested in hearing it." His voice was soft, and echoes of old hurts vibrated.

She remembered other times when they'd skirted the edges of the past. Carefully, afraid to believe it, she said, "But when I came back to Boston you already were married. I was…so shocked. And…hurt, too."

His face grew even more sober. "I gave up. When you went south, I knew I didn't have a chance. Then Wendy came along—"

"Don't." Quickly she reached up and placed her palm across his lips. "I understand. I don't ever expect to take her place."

"No," he agreed. "You can never take her place."

The words twisted like a knife deep in a wound, and she grimaced, lowering her head to hide her expression from him. *You can deal with it,* she thought to herself. *He said he loves you, too.*

"But that's because you owned the largest piece of my heart long before I ever met Wendy." His voice dropped. "I *did* love her, but there was a part of me that always recognized—and regretted—that she wasn't you."

Shock rippled through her and she sagged in his grip.

He made a sound of alarm, then maneuvered her to the edge of the bed, lowering himself to sit beside her with one heavy arm around her back. "Are you all right?"

She nodded. Then she raised a palm to the side of his face, closing her eyes briefly in pleasure at the feel of his warm, beard-stubbled jaw beneath her hand. "All these months," she whispered, "I wanted you to love *me*. And now…you do." She shook her head. "Pinch me. This is a dream."

Ryan chuckled, the sound filled with relief. "I can think of a lot of things I'd like to do to you, but pinching you isn't on the list." He turned his face into her hand, pressing a slow kiss into the softness of her palm. "God, I love you. I've loved you forever, it seems." He raised his gaze to hers. "Tell me."

"I love you." Her words were low and intense, and she leaned forward, inviting him to set his mouth on hers.

He gathered her closer, one arm around her, the other resting on her bulging belly. Gently, tenderly, he took her mouth in a kiss so sweet she felt more tears rising. "I have got to be the luckiest guy in the world."

"And I'm the luckiest woman," she added.

"Does this mean you'll reconsider moving out?"

Her face fell as she remembered his reaction to her lease renewal. "I'm sorry I didn't trust you. I guess…it's hard for me to let go of my independence."

"Because you've never been able to depend on anyone else," he said. "But I promise you that I will always be here, for whatever you need. If you don't want my money, that's fine. If you want it all, that's fine, too. We're one now, in all the ways that count."

And she felt the same way. Once she'd feared commitment, her fear buried deep down in a place she hadn't even been able to acknowledge. She'd been afraid that letting herself love would open her up to more of the heartache she'd experienced as a child, when she'd longed for love from people who didn't have it to give. And because they hadn't, she'd told herself it was better to live without it.

She smiled, tracing his lips with a tender finger. "Actually, we'll soon be *four*. Isn't that a scary thought?"

He shook his head. "Not in the least. Not when I know I'll be sharing the future with you."

Epilogue

"Catch, Daddy!"

Ryan put up a hand almost reflexively as a surprisingly well-aimed baseball came flying straight at his chest the moment he stepped out of the garage. "Hey!" he said, wincing as the ball stung his bare palm. "Wait until I change clothes and get a glove, okay, Liv?"

Olivia Shaughnessy spit elaborately onto the ground as only a four-year-old could and came swaggering toward her father. "Okay."

"Where's your sister?" Ryan scooped his eldest terror up in one arm and nuzzled her neck as she shrieked.

A window opened on the second floor. "Olivia!" Jessie's dark head emerged. "I just got Tyler to sleep, and if you wake him, I swear I'll serve you for dinner. Oh, hi!" Her face lit up as she saw that her husband was home. "Be right down." And she vanished.

"Lanie's helpin' Finn paint Matthew's room," Livvie informed her father. "I was, too, but I got tired of painting."

"I see." As the back door opened, he glanced over his daughter's shining copper curls, drinking in the sight of his wife standing on the stoop. She held a struggling tot on her hip, and she blew her hair out of her eyes with pursed lips as she smiled at Ryan.

"Look, Mattie! Daddy's home." The little boy squirmed down and raced over to attach himself to Ryan's kneecap.

"Hi, squirt." Ryan scooped up his nearly three-year-old son in his free arm and kissed him noisily, noticing splatters of blue paint liberally applied to the little hands. "Were you helping Finn, too?"

"Uh-huh." Matthew held up his hands and regarded them, frowning. "Dirty."

"Yeah." Ryan squatted and set both children down. "Why don't you guys go in and tell Finn it's quitting time. Then wash your hands and get ready for dinner."

He stood, smiling as they raced off, and opened his arms. Jessie came into them, sliding her hands around his waist and up his back beneath his summer suitcoat. "Hi, handsome."

His heart skipped a beat at the warm, loving glow in her eyes. Dropping his head, he sought her mouth, enjoying the feel of her still-slim curves pressed against him. Would he ever get used to being loved by her? Even now, after five years and four children, she still had the power to turn his knees to jelly when she smiled. Her love was a miracle in his life.

"How was your day?" he asked. "Tyler still so bent out of shape?" Their youngest son would be six months old tomorrow and he was teething. Last night they had taken turns walking the fussing baby.

"Not so bad." She pressed a kiss to the side of his neck, speaking against his skin. "That tooth is finally through. He took good naps today, and I bet he'll sleep better tonight."

A shiver of sexual pleasure ran down his spine at the feel of her soft, open mouth on him, and he ran his hands down her back to cup the warm curves of her bottom. "I hope so. I have big plans for tonight."

She laughed, pressing herself closer against the unmistakable evidence of his "plans." "You certainly do," she murmured.

"Only if you're not too tired, though." Although his need for her was as strong as it had been the day they'd first made love, he knew that overseeing four children and a thriving business, even with the help of Finn and Penny, could be exhausting. The nights when he did nothing more than hold her in his arms were as sweet as the nights when they wrecked the bed, simply because there was no one else in the world with whom he'd rather spend his life.

"I got a nap today," she said, unaware of the direction of his thoughts.

"Good." He kissed her again, lingering over her, leisurely drawing her tongue into his mouth and tenderly exploring hers as he drew her closer against him. "I love you," he whispered against her lips. "The day you decided you wanted to have a baby was the luckiest day of my life."

"The day I decided it should be fathered by an 'eminently available hunk' was mine," she said, her eyes

dancing as he picked her up and carried her into the home
that rang with the joyous sounds of the family they'd created together.

*   *   *   *   *

Billionaire Bachelors: Stone

ANNE MARIE WINSTON

To all the nurses at the Waynesboro Hospital
who have shared my midnight vigils.
My thanks do not begin to express my
appreciation for your kindnesses.

Prologue

"**S**mythe Corp. will be yours…on one condition." Eliza Smythe's eyes narrowed as she studied her only son.

Stone Lachlan stood with one arm negligently braced on the mantel above the marble fireplace in his mother's Park Avenue apartment in New York City. Not even the flicker of an eyelash betrayed any emotion. He wasn't about to let his mother know what her offer meant to him. Not until it was his and she couldn't take it away.

"And what might that condition be?" He lifted the crystal highball glass to his lips and drank, keeping the movement slow and lazy. Disinterested.

"You get married—"

"Married!" Stone nearly choked on the fine Scotch malt whiskey.

"And settle down," his mother added. "I want

grandchildren one of these days while I'm still young enough to enjoy them."

He set his glass on a nearby marble-topped table with a snap. It took him a moment to push away the hurtful memories of a small boy whose mother had been too busy to bother with him. His mouth twisted cynically. "If you plan to devote yourself to grandchildren as totally as you did me, why are you planning to retire? It doesn't take much time to give a nanny instructions once a week or so."

His mother flinched. "If it's any consolation to you, I regret the way you were raised," she said, and he could hear pain in her voice. "If I had it to do over..."

"If you had it to do over, you'd do exactly the same thing," Stone interrupted her. The last thing he needed was to have his mother pretending she cared. "You'd immerse yourself in your family's company until you'd dragged it back from the brink of bankruptcy. And you'd keep on running it because you were the only one left."

His mother bowed her head, acknowledging the truth of his words. "Perhaps." Then she squared her shoulders and he could see her shaking off the moment of emotion. Just as she'd shaken him off so many times. "So what's your decision? Do you accept my offer?"

"I'm thinking," he said coolly. "You drive a hard bargain. Why the wife?"

"It's time for you to think about heirs," his mother said. "You're nearly thirty years old. You'll have responsibilities to both Smythe Corp. and Lachlan International and you should have children to follow in your footsteps."

God, he wished she was kidding but he doubted his mother had ever seen the point of a joke in her entire life. A wife…? He didn't want to get married. Hadn't ever really been tempted, even. A shrink would have a field day with that sentiment, would probably pronounce him scarred by his childhood. But the truth, as Stone saw it, was simply that he didn't want to have to answer to anyone other than himself.

Where in hell was he going to get a wife, anyway? Oh, finding a woman to marry him would be easy. There were dozens of fresh young debutantes around looking for Mr. Rich and Right. The problem would be finding one he could stand for more than five minutes, one that wouldn't attempt to take him to the cleaners when the marriage ended. When the marriage ended…that was it! He'd make a temporary marriage, pay some willing woman a lump sum for the job of acting as his wife for a few weeks.

"Draw up the papers, Mother." His voice was clipped. "I'll find a wife."

"Which is why it's conditional."

That got his attention. "Conditional? What—you want final approval?" Another thought occurred to him. "Or you're giving me some time limit by which I have to tie the knot?"

Eliza shook her head. "The last thing I want you to do is rush into marriage. I'd rather you wait until you find the right woman. But at least now I know you'll be thinking about it. The condition is that once you marry, the marriage has to last for one year— with both of you living under the same roof—before the company becomes yours."

One year… His agile mind immediately saw the

fine print. He would find a bride, all right. And the minute the ink was dry on the contract with his mother, there would be a quiet annulment. A twinge of guilt pricked at his conscience but he shrugged it off. He didn't owe his mother *anything*. And it would serve her right for thinking she could manipulate his life this way.

He smiled, trying to mask his newfound satisfaction. "All right, Mother. You've got a deal. I find a bride, you give me your dearest possession."

Eliza stood, her motions jerky. "I know I haven't been much of a mother to you, Stone, but I do care. That's why I want you to start looking for a wife. Being single might seem appealing for a while, but it gets awfully lonely."

He shrugged negligently, letting the words hit him and bounce off. No way was he going to let her start tugging at his heartstrings after all this time. She was the one who had chosen to leave. "Whatever."

Eliza started for the door. "At least give it some thought." She sighed. "I never thought I'd say it, but I'm actually looking forward to having some free time."

"I never thought you'd say it, either." And he hadn't. His mother lived and breathed the company that had come to her on her father's death when she was barely twenty-five. She'd loved it far more than she had Stone or his father, as his dad had pointed out.

Smythe Corp. He'd resigned himself to waiting for years to inherit his mother's corporation. But he'd never stopped dreaming. Now he would be able to implement the plans he'd considered for years. He'd merge Smythe Corp. with Lachlan Enterprises, the company that had been his father's until his death eight years ago.

As his mother took her leave, he moved into his office, still thinking about finding the right woman to agree to what sounded like an insane idea. A temporary wife. Why not? Marriage, as far as he could tell, was a temporary institution anyway. One he had never planned to enter. But if marriage was what it took, then marriage was what his mother would get.

While he turned the problem over in his head, he thumbed through the day's mail. His hand slowed as he came to a plain brown envelope. In the envelope was the report he received quarterly, giving him updates on his ward, Faith Harrell.

Faith. She'd been a gawky twelve-year-old the first time he'd seen her. He'd been fresh out of college, and they both were reeling from the death of their two fathers in a boating accident a month earlier. He'd been absolutely stunned, he recalled, when Faith's mother had begged him to become her guardian.

A guardian...him? It sounded like something out of the last century. But he hadn't been able to refuse. Mrs. Harrell had multiple sclerosis. She feared the disease's advance. And worse, she'd been a quietly well-to-do socialite for her entire married life, pursuing genteel volunteer work and keeping her home a charming, comfortable refuge for her husband. She knew nothing of finances and the world of business. They'd been married for a long, long time before they'd had Faith and their world had revolved around her. His father would have wanted him to make sure Randall Harrell's family was taken care of.

And so Faith became his ward. He'd taken care of

her, and of her mother, in a far more tangible way when he'd discovered the dismal state of Randall's investments. The man had been on the brink of ruin. Faith and her mother were practically penniless. And so Stone had quietly directed all their bills to him throughout the following years. He'd seen no reason to distress the fragile widow with her situation, and even less to burden a young girl with it. It was what his father would have done, and it certainly wasn't as if it imposed a financial strain on his own immense resources.

Faith. Her name conjured up an image of a slender schoolgirl in a neat uniform though he knew she hadn't worn uniforms since leaving her boarding school. It had been more than a year since he'd seen her. She'd become a lovely young thing as she'd grown up and she probably was even prettier now. She would be finishing her junior year at college in a few months. And though he hadn't seen her in person recently, he looked forward to reading the update on her from the lawyer who had overseen the monetary disbursements to Faith and her mother.

He slit the envelope absently as he returned to the problem of where to find a temporary wife.

Five minutes later, he was rubbing the back of his neck in frustration as he spoke to the man who provided the updates on Faith Harrell. "What do you mean, she withdrew from school two weeks ago?"

One

A huge, hard hand clamped firmly about her wrist as Faith Harrell turned from the Carolina Herrerra display she was creating in the women's department of Saks Fifth Avenue.

"What in *hell* are you doing?" a deep, masculine voice growled.

Startled, Faith looked up. A long way up, into the furious face of Stone Lachlan. Her heart leaped, then began to tap-dance in her chest as pleasure rose so swiftly it nearly choked her. She hadn't seen Stone since he'd taken her out for lunch one day last year—he was the last person she had imagined meeting today! Her pulse had begun to race at the sound of his growling tones and she hoped he didn't feel it beneath his strong fingers.

"Hello," she said, smiling. "It's nice to see you, too."

He merely stared at her, one dark eyebrow rising. "I'm waiting for an explanation."

Stone was nearly ten years her senior. His father and hers had been best friends and she'd grown up visiting with Stone and his father occasionally, chasing the big boy who gave her piggyback rides and helped her dance by letting her stand on his feet. He'd been merely a pleasant, distant-relation sort of person until their fathers had died together in a squall off Martha's Vineyard eight years ago. Since then, Stone had been her guardian, making sure her mother's multiple sclerosis wasn't worsened by any sort of stress. Technically she supposed she still was his ward, despite the fact that she'd be twenty-one in November, just eight months away. And despite the additional fact that she was penniless and didn't need a guardian anyway.

Stone. Her stomach fluttered with nervous delight and she silently admonished herself to settle down and behave like an adult. She'd been terribly infatuated with him by the time she was a young teenager.

He'd teased her, told her jokes and tossed her in the air. And she'd been smitten with the fierce pain of unrequited love. Though she'd told herself it was just a crush and she'd outgrown him, her body's involuntary reactions to his nearness now called her a liar. *Ridiculous,* she told herself sternly. *You haven't seen the man in months. You barely know him.*

But Stone had kept tabs on her since their fathers' deaths, though his busy schedule apparently hadn't permitted him to visit often. He'd remembered her at Christmas and on her birthday, and she'd occasionally gotten postcards from wherever he happened to be in the world, quick pleasantries scrawled in a

strong masculine hand. It hadn't been much, she supposed, but to a young girl at a quiet boarding school,
it had been enough.

And she knew from comments he'd made in his
infrequent letters that he had checked on her progress
at boarding school and at college, which she'd attended for two and a half years.

Until she'd learned the truth.

The truth. Her pleasure in his appearance faded.

"I work here," she said quietly, gathering her dig-
nity around her. She should be furious with Stone for
what he'd done, but she couldn't stop herself from
drinking in the sight of his large, dark-haired form,
so enormous and out of place among the delicate,
feminine clothing displays.

"You quit school," he said, his strong, tanned features dark with displeasure.

"I temporarily stopped taking classes," she corrected. "I hope to return part-time eventually." Then
she remembered her shock and humiliation on the
day she'd learned that Stone had paid for her education and every other single thing in her life since
her father's death. "And in any case, I couldn't have
stayed. I needed a job."

Stone went still, his fingers relaxing on her wrist
although he didn't release her, and she sensed his
sudden wariness. "Why do you say that?"

She shook the index finger of her free hand at him.
"You know very well why, so don't pretend innocence." She surveyed him for a moment, unable to
prevent the wry smile that tugged at her lips. "You'd
never pull it off."

He didn't smile back. "Have lunch with me. I
want to talk to you."

She thought for a moment. "About what?"

"Things," he said repressively. His blue eyes were dark and stormy and he took a moment to look at their surroundings. "You can't keep this up."

She smiled at his ill temper. "Of course I can. I'm not a millionaire, it helps to pay the rent." Then she remembered the money. "Actually, I want to talk to you, too."

"Good. Let's go." Stone started to tow her toward the escalator, but Faith stiffened her legs and resisted.

"Stone! I'm working. I can't just leave." She waved a hand toward the rear of the department. "Let me check with my supervisor and see what time I can take my lunch break."

He still held her wrist and she wondered if he could feel her pulse scramble beneath his fingers. He searched her face for a long moment before he nodded once, short and sharp. "All right. Hurry."

Faith turned and walked to the back of the store at a ladylike pace. She refused to let Stone see how much his presence unsettled her. Memories ran through her head in a steady stream.

When he'd come to visit a few months after the funeral to help her mother tell her what they had decided, he'd been grieving, but even set in unsmiling severe lines, his face had been handsome. She'd been drawn even more than ever to his steady strength and charismatic presence. He talked about the friendship their fathers had shared since their days as fraternity brothers in college but she'd known even before he started to talk that he'd feel responsible for her. He was just that kind of man.

He intended to continue to send her to a nearby private school in Massachusetts, he told her, and to make sure that her mother's care was uninterrupted and her days free of worry. And though she hadn't known it at the time, Stone had taken over the burden of those debts. At the time of his death, her father had been nearly insolvent.

"Faith!" One of the other saleswomen whispered at her as she rushed by. "Who is that gorgeous, gorgeous man standing over there? I saw you talking to him."

Faith threaded her way through the salespeople gathering in the aisle. "A family friend," she replied. Then she saw Doro, her manager. "What time will I have my break today?"

Doro's eyes were alive with the same avid curiosity dancing in the other womens' faces. "Does *he* want you to have lunch with him?"

Wordlessly Faith nodded.

"That's Stone Lachlan!" One of the other clerks rushed up, dramatically patting her chest. "Of the steel fortune Lachlans. And his mother is the CEO of Smythe Corp. Do you know how much he's worth?"

"Who cares?" asked another. "He could be penniless and I'd still follow him anywhere. What a total babe!"

"Sh-h-h." Doro hustled the others back to work. Then she turned back to Faith. "Go right now!" The manager all but took her by the shoulders and shoved her back in Stone's direction.

Faith was amused, but she understood Stone's potent appeal. Even if he hadn't been so good-looking, he exuded an aura of power that drew women irresistibly.

Quietly she gathered her purse and her long black

wool coat, still a necessity in New York City in March. Then she walked back to the front of the women's department where Stone waited. He put a hand beneath her elbow as he escorted her from the store and she shivered at the touch of his hard, warm fingers on the tender bare flesh of her neck as he helped her into her coat and gently drew her hair from beneath the collar.

He had a taxi waiting at the curb and after he'd handed her into the car, he took a seat at her side. "The Rainbow Room," he said to the driver.

Faith sat quietly, absorbing as much of the moment as she could. This could very well be the last time she ever shared a meal with him. Indeed, this could be the last time she ever saw him, she realized. He had taken her out to eat from time to time when she was younger and he'd come to visit her at school. She'd never known when he was going to show up and whisk her off for the afternoon—Lord, she'd lived for those visits. But she and Stone lived in different worlds now and it was unlikely their paths would cross.

At the restaurant, they were seated immediately. She sat quietly until Stone had ordered their meals. Then he squared his big shoulders, spearing her with an intense look. "You can't work as a shop girl."

"Why not? Millions of women do and it hasn't seemed to harm them." Faith toyed with her water glass, meeting his gaze. "Besides, I don't have a choice. You know as well as I do that I have no money."

He had the grace to look away. "You'd have been taken care of," he said gruffly.

"I know, and I appreciate that." She folded her

hands in her lap. "But I can't accept your charity. I'd like to know how much I owe you for everything you did in the past eight years—"

"I didn't ask you to pay me back." He leaned forward and she actually found herself shrinking back from the fierce scowl on his face.

"Nonetheless," she said as firmly as she could manage, given the way her stomach was quivering, "I intend to. It will take me some time, but if we draw up a schedule—"

"No."

"I beg your pardon?"

"I said no, you may not pay me back." His voice rose. "Dammit, Faith, your father would have done the same if I'd been in your shoes. I promised your mother I'd take care of you. She trusts me. Besides, it's an honor thing. I'm only doing what I know my father would have done."

"Ah, but your father didn't make risky investments that destroyed his fortune," she said, unable to prevent a hot wash of humiliation from warming her cheeks.

"He could have." Stone's chin jutted forward in a movement she recognized from the time he'd descended on the school to talk to her math teacher about giving her a failing grade on a test she'd been unable to take because she'd had pneumonia. "Besides," he said, "it's not as if it's made a big dent in my pocketbook. Last time I checked, there were a few million left."

She shook her head. "I still don't feel right about taking your money. Do you have any idea how I felt when I learned that you'd been paying my way for years?"

"How did you find out, anyway?" He ignored her question.

"In February I went to the bank to talk about my father's investments—I thought it would be good for me to start getting a handle on them since you'd no longer be responsible for me after my twenty-first birthday, which is coming up later this year. I assumed I'd take on responsibility for my mother's finances then, as well. That's when I learned that every item in my family's budget for *eight years* had been paid for by you." Despite her vow to remain calm, tears welled in her eyes. "I was appalled. Someone should have told me."

"And what good would that have done, other than to distress you needlessly?"

"I could have gotten a job right out of high school, begun to support myself."

"Faith," he said with ill-concealed impatience. "You were not quite thirteen years old when your father died. Do you really think I would have left you and your mother to struggle alone?"

"It wasn't your decision to make," she insisted with stubborn pride, swallowing the tears.

"It was," he said in a tone that brooked no opposition. "It *is*. Your mother appointed me your guardian. Besides, if you finish your education you'll be able to get a heck of a lot better job than working as a salesclerk at Saks."

"Does my mother know the truth?"

Stone shook his head. "She believes I oversee your investments and take care of the bills out of the income. Her doctors tell me stress is bad for MS patients. Why distress her needlessly?"

It made sense. And in an objective way, she admired his compassion. But it still horrified her to think of the money he'd spent.

The waiter returned then with their meal and the conversation paused until he'd set their entrées before them. They both were quiet for the next few moments.

Stone ate with deep concentration, his dark brows drawn together, obviously preoccupied with something.

She hated to be keeping him from something important but when she said as much, he replied, "You were the only thing on my agenda for today."

Really, there wasn't anything she could say in response to *that,* she thought, suppressing a smile. "Since that's the case," she finally said, "I'd really like to have an accounting of how much I owe you—"

"*Do not* ask me that one more time." Stone's deep voice vibrated with suppressed anger.

She gave up. If Stone wouldn't tell her, she could figure out a rough estimate, at least, by combining tuition fees with a living allowance. And she should be able to get a record of her mother's fees from her doctor. "I have to get back to work soon," she said in the coolest, most polite manner she could muster.

Stone's head came up; he eyed her expression. "Hell," he said. "You're already mad at me; I might as well get it all over with at once."

"I'd prefer that you don't swear in my presence." She lifted her chin. Then his words penetrated. "What do you mean?"

"You're not going back to work."

"Excuse me?" Her voice was frosty.

He hesitated. "I phrased that badly. I want you to quit work."

She stared at him. "Are you crazy? And live on what?"

He scowled. "I told you I'd take care of you."

"I can take care of myself. I won't always be a salesclerk. I'm taking night classes starting in the summer," she said. Despite her efforts to remain calm, her voice began to rise. "It's going to take longer this way but I'll finish."

"What are you studying?" His sudden capitulation wasn't expected.

She eyed him with suspicion. "Business administration and computer programming. I'd like to start my own business in Web design one of these days."

His eyebrows rose. "Ambitious."

"And necessary," she said. "Mama's getting worse. She's going to need 'round-the-clock care one of these days. I need to be able to provide the means for her to have it."

"You know I'll always take care of your mother."

"That's not the point!" She wanted to bang her head—or his—against the table in frustration.

"My father would have expected me to take care of you. *That's* the point." He calmly sat back against the banquette, unfazed by her aggravation, an elegant giant with the classic features of a Greek god, and she was struck again by how handsome he was. When they'd entered The Rainbow Room, she'd been aware of the ripple of feminine interest that his presence had attracted. She'd been ridiculously glad that she was wearing her black Donna Karan today. It might be a few years old but it was a gorgeous garment and she felt more confident simply slipping it on. Then she remembered that *his* money had paid for the dress, and her pleasure in her appearance drained away.

"I'm sure your father would be pleased that you've done your duty," she said with a note of asperity. "But we will *not* continue to accept your charity."

He grimaced. "Bullhead."

"Look who's talking." But she couldn't resist the gleam in his eye and she smiled back at him despite the gnawing feeling of humiliation that had been lodged in her belly since the day she'd found out she was essentially a pauper. "Now take me back to work. My lunch hour is almost over."

He heaved an impatient sigh. "This is against my better judgment."

She leaned forward, making her best effort to look intimidating. "Just think about how miserable I will make your life if you don't. I'm sure your judgment will improve quickly."

He shot her a quirky grin. "I'm shaking in my boots."

He didn't want to notice her.

She had been an unofficial little sister during his youth, and his responsibility since her father had died. She was ten years younger than he was. He was her guardian, for God's sake!

But as he handed her back into the car after their meal, his eye was caught by the slim length of her leg in the elegant high heels as she stepped in, by the way her simple dress hugged the taut curve of her thigh as she slid across the seat, by the soft press of pert young breasts against the fabric of the black coat as she reached for her seat belt.

He'd seen her standing in the store long before she had noticed him, her slender figure strikingly displayed in a black dress that, although it was perfectly discreet, clung to her in a way that made a man want to strip it off and slide his hands over the smooth curves beneath. Made *him* want to touch, to pull the pins out of her shining coil of pale hair and watch it slither down over her shoulders and breasts, to set his mouth to the pulse that beat just beneath the delicate skin along her white throat and taste—

Enough! *She's not for you.*

Grimly he dragged his mind back from the direction in which it wanted to stray.

He hated the idea of her wearing herself out hustling in retail for eight hours a day, and he figured he'd give it one more try. The only woman he'd ever known who really enjoyed working was his mother. Faith shouldn't be working herself into exhaustion. She should be gracing someone's home, casting her gentle influence around a man, making his life an easier place to be. He knew it was an archaic attitude and that most modern women would hit him over the head for voicing such a thought. But he'd lived a childhood without two parents because his own mother had put business before family. He *knew,* despite all the Superwoman claims of the feminist movement, that a woman couldn't do it all.

Diplomatically he only said, "Why don't you go back to school for the rest of the semester? Then this summer we can talk about you finding a job."

Her eyes grew dark and her delicate brows snapped together. "You will *not* give me money.

More money," she amended. "I'm not quitting work. I need the money. Besides, it's too late in the semester to reenroll. I've missed too much."

He looked across the car at her, seated decorously with her slender feet placed side by side, her hands folded in her lap and her back straight as a ramrod. Her hair was so fair it nearly had a silver sheen to it where the winter sun struck it, and her eyes were a pure lake-gray above the straight little nose. She had one of the most classically lovely faces he'd ever seen, and she looked far too fragile to be working so hard. The only thing that marred the picture of the perfect lady was the frown she was aiming his way. The contrast was adorable and he caught himself before he blurted out how beautiful she was in a snit.

Then he realized that beautiful or not, she was as intransigent as a mule who thought she was carrying too heavy a load. "All right," he said. "You can keep doing whatever you want. Within reason."

"Your definition of reason and mine could be quite different." Her tone was wry and her frown had relaxed. "Besides, in eight more months, you won't have any authority to tell me what to do. Why don't you start practicing now?"

He took a deep breath, refusing to snarl. He nearly told her that no matter how old she got she'd always be his responsibility, but the last thing he needed was for her to get her back up even more. Then he recalled the image of her stricken face, great gray eyes swimming with the tears she refused to give in to as she told him how she'd found out about her financial affairs, and he gentled his response to a more reasonable request. "Would you at least consider a different kind of job? Something that isn't so demanding?''

She was giving him another distinctly suspicious look. ''Maybe. But I won't quit today.''

He exhaled, a deep, exaggeratedly patient sigh. ''Of course not.''

When the taxi rolled to a stop in front of Saks, he took her elbow as she turned toward the door. ''Wait,'' he said before she could scramble out.

She turned back and looked at him, her gray eyes questioning.

''Have dinner with me tonight.''

Could her eyes get any wider? ''Dinner?''

He knew how she felt. He hadn't planned to ask her; the words had slipped out before he'd thought about them. Good Lord. ''Um, yes,'' he said, wondering if thirty was too early for the onset of senility. ''I'll pick you up. What's your address?''

She lived on the upper West Side, in a small apartment that would have been adequate for two. But he knew from the talk they had shared over lunch that she had at least two roommates from the names she'd mentioned.

''How many people do you live with?'' he asked dubiously, looking around as she unlocked the door and ushered him in.

''Three other girls,'' she answered. ''Two to each bedroom. Two of us work days and two work nights so it's rare that we're all here at the same time.''

Just then, a door opened and a girl in a black leotard and denim overalls came down the hall. Stone examined her with disbelief. She was a redhead, at least mostly. There was a blue streak boldly marching through the red near the left front side of her curly hair. She had a wide, friendly smile and green eyes that were sparkling with interest.

"Well, hey," she said. "Like, I hate to tell you, handsome, but you *so* do not fit in here."

He couldn't keep himself from returning the grin. "My Rolex gave me away?"

"Gretchen, this is Stone Lachlan," Faith said. "Stone, one of my roommates, Gretchen Vandreau."

"Pleased to meet you." Gretchen dropped a mock-curtsy, still beaming.

"You also, Miss Vandreau." He grinned again as her eyes widened.

"Are you—oh, wow, you are! *The* Lachlans." Her eyebrows shot up as she eyed Faith. "Where did you find him?"

"Actually I found her," Stone said. "Faith and I are old friends." He turned to Faith. "Are you ready?"

"Ready? Like, to go out?" Gretchen looked from one to the other with delight. "You go, girlfriend."

"It's not like *that,*" she said to Gretchen.

"Depends on what *that* is," Stone inserted.

Faith turned and glared at him. "Stone—"

"Better hurry, I have reservations for eight." He felt an odd sense of panic as he gauged the mulish expression on her face. Was she having second thoughts? Was she going to back out? He had to battle the urge to simply pick her up and carry her back down to the car.

She retrieved a black cape from the small coat closet with her friend chattering along behind her. He stepped in to help her on with the garment, and they went out the door to the sound of Gretchen's enthusiastic, "Have a blast!"

He took her elbow and urged her into the elevator, conscious of a ridiculous sense of relief sweeping through him as they exited the cramped apartment. It was only that he felt it was his duty to take care of her, he assured himself. Faith didn't belong in a crowded apartment or behind a counter in a department store. Her family had intended that she be gently raised, probably with the idea that she'd marry a polite young man of the upper class one day and raise polite, well-mannered upper-class children. After all, she'd been sent to the best private schools, had learned the sometimes ridiculous rules that accompanied moving in society.

He wished the idea didn't fill him with such a sense of…unease. That was all it was. He wanted the best for her and it would be up to him to be sure any suitors were suitable.

He surveyed her covertly as they stood in the elevator, waiting for the ground floor. Her blond hair was smoothly swept back into a shining knot at the back of her head and the harsh lighting in the elevator made it gleam with silvery highlights. She was chewing on her bottom lip; he reached out and touched it with his index finger to get her to stop. Alarm bells went off in his head as a strange jolt of electric awareness shot through his body.

He stared down at her. She had her gaze fixed on the floor and he had to restrain himself from reaching for her chin and covering her lips with his own. What would she taste like?

Then he realized what he was thinking…totally

inappropriate thought to be having about a girl who was like his little sister. Again.

Little sister? Since when do you wonder how your little sister's curves would feel pressed up against you?

He almost growled aloud to banish his unruly thoughts and Faith's gray eyes flashed to his face with a wary look he thought was probably normally aimed at large predators.

"Something wrong?" he asked.

"No." Then she shook her head. "That's not true. Why are you doing this?"

He gazed calmly back at her. "Dinner, you mean?"

She nodded.

"I'm your guardian. It struck me today that I haven't done a very good job of it, either, so I thought we'd spend a little more time together. You can tell me more about your plans."

She nodded again, as if his explanation made sense.

The ride to the small, quiet Italian restaurant where he'd made reservations was a short one. As the maître d' showed them to their table, Faith caught his eye. As the man walked away, she whispered, "If this isn't a Mafia haven, I don't know what is!"

He chuckled, surprised she'd picked up on it. He'd been coming here for years—the food was reputed to be some of the best Northern Italian cuisine in the city. But the waiters, the bartender, certainly the man who appeared to be the owner greeting guests, had an air of authority, underlaid with an indefinable air of menace. "It's probably the safest place to be in Manhattan," he said.

Over dinner, he asked her questions about her interest in computers.

"I had a knack for it," she told him, "and I started helping out in the computer lab at school. It got so that the instructors were coming to me with questions about how to do things, and how to fix things they'd messed up. That led me into programming and eventually I set up the school's Web site. And once I did that, other people began to ask me to design their sites. It occurred to me that I could make a living doing something I really enjoy, so I decided on a double major in computers and business."

"You're planning to open your own company when you get your degree?"

She nodded, and her eyes shone with enthusiasm. "Eventually. I think I'd like the challenge. But I'll probably start at an established firm." She paused and her gaze grew speculative. "You had to take over Lachlan after your father passed away, and you've clearly been successful at it. You can give me some pointers."

He shrugged. Discussing business with Faith was hardly at the top of his list of things he wanted to do. "I'm sure you'll have no trouble."

Their dinners arrived and while they ate, he inquired about her mother's health.

"She isn't able to get around without using a motorized scooter now," she said, her face sobering. "She's sixty, and the disease has started to accelerate. Recently she's been having a lot of trouble with her vision. Some days are better than others. But it's only a matter of time before she needs live-in assistance or she has to go to some kind of assisted care facility. She wasn't happy that I'm working, either, but we're going to be facing some serious expenses one of these days." He could hear the frustration in her voice.

"She's only thinking of you," he said. "She wants you to have the freedom and enjoy normal experiences for a young woman your age."

Moments later, Faith excused herself from the table and made her way to the ladies' room. As he watched her walk across the room, he was struck again by her elegance and poise. Every man in the room watched her and he caught himself frowning at a few of them in warning.

That was ridiculous. He wasn't her keeper.

Well, in fact he supposed he was. But this wasn't the Dark Ages and she didn't need his permission to accept a suitor. Or a husband, for that matter.

He didn't like that thought. Not at all. Faith was still very young, and she fairly screamed, "Innocent." She could easily be taken advantage of now that she wasn't in the somewhat protected environment of an all-girls' college. She was still his ward, though in her mind, at least, it was a mere technicality. In his, it was altogether different. He was supposed to take care of her. And he'd never forgive himself if she came to harm, even if it was only getting her heart broken by some cad. It frustrated the hell out of him that he wasn't going to be able to keep her safe.

Then the perfect solution to his frustration popped into his head. He could marry her!

Marry her? Was he insane? They were ten years apart in age, far more than that in experience. But, he decided, the kind of experience he was thinking of could play no part in a marriage with Faith. It would be strictly a platonic arrangement, he assured himself. Simply an arrangement that would help him achieve a goal and protect her at the same time. If she was married, Faith wouldn't be a target for trouble. In another year or so she'd be more worldly, and the best part was that he would be able to keep her safe during that time.

He was going to have to marry to satisfy his mother's conditions anyway. And if they married soon, as soon as possible, then he'd be only a year away from achieving the goal of which he'd dreamed for years. He would be able to merge Smythe Corp. and Lachlan Industries into one bigger and better entity.

Then he forgot about business as Faith appeared again. She walked toward him as if he'd called to her, and as she drew closer he could see her smiling at him. He smiled back, knowing that the other men in the place had to be envying him. Long and lean, she had a smooth, easy walk with a regal carriage that ensured instant attention when paired with that angelic face. He doubted she even realized it.

As she passed one of the waiters, the man flashed a white smile at her. She gave him a warm smile in return, and she had no idea that he'd turned to watch her back view as she continued on through the restaurant to their table.

And *that* was exactly why she needed his protection, Stone thought grimly. He stood as she arrived and walked around to settle her in her chair. She glanced up at him over her shoulder with the same sweet smile she'd just given the waiter, and he felt his gut clench in response. She was far too potent for her own good.

"So," he said, picking up his water and taking a healthy gulp, "while you were gone I was doing some thinking, and I have a proposition for you."

"A proposition?" Her eyes lit with interest. "Are we talking about a job here?"

"In a sense." He hesitated, then plunged ahead. "Are you serious about paying me back?"

"Yes," she said immediately.

God, he hadn't been this nervous since the first day he'd stood in front of the assembled employees of his father's company for the first time. "I could use your help with something," he said slowly.

Faith's gaze searched his expression, clearly looking for clues. "You need my help?"

He nodded. Then he took a deep breath and leaned forward. "I need a wife."

She stared at him, apparently sure she hadn't heard him correctly. He couldn't blame her. As soon as the words were out, he'd decided he was crazy. "You need *what?*"

"A wife." He could hear the embarrassment and impatience in his tone and he forced himself to take deep, slow breaths. Calming breaths.

She spread her hands in confusion and her smooth brow wrinkled in bewilderment. "But how can I help you with that? I doubt I know anyone who—"

"Faith." His deep voice stopped her tumbling words. "I'd like *you* to be my wife."

Her eyes widened. Her mouth formed a perfect O of surprise. She put a hand up and pointed to herself as if she needed confirmation that she hadn't lost her mind, and her lips soundlessly formed the word, "Me?"

He nodded, feeling an unaccustomed heat rising into his face. "Yes. You."

Two

Stone couldn't have shocked her more if he'd asked her to stand and start stripping. Faith stared at him, convinced he'd lost his mind.

"Not," he said hastily, "a *real* wife. Let me explain." He took a deep breath. He was looking down at his drink instead of at her, and she was surprised to see a dull bronze flush rising in his cheeks. "My mother is beginning to think about retirement. She's offered me her company, but before she'll turn it over she wants me to be married."

"Why would she do that?" She was completely baffled. What kind of mother would put her own child in a position like that?

"She thinks I need to settle down and give her some grandchildren." He snorted. "Although I can't imagine why. She's not exactly the most maternal person in the world."

She wondered if he heard the note of resentment and what else? Longing, perhaps, for something that hadn't been, in his voice. "Forcing you into marriage seems a little...extreme," she said carefully.

His face was grim. "My mother's a control freak. This is just one more little trick she's playing to try to arrange my life to suit herself." He bared his teeth in what she felt sure he thought was a smile. "So this time I intend to outfox her."

"What happens if you refuse to get married?"

He shrugged. "I guess she liquidates or sells. I didn't ask." He leaned forward, his eyes blazing a brilliant blue in the candlelight. "It would mean a lot to me, Faith. I want to keep Smythe Corp. a Lachlan holding."

"Why?"

He stared at her, clearly taken aback. "Why?" When she nodded, he sat back, as if to distance himself from the question. "Well, because it's a good business decision."

"But surely there are other companies out there that fit the bill. Why *this* company?"

"Because it's my heritage. My great-grandfather founded Smythe Corp. It would be a shame to see it pass out of the family."

There was something more there, she realized as she registered the tension in his posture, something she couldn't put her finger on, that underlay his stated reasons for wanting that particular company. But she had a feeling he wouldn't take kindly to being pushed any further.

"Will you do it?" he asked.

"I don't know." She chewed her lip. "It seems so dishonest—"

"Any less dishonest than trying to force me into marriage just because she's decreed it's time?" he demanded. For the first time, his control slipped and she caught a glimpse of the desperation lurking beneath his stoic facade. But he quickly controlled it, and when he spoke, his voice was calm again. "It would only be for a year," he said, "or a bit more. Strictly temporary. Strictly platonic. Except that we'd have to convince my mother that it's a real marriage. I'm not asking you to lie about anything that would hurt anyone." He stared deep into her eyes. "Think about that company, Faith. It's been in my family for three generations. If it's sold to an outsider, who knows what kind of restructuring might occur? Hundreds of people might lose their jobs."

She frowned at him. "That's emotional blackmail."

He grinned ruefully. "Did it work?"

She stared at him, her thoughts crashing over each other in chaotic patterns. "Would we live together?"

He nodded. "You'd have to move into my place for the duration. But we'd get an annulment when the time comes. And I'd expect to pay you for your time."

Pay you. She was almost ashamed of the mercenary thoughts that rushed through her head. Practical, she told herself, not mercenary. Not much. She couldn't possibly let him pay her. Not after all he'd done for her. This would be a good way to do something for him in return. Besides, if she moved in with him, she wouldn't have to keep renting her apartment.

She could go back to school, get a lot farther along in her education more quickly, if she didn't have living expenses. She only had a year and a half to go. Which meant that she'd be able to start repaying him sooner. Because regardless of what he said, she *was* going to pay back everything he'd done for her and her mother in the years since her father had died. And suddenly, that goal didn't seem so totally out of reach.

A profound relief washed over her and she closed her eyes for a moment.

"Are you all right?" He reached across the table and cupped her chin in his hand.

She swallowed, very aware of the warmth of his strong fingers on her skin. His touch sent small sizzling streamers of excitement coursing through her and she suppressed a shiver of longing. "Yes." But it came out a whisper. She cleared her throat. "But you can't pay me."

He released her chin, his brows snapping together. "Of course I'll—"

"No. I'm in your debt already."

"All right," he said promptly. "How about this: if you marry me for the time I need to get Smythe Corp., I'll consider all the debt you imagine you owe me to be paid in full."

She froze for a moment as hope blossomed. Then she realized she couldn't possibly make a deal like that. It wouldn't be fair to him. She started to shake her head, but before she could speak, Stone raised a hand.

"Hear me out. Marriage would be a sacrifice. You'd lose a year of your freedom. You'd be expected to attend social functions with me and play the part of hostess when we entertain. We'd have to convince my mother it was a real marriage for real reasons.''

She didn't ask what he meant, but she could feel a blush heating her own face now as she sat silently considering his proposal.

''It's a fair deal,'' he urged. ''An exchange of favors, if you like.''

She wasn't so sure of that. Taking care of her mother and her for eight years weighed a lot more on her scale than one measly year of marriage did. But when she met his gaze, she could see the iron determination there. If she didn't agree to this, he was liable to start in about paying her again.

And there was another factor, one that outweighed even her concerns about her finances. A moment ago, she'd seen naked panic in his eyes at the thought of losing that company. It wasn't financial, she was sure. But it was terribly important to Stone for some reason. And because she'd discerned that, she knew what her answer had to be.

''All right,'' she said hoarsely. ''It's a deal. But there are three conditions.''

He only raised one eyebrow.

''I'd like to continue with my education—''

''You don't need to finish school.'' Impatience quivered in every line of his big body. ''You'll be doing me an enormous favor with this marriage. The least I can do is settle a sum on you at the end of the year. You won't need to work at all.''

''I *want* to work,'' she insisted. ''And I want to go back to school.''

''You won't be able to work,'' he said. ''Can you imagine what the press would do with that?''

Unfortunately she could. As one of the richest men

in the country, Stone dealt with a ridiculous amount of intrusive press.

"You'd have to consider being my wife your job," he said. "But I'll pay your tuition if you insist on taking classes."

"I do," she said firmly. "I'll reenroll for the summer session."

"All right. Now what's the third thing?"

She hated that she had to ask him for help with anything, but she had no choice. And it wasn't for her. "My mother," she said quietly. "The cost of her care—"

"Is not a problem for me," he said firmly. Then he leaned forward. "In fact, if you like, we could move your mother into my home. There's an apartment on the main floor for live-in help but I've never had anyone live in. She could stay there."

It was a generous offer and a generous thought, even if he was doing it for selfish reasons. She swallowed, more tempted by the thought than she should be. It would make her life much easier in many ways. And she'd be able to see her mother every day, perhaps even help with her care

"Please," Stone said. "I'd really like you to do this, Faith."

She studied his handsome face, serious and unsmiling, his eyes intense with the force of his will and an odd feeling rippled through her. "All right," she said. Then she cleared her throat and spoke more firmly. "I'll marry you."

The next morning, Saturday, he picked her up in his silver Lexus and took her to his home so that she could see where she'd be living and check out the apartment for her mother. He'd asked her to stop working immediately, and though he could tell she didn't like it, she'd informed him when he picked her up that she was no longer employed.

"Don't think of it as unemployed," he advised. "You just switched jobs."

She was silent as he maneuvered the car through Manhattan's insanely crowded streets to the quieter area where he made his home.

He could see her chewing her lip as she had the night before and he wondered what she was thinking. Worrying, probably, about whether or not she'd made a bad decision.

As he braked for a light, he said, "Thank you. I know this isn't an easy thing for you to do." He put his hand over hers where it lay in her lap and squeezed. This time he was prepared for the sensation her soft flesh aroused. Or so he told himself. Still, the shock he'd absorbed when he'd touched her last night reverberated through him. All he'd done was place his hand beneath her chin, letting his fingers rest against the silken skin of her cheek.

He thought he'd steeled himself for the same reaction that had hit him yesterday when he'd touched her lip.

But he hadn't been prepared for the strong current of attraction that tore through him, making him want to deepen the skin-to-skin contact in a very basic way. It was as if she was a live circuit and touching her plugged him in to her special current. He mentally shook his head. What was he doing, asking the girl to live in his home? Putting temptation right under his nose probably wasn't the smartest thing he'd ever done.

Still, as he drew her from the car and took the elevator from the garage to his Fifth Avenue town house across from Central Park, he felt an immense relief. Faith had been sheltered her entire life. Who knew what kind of things might happen to a naive girl like her on her own? He'd promised his father's memory that he'd take care of Faith, and he would.

Unlocking the door, he ushered her into his home. Inside the door, Faith stopped in the large central foyer, looking around. Though she'd spent her early years in a family that wanted for little, he imagined that the place seemed luxurious compared to the seedy little apartment in which she was living. Looking at it through her eyes, he watched her as he realized he was holding his breath waiting for her reaction.

"This is lovely," she said quietly. "Simply lovely."

He smiled, relieved. Straight ahead of them, a hallway led to the back of the house while a staircase just to the right of the hall climbed graciously to a landing that led to an upper floor. To the left was a formal living room with an equally formal dining room through an archway behind it; to their right was Stone's office, with its masculine desk, lined shelves of books and office equipment that filled the surfaces of the built-in counters along one wall.

"I'm glad you like it." He stepped around her and indicated the stairs. "Would you like to see the upstairs? I'll show you your room."

She moved obediently in the direction he indicated, climbing the stairs as he followed. He took her down the hallway past an open set of double doors, pausing briefly to indicate the masculine-looking master suite done in striking shades of burgundy, black and gold. "That's my room." Turning, he pointed to the doors just opposite. "And across the hall is a guest suite. Your room will be the next one on the right. It should suit you. It belonged to my mother years ago and I've never changed it." He shook his head. "She may have her flaws but I can't fault her taste."

Leading her to her room, he pushed open both doors.

"Oh," she said on a sigh, "it's *perfect*."

It was a charming, feminine suite decorated in soft lavenders and blues accented with pure white. Though it was slightly smaller than his, it was still spacious, with a walk-in closet, a sitting area and a large full bath. He walked past her into the bathroom. "Our rooms are connected," he told her, sliding back a large set of louvered doors to reveal his bath and bedroom beyond. "No one will have to know we don't share a room."

She couldn't look him in the eye. "All right," she said in a muffled tone.

"Faith." He waited patiently until finally, she gazed across the room at him. "This will be a good arrangement for both of us. I promise to respect your privacy."

She nodded. Her cheeks had grown pink and he knew that she understood that he was telling her, in as gentle a way as he could, that she had nothing to fear from him sexually. No, appealing as she might be, he had no intention of changing the platonic status of their relationship.

By the time they had finished the house tour, it was lunchtime. He'd decided to show her how it would be when they lived together so he took her into the kitchen and seated her on a stool at the large island while he made tuna salad, sliced tomatoes and piled the combination between two halves of a crois- sant with cheese. He grilled the sandwiches while he sliced up a fresh pineapple.

"I didn't expect you to know your way around a kitchen," she told him, filling two glasses with ice and water as he'd asked her to do.

He grinned. "Figured I'd have a chef on standby waiting to fulfill my every wish?"

"Something like that." She glanced up at him and smiled. "I can cook, although I'm no Julia Child. I'd be happy to do the cooking."

"Actually," he admitted, "I do have a woman who comes in Monday through Thursday unless I have to be away. Why don't we keep her for the time being until you see how much free time you're going to have?"

"I'll have free time from nine-to-five every day of the week," she said. "If there's anything I can help with, all you have to do is ask."

He couldn't imagine asking her to get involved in any of his business dealings except in a social fash- ion, and he had someone to clean the house, so he couldn't think of anything he'd want her to do. "You'll have studying to do as soon as the summer term starts," he said instead. "And you'll be able to spend some time with your mother."

She brightened, and he remembered her pleasure last night at the idea of spending time with her mother. It was ironic, really, that they both had been deprived of their mothers for part of their childhoods. The difference was, she looked forward to spending precious time with her mother while he went out of his way to avoid close contact with his. "That will be nice." Her light voice broke into the dark thought. "We haven't had a lot of time together since I went away to school."

Which was not long after the accident in which their fathers had died, he thought, as an awkward silence fell.

"Sometimes it doesn't seem possible that Daddy's been gone for eight years." Her voice, quiet and subdued, broke the moment.

A stab of grief sharper than any he'd allowed himself to feel in a long time pierced his heart. "I know what you mean. Sometimes I still expect mine to walk through the door."

Her gaze flew to his. "This was your childhood home?"

He nodded. "Dad and Mother lived here when they were first married. After the divorce, she moved out."

"That must have been hard," she offered. "How old were you?"

"Six. And no, it wasn't particularly hard." He willed away the memories of his youth, of the nights he'd spent crying into his pillow, wondering what he'd done to make his mother leave. Of the days he'd envied schoolmates who had had mothers who cared enough to show up for visitors' days and school plays, mothers who sat in the stands during baseball games and cheered, mothers who planned birthday parties and actually remembered cake and presents. "My mother was rarely here and when she was, she and Dad were shouting the walls down half the time."

The sympathy shining in her silvery eyes moved him more than he wanted to admit. "My childhood was just the opposite. Extremely quiet. My mother's illness was diagnosed when I was less than two years old, and my father and I did our best to keep her from getting upset about anything." She rested her elbows on the bar and crossed her arms. "In that respect, we have something in common. I went to my dad with my problems, because I couldn't go to my mother."

He smiled. "Did you know I used to go to the Mets games with your father and mine?" He shook his head. "Dad had great seats right along the third base line and we never missed a home game. Those two knew every player's stats going back to the beginning of time. And they used to argue about who the MVP was each season, who should go to the All-Star team, who ought to be traded…looking back, I think they just argued because it was fun."

Her eyes were crinkled in laughter. "I've never heard about this before." Her smile faded slightly, wobbled. "I guess you probably have a lot of memories of my father that I don't."

He hesitated, torn between lying to spare her feelings and telling her the truth. Truth won. "Yeah, I guess I do. Some of my best memories are of times I spent with my dad and yours. I'll tell you some more when we have time." He rose and took the lunch plates to the sink for the housekeeper. "This afternoon, I'd like to go pick out rings. Is that all right with you?"

Her gray eyes widened. "Rings? Is that really necessary?"

He nodded, a little disappointed that she didn't yet

seem to grasp the seriousness of his proposal. "Yes. This will be a real marriage, Faith." He almost reached for her shoulders, then stopped himself, remembering the desire that had knocked him over the last time he'd touched her. "Our reasons might be a little different from most people's but we'll be as legally wed as the next couple. So let's go get rings."

He called ahead, so that they would have some privacy while they shopped, and thirty minutes later, he handed her out of a cab in front of Tiffany & Company. Faith was a quiet presence at his side as they waited for the doors to be unlocked.

As they stepped into the cool hush of the store, a beaming saleswoman was upon them. "Welcome, Mr. Lachlan. It is Tiffany's pleasure and mine to serve you. How can we help you today?"

"Wedding rings," he said.

The woman's eyes widened as did those of the other employees ranged behind her, and he wondered how many minutes it would be until the press got wind of his marriage. He supposed he should warn Faith, though certainly she knew how ridiculously newsworthy his life was. Then he realized that they had better each tell their mothers about their plans before they read it in tomorrow's paper.

"We have a lovely selection right back here." The saleswoman had recovered quickly and was indicating that they should follow her.

Twenty minutes later, Faith was still perched on the edge of a comfortable chair, quietly staring at the array of precious stones scattered across the black velvet before her. She shook her head. "I couldn't possibly—"

From where he stood behind her, Stone said, "All

right. If you can't decide, I'll choose one.'' He knew she'd been going to say something ridiculous, like, ''I couldn't possibly accept such an expensive ring when you've already done so much for me.'' It bothered him that the salespeople hovering around with their antennae primed for gossip would find rich pickings if they knew the truth about this marriage. Only, of course, because he couldn't risk having his mother find out. Of course.

He bent down to Faith and murmured in her ear. ''Be careful what you say in here—it will get into the papers.''

That startled her, he could tell by the way she jerked around and stared up at him, her face wearing an expression of shock. While she was still staring at him, he reached for a stunning square, brilliant-cut diamond ring with progressively smaller diamonds trailing down each side. It was set in platinum. He'd liked it the moment the woman had pulled it out of the case, and he suspected Faith liked it, too, from the way her eyes had caressed it. He lifted her left hand from her lap and immediately felt the tingling electricity that arced between them as their flesh connected. He took a deep breath and slipped the ring onto her third finger. There was just a hint of resistance at the knuckle before it slid smoothly into place and he quickly dropped her hand as if it burned. It was the same feeling he'd convinced himself he hadn't felt when he'd taken her chin in his hand, indeed when he touched her in any way.

''A perfect fit.'' He caught her gaze, forcing himself to behave as if nothing out of the ordinary had happened. ''Do you like this one?''

"It's…" She shrugged, lifting dazed eyes to his. "It's beautiful," she whispered.

"Good." He studied the way her long, elegant fingers set off the ring, a deep satisfaction spreading through him. His ring. His wife. He was surprised at how much he liked the thought. Maybe this year wouldn't be such a trial at all, with Faith at his side. The more he thought about Faith and marriage, the better he realized his solution was. She could protest all she liked, but he would set up a trust fund for her and her mother so that once this arrangement ended she wouldn't be afraid of where her next meal would come from or how her mother's next medical bill would be paid.

He turned her hand and linked his fingers through hers. To the saleswoman, he said, "We'll take the matching wedding bands."

"Stone!"

"Faith!" he teased. "Did you think I was going to let you get away without a wedding band?"

The saleswoman had flown off in a twitter to get the proper ring sizes. He followed her across the room, catching her attention and motioning for quiet. "I'd also like the sapphire-and-diamond choker and matching earrings in the display window. But don't let my fiancée see them."

The woman's eyes got even wider. "Very good, Mr. Lachlan. And may I congratulate you on your engagement, sir."

"Thank you," he replied, resigned to the fact that tomorrow's paper would carry a mention of his upcoming wedding. His only consolation was that it would take them a day or two before they figured out who the bride-to-be was. "I'd like you to deliver the wedding rings and the sapphire set to my home. She'll wear the engagement ring.''

He called his mother the moment they got back into a cab. She wasn't available so he told her assistant that he'd gotten engaged that afternoon and that he'd like her to come for dinner and meet his bride Saturday evening, and hung up.

Within thirty seconds, the cell phone rang. He chuckled as he punched the speaker button on the phone. ''Hello, Mother.''

''Was that a joke?'' Eliza Smythe demanded.

''Not in the least.'' He kept his tone pleasant. ''We'd like you to come to dinner tonight to make her acquaintance.''

''So I don't know her?'' The tone was exasperated.

''You know of her, I believe,'' he replied. ''Faith Harrell. She's the daughter of—''

''Randall.'' His mother's tone was softer. ''He was a good man. I was so sorry when he—good Lord!'' she said suddenly. ''Stone, that girl isn't even legal! Are you crazy?''

''Faith will be twenty-one this year,'' he said coolly.

''All right.'' Eliza Smythe changed tactics abruptly. ''I'll come to dinner. I can't wait to meet Miss Harrell.''

''She'll be Mrs. Lachlan soon,'' he reminded her. ''Why don't we say seven o'clock? See you then.''

She couldn't stop staring at the engagement ring. It was breathtaking, the central stone over three carats. He'd paid an obscene amount of money for it, she was sure, though no one on the Tiffany staff had been indiscreet enough to actually mention payment in front of her. She had noticed Stone placing a hasty phone call to his insurance agent, so at least if she left it lying in the ladies' room somewhere it would be covered.

Not that she ever intended to take it off her finger.

She was so preoccupied that when Stone opened the cab door and put a hand beneath her elbow, she looked up at him in confusion. "Where are we going now?"

"Shopping." He helped her from the car. "You probably need some things for the formal occasions we'll be going to from time to time. Next weekend, we'll attend a charity ball. That will give everyone an opportunity to hear about our marriage and gawk at you. After that, things should settle down."

A charity ball? She'd never had any experience with such things although her family had been modestly wealthy—unless you compared them to Stone, in which case they didn't even register on the personal fortune scale.

"Um, no, that would be fine," she said. "I suppose the sooner the news of this gets out, the sooner the fuss will die down."

He glanced down at her. "I'm sorry if the thought of the media unnerves you. I generally don't do much that excites them. This will make a splash but it'll fade the minute there's a scandal or someone bigger crosses their sights."

She shook her head, smiling at him pityingly. "You underestimate your appeal."

He grinned at her, so handsome and confident her heart skipped a beat. "You'll see." Then his face sobered. "I'd like to get married soon," he said.

"Well, it shouldn't take long to get things organized," she said. If the mere thought of marrying him
unnerved her like this, how was she going to get
through the real thing? "I'm assuming you don't
want to make a fuss of this wedding so we probably
could get it together in three months—"

"Faith."

She stopped.

"If I apply for the license tomorrow we could be
married on Thursday or Friday."

She blinked, shook her head to clear her ears.
"*Next* Friday?"

"Mmm-hmm."

"But how can we possibly...never mind." She
smiled feebly. "I guess you have people who can
arrange these things."

He nodded. "I do. Do you prefer a church or the
courthouse?"

"Courthouse," she said hastily. Getting married
in a church would feel sacrilegious, when they had
no intention of honoring the vows they would be
taking. A dull sense of disappointment spread
through her, and she gave herself a mental shake.

"All right." As far as he was concerned, the matter appeared to be settled. "Then let's go get you a
wedding dress."

"Oh, I don't need—" She felt as if she'd hopped
a train only to find it racing along at top speed, skipping its regular stops.

"Yes," he said positively. "You do."

Shopping with Stone was an education. *More like
a nightmare,* she thought, suppressing a smile as he
fired orders at a salesperson. She tried repeatedly to
tell him she didn't need all these clothes; he rolled

right over her objections. She supposed she should be grateful for small mercies. At least he hadn't followed her into the dressing room or insisted she model for him.

He dragged her from one shop to the next. Neiman Marcus, Barney's, the new Celine flagship store. For day, a short black Prada, a Celine herringbone suit and a striking black-and-pink Cavalli blouse with Red Tape jeans. Everywhere they went, he was recognized sooner or later. She could tell exactly when it happened from the appraising looks that began to fly her way. For the first time, it occurred to her that marrying Stone might change her life forever. He was a public figure and without a doubt, she would become one for the duration of their marriage. But would she be able to resume her normal anonymous lifestyle after they parted?

"We'll take all three of those gowns she liked," he said, oblivious to the direction of her thoughts as he nodded at the fawning saleswomen.

"All three" included an Emanuel Ungaro seafoam-green silk mousseline wrap dress with a halter collar, no back and a slit clear up her thigh, a strapless Escada with a fitted, silver-embroidered bodice and a full, Cinderella-like skirt with tulle underlayers in silver and blue, and a classic black organza with laser-cut trim by Givenchy.

And there were shoes. Walter Steiger pumps for the day dresses. Sergio Rossi mules in black for the jeans. Silver heels from Ferretti, a pair of Jimmy Choo Swarovski crystal-and-satin slip-ons in the same soft green as one of the dresses. And for the classic black, equally classic open-toe Versace heels. All with matching bags.

It was mind-boggling, she thought, as he hustled her back into the car after the final store. When Stone made a decision, he didn't let time lapse before carrying out his plans. It might be something to remember.

It was actually a relief to see the sturdy stone facade of her soon-to-be residence appear. Stone's home overlooking Central Park was everything she'd expected the first time she'd seen it that morning. And more. Much more. Brass and glass. Modern cleverly blended with antique. Fresh flowers and thriving potted plants. Understated elegance.

At his direction, all of their recent purchases had been sent to his home since, as he pointed out, they'd simply have to move them again when she moved in. When they arrived, everything had been delivered and the housekeeper had it all piled in Faith's room.

Her room. She couldn't believe she would be living here with him, *sleeping* just one room away from him, in only a few days. Since they didn't have a lot of time, she'd brought over what she would need for this evening's dinner with his mother and planned to change there.

"I'll meet you back down here in…forty-five minutes?" Stone was consulting his watch. "That will give us a few minutes to relax before my mother arrives."

His mother. Her stomach jumped as she nodded and went to her room. She'd never met Eliza Smythe and knew only what she'd read in the news about the hard-hitting, hardworking female who had taken over Smythe Corp. after her father's unexpected death from a heart attack at a young age. She took deep breaths and tried to settle the nerves that arose at the thought of being vetted by the woman. What if his mother didn't like her?

Three

She was right on the button when she descended the steps a few minutes after he did. Stone, in the act of entering the drawing room, glanced up—and froze where he was.

Faith wore what at first glance appeared to be a simple dress in a lightweight Black Watch plaid. But a second glance at her figure in the soft brushed fabric dispelled any doubt that this was a demure dress for the classroom or office. She wore the collar open and turned up, framing a long, delicate neck and fragile collarbone, and her hair was up in a classic, shining twist. A matching fabric belt encircled her slender waist. The sleeves were three-quarter-length and tiny buttons ran from a point between her breasts to midthigh, allowing a slight glimpse of smooth, slim leg as she came down the stairs.

And as he realized that those thighs were encased

in black fishnet stockings and incredibly well-displayed in a pair of the new heels they'd just bought, his blood pressure shot straight through the roof. He'd never thought he was a leg man, but he sure wasn't having much success keeping his mind off Faith's legs. Or any of her other perfectly rounded feminine attributes, either, for that matter.

"You look very...nice," he said, and then winced at the banality.

But she smiled. "Good. I know your mother will be coming straight from the office and I thought this would work better than something that's really for evening. It's a Ralph Lauren," she added smugly. "I got it at a secondhand shop for a pittance!"

He grinned. She hadn't realized yet that cost was a concept she no longer needed to consider. "Would you like a drink?"

She hesitated. "I'm not really much of a drinker. A glass of wine, perhaps?"

"How about champagne? Since we are celebrating our engagement." He gestured for her to precede him into the drawing room, which gave him a chance to scrutinize the back view of her dress. Yeow. It was a good thing this marriage wasn't for real. He could imagine getting overly possessive at the thought of other men putting their hands on her, even in a correct public dance position.

Duh. What was he thinking about that for? Wasn't going to happen. Was. Not. Besides, he reminded himself, he shouldn't be ogling her, either. She was his ward.

The caterer he'd hired had set out an assortment of hors d'oeuvres on a table in a corner. A small flame beneath a silver chafing dish kept some crab balls warm, and around it, a selection of fruits, vegetables and a paté with crackers made an attractive display.

"Pretty," she commented, picking up a strawberry and biting into it. "I've never had champagne. Will I like it?"

"Probably, if you like wine," he said, crossing to the bar where an ice bucket contained a tall-necked French bottle. Watching the way she savored the luscious red fruit, the way her lips had closed around the morsel as her eyelids fluttered down in unconscious ecstasy, he was uncomfortably aware of the stirring pulses of arousal that threatened to turn his trousers into an article of torture. He might be her guardian but he was also a human male…with a healthy sexual appetite. And right now, he was hungry for *her*. Hastily he turned away and poured a glass of the pale golden sparkling liquid for her and one for himself.

Taking a deep breath and reaching for self-control, he came to where she stood in the middle of the room. He handed her one flute and held his aloft in a toast. "To a successful partnership."

"To a successful partnership," she repeated, lifting her gaze to his as their glasses sounded a pure chime and they each lifted them to drink. Their eyes met and held for a moment before she looked away, a warm pink blush rising in her cheeks.

He watched her over the rim of his glass as she tasted her first champagne. Her eyes widened slightly as she inhaled the fruity fragrance, and then she promptly sneezed as the bubbles tickled her nose.

"Bless you," he said, laughing, glad for the distraction. "You have to watch that."

"It's delicious," she said, taking an experimental sip. Then she slanted a flirtatious smile at him from beneath her lashes. "Is this one of the benefits of being married to a millionaire?"

He felt his whole body tighten in reaction to that teasing smile. He was sure she had no idea what that smile made a man want to do, and he forced himself to ignore the urge to reach out and pull her against him to erase it with his mouth. "This is one of the benefits of being married to a man who likes a good wine,' he said. "Listen, we need to talk a little bit before my mother arrives."

"About what?" She held her glass very correctly by the stem and he was reminded that although she didn't have a lot of money, she'd grown up in a very genteel home and a carefully selected school which had only enhanced her ladylike ways.

"My mother," he said carefully, "has to be convinced that we married for...the reasons normal couples get married."

He watched as she processed that. "You mean you want me to pretend to be in love with you," she pronounced.

"Uh, right." He'd expected some coy reaction, not such a straightforward response, and he forced himself to acknowledge that a corner of his pride might be dented just the smallest bit. She appeared completely unaffected by the idea of being in love with him. That was good, he assured himself, since that particular emotion would royally foul up their arrangement for the coming year.

"Okay."

"Okay? It might not be easy," he warned, dragging his mind back to the topic. "She's going to walk in here in a foul temper. So just follow my lead.''

"Yes, o master.'' She smiled as she took another sip of her drink.

He took her glass of champagne and set it firmly aside, guiding her to the food. "Get yourself a bite to eat. The last thing I need is for you to be silly with drink when my mother arrives.''

"I've only had half a glass," she said serenely. But she allowed him to spread paté on a cracker and lift it to her mouth. She leaned forward and opened her lips, closing them around a portion of the cracker, crunching cleanly into it with straight white teeth. Her lips brushed his fingers, closed briefly over the very tip of one, and then withdrew.

And he realized immediately he'd made a monumental mistake. The sensation of her warm, slick mouth on him brought erotic images to flood his brain and his body stirred with a powerful surge of sensual intensity. Hastily he stepped back, hoping she hadn't noticed his discomfort. His fingers were wet from her lips and he almost lifted them to his own mouth before he realized what he was doing. Wiping them on a napkin, he tried desperately to fix his thoughts on something, anything other than the unconscious sensuality that his ward—his wife, soon—wore like other women wore perfume.

She chewed the bite for a time, then licked her lips. "That's excellent!''

Watching her pink tongue delicately flick along the outer corner of her mouth, he couldn't agree more. God, she was driving him crazy.

Faith was practically a sister to him, he reminded himself sternly. This was merely a business type of arrangement from which they both would benefit. He'd fulfill his mother's wishes, in his own fashion and get Smythe Corp. Faith could finish her education, which she seemed determined to do. And it had the added benefit of making her feel as if she was paying him back, of divesting herself of the debt she imagined she owed him for the years he'd taken care of her and her mother.

Yes, it was going to be a good arrangement. And if he couldn't stop his overactive imagination from leaping straight to thoughts of what it would be like to have her writhing beneath him in a big, soft bed, at least he could keep her from knowing it.

The doorbell rang then and he glanced at his watch. His mother, ever-punctual. "Brace yourself," he warned Faith as he started for the foyer. "I'll let her in."

Faith looked up from the grape she was about to eat. "Surely she isn't that bad."

He merely raised one eyebrow.

The doorbell rang again, impatiently, and she made a shooing motion as she set down her plate. "Go! Let her in. And be nice."

Be nice. He snorted with amusement as he walked to the massive front door and twisted the knob. Like his mother had ever needed anyone to be nice to her. She'd probably steamroll them right into the pavement as she moved past.

"Good evening, Mother." He stepped aside and ushered in the petite woman whose dark hair was still the same shade as his own, with the added distinction of a few silver streaks at her temples.

"Hello." His mother whipped off her gloves and coat and thrust them unceremoniously into his arms as she stalked in. "Would you care to explain to me exactly what you think you're doing?"

"Excuse me?" He deliberately infused his tone with innocence.

Eliza made a rude noise. "Where's this woman you've talked into marrying you? And how much did you have to pay her?"

"I didn't pay her anything." That was absolutely true, so far. "My bride-to-be is in the drawing room." He indicated the archway and his mother strode forward.

As Eliza entered the drawing room, he hastily disposed of her outerwear and followed her. Faith came across the room as they appeared, her hand extended. For a moment, he couldn't take his eyes off her. She wore a welcoming smile that looked too genuine to be faked, and her slender body moved gracefully beneath the soft fabric of the fitted dress.

"Hello, Ms. Smythe," she said, her gray eyes warm. "It's a pleasure to meet you."

The older woman took her hand and Stone watched her give Faith a firmer than necessary handshake. "I wish I could say the same," she said coolly. "What did my son promise you for going through with this ridiculous charade?"

Faith's eyes widened. Shock filled them, then he could see the distress rush in. "I, uh, we—"

"Mother." He spoke sharply, diverting her attention from Faith. "You can either be courteous to my fiancée in my home or you can leave. You should have no trouble remembering the way out," he added, unable to prevent the acid edge to the words.

His mother had the grace to flush. "Please forgive my rudeness," she said to Faith, sounding like she meant it. Then she turned one gimlet eye on her son. "But I believe this hasty union was arranged for the purpose of circumventing my wishes in regard to an offer I made my son."

"How could you possibly know why I want to marry her?" he demanded. "You don't know enough about my life to be making snap judgments."

"She's a child." His mother dismissed Faith with one curt sentence. "I'm no fool, Stone. If you think you're going to con me into believe—"

"I don't care what you believe." He put a hand on Faith's back, feeling the rigid tension in every muscle. Deliberately he slid his palm under her collar to the smooth, bare flesh at her nape, gently massaging the taut cords, his big hand curving possessively around her slender neck. "Faith and I have known each other since we both were children. I've been waiting for her to grow up and she has. When you made me your offer, I realized there was no reason to wait anymore." He exerted a small amount of pressure with his fingers, tugging Faith backward against him. "Right, darling?"

She turned her head to look up at him and he could see the uncertainty in the depths of her bottomless gray eyes. "Right," she replied, her voice barely audible. Her face was white, probably from shock. He doubted she'd ever had words with *her* mother that were anything like this scene. She couldn't have looked less like a thrilled bride-to-be, so he did the only thing he could think of to make his case more convincing: he kissed her.

As he bent his head and took her lips, he put his arms around her and turned her to him, pulling her unresisting frame close. The moment their lips met, he felt that punch of desire in his diaphragm, a sensation he still hadn't gotten accustomed to. His head began to spin.

Her lips were soft and warm beneath his, and as he molded her mouth, she made a quiet murmur deep in her throat. The small sound set a match to his barely banked desire, and he slid his arms more fully around her, pressing her long, slender curves to him. Faith lifted her arms around his shoulders and as her gentle fingers brushed the back of his neck, he shuddered. The intimate action moved the sweet swell of her breasts across his chest and rational thought fled as he gathered her even closer.

"Good grief," his mother said. "You can stop now. You've convinced me."

It took him a moment to remember that they had an audience, to make sense of the words. Faith's mouth was soft and yielding, still clinging to his when he broke the kiss and dragged in a steadying breath of air. She kept her arms looped around his neck, her face buried in his throat, and as her warm breath feathered across his throat, his hands clenched spasmodically on her back with the effort it took him not to drag her into a private room to finish what they'd started.

Taking a deep breath, he forced his fingers to relax. He raised his head and looked at his mother over Faith's fair hair. "We weren't trying to convince you," he said roughly. And it was true. He might have started the kiss with that intent, but the moment Faith surrendered to the sensual need that enveloped him every time he touched her, he'd forgotten all about convincing anyone of anything.

Then Faith stirred in his arms, pushing against his

chest until he released her. She straightened her dress and smoothed her hair, uttering a small laugh. "I apologize if we made you uncomfortable," she said to his mother. "When Stone kisses me like that, I have a hard time remembering my name, much less my manners or anything else." She turned to Stone and her voice was steady although her eyes were still soft and dazed. "I'm sure your mother would like a drink, darling."

He had to force himself not to let his jaw drop. She was a better actress than he'd expected, and his own tense demeanor eased as he saw the suspicion in his mother's eyes fade. "Will you join us in a glass of champagne, Mother?" he asked her. "And help us celebrate this special time?"

The rest of the evening went smoothly. He kept Faith close to him, holding her hand or with his arm loosely around her waist, most of the time when they weren't at the table, not giving his mother any opportunity to corner her alone and harass her. It was both heaven and hell to feel her warm curves at his side, and he told himself he was only trying to convince his mother that their marriage was a love match. But he couldn't quite ignore the leaping pleasure in every nerve ending. God, what he wouldn't give to have the right to make her his wife in the fullest sense of the word!

She had recovered her innate elegant manners by the time they went in to dinner. And though she was quiet, he imagined it was simply because he and his mother were discussing business matters much of the time.

Touching her, he decided as they settled on the love seat in the drawing room again after the meal, was like a damned drug. Addictive. He had his arm around her and he idly smoothed his thumb over the ball of her shoulder joint as his mother turned to her and said, "Faith, I hope you'll forgive my earlier behavior. Welcome to the family."

Faith smiled. "Thank you."

"Faith's mother will be moving in with us soon." He didn't know why he was telling his mother this, but he plowed on. "She suffers from multiple sclerosis and we're fixing up an apartment for her on the main floor."

Eliza turned to Faith. "I never met your mother. Has she had MS long?"

"Almost all my life," Faith responded, her smile fading. "I was a late baby and she was diagnosed just over a year later. But I think she had symptoms years before that and ignored them."

His mother nodded. "My first secretary, who was absolutely invaluable during the first years when I stepped into my father's shoes, was diagnosed when she was forty-four. It was terribly difficult to watch her slowly lose capabilities. She passed away last year." Her eyes brimmed with tears; he was amazed. He'd never seen his mother cry, had never even imagined that she could. Which, he supposed, was a sad indicator of the degree to which they'd stayed out of each other's lives. Still, she was the one who had initiated the estrangement, if it could even be called that. There was no reason for him to feel guilty about it.

At his side, Faith stirred and he realized she was passing his mother a cocktail napkin so she could wipe her eyes. "It *is* difficult to accept that there's so little we can do to combat it," she said. "After my father died, my mother's condition worsened rapidly.''

After a few more moments of conversation, Eliza set down her drink and rose. ''Call me a taxi, please, Stone. It's time for me to be going.''

He did so, then helped her on with her coat and they stood in the foyer for a few moments until the car rolled down the street and stopped in front of the house.

As he closed the door behind her, he turned to Faith, still standing at his side in the foyer. ''We did it! We convinced her.'' He took her hands, squeezing lightly. ''Thank you.''

''You're welcome.'' She smiled slightly but he noticed her gaze didn't reach any higher than his chin as she eased her hands free of his and turned. ''It's been a tiring day. Could you take me home now?''

''Of course.'' His elation floated away, leaving him feeling flat and depressed. And there was no reason for it, he told himself firmly. He'd accomplished what he'd intended. So what if he had a raging physical attraction to Faith? She wasn't indifferent to him, either. He was certain of it after that smoking kiss before dinner, but she clearly wasn't any more prepared to step over the line than he was.

And he knew he should be glad for that. Because if she encouraged him, he was fairly certain he'd forget he'd ever drawn that line in the first place.

Faith spent the following Monday packing most of her things and answering breathless questions from Gretchen about her upcoming marriage. The morning paper had carried a tantalizing mention of Stone's impending nuptials and Gretchen had been quick to add up the details and come to the right conclusion.

Stone picked her up just after two o'clock and they made the drive into rural Connecticut where her mother lived in a beautifully landscaped condominium. Her apartment was on the ground floor and was handicap-accessible. Faith had helped her find the place during one of her infrequent vacations from school. Only now did it occur to her that Stone had probably helped her mother sell their old house. And rather than using it to finance this purchase, she was willing to bet he'd used it to pay off her father's debts and had spent his own money on her mother since then.

The thought of him assuming the full financial burden of caring for her mother and her still pricked at her pride, but she was grateful, too. She was practical enough to recognize that she never could have provided her mother with a stable, comfortable home. God only knew what would have become of them if Stone hadn't stepped in. What had her father been thinking?

They probably would never know. Her throat tightened as she thought of the laughing man with hair as pale as her own who had tossed her into the air and tucked her into bed every night. Clearly he hadn't been perfect, but she would always think of him with love.

Thank God, she thought again, for Stone. He'd provided desperately needed tranquillity for her mother and also had given Faith the tools to make her own way in the world one day. And she was all the more determined to repay his kindness during the upcoming year. She'd be such an asset to him he would wonder what he'd done before he had a wife! A momentary flash of disquiet accompanied the thought. Already, it was as though she'd been with Stone for months rather than days. What would it be like to lose him after a year?

Clarice, her mother's day help, answered the door when Stone rang the bell. "Hello, honey," the older woman greeted Faith. "She's really looking forward to your visit."

Faith hugged her. Clarice was a godsend. Widowed at sixty, Clarice had little in the way of retirement savings and was forced to continue to work. Faith and her mother had tried three other aides before they found Clarice, and Faith knew a gem when she saw one. Clarice, in addition, appeared to genuinely enjoy Mrs. Harrell and swore the work was well within her capabilities. Fortunately Faith's mother wasn't a large woman, so it wasn't terribly difficult for Clarice to assist her for tasks like getting in and out of the bath.

Still, Faith worried. Her mother was steadily losing mobility and motor control and the day was coming when she would need more than occasional assistance and handicapped facilities in her home. But as she entered the condo with Stone behind her, she felt less burdened, less worried than she had in some time. For the next year, her mother would want for nothing. And as soon as Faith got her degree and a job with decent pay, she planned to find a place she could share with her mother that would meet both their needs.

"Clarice," she said, "this is Stone Lachlan, my fiancé." She was proud that she didn't stumble over the word—she'd practiced it in her head fully half of the trip.

"Hello," said Clarice, "Faith's never brought—" Then the import of Faith's words struck her. "Well, my lands! Come in, come in. Congratulations!" She pumped Stone's hand, then hugged Faith. "Does your mother know?"

Faith shook her head. "Not yet. Is she in the living room?"

The older woman nodded. "By the window. She loves to look out at the birds. I put some feeders up to attract them and we've been seeing all kinds."

Faith felt another rush of gratitude. Clarice was indeed a gem. She wondered if there was any possibility of convincing her to come with her mother to live in New York. Deciding not to get ahead of herself, she let Clarice lead them into the living room.

"Mama." She went to the wheelchair by the window and knelt to embrace her mother, tears stinging her eyes.

"Hello, my little love." Her mother's arms fumbled up to pat at her. Her speech was slow but still reasonably clear, although Faith had noticed some change over the past year. Then her mother said, "Stone!"

"Hello, Mrs. Harrell." He came forward and Faith was surprised when he knelt at her side and gave her mother his hand. "It's nice to see you again."

"You, also." Naomi Harrell clung to his hand. "Did you drive Faith up?"

He nodded. Then he looked at Faith, and she smiled at him, grateful to him for sensing that she wanted to be the one to tell her mother of their marriage.

"Mama, I—we have some news. Stone and I are engaged to be married."

"Engaged?" Naomi slurred the second "g" and her eyes, magnified by the thick glasses she wore, went wide. "You're getting married?"

Stone looked at Faith again, still smiling, and for a moment, she was dizzied by the warm promise in his eyes, until she realized he was putting on a show for her mother's sake. "We are," he said. "This Friday, at eleven o'clock. We'd like you to be there, if you are able."

Naomi Harrell looked from one of them to the other. "I didn't even know you were dating," she said to Faith.

The comment shouldn't have caught her off guard but it did. "We, um, haven't been going out long," she said. Understatement of the year.

Stone slipped one steely arm around her shoulders, pulling her against his side. "I swept her off her feet," he told her mother, then turned again to smile down at her. "I was afraid if I waited until she was finished with school, the competition might edge me out." He paused, looking back at her mother. "I wasn't about to lose her."

Her mother nodded slowly, and Faith wasn't surprised to see tears welling in her eyes. Naomi Harrell had known that kind of love for real. She accepted the idea that her daughter had found the same happiness more easily than Stone's mother had. "I'm glad," Naomi said. "Faith needs somebody."

Faith knew her mother only meant that she didn't want Faith to be alone in the event anything happened to her. It was an upsetting thought. "That's not all, Mama," she said, anxious to get it all said and done. "Stone and I would like you to come and live with us after we're married. Stone has an apartment on the main floor of his home that you could have. There's plenty of room for you and Clarice, too, if she'd consider leaving this area."

But Naomi was shaking her head. "New-ly-weds," she said, enunciating carefully, "should have some time alone."

Stone chuckled. "Mrs. Harrell, my home is big enough for all of us. Your apartment can be completely self-contained. There's even an entrance from the back. You don't even have to see us if you don't want to."

Naomi smiled. "I want to. But I don't want to be in the way."

"Mama, I'd really, really love it if you'd come to live with me." Faith took her mother's hands. "I miss you."

"And besides," Clarice piped up, "this way we'll be right there when the grandbabies start arriving!"

Oh my Lord. If there was any way she could put those words back in Clarice's mouth…she felt herself begin to blush.

At her side, Stone stirred, bringing his other hand up to rest over hers and her mother's. "We aren't ready to think about that yet," he said. "I want Faith all to myself for a while. A long while."

"And besides," she added, "I have to finish school and get established in my career." Well, at least *that* wasn't a lie.

"Yes, I can't seem to talk her out of this obsession with working." Stone's voice was easy and colored with humor, but she sensed a grain of truth beneath the light tone. She was sure it wasn't her imagination. Thinking of the tension between him and his own mother, she wondered just how deeply he'd been scarred by his parents' split when he was a child.

She recalled the acid in his voice the night he'd suggested that his mother knew the way out—it had been a deliberate attempt to hurt. And judging from his mother's slight flinch before she controlled her expression, the shot had hit its mark. She felt badly for Eliza Smythe even though she didn't agree with the way she'd apparently put business before her young son more than two decades ago. Eliza's face had shown a heartbreaking moment of envy when Stone had told her about Faith's mother moving in with them. Again, she suspected he'd done it because he knew it would hurt. Or maybe he'd *hoped* it would, she thought with a sudden flash of insight. Children who had been rejected often continued to try to win their parent's attention, even in negative ways.

She sighed. She'd *liked* her new mother-in-law-to-be. Was it too much to hope that during her year with Stone she could contribute to mending the obvious rift between them?

Her year with Stone. As they said farewell to her mother and Clarice, Faith was conscious of the large warm shape of him at her side, one big hand gently resting in the middle of her back. He smelled like the subtle, but expensive, cologne he always wore, and abruptly she was catapulted back to Saturday night, when he'd taken her in his arms. That scent had enveloped her as he'd pulled her to him and kissed her.

He'd kissed her! She still thought it might have been a dream, except that she could recall his mother's wry, amused expression far too well. No wonder she'd been amused. For Faith, the world had changed forever the moment he'd touched her. And when his firm, warm lips had come down on hers and his arms had brought her against every muscled inch of his hard body, she'd forgotten everything but the wonderfully strange sensations rushing through her. Her body had begun to heat beneath his hands. She'd wanted more, although she didn't quite know what to do next to get it. But when she'd lifted her arms and circled his broad shoulders, the action had brushed her sensitive breasts against him and she'd wanted to *move,* to cuddle her body as close to his as she could get, to press herself against him even more. When he'd lifted his head, she'd simply hung in his arms as he'd spoken to his mother. God, the man was potent! She had been too embarrassed to face Eliza Smythe for a moment, then she'd simply told her the truth. She *did* forget everything when Stone kissed her.

Covertly she studied him from beneath her lashes. Stone's big hands looked comfortable and confident on the wheel of the Lexus and she shivered as she remembered the way they'd slid restlessly over her body as he'd kissed her. Would he do it again?

She wanted him to. Badly. In fact, she wanted far more than his kisses. She was almost twenty-one years old and she'd never even had a serious boyfriend. Soon she would have a husband. She studied his chiseled profile, the jut of his chin, the solid jaw, the way his hair curled just the smallest bit around his ears. She'd been half in love with him practically her whole life and being with him constantly over the past few days had only shown her how much more she could feel.

Quickly she turned her head and looked out the window before he could catch her staring at him like a lovesick fool. He didn't love her, only needed her for the most practical of reasons. But still...her heart was young and optimistic, unbruised and whole. He might not love her, but he certainly seemed to desire her. Wasn't that a start? Maybe, in time, if they got close...physically, he'd begin to need her the way she was realizing she needed him. It was too new to analyze. But she knew, with a not entirely pleasant certainty, that if she couldn't change his mind about making this a longer than one-year marriage, she wouldn't be able to leave him behind easily.

Not easily at all. In fact, she wasn't sure she could ever forget him. What man would ever measure up to Stone in her estimation?

She was afraid she knew the answer to that.

Four

Back in Manhattan, he headed home.

"Where are you going?" Faith asked.

He glanced across at her. She'd been very quiet the whole ride, apparently lost in her own thoughts. "Home."

"My home or your home?"

"Our home." He put a slight emphasis on the pronoun.

"It won't be our home until Friday," she said, using the same emphasis. "And I need to go to my apartment in any case. I still have things to pack."

"I can send someone to finish the job. We have things to do."

"I'd rather you didn't," she said mildly.

"It's no problem. And it will save you—"

"No, thank you." She shook her head, her blond hair flying and her tone was definite enough to warn him that he was traveling a narrow path here. "No. I would like to pack myself. There's not that much."

"Can I at least send someone to pick everything up and move it for you?"

She smiled, and a small dimple appeared in her soft cheek, enchanting him. "That would be nice. They could come Friday afternoon."

"Friday afternoon? Why not tomorrow? Surely you don't have that much stuff to move."

The smile had disappeared. "I'm not planning on moving in until after the ceremony on Friday."

"That's silly," he said sharply, acknowledging more disappointment than he ought to be feeling. There was an unaccustomed tightness in his chest. "I want you there as soon as possible. Why wait until Friday?"

"Because my mother would expect it," she said heatedly.

"Your mother would—oh." Belatedly he realized what she meant. He almost laughed aloud, to think that someone would still be so concerned with observing the proprieties. Then he saw that she was dead serious. He sighed in frustration, bringing one hand up to roughly massage his chest. "All right. But I still think it's silly." *Especially given the fact that nothing will be changing after you do move in.*

"Fortunately," she said in a honeyed tone, "I don't particularly care what you think."

"Yes, you've already made that plain," he said; recalling the way he'd found out she quit school after the fact.

Then she homed in on the rest of his original statement. "What things do we have to do?"

"Wedding dress," he said briefly, glancing at her

again to gauge her reaction. "And wedding plans."
Faith wasn't quite as pliable as her quiet nature suggested, a fact he seemed to be learning the hard way.

Her eyes went wide and then her fair elegant
brows drew together. "Absolutely not. I'm not wearing a real wedding dress. I have an ivory silk suit,
fairly dressy, that ought to do."

"I have a woman meeting us at the house at one
with a large selection." He took a deep breath, fighting the urge to bark out orders. Faith wasn't one of
his employees and if he shouted at her, she was liable
to bolt. "If you don't want a big, fluffy wedding
dress, that's fine. But our mothers—not to mention
the press—are going to expect you to look something
like a bride."

"It's really none of the press's business."

"I know. But when you have as much money as
I do, you wield a certain amount of influence. And
influence leads to attention, even though I don't seek
it out." A quick glance at her expression told him
she hadn't bought it yet. "Like it or not, we're going
to be of interest to the public. Think of yourself
as…sort of a princess of a minor kingdom. Royalty
interests everyone. And since there's no royalty in
America, the wealthy get pestered."

She sighed. "It's that important to you?"

He hesitated. There was an odd note in her voice,
though he couldn't decipher it. "Yes," he said finally. "It's that important to me. This has to look
real. If anyone should suspect it isn't…" He looked
over at her while he waited at a light, but she had
linked her hands in her lap and was studying them.
He was sure she was going to object again, or perhaps even refuse to marry him. He took a deep

breath, deliberately expanding his lungs to full capacity, but still he had that taut, binding sensation gripping him.

Then she said, "All right. I'll come to your home and see these dresses."

His whole body relaxed and the air whooshed from his lungs with an audible sound.

She shot a questioning glance at him. He'd better get a grip. She was going to think this meant more to him than it did. All he wanted, he reminded himself, was to inherit the company that had been his mother's family's. He'd known before he'd ever embarked on this course of action that this was to be a marriage with a finite limit of time. And in any case, he had no business even thinking about Faith in any terms other than those of a…a what? A guardian and his ward was definitely too archaic. A sister? No, there was no way he could ever condition himself to think of her as a sister. A friend? There. They could be friends. That was by far the most suitable description of their relationship, both now and in the future.

Inside him, though, there was a little voice laughing uproariously. *A friend? Does kissing a friend get you so hot and bothered you barely remember your own mother is in the room?*

Shut up, he told the voice. Just—shut—up.

But all he said aloud to Faith was "That's great. Thank you."

Friday morning finally arrived. Standing in the courthouse with his mother, he checked his watch. Almost time. Where the hell was Faith? He knew he should have made her move in before this. Then he could have kept an eye on her, made sure she didn't get cold feet.

It had been a surprisingly long week. He'd caught himself glancing at his watch throughout meetings and conference calls practically every hour since he'd dropped Faith off at her apartment to pack on Monday after her private showing of wedding dresses.

Which she hadn't let him see.

He frowned. Whoever would have suspected the stubborn streak hiding behind that angelic face? It would be bad luck, she'd told him.

Just then, an older woman walked around the corner. Spying him, her face lit up and she hurried forward. "Hello, Mr. Lachlan. We're here."

It was…what was her name? Clarice. Faith's mother's…friend. Caregiver. Whatever.

"Hello, Clarice," he said. "Have you seen Faith?"

"Oh, she's here. We all came together." Clarice extended a hand to his mother. "Hello. I'm Clarice Nealy, Faith's mother's companion."

He felt a dull embarrassment at his lapse of manners. "Oh, sorry. Clarice, this is my mother, Eliza Smythe." The two women shook hands.

His mother only smiled at him. "We forgive you." To Clarice, she said, "He's going to have a stroke if he doesn't get to see his bride soon."

Stone ignored that and consulted his watch. "It's our turn. What is she doing?" Impatiently he strode toward the corner, but Clarice's voice stopped him.

"No, no. You go in. Faith and her mother will be here in a moment."

He frowned, but when his mother took his arm, he sighed and led her into the room.

The justice of the peace stood at the front of the room in front of a wooden rail. To one side of him was a massive raised bench behind which the man presided over his courtroom, with state and national flags displayed behind it. He looked a little startled as Stone and his mother walked forward. "Hello. You are Stone Lachlan and Faith Harrell?"

Eliza Smythe started to chuckle. "No. The bride isn't here yet."

Just then, the door to the small chamber opened and he caught a glimpse of Clarice's beaming face as she held it wide. Faith's mother, seated on a motorized scooter, whirred into the room and stopped just inside the door. Then Faith stepped into the doorway and reached for her mother's hand.

The whole room seemed to freeze for one long moment as he simply stared. His heart leaped, then settled down to a fast thudding in his chest.

She looked stunning. As she walked toward him, pacing herself to the speed of her mother's scooter at her side, he had to remind himself to breathe.

She had chosen a short dress rather than anything long and formal. An underlayer was made of some shiny satiny fabric that fit her like a second skin, showcasing her slender figure. The satin, covered by a thin, lacy overlayer, was strapless and low-cut and against his will his eyes were drawn to the shadowed swell of creamy flesh revealed above its edge. Over the satin, the sheath of fine sheer lace covered her up to the neck, though it clearly wasn't designed to hide anything, but rather to enhance. This layer had long close-fitting sleeves and extended in a lacy scallop just below the hem of the underdress.

He took in the rest of her. Her hair was up in a smooth, gleaming fancy twist of some kind and she wore flowers in it, arranged around a crown of shining gems. As he recalled his reference to royalty, he had to suppress a grin. She'd done that deliberately, the little tease. She carried the small but exquisite trailing bouquet of palest peach roses, Peruvian lilies and white dendrobium orchids with touches of feathery greens that he'd sent to her. The subtle touch of color was the perfect enhancement for the glowing white of the dress.

It didn't escape his notice that she'd chosen pure, virginal white for her wedding day. Probably a good thing, since it served to remind him of the liaison they had—and its limits.

Limits. God, what he wouldn't give to be able to show her the pleasures of lovemaking. For an instant, he allowed himself to imagine that this was real, that the beautiful, desirable woman coming toward him would be his wife in every way. If this was real, it would be just the beginning. He would enjoy the incredible pleasures her soft body promised, and come home to her warm arms every night. In due course they would add children to their family—

Whoa! *Children?* He gave himself a firm mental kick in the butt.

Faith had reached his side by now and he surveyed her face as she turned to kiss her mother and then his. She wore more makeup than usual and the normal beauty of her features now approached a porcelain perfection. Her skin seemed lit by an inner radiance. She'd curled small wisps of her hair and it

gently bounced around her face in soft, shining
waves that made him want to sink his fingers into it
simply to experience the texture. But he couldn't do
that. He couldn't touch her in any but the most in-
nocuous of ways.

The justice cleared his throat and Stone realized
the ceremony was about to begin. His mother flanked
him and Naomi maneuvered her scooter to Faith's
far side. Clarice took a seat in the small rows of
chairs behind them. He extended his arm to Faith and
she took it, smiling up at him tentatively.

He didn't smile back. The reminder that this was
a forced union of sorts had ruined the moment for
him. This was a ridiculous charade, necessitated by
the intransigence of his mother. It was, at best, an
inconvenience, an interruption, in his life as well as
Faith's. There was nothing to smile about.

The smile faded from her face when he didn't respond and she dropped her gaze. Her face abruptly
assumed the serene contours he knew meant she was
hiding her thoughts from the world, and she turned
toward the official who was beginning the ceremony.

Too late to catch her eye, he regretted his action.
Now he felt like a real bastard. She'd clearly wanted
a little reassurance. He glanced down at her fine profile as she stood beside him, one small hand resting
in the crook of his arm. To his dismay, he realized
she was blinking rapidly, her silver eyes misted with
a sheen of tears. Damn!

Acting on instinct, he raised his free hand and covered hers on his opposite arm, squeezing gently.

She looked up at him again and offered him a
wobbly smile. Remorse shot through him. She was
only twenty years old. He doubted this was what

she'd envisioned when she'd dreamed of her wedding day, even though she'd insisted on this extreme simplicity when they'd discussed it.

He smiled down at her as he passed an arm behind her back and gave her shoulders a gentle hug. She felt small and soft beneath his hand, and he liked the way her slender curves pressed against his side far too well. Tough. He wasn't going to do anything about *that* but he could make this day less of a chore for each of them.

The ceremony was short and impersonal as the justice of the peace sealed the bonds of matrimony with swift efficiency. Faith spoke her responses in a quiet, steady tone, looking down at their hands as they exchanged rings and in a shockingly brief matter of minutes, they were legally bound.

The justice looked incredibly bored; how many of these things did he perform in a week's time? "You may kiss your bride," the man intoned.

Stone set his hands at Faith's waist and drew her toward him. As his mouth descended, she raised her face to his and his lips slid onto hers. He froze for an instant, nearly seduced by the sweet, soft flesh of her full lips and the memory of the way she'd melted in his arms on Sunday night. But this couldn't be. It *couldn't be,* he told himself fiercely. Faith wasn't experienced enough to know that sex and love were two distinct issues in a man's mind. He would be courting a messy, emotional disaster if he couldn't keep his distance from her. And so, steeling himself to the powerful allure of her person, he kept the kiss brief and impersonal, then drew back.

He felt her go rigid beneath his hands, and he nearly apologized, but as the words formed, he realized how strange *that* would sound to the witnesses, so he swallowed the apology and settled instead for, "Are you ready to go?"

Faith nodded. She wouldn't look at him and he gritted his teeth against the urge to raise her chin and cover her lips with his own again.

Oh, hell. No, no, and *no!* He wasn't going to do anything stupid with Randall Harrell's daughter. His ward. This marriage was just a business arrangement, of a sort.

Of course it was.

Faith woke early on her first morning as a married woman. For a moment, she didn't recognize her surroundings and then it all came flooding back. Yesterday she had married Stone.

Married. She raised her left hand and her new rings sparkled as the faceted stones caught the light. If it weren't for these she'd think it had been a dream. Slowly she got to her feet and headed for the bathroom. As she showered and dressed, she couldn't keep herself from reviewing the wedding ceremony, like a child who couldn't resist picking at a healing wound.

Stone had looked so handsome in the severe cut of the morning suit he'd worn. As she'd come into the courtroom, she'd allowed herself to fantasize, for one brief instant, that she was a real bride, flushed and brimming with love for her husband, taking his name and becoming part of his life forever. But then she'd looked into Stone's eyes and seen nothing. Nothing. No feeling, no warmth. No love. He'd quickly tried to cover it up, but that first impression was indelibly stamped on her mind.

She felt her bottom lip tremble and she bit down on it fiercely. For the first time, she allowed herself to acknowledge the depths of her disappointment. She hadn't married Stone entirely because of their bargain. She'd married him because somewhere in the past week her silly, girlish crush had gelled into a deeper, more mature emotion.

Oh, it hurt even to think it and she shied away from deeper examination of her feelings.

Instead she replayed the wedding scene in her mind again. And she realized her shattered heart had forgotten something. He did have *some* feelings for her. Recalling the look in his eye the first night he'd kissed her, she knew with a deep inner feeling of feminine certainty that he wanted her, at least in the physical sense. And yesterday, for the briefest instant before his gaze had grown cool and distant, she'd seen the poleaxed look on his face as he absorbed the sight of her in her wedding dress. And she'd been gratified, because she'd chosen the unconventional wedding dress, her makeup and the soft, pretty hairstyle for the express purpose of making him notice her.

Yes, for that one unguarded moment, there had been no doubt that he wanted her. If she was going to remember the cold shoulder, she needed to cling to this memory, too. And though she knew it was foolish to believe she could parlay that basic sexual desire into a more lasting emotion, that was exactly what she hoped.

He wanted her. It was a start. And she…she wanted him as well. Wanted him to be the one to teach her the intimacies of the sexual act, wanted him to make love to her. Maybe she could attract his feelings the same way her body attracted his.

Perhaps they would begin to communicate better when they went on their honeymoon. Though she knew Stone hadn't planned one, he'd told his mother they would be going away a few weeks from now. He'd only said it because Eliza had very pointedly asked where he intended to take Faith, she was certain. And she knew he would follow through if only to assuage any doubt in his mother's mind about the veracity of their marriage.

Buoyed by the thought, she made her bed and headed downstairs. The newspaper was lying on the kitchen counter and there was fresh coffee, signs that Stone must already be up. She hunted through the cupboards until she found cereal and dishes, and ate while she leafed through the paper. But all her nerve endings were quivering, alert, waiting for him to enter the room.

When she heard him coming down the hall, she quickly ducked her head behind the paper again, looking up innocently as he entered. "Good morning."

"Good morning. Did you sleep well?" He barely glanced at her as he headed for the coffeepot and poured himself a cup.

"Quite, thank you. And you?"

"Fine." He sounded grumpy. Maybe he wasn't a morning person, though he certainly looked like he was awake and alert. Lord, it simply wasn't fair for the man to look so absolutely stunning first thing in the morning. He was as handsome to her as always and her heart rate increased as a wave of tenderness swept through her. She was his *wife!* Then she realized he was saying something else.

"Your mother and Clarice will be moving in today. I have a company bringing her household up late this morning. Will you help her arrange everything when it arrives?"

"Of course." It shouldn't bother her that he hadn't asked her opinion. Although she'd have preferred to go down and help Clarice pack, she knew this way would be much faster and more efficient.

Stone seemed unaware of her thoughts. "I know it's Saturday but I have to go in to my office for a few hours, so I'll leave that to you." He opened the door of the refrigerator and she saw a large casserole dish. "That's a chicken and broccoli casserole the housekeeper made and froze. I set it in there to thaw. If you want to invite your mother and Clarice to eat with us tonight, that's fine with me."

She nodded. "Is there anything else you'd like me to do? Until the summer sessions begin, I'm going to have a ton of time on my hands. I have some accounting skills and I know my way around a computer. Maybe I could help in your office—"

But he was chuckling. "I employ people to do all that," he said. "Just consider the next two months a vacation."

Disappointment rushed through her for more than one reason. She hated to be idle. And working for him would give them something in common. "Oh, but I could use the experience—"

"Tell you what," he said, cutting her off again. "I know something you could do that would help immensely."

Thrilled, she sat up straighter. "What?"

"The den," he said.

The den? *What* in the den?

"I've never had it redecorated," he continued. "It's something I've thought about a lot and just never gotten around to doing. But it needs a facelift desperately. The easy chair my father sat in for years is still in there." Now he looked at her hopefully. "Would you consider taking on that project?"

"Of course," she said. "Just tell me what color scheme you like. But also, I—"

"I trust your judgment," he said. "Anything fairly neutral." He headed for the door, coffee cup in hand. "I've got to get going. I have an early meeting this morning. Enjoy your day."

"Oh, yeah, it ought to be a blast," she muttered as she heard the front door close. Redecorate the den. Was he serious? She'd intended to help him at the office. She didn't care if she was a receptionist. It would certainly be better experience than redecorating the stupid den! She should have told him how insulting she'd found that...giving her a little wifely project to do when what she really wanted was to be working for him, in whatever capacity he could use her.

Yikes. Her mind took that last thought and gave it a distinctly sexual twist as the memory of his hard, hot body pressed against her side while they spoke their vows set her heart racing again. She still was trying to get used to the perpetual breathless state that being around Stone left her in since the night he'd kissed her in front of his mother and turned her world upside down.

He'd kissed her when they'd gotten married, too, and though that had been only the merest correct meeting of lips, she was sure it had short-circuited some of her brain cells. It certainly had sealed her fate. And with that thought, she forced herself to face the truth.

She hadn't married Stone Lachlan because he needed her help. And she hadn't married him because it was a way to pay him back for his financial support, or because he'd promised to take care of her mother, or because he had promised to help her finish school. No, she'd married him because she was in love with him.

She took a deep breath. *Okay, you've admitted it.* She'd loved him, she supposed, for years under the guise of having a crush. Only the crush had deepened more and more as she'd come to know him, as she'd seen what a decent, honorable man he was, what a thoughtful, caring person—and how incredibly potent his appeal was.

And that was her misfortune. He'd made it abundantly clear, over and over again, that this was a business arrangement, not one in which emotion was welcome.

Well, tough. He might consider it business, but she was declaring war. She had a year. Three hundred and sixty-five days. Surely within that time she could make herself such an integral part of his life that he'd wake up one day and realize he loved her, too.

Having Faith's mother and Clarice around the house wasn't the burden he'd expected it to be, Stone thought a week later as he sat at the kitchen counter nursing a cup of coffee. In fact, it was a distinct blessing.

He'd encouraged the older women to join them for

dinner each night. And though they'd both protested at first, he'd made it his goal to charm them. And he'd succeeded. He hadn't had to spend more than a few moments alone with Faith all week. Yes, inviting her mother here had been a great idea.

It might be the only thing that kept him from grabbing his young bride and ravishing her for the remaining fifty-one weeks of what was shaping up to be one damned long year.

He heaved a sigh, propping his elbows on the counter and pressing the heels of his palms against his temples. God, but Faith was making it difficult to be noble! He had no intention of seducing her. It would be despicable of him to use her that way for the brief term of their marriage and then discard her when they split up, as they intended to do.

And maybe if he kept telling himself that long enough, he'd believe it. He could hear her first thing in the morning, moving around in her bathroom, humming in the shower, removing hangers from her closet and replacing them. His active imagination supplied visual details in Technicolor. She joined him over breakfast, no matter how early he got up, and her soft farewell was the last thing he heard before he left. In the evening, she always came to greet him at the door with a smile, taking his coat and preparing dinner while he changed into casual clothes. It was a treat not to have to eat alone all the time.

And then there was her relationship with her mother. Faith and Naomi were closer than they had any right to be, considering how little they'd really seen of each other during Faith's adolescent years. They teased and smiled, shared stories about Faith's father, worked crossword puzzles together, and genuinely seemed to treasure each moment spent together. It was such a marked contrast to his relationship with his own mother that he could get jealous if he let himself think about it long enough. Sure, he'd imagined that normal families had relationships like that, but until he'd seen exactly how close and loving Faith and her mother were, it had been an abstract concept. Now, thanks to them, it was a reality.

He could hear them laughing right now as they came in from an early walk—or drive, in Naomi's case—through Central Park, across the street from the town house. In a moment, they were in the kitchen.

"We're back." Faith greeted him with a smile as she helped her mother out of her coat and took it to hang in the closet. "It's a beautiful day. Spring is definitely on the way."

"The prediction is for snow by the first of the week," he warned her.

"But it won't last," she said confidently.

Naomi directed her motorized scooter toward her own apartment down the hall from the kitchen and the two of them were left alone. An awkward moment of silence passed.

Then Faith cleared her throat. "Do you have anything planned for today?"

"Um, nothing special," he said. "Tonight there's a dinner and ball but we have most of the day before we have to start getting ready for that."

"That reminds me," she said, snapping her fingers. "Is there anything in particular you'd like me to wear to the ball? I have those dresses we bought last week, remember?''

He remembered. And his blood heated. Though she hadn't modeled them for him, he'd had several long, detailed daydreams. "How about the blue?" he said.

"All right." She cleared her throat. "Actually, if you have time, I'd like you to look at some fabric swatches and paint colors for the den. I can order things next week."

He didn't really want to spend any more time alone with her than he absolutely had to, but she vanished before he could think of a good reason not to look at the samples. A few moments later she reappeared clutching a large folder and two wallpaper books. He folded up his paper and efficiently, she spread everything out on the counter. Her slim figure, clad in blue jeans and a clinging pale yellow sweater, was so close he could smell the clean scent of her hair, and her shoulder brushed against his side as she moved. "Here you go." She pulled one of the wallpaper books toward them. "The first thing you need to do is decide on the walls. Then we'll go from there."

"You're really happy to have your mother here, aren't you?" Good God. Why had he said that?

Her fingers stilled on the books. "Yes. Thank you again."

"No," he said impatiently. Hell, he'd started this, he might as well find out what he really wanted to know. "I mean, you're enjoying her company, not just putting on a polite act."

Her eyebrows rose. "Why on earth would I do that? Of course I'm enjoying her company. No, I take that back. I'm *loving* it. At school, there were nights when I cried myself to sleep, missing her so much. It wasn't that the school was a terrible place," she said hastily as he frowned. "The staff members were actually very caring and mostly I was happy. And I could call Mama every day if I liked. But it still wasn't the same."

"No, I guess it wasn't." He could hear the longing in her voice as she relived those days and he felt a surprising kinship. "But you understood how difficult it would have been for her to try to care for you at home. You knew she would have done it if she could."

She turned and looked at him, her gray eyes far too wise and understanding. "I think your mother cares, too. Maybe it wasn't as easy for her to leave you as you think."

"I don't think about it," he said. He didn't want her pitying him, thinking he'd had a miserable childhood. "My father and I got along fine without her."

She didn't say a word, only studied him.

"She could have pretended she cared," he said, goaded by her silence. "Would it have killed her to let a little kid think he meant something special to her?"

Faith laid her small hand on his arm and he realized how tense he was. "I don't know," she said. "Have you ever asked her?"

He consciously relaxed his muscles, feeling the tension drain out of him. "No." He reached forward and pulled the wallpaper books toward him. This conversation was pointless. "It doesn't matter anymore. Now why don't you show me what you have in mind?"

She continued to gaze at him for a long moment, and he kept his eyes on the books. He didn't want her pity. Sure, he'd been hurt by his mother's indifference when he was small, but he was a grown man now, and her approval had long ceased to matter to him.

"All right," she finally said. She rested one hand on the back of his chair and opened the topmost book with the other. The action placed her breasts just below eye level, inches away, and he couldn't prevent himself from covertly assessing the rounded mounds. "Here you go. The first thing to decide on is—"

"Look." He pushed back his chair and rose before he gave in to the fantasy that had leaped into his head. "I want you to like the den, too," he said. "I don't need to approve it. I'm sure whatever you choose will be fine."

"You're the one who's going to have to live with it after I leave," she pointed out.

After I leave… The words echoed in the air around them and he was shocked by the strong urge to blurt out "Don't leave!"

But he didn't say it. Instead images of his life a year from now, when Faith and her family were gone and he was rattling around this place alone again, bombarded him. He *liked* having Naomi and Clarice around, dammit! And he more than liked having Faith around. For one brief instant he allowed himself to imagine what it would be like to grow old with her, to stay married to her on a permanent basis. The thought was so tantalizingly appealing that he immediately shoved it away.

Abruptly he turned his back and started out of the room. "I don't have time to deal with this now."

Five

That evening, Faith showered and shampooed, then rubbed silky cream into her skin and rolled her hair in large hot rollers that left it frothy and bouncy around her shoulders. It would be a lie, she thought as she applied a heavier-than-normal makeup suitable for evening, if she didn't feel the slightest bit pleased by his reaction to her in the morning. When she'd stood close to Stone at the breakfast bar, he definitely had been uncomfortable. And she was pretty sure it wasn't because he was worried about her decorating skills. She'd noticed him looking at her body out of the corner of his eye. And before that, he'd talked about his mother.

Okay, those few sentences weren't much to go on, but she couldn't expect him to be too voluble at first. That would come later, after they'd gotten closer, she hoped. She slipped into a strapless bra and panties and donned the pretty Escada with the silver trim that Stone had asked her to wear. The Prada heels and a small silver clutch bag completed the ensemble and as she glanced into the full-length mirror in the bathroom, a small thrill ran through her.

She'd never owned anything so beautiful before. Thanks to the snug bodice of the strapless dress and the bra beneath it, she had genuinely respectable cleavage. The silver and blue layers of the full skirt swayed as she left her room and walked down the stairs to meet Stone.

He was standing in the archway to the formal front room with his back to her as she rounded the turn on the landing and continued down toward him, one hand lightly trailing on the banister as a precaution, since she wasn't used to such high heels. When he heard her footsteps he turned—

And for one long, strangely intense moment, the air seemed to shimmer between them. His gaze started at her toes and swept up her body, leaving her quivering in reaction and her steps slowed and stopped as his eyes bored into hers. She simply stood, halfway down the steps, held immobile by that gaze and she felt her breath quicken as a heavy, unfamiliar pressure coiled low in her abdomen.

Finally Stone cleared his throat. "I'll be the envy of every man in the room."

The spell was broken but she was warmed by his words. "That would be nice," she said, finishing her descent and stopping in front of him. "I'll try to be an asset to you."

Stone smiled but it looked a little strained and she realized the barrier he'd put between them earlier in the day was still firmly in place. Then he smiled.

"The first time I ever met you, you had a ponytail so long you could sit on the end of it. It's a little disconcerting to see you looking so grown-up and gorgeous."

"Thank you. I think." She wasn't particularly pleased with the hint that he still thought of her as a child, and she knew he'd done it deliberately. But she didn't comment. "You look very nice, too. I've never seen you in a tux before."

"A necessary evil." He dropped her hand and turned away, picking up a small box from an etagere beneath a large gilt-framed mirror. "I have a wedding gift for you."

She was dismayed. "But...I didn't get anything for you."

"Agreeing to this charade was gift enough." He lifted her limp hand from her side and pressed the velvet case into it. "Open it."

Automatically she lifted the other hand to support the box, which was heavier than she'd expected. "Stone, I—"

"Open it," he said again, impatience ripe in his tone. "Don't forget you're Mrs. Stone Lachlan now. People would talk if I didn't have you dripping with gems."

Slowly she nodded, then bent her head and pried open the hinged box. And gasped.

Nestled on black velvet was a necklace of brilliant blue sapphires and diamonds. The alternating colored stones glinted gaily in the light from the crystal chandelier overhead, smaller stones back near the ornate platinum clasp gently graduating in size to a significant sapphire anchor in the middle. Matching teardrop earrings were fastened to the velvet as well.

She was speechless. Literally. Her mouth was as dry as a bone. There was nothing she could do but stare at the striking jewelry, not even blinking. Never, in her entire life, had she seen stones like these up close and personal. Unless you counted the glass display behind which the Hope Diamond rested at the Smithsonian in Washington.

Stone took the box from her and removed the necklace. "Turn around."

Obediently she turned around, and in a moment she felt the cool weight of the platinum and gems against her skin as Stone's fingers grazed her nape. This felt like a dream. Just weeks ago, she'd been waiting on customers at Saks; today she was married to one of the wealthiest men in the country and he was showering her with clothing and jewels. A few months ago, she'd been a college student with no idea that every penny of her education was being paid for out of the goodness of someone's heart.

Flustered and agitated, she whipped around to face Stone. "I can't do this."

"Do what?" He raised his hands and clasped her upper arms gently, rubbing his thumbs back and forth over the sensitive flesh.

She shivered as goose bumps popped up all over her body and a quick *zing* of mouth-drying, breath-shortening attraction shot through her. She was so close she could see the flecks of amber and gold amid the blue in his irises when she looked up and abruptly she realized her change of position had placed them in a decidedly intimate pose. Her breasts grazed the solid expanse of tuxedo-clad chest and the way in which he held her made her feel strangely small and delicate.

"You know." She stepped back a pace and raised her hands to try to unclasp the necklace. "Pretend to be your wife—"

"There's nothing pretend about it, Faith," he said. "You *are* my wife."

"Not in every way," she said steadily though she knew she was blushing and her whole body felt trembly and weak.

His hands dropped away from her as if her skin burned his flesh. "No," he said. "That was our agreement."

"We could...change the terms, if we wanted to." She didn't know where she'd found the courage to speak to him so frankly, but she was conscious of every hour of her year sliding by.

But he was shaking his head. "No. It's normal for us to be attracted to each other in a situation like this. But acting on it would be a huge mistake." He took the box from her and removed the earrings, then handed them to her as matter-of-factly as if they hadn't just had the most intimate conversation of their acquaintance. "Put these on and then we'll go."

She wanted to say more but she didn't have the courage. He'd turned her down flat, crushing her hopes. Numbly she fastened the earrings through her ears and picked up her small purse again.

"Aren't you even going to look at them?" Stone took her shoulders and angled her to look in the mirror over the table. Reflected back was an elegant, beautiful woman wearing a stunning sapphire-and-diamond collar and matching earrings. Behind her, his hands possessively cupping her shoulders, was a tall, handsome man in a tuxedo, confidence oozing from every pore.

A perfect match. She turned away from the mirror, fighting tears. They looked so right together, confirming her feelings. How could he think making love would be a mistake?

"What is this fund-raiser for?" Faith asked as they stepped into the grand ballroom a little while later.

Stone grinned, feeling a spark of genuine amusement as he anticipated her response. "It's not quite the typical political occasion," he said. "It's for WARR."

"War?" Her eyebrows rose.

"Wild Animal Rescue and Rehabilitation. The organization rescues lions, cheetahs, tigers, elephants, bears…you name it, from bad situations. They restore them to health and place them in zoos, parks and other habitats where they'll be able to live in peace."

She nodded, her eyes lighting up. "That's wonderful. I read an article about Tippi Hedren's efforts with the great cats recently. It's horrifying to hear some of the stories about the way those poor animals are forced to live."

"It's also horrifying that people think they'll make great pets." He took her hand and directed her toward a large display near the entrance, where guests were perusing photos and stories about WARR's work. "A child in Wyoming recently was killed by a tiger that her neighbor owned as a pet—uh-oh." Catching sight of the woman bearing down on them, he squeezed her hand once in warning. "Brace yourself. We're about to face the inquisition."

"Stone Lachlan!" It was a woman's voice, booming and imperious. "Where have you been hiding yourself?"

Stone kissed the rouged cheek of the tiny woman who approached. "Mrs. deLatoure. What a pleasure. I've been working rather than hiding, but I'm glad I took a break tonight. Otherwise, I might have missed seeing you."

The little woman beamed. "Outrageous flattery. Feel free to continue."

Eunicia deLatoure was the widowed matriarch of one of the country's wealthiest, oldest wine-making families. Her sons had taken over the business a few years ago when her husband had passed away but the widow deLatoure was still a force to be reckoned with. Rumor had it that her sons ran every major decision by her before plunging into anything. Having met her quiet, deferential sons before, Stone didn't doubt it.

He slipped an arm around Faith's waist then and drew her forward, enjoying the feel of her slender body in his grasp as he made a perfunctory introduction. This night was going to be both heaven and hell. Especially now that he knew what she was thinking. Did she have any idea what she was asking for? He seriously doubted it. He was pretty sure she was still a virgin. Damn, *that* was the wrong thing to think about!

"Your bride! I just read about your engagement a few days ago." The woman's eyes flew wide and the stentorian tones turned heads throughout a solid quadrant of the ballroom. She leveled a piercing gaze on Faith. "Congratulations, my dear. I assume this is a recent development."

"Very recent. We're still in the honeymoon stage."

Stone answered before Faith could open her mouth. "And we're feeling quite smug to have kept it a secret from the press."

The matriarch chuckled. Then her gaze sharpened as she pinned Faith with that gimlet eye again. "It's delightful to meet you. Is your family in attendance tonight?"

It was a blatant attempt to ferret out Faith's pedigree, he knew. "No." He answered before she could speak. "Just me." He pulled her closer to his side. "It's good to see you, Mrs. D. Say hello to Luc and Henri for me."

As he steered Faith away, she said, "I could have spoken for myself, you know. The woman probably thinks you married a mute."

He registered the slightly testy tone in her voice. "Sorry. I just didn't want her to grill you. She can be merciless." As he continued across the room, he muttered in her ear, "We don't have to worry about spreading the news anymore. I bet every person in this ballroom knows we're married within ten minutes."

"That's what you wanted, isn't it?" Her gaze was steady and there were unspoken issues dancing between them.

"Yeah," he said, ignoring everything but the words. "That's what I wanted." Purposefully he moved through the crowd enjoying drinks and canapés, introducing Faith as they went.

The band switched from background music to dance tunes and the floor filled immediately. When he heard the strains of the first slow dance, he took her glass and his and set them both aside. "Do you

like to dance?'' he asked as he escorted her to the
floor.

"I don't really know," she said. "I've never done
much of it."

"You're kidding. What did they teach you at that
school?"

"Latin, physics, biology...little things like that. It
was a *real* school."

"Point taken," he said, amused. "All right, I'll
teach you to dance. Just step where I step and hold
on to me."

"How about I just stand on your feet like I used
to?"

He laughed. "Let's see how you do learning the
steps before we resort to that."

When they reached the dance floor, he pulled her
into the rhythm of the steps with ease, guiding her
with one big hand on her back. His fingers grazed
her skin just above the place where her dress stopped.
God, he wanted to touch her in so many other ways.
This was torture. But it was necessary. They had to
appear to be a happy newly married couple. The first
few weeks were bound to be the toughest, until their
marriage faded from the radar screens of the gossip-
mongers.

"Are you doing all right?" he asked. She was following his lead easily, as if they had danced together
a hundred times before.

She nodded, the action stirring the soft curls
against her neck. "Fine."

"Good." He hesitated, then said, "I'm going to
hold you closer. The world is watching and I want
them to be convinced we're newlyweds." *Uh-huh,*

ri-i-ight, said his conscience, but he firmly squashed it.

"All right." Her voice was breathy, her color high. Her gaze flashed to his, then away, and the desire she felt was so transparent he felt scorched by the heat that leaped between them.

Dammit, this was impossible. Knowing that she wanted him was the worst kind of aphrodisiac in the world. If she were more experienced, he wouldn't hesitate to take what she offered. But she wasn't. And he had no intention of changing their situation. Someday she would thank him for it. He hoped so, anyhow, because if she didn't appreciate how hard this was for him, he might just strangle her.

How hard…bad choice of words. Very bad choice of words. He drew her in, tucking their clasped hands to his chest and sliding his arm more fully around her, bringing her body closer to his without pressing her torso against his. Thank God she was wearing that puffy-skirted dress that made it hard, er, *difficult* for him to get too close. She'd probably be shocked silly if she realized exactly what she was pressed against, because for all her delicate dancing around a very touchy subject, he knew her experience was extremely limited. The first time he'd kissed her he'd sensed that she hadn't had a lot of practice at it. But she'd learned fast. Thinking about her passionate, searing response to his kiss was a bad idea. A really, really lousy idea, in fact. He tried to concentrate on the music, the couples around them, but all he could seem to absorb was the feel of her in his arms. She startled him then by turning her face into his throat, tilting it slightly upward so that her breath caressed his throat and resting her head against his shoulder and without thinking, he slid his hand up over the bare skin of her back to caress her nape.

She shivered involuntarily, and he smiled against her hair. "Sorry. Did I tickle you?"

"N-no."

"Good. Relax." *Was she kissing his neck?* No, of course she wasn't. It was only his prurient imagination in overdrive. "People are watching us. You do realize we're going to be the hot topic of tomorrow's gossip column, don't you?"

"I hope not." Her breath lightly feathered his skin.

"We are. But as I said, they'll soon be on to some newer gossip. We'll be so boring they won't have anything to write about."

"Good." Her answer was heartfelt.

They danced in silence for a long while as the music flowed from one song into another. He thought he probably could hold her, just like this, all night. Their silence wasn't strained, and though his body was well aware of her nearness, there was a strangely satisfying peaceful sweetness in simply dancing with her in his arms. The thought of doing this week after week for an entire year was powerfully appealing. His blood fizzed and bubbled like fine sparkling wine in his veins and reluctantly, he acknowledged that he was going to have to put some space between them or he was going to do something he would definitely regret.

"Faith?"

"Hmm?"

"When this song ends, we're leaving."

She raised her head from his shoulder and immediately he missed the warmth. "It's barely ten o'clock. Isn't that a bit early?"

"Not for newlyweds. They'll think they know exactly where we're going."

"Oh." Her eyes widened and her gaze clung to his for a long moment. Then she dropped the contact and looked steadily at his right shoulder, which he knew was all she could see from her angle. She'd withdrawn from him, he realized. And a second later, he also realized he didn't like it one damn bit.

"Faith?"

"Yes?" She didn't look at him.

The hell with distance. He had to taste her again or die. "I'm going to kiss you."

"Wha—?" Her eyes flew open and she instinctively tried to pull away from him, but he controlled her with such ease that he doubted anyone even realized she'd just lost a bid for freedom. "Why?" she asked bluntly. "You said I—you said you didn't want me—"

"Appearances." His voice sounded strained to his own ears. "I'm going to kiss you so there's no doubt in anyone's mind why we're leaving." *Liar.*

"Oh." It took the wind out of her sails and he almost could feel her droop against him. She was so vulnerable that one short comment had wounded her. It was a puzzle. How could a woman as lovely as Faith think she wasn't attractive? Then he realized that she'd simply never been exposed to large quantities of men who would undoubtedly drool over her. He sighed, unable to let her continue thinking that she didn't turn him on.

"It's not you," he said gruffly. "You're the most desirable woman I've ever known and if you want the truth, I'm having a hell of a time keeping myself from, uh, doing something rash.''

There was a silence between them.

Finally she said, ''Really?'' and her tone was distinctly doubtful.

''Really,'' he responded dryly.

''It, um, wouldn't be rash,'' she said, looking up at him with such hope in her eyes that he felt ten feet tall.

His body urged him to take her somewhere private and plunge into the maelstrom of passion she offered—but he resisted. He still wasn't going to make any moves they both would regret later. He had to kiss her, but he would keep it short. Just a taste to get him through this ridiculously adolescent longing. ''Selfish, then. Your whole life is ahead of you. You need time to experience the world.''

She didn't say anything, just lowered her gaze to his shoulder again, giving him a subtle but definite cold shoulder.

Now he knew exactly what his married buddies called ''the silent treatment.'' And he knew why they didn't like it. Well, the hell with that. Letting go of the hand he held in closed dance position, he took her stubborn little chin in his fingers and tipped her face up to his. And then his lips slid onto hers and the world exploded.

He initially had intended to give her a light, gentle kiss that would look romantic to the many eyes covertly directed their way. But the minute he began to kiss her, Faith relaxed against him with a quiet hum of approval, delighting him and pushing his already eager body into a far-too-serious awareness of the girl who was, in the strictest sense of the word, his ward until her twenty-first birthday. God, she was so innocent! He could taste the inexperience in the sweet soft line of her lips as she passively let him mold them, and he moved carefully, determined not to scare her.

But she didn't seem to be in any danger of being frightened. He suppressed a groan as her lips began to move beneath his. Slowly he lifted his mouth a breath away from hers, knowing he couldn't take much more. They were on a dance floor in the middle of a crowded ballroom; even if he intended to deepen the kiss and teach her how to kiss him back the way he longed for her to do, he wasn't going to do it here.

You aren't going to do it ever.

Ever. He looked down at her, taking in the glaze of passion in her eyes and the way she ran her tongue over her lips in reaction as she said, "Stone?" in a bewildered tone.

"That should convince them." He forced out the words, ignoring her unspoken appeal. "Thanks."

Her eyes widened and her body went stiff in his arms. Carefully she pushed herself away from the close contact and let him continue to lead her through the motions of the dance. But she'd lowered her head and withdrawn into herself again. He could feel the distance between them and abruptly, he led her off the dance floor.

No matter how much he wanted to pull her back against him and teach her all the things that were playing in his mind right now, he wasn't going to. They had to live in each other's pockets for twelve months. He was her guardian, he reminded himself rather desperately. He respected her too much to cheapen their relationship with casual sex. He was almost thirty years old and he'd learned by now that sex without commitment wasn't all it was cracked up to be. He didn't love Faith that way and though he wanted her badly, he didn't want to mislead her. She was so innocent she'd probably confuse sex with love. Which wasn't what was between them. Not at all.

Love wasn't an emotion with which he was familiar. In fact, he was pretty sure it didn't exist, except in poets' imaginations. It was just a pretty word to dress up desire. Physical attraction. He'd never seen two people in love yet who weren't physically attracted to each other, proving his point. And when that attraction wore off, there often wasn't enough basic compatibility to keep them together. His parents were a prime example of that.

Things were strained between them during the rest of the evening, though he doubted anyone else would notice. Faith dutifully smiled and made small talk as he took her around the room to introduce her to a few more people who would be offended if he didn't. But she didn't meet his eyes. He kept a hand at the small of her back or lightly around her waist most of the time, just for show.

She was still silent on the drive home.

He said good-night to her at the foot of the stairs, then left her to rustle up the stairs in her pretty gown alone while he moved into his study on the pretext of checking his e-mail. In truth, he didn't really want to be in his room, imagining her disrobing just on the other side of an unlocked door. He trusted his willpower but there was no sense in being stupid.

She was young and beautiful, slim and warm, and his body knew she was available.

Just say no, he reminded himself. He'd seen Nancy Reagan's famous slogan, intended to help kids resist drugs, plastered on billboards. Somehow, it seemed appropriate under the circumstances.

Two weeks passed. Forty-nine more weeks with Stone after this one, she thought to herself one Wednesday morning. Although that time would do her little good, she thought morosely, when the man barely set foot in the same room with her. He left for work at dawn and often worked well past the dinner hour. She'd eaten dinner with her mother and Clarice almost every night and kept a plate warm in the oven for him. Her days were incredibly long and, well, boring.

The one bright spot in the tedium of her current situation was the time she got to spend with her mother. Yesterday, they'd gone across Central Park to the West Side and toured part of the Natural History Museum. Naomi's face had been one big smile the whole time, although Faith worried a little bit that the trip was too tiring for her.

"Tiring?" her mother had said. "How can it be tiring? All I'm doing is driving this scooter."

But privately, Faith could see that her mother had lost a lot of ground in the past year. She was unable to get from bed or chair to her scooter without Faith's or Clarice's assistance. Eating was becoming more difficult due to the tremors that often shook her hands and arms. And on Monday, they'd taken her to the ophthalmologist because Naomi had thought she needed stronger glasses. The ophthalmologist did give her a new prescription, but while she was picking out new frames with Clarice, he'd taken Faith aside and told her that her mother was developing double vision, a common problem with MS. She should see her primary care physician, he'd emphasized, since there were advances in medicine all the time and he didn't know that much about multiple sclerosis.

The worries about her mother's health made every moment they spent together even more special. She thought of Stone, and the way he'd reacted to his mother, and she remembered what he'd said: *Would it have killed her to let a little kid think he meant something special to her?* His resentment was deep-seated and not without cause. But she'd also seen the pain in Eliza's eyes on more than one occasion when Stone had brushed her off. Whatever she'd been or done in the past, she cared about him. And Faith couldn't imagine that a woman who cared about her child would absent herself from his life for extended periods without good reason.

Acting on impulse, she went to the kitchen and found the telephone book, then placed a call. A few moments and two receptionists later, she was speaking with her mother-in-law.

"Faith! What a pleasant surprise!" The CEO of Smythe Corp. sounded delighted to hear from her. "How are you adjusting to marriage?"

"Quite well, thank you." Dangerous subject. She'd better move to the reason for her call. "I was hoping you could join us for lunch one day soon if you're not too busy."

There was a momentary silence on the other end.

"I would love to," Eliza said, and Faith could tell she meant it. "When and what time?"

On Saturday night, Faith and Stone attended the opening of a new Broadway show in the Marriott Marquis. It was a stirring musical based on the life of Abraham Lincoln. It ended with shocking effect with the shot that took Lincoln's life and the audience held their applause for a hushed moment of silence before breaking into wild clapping.

Faith wore another of the dresses Stone had purchased for her and the sapphires again. Might as well let him get his money's worth. She felt constrained in his presence tonight, all too aware of the distance he insisted on imposing. He'd been that way in the weeks since the WARR ball, staying so busy she barely saw him, spending what time he was at home in his office working. Some days she hadn't seen him at all. Others, he'd made charming small talk with her mother and Clarice over dinner, including Faith just enough to make a good showing for the older women. She resented it, but she knew she had no real reason to complain. This was the bargain they'd made. He was living up to his end and expected her to do the same.

"Well," Stone said as they moved toward the room where a private reception to celebrate the opening night was being held, "I predict a long and healthy run." He didn't meet her eyes, though, as he spoke, and she was all too aware this was a public performance.

"I agree." She pointed as they entered the ballroom. "Oh, look at the ice sculpture." There were several stations scattered around the room for hors d'oeuvres and at each one was a towering ice sculpture. The one nearest them was a stunningly faithful representation of Lincoln in profile.

They got plates of pretty sandwiches and other bite-size morsels and Stone brought her a glass of club soda as she'd requested. But he didn't sit down when he returned with her drink. "I see some people I need to speak to," he told her. "I'll be back in a few minutes."

"Oh, I'll go with you." She started to rise, but he put a hand on her shoulder.

"No, it's business. Go ahead and eat. We'll dance when I get back."

She watched him walk away through the crowd. *It's business.* He was determined to keep that part of his life separate from her, it seemed. And to keep himself away as much as possible, too. She ate, and waited. And waited some more. She was getting quite tired of waiting when she saw a small knot of people off to her left. As she scrutinized the group, she realized that they were clustered around a youngish looking dark-haired man. And a moment later, she recognized him as one of the actors from the play.

Well. If Stone wasn't going to entertain her, she'd find someone to talk to on her own. She might never have had the nerve to approach the actor if there hadn't been a ring of fans already around him, but she'd been quite impressed with his performance and wanted to tell him so. Rising, she walked toward the crowd and waited patiently as person after person shook the actor's hand and effused about the show. The man glanced up, and his gaze sharpened as he caught her eye. She smiled and extended her hand.

"I wanted to tell you what a fine performance you gave tonight. I suspect this will keep you employed for quite some time."

The actor laughed, displaying dimples and perfect white teeth. "That would be nice!" He didn't let go of her hand, but turned, tucking it through his arm. "I'm starving. Will you accompany me to the buffet?"

She allowed him to turn her in the right direction.

"What's your name? I'm at a disadvantage—you know mine." His blue eyes twinkled as he looked down at her.

And indeed she did. "I'm Faith," she said. "Faith—Lachlan."

"It's nice to meet you, Faith. Please tell me you aren't here with anyone."

Vaguely alarmed, she released his arm. "Sorry," she said. "My husband is here with me."

"He doesn't seem to be taking very good care of you."

"He is now."

Faith jumped and half turned. Stone had approached behind her. His voice was distinctly chilly. She felt his left hand settle at her waist; the right he extended to the other man. "Stone Lachlan. I take it you've met my wife."

"Sorry," said the actor, backing away, a wry grin on his face. "She was alone. I assumed she was single because no man in his right mind would leave a woman like her alone..." and he turned and headed in the other direction.

Stone's hand slid from her waist and he braceleted her wrist with hard fingers. "Dance with me."

"All right." But he was practically dragging her toward the dance floor.

"Did you tell him," he said through gritted teeth as he swung her into dance position, "that in eleven more months you'll be free to flirt with anyone you want?"

What? She was so shocked by the unexpected attack that she was speechless as he took her in his arms and began to move across the dance floor. "I wasn't—"

"Save it for later, when we don't have an audience," he said curtly.

"I will not!" Finding her voice as outrage rose, she stopped dancing, forcing him to halt as well.

"Faith, you're making a scene." His voice was tight.

"Maybe you should have thought of that before you started slinging around unfair accusations." She tugged at his arm around her waist but it was like pulling on a steel bar. He didn't give an inch. "Let me go," she said. "I want to go home."

"Fine. We'll go home."

"I said I, not we." To her utter mortification, tears rose in her eyes. "I did nothing to deserve to be treated like that. Let me go!"

"Faith—" He hesitated and there was an odd note in his voice. "Don't cry."

"I'm not crying. I'm *furious!*" But that wasn't strictly true. She was devastated that he would accuse her of such a low action. "I wasn't flirting. And if you didn't want me talking to other people, you shouldn't have left me sitting alone for an hour."

She tried to wrench herself away from him but instead of releasing her, Stone merely wrapped his arms around her and lifted her off her feet, moving from the dance floor to a partially private spot beside a large pillar. "Baby," he said roughly, "I'm sorry—"

"Not as sorry as I am," she said. She deliberately made her voice and her face expressionless, retreating in the only way she knew how, forcing herself to ignore his big, hard body so intimately pressed to her own.

"Look," he said desperately, "I was wrong. I was jealous and I didn't handle it very well. Please don't cry." And before she could evade him, he bent his head and covered her lips with his.

She'd longed for his kisses, dreamed of them constantly. As his warm mouth moved persuasively on hers, she tried to hold onto her anger but it was quickly overridden by her body's clamoring response to the man she loved. With a small whimper, she put her arms around his neck and tried to drag him closer, and between that heartbeat and the next, the kiss changed. Stone growled deep in his throat and his arms tightened. He slid one hand down her back to press her up against him and she gasped as his tongue slipped along the line of her lips.

Oh, she wanted him! Her pulse beat wildly at the realization that he wanted her, too. *I was jealous...* The husky words echoed in her head, melting her anger and softening her heart as wonder stole in. He'd been jealous. She could hardly credit that in light of the way he'd been carefully avoiding any contact with her, but...he was *kissing* her now, his mouth moving possessively, his big hands splayed over her body, holding her tightly against him.

But in a moment, he began to lessen his grip and

his kisses became shallower and more conventional. "My wife," he murmured against her lips as he finally set her free. "You're *my* wife."

His wife…was that all she was to him? Her rising hopes crashed into a flaming abyss once again. Had he only kissed her to establish a claim? To show the world that she was his?

She couldn't quite let herself believe that, not after that kiss. She looked up at him, but he already was leading her out of the ballroom, claiming their coats, hailing a taxi and bundling her in. As he tipped the parking attendant who'd gotten the cab and slid in beside her, she cleared her throat. "Stone?"

"Hmm?"

"Where do we go from here?"

He looked at her questioningly. "Home."

"No." She waited until he braked at a red light and she caught his eye again. "I mean, you and I. Our relationship."

"Faith." His gaze slid back to the street and his voice was firm and resolute. "We've had this discussion before."

"Yes, but—"

"The answer is no. It doesn't matter what you want, or what I want. It would be a huge mistake for us to get involved in a physical relationship."

"Are you trying to convince me or yourself?" she challenged, frustrated beyond belief by his hard-headed refusal to see what they could have together.

"Both, probably," he said grimly.

Six

"Hello, Faith. Thank you for inviting me." Eliza Smythe entered the foyer two weeks later and handed Faith her coat and handbag. "I've been hoping we could get to know each other better."

"So have I," Faith responded, leading her mother-in-law into the dining room, where she had set two places at a small round table near the fireplace. "Please, sit down." She waited until the older woman was seated before she took her own place. "I'm so sorry Stone couldn't be here. He had some pressing things to take care of at his office."

"Pressing things?" Eliza laughed cynically. "I bet they became a whole lot more pressing when he found out I was coming for lunch."

Faith felt herself flushing. She was unable to deny it.

Eliza leaned forward, her face growing serious. "I

hope your invitation didn't cause trouble between you and Stone."

"It didn't." That was perfectly truthful. For there to be trouble between them, they first would have to talk. Stone's only reaction, when she'd told him his mother would be coming to lunch was a curt, "I have meetings all day, so count me out." Gee, what a shock.

"Good." Faith's mother-in-law smiled warmly at her. "So tell me how you like married life. Has the press been too intrusive?"

"Not as bad as I feared, actually," Faith confessed. "But Stone has taught me to keep a low profile in public. That's helped."

"He'll be less interesting now that he's married," predicted Eliza. "Unless," she added, smiling wickedly, "you keep giving them moments like those photos from the Lincoln reception. That was hardly what I'd call low-profile."

Faith felt the heat rise in her face. The week after the disastrous evening, there had been a series of three photos of them in the Star Tracks section of *People* magazine. In the first frame, Faith was with the actor she'd met, with her arm tucked warmly through his. The man's head was tilted down so that he could hear something she was saying. It was a decidedly intimate-looking pose.

The second photo showed Stone, scowling, pulling her toward the dance floor and the other man could clearly be seen walking away in the background. But the third shot was the one that had made her cringe. It had been taken during their heated kiss behind the pillar. Stone had her locked against him, nearly bent backward beneath the force of his kiss. She clung to him on tiptoe, one hand in his hair. The sly, amusing captions had mentioned his jealous reaction—and she doubted the author would ever know how true it had been. Unfortunately, she thought, Stone hadn't been reacting out of any personal feeling. He just didn't want anyone coming on to his wife. She was pretty sure he viewed her as an extension of property.

She ducked her head. "Stone wasn't very happy with that," she admitted. "We'll have to be more careful in the future." Her mother-in-law was still smiling, though, and she decided that the revealing photos probably had helped Stone's cause in his quest to convince his mother of the authenticity of his marriage.

Faith picked up a spoon then and started on the soup she'd set out for the first course. Her mother-in-law followed suit and they talked of other things during the meal. Eliza asked after Faith's mother, and Faith found herself sharing some of her concerns about the future. To her pleasure, Eliza spoke freely about her business. If only Stone would do the same! She longed to share his life, but it seemed he was never going to give her the chance.

"So," the older woman said as they relaxed with coffee an hour later, "we got sidetracked after I asked you how you liked married life. Has it been a big adjustment?"

"In some ways." Faith hesitated, then decided it wouldn't be inappropriate to share her feelings with her mother-in-law. "The boredom is driving me crazy," she confessed, "if you want the truth. I can only spend so much time with Mama—she needs a lot of rest and quiet."

"I thought you were a student. Don't you have classes?"

"I took this semester off." Faith doubted Eliza even knew about Stone taking on financial responsibility for two additional people. In any case, she couldn't explain the details of her "semester off" without the risk of giving away the true reasons for her marriage. "My classes don't start again until June."

"That's not so far away," Eliza pointed out.

Faith raised her eyebrows. "You wouldn't say that if you were the one sitting here twiddling your thumbs. I've asked Stone if I could help at the office but—" she rolled her eyes and tried to sound mildly aggravated as an indulgent wife might "—he told me to redecorate the den." Her opinion of *that* was evident in her voice.

"Well, it is a project," his mother said, playing devil's advocate.

"One I accomplished in a few days," Faith said. "The painters are here right now. The wallpaper, carpet and new furniture have been ordered."

Eliza chuckled. "And you're twiddling your thumbs again." As Faith nodded, the older woman cleared her throat. "I might have a project for you, if you're interested."

A project? Faith was cautious. "Such as?"

"I have a significant amount of data from one of my plants that recently was restructured. The last man was an incompetent idiot and he left a huge mess with a number of damaged files that need to be recovered. It needs to be straightened out. It would be a short-term job, of course, but it might be perfect for your situation."

Faith's spirits soared immediately. She nearly clapped her hands. Then something occurred to her. "Wait a minute. How do you know I'm capable of doing this job?"

Eliza's slim shoulders rose and fell in a wry gesture. "I confess I did look into your background a little bit. You have quite a gift with computers, it seems."

She didn't know whether to be flattered or annoyed. "I'm beginning to see where Stone gets his autocratic nature."

Her mother-in-law winced. "I'm sorry if I've made you angry."

"It's all right." She wasn't really angry. "The job sounds like a challenge. I like challenges. But I'll need to talk to Stone about it."

"All right." Eliza rose. "Thank you for lunch. Whether or not you take the job, I hope we can continue to get together from time to time."

"That would be nice." And it would be. "Perhaps Stone will be able to join us next time."

Eliza made a distinctly unladylike sound. "Not if he finds out I'm going to be there."

The words were filled with pain, as were her eyes. Faith hesitated. She knew Stone wouldn't thank her for getting in the middle of his relationship with his mother...still, she couldn't simply ignore this. "I'm sorry," she said. "Maybe, in time, he'll soften." But she doubted it.

Eliza sighed. "You don't believe that and neither do I. Stone thinks I abandoned him. And he's right. I did." Her face looked as rigid as marble. The only sign of life was the leaping, snapping flames in her eyes. "When my father died, I was a young wife with a small child. And suddenly, I was the heir to this company—which was struggling to keep its head above water, something my father had never told me. I was determined to keep Smythe for my son. Maybe I should have hired someone else to lead it, but at the time I felt like…oh, I don't know, like it was my destiny or something.'' She tried to smile. ''Or maybe it just makes me feel better to tell myself I had no other choice but to take over and lead the company myself.''

''It must have been a good decision,'' Faith said, realizing what a difficult choice Eliza had been forced to make. ''Look at what you've accomplished.''

The Smythe Corp. CEO shrugged. ''But look at what I sacrificed. My marriage fell apart when my husband realized I had no intention of walking away from Smythe Corp. I should have refused to cooperate when he told me to leave. I should have taken Stone with me. But he was so close to his father…I didn't think it would be fair.'' She shook her head. ''Of course, I never thought my husband would try to keep me from seeing my son, either. And once I'd moved out, the courts *did* view me as a poor parent.'' Her shoulders slumped. ''I guess we all have things we wish we had done differently.''

Faith was stunned. Stone thought his mother hadn't wanted him! All these years he'd thought she didn't care…he couldn't have been more wrong.

''You, ah, wanted to see him more often?''

His mother looked beaten. ''Yes, but when his father got full custody he was able to severely limit the time I spent with Stone. After a while, Stone seemed to view my visits as a chore and it was easier not to go as often." She shook her head regretfully. "I'm very sorry now that I didn't continue to be a presence in Stone's life no matter what."

Then she glanced at her watch, and Faith could see her shaking off the moment of painful truth. "I have enjoyed this tremendously, Faith. Thank you again for inviting me. It's time for me to get back to the office."

"Thank you for joining me." Faith rose and laid her napkin aside, then led the way to the front door.

Eliza put on her coat, then turned once more. "Let me know if you're interested in that job. It wouldn't just be something I've made up to keep you busy. I really do need to get someone on that project soon."

"I'll let you know by the end of the week," Faith promised. "I appreciate the offer more than you know."

She was just coming down the stairs to breakfast two days later when she heard Stone calling her name. His voice sounded alarmed, unusual for him, and immediately she doubled her speed.

He was in the breakfast room. So was her mother. But Naomi was lying on the floor near the table with him crouched at her side.

"Mama!" Faith rushed forward, taking in the scene. Her mother was conscious, though she lay awkwardly on her side. "What happened?"

"She says she was transferring from her scooter to the table. She had a muscle spasm and she slipped," Stone said. As Faith dropped to her knees, Stone rose and left the room, returning a moment later with the telephone as well as a blanket, which he draped over her mother. "It's a good thing it's

Saturday," he said, "or I might not still have been home. She could have lain here for a while except that I was in the kitchen and I heard her."

"Where's Clarice? And why were you trying to do this alone?" Faith knew her voice was too shrill but she was frightened. Naomi shouldn't have been trying to move without supervision.

Clarice had agreeably offered to work six days a week. Sunday was the only day she took off and even then, she often was gone only a few hours. She had no children and, Faith assumed, no other family.

"I sent her to the deli," said Naomi. "They have wonderful fresh bagels. I thought I could...I thought..." Her voice trailed off and she started to cry.

"It's okay, Mama." Faith stroked her hair. "It's okay. How do you feel? Do you think anything is broken?"

"Don't try to move." Stone's voice brooked no opposition. "Let me call an ambulance and we'll go to the hospital so you can be checked."

"No emergency service," Naomi begged.

Stone shook his head as he punched a speed dial button. "I won't call 9-1-1. I'm calling your doctor first."

Clarice returned just as Stone hung up from explaining the situation to Naomi's doctor. The caregiver was as upset as Faith had ever seen her, and it was as much work to calm Clarice as it was to comfort her mother. Things moved rapidly after that. Naomi's doctor sent a private ambulance and she was transported to the hospital where she was met by her doctor. Faith, Stone and Clarice waited impatiently until a nurse appeared to take them to the room in which they'd settled Naomi.

The doctor who oversaw her care met them in the hallway and took all three of them into a small visitors' lounge before they saw Faith's mother.

"Your mother is experiencing an increase in spasticity that worries me. It's important that we begin a physical therapy program in order to keep it from worsening. Passive stretching, maybe some swimming, that kind of thing. Also, she absolutely should not attempt transfers from one place to another without physical assistance. Sometimes the spasms can be severe enough to knock a patient right out of their wheelchair."

"Is she going to have to start using a wheelchair now?" Faith asked apprehensively.

"I'm not ready to take that step yet," the doctor replied. "Let's see if we can't control the spasticity first."

"Exactly what do you want us to do?" Stone's voice was authoritative and Faith was happy to let him direct the conversation.

"I would recommend one of two things: either hire trained therapists who can work with Mrs. Harrell, or consider placing her in a facility where she can be cared for."

"You mean a nursing home," Faith said dully. She'd worried about this edict for years. Now, suddenly, here it was. And she was no closer to accepting it than she had been before.

"She won't need a nursing home." Stone put his arm comfortingly around her shoulder as he addressed the doctor. "But if you could give us the names of some reliable sources of personnel, we'll get more help at home."

Stunned, Faith stared at him and he glanced down at her and smiled.

A moment later, the doctor left.

Clarice rose. "I guess you won't need me now," she said in a small voice. "I don't know how to help her exercise."

"Oh, you're not getting away from us," Stone told her in a firm voice, removing his arm from around Faith and standing. He took Clarice's hands in his. "Unless you want to, that is. Naomi depends on you, and so do Faith and I. If you agree to stay, you'll be in charge of any personnel who come in to help. It'll be your job to make sure they're doing theirs, and that everything is going smoothly."

Clarice stared at Stone for a long moment. She opened her mouth, but no sound came out. Faith realized the older woman was on the verge of tears. Finally she said, "Thank you. Thank you so much. I don't have any family and I've gotten really fond of Naomi. I would have hated leaving all of you."

"And we would hate to lose you," Faith said, rising and hugging the older lady. "We're your family now."

Clarice went ahead of them to see Naomi as Faith turned to Stone. She swallowed with difficulty and took a deep breath. "I appreciate your support but I know you hadn't counted on this when we made our agreement. I won't hold you to anything you said to that doctor."

"I know you won't. But I still intend to hire additional help and keep your mother in our home."

"You've done enough for us already," she told

him unsteadily. "I don't think your father meant for you to support us for the rest of our natural lives." She tried to smile at the weak joke.

Stone put his arms around her and pulled her head to his shoulder, just holding her for a long, sweet moment. "Your mother means a lot to me, too," he told her. "She and Clarice have made the house a warmer, livelier place."

She pulled back and searched his gaze for a long moment. He appeared to be completely serious. "Thank you." She didn't know how she ever would repay him, but she would swallow her pride to make sure her mother was happy and well-cared-for. Putting Naomi in a nursing home would have been devastating for her as well as for Faith.

"Don't thank me," he said, still holding her loosely in his arms. "I mean it. Keeping her at home is really an act of selfishness on my part."

"Right." Although she could have stayed in the comforting embrace forever, she forced herself to move away from him. "You're a good man," she said quietly, touching his cheek with a gentle hand before turning to leave the room.

They visited briefly with her mother. She hadn't been badly hurt, just severely bruised and she'd broken a bone in her wrist. She would be staying overnight at the hospital for some additional tests and would be released tomorrow. Faith was relieved the fall hadn't been worse.

Clarice decided to stay at the hospital for a few hours and told them she would take a cab home later. On the ride home, Stone said, "I haven't told you how good the den looks. I really like my new chair." He flexed his fingers on the wheel. "I believe my mother must have chosen the old furnishings. I don't ever remember it looking any different.''

''Your mother did a lovely job,'' she told him. ''The things she chose lasted a long time.''

''Longer than she did.''

''I'm not sure that was her choice, entirely.'' It was a risk, talking about his mother, but she felt she had to try to share with him his mother's version of the past.

The car was uncomfortably quiet for a moment. Then he said, ''It's old news.'' He shrugged, frowning as he drove. ''Who cares anymore?''

You do. ''She does,'' Faith said. ''She didn't want to leave you behind but your father fought her for custody. And limited her visits. She's always wanted to be a bigger part of your life than she was permitted to be.''

''And I suppose she told you this during your cozy little luncheon.'' His voice was expressionless.

''Yes.'' There was another awkward silence. She waited for him to ask her what she meant, what his mother had said. But he never did.

Instead he finally said, ''We got off the track, I believe. We were talking about the changes in the den.''

''I'm glad you like the new look and the new furniture.'' She was disappointed that he hadn't listened to more of his mother's story, but at least he hadn't bitten her head off. ''I really wasn't sure about it, but since you told me to go ahead...'' Then she followed up on the opening he'd given her. She'd been trying to figure out a way to approach him again for several days. ''Now that the job is finished, I'm finding myself with a lot of free time. You know, I'm not sure you appreciate the extent of my computer skills. Surely there's something at your company that I could—''

"There really isn't," he interrupted her. "But I did want to ask you to do something else." Without giving her a chance to respond, he said, "I've received several wedding gifts at the office and I know we've begun to get quite a few more at the house. Would you please write thank-you notes to everyone? I'll supply you with the addresses you need."

"I've kept a list of everything. The files are on the computer in your home office," she told him, disappointment shading her tone. "I'd thought perhaps it was something we could do together."

But he shook his head. "I really don't have the time. I'm sorry. At the end of the week I'll be leaving for China for a nine-day trip."

"China!" She couldn't believe he hadn't mentioned this before. How long had he intended to wait before telling her?

"Yes. We have an incredible opportunity to get our foot in the door with some steel exports." Unaware of her thoughts, he sounded as excited as she had ever heard him. "And I want to investigate the possibilities of setting up an American division of Lachlan Industries in Beijing."

It had been a strange conversation. He'd taken her to the heights of exasperation but now he was sharing his business plans with her...something she'd wanted for so long. Cautiously, afraid he would clam up again, she said. "Lachlan Industries in Beijing?"

"Uh-huh. The world really has become a global marketplace. If I want Lachlan to be a player on more than a national level, I have to establish a pres-

ence around the world. Our plants in Germany produce a number of products for the European market.
One in Beijing could serve a sizable portion of the
Far East, including Taiwan and Japan.'' He was
warming to his theme and his tone was enthusiastic.

''Now I understand why people say you have the
Midas touch,'' she said. ''You never stop thinking
of ways to improve.''

''I can't,'' he said simply, ''if I want to stay on
top. I'm always looking for the next opportunity. It's
a full-time effort.''

''When you take over your mother's corporation,
how will you manage both companies?''

Instantly the light in his eyes flattened and cooled.
She saw immediately that she'd said the wrong thing.
He shrugged, elaborately casual. ''I'll probably work
out some kind of merger. Get everything under one
umbrella so I don't have so many balls to juggle.''

His too-casual tone, coupled with an explanation
that sounded wooden and rehearsed, alerted her to
the realization that this wasn't just business for
Stone. Merge the two companies?

Some of the pieces of the puzzle that was her husband clicked into place as she recalled the odd note
of near-desperation in his tone on the night he'd laid
out his proposal. Her heart ached for him as a flash
of insight showed her the truth. He didn't want
Smythe Corp. because it was a good deal, or even
because it was a family tradition. A merger was
something he could control as he hadn't been able to
control the disintegration of his family when he'd
been a child—and in a very tangible if symbolic
sense, he would be putting his family back together
again.

She wondered if he understood that some things could never be fixed. Quietly she said, "You know, merging these companies is nice, but it isn't going to help you resolve your differences with your mother. You really ought to sit down and talk with her."

But she could tell her impassioned words had fallen on deaf ears. His face drained of expression and when he looked at her, his eyes were as cool as the blustery spring weather outside. "Funny, but I don't remember asking you for your opinion on what I ought to do with my mother. All I require of you is that you play a part for ten more months."

She felt as though he'd slapped her. As a reminder of the time limit she had, it was fairly brutal. She didn't speak again, and when they arrived home, she got out of the car before he could open her door and hurried inside, heading for her room. *Fine,* she thought angrily. *Let him go to China. Let him count down the days until he rids himself of me. Let him refuse to give me anything meaningful to do.*

With that thought, she remembered Eliza's offer. And she reached for the phone.

"This place is awesome!" Faith's former room-mate Gretchen bounced into the kitchen of the town house as they completed a short tour of the house several days later. She turned to face Faith, her expressive pixie face alight. "I still can't believe you're married to him."

"I can't believe it, either," Faith said wryly. "It's a little overwhelming sometimes."

"He's really been great about your mom living here." Gretchen flung herself onto one of the bar stools. "Tim would wig out if I asked him to let my mother live with us."

"It's a slightly different situation." Faith felt compelled to defend Gretchen's steady beau, one of the nicest guys she'd ever met. "I mean, it's not as though we're tripping over each other like we would in a small place."

"Yeah, I guess the money makes a difference." The redhead made a little moue of frustration. "Money. I wish it didn't exist."

"Amen." Gretchen couldn't know how much Faith meant that. Then her friend's woebegone expression registered, and she focused on Gretchen. "What's wrong?"

Gretchen shrugged. "Nothing, really. Tim asked me to marry him—"

"When? Why didn't you tell me?" Faith leaped from her own seat and embraced her friend. "Congratulations!"

But Gretchen raised a hand and indicated that she should calm down. "Well, frankly, it isn't that big a deal yet. Tim says he wants to marry me, but he wants us to save some money first. He's thinking we should buy a house in New Jersey."

"And you don't want to do that?"

"Are you kidding? I'd love it!" Gretchen waved her hands about. "Big old trees, a little white picket fence and a house with shutters. We could get a dog…we've even talked about children." Her big eyes sparkled with tears. "But he wants to wait until we can make a down payment on a home to get married. I love the stupid man and I want to marry him *now!*"

"Why should you wait?" Faith tried to think

about it from Tim's point of view. And failed. People who loved each other should marry. What did money have to do with love?

"Beats me."

"I don't get it, either." Faith sighed heavily. "I'm sorry. Men are such dolts sometimes."

"You said it, girlfriend." Shedding her sad mood, Gretchen eyed Faith over the rim of her coffee cup. "That sounded like you had one specific man in mind."

Faith smiled slightly. "Without question."

"Problems with the tycoon?"

"A few." If her friend only knew!

"Sex," said Gretchen.

Faith nearly choked on the coffee she'd just swallowed. "What?"

"Men are amazingly easy to manipulate if you start with a little physical T.L.C."

"They are not."

"That's what all the magazines say." And that, as far as Gretchen was concerned, made it fact. "So you just have to dazzle him with incredible, unforgettable sex and then talk about whatever's bothering you. He'll be much more malleable then."

"You are *terrible!*" Faith began to giggle as she saw the glint of humor lurking in her friend's eyes. But her amusement faded away as she thought about her marriage. "Anyway, that's not an option. We don't—" Oh, my God. She stopped, appalled at her runaway tongue.

Gretchen was staring at her as if she'd sprouted a second head. "Tell me you are kidding. You have a platonic relationship with one of the most gorgeous men in North America?"

"Um, yes, that's about right." Faith squirmed beneath the incredulous stare.

"Don't you love him?"

Faith nodded sadly. "I do. I never knew it was possible to care for someone the way I care for him. But that doesn't mean it's mutual."

"Well, if he doesn't love you and you're not having wild, bed-wrecking sex every night, then why the heck did he *marry* you?"

Well, there was no backing out of it now. If there was a more persistent woman than her redheaded friend on the face of the planet, Faith would have to meet her to be convinced. "He married me because he feels responsible for me," she said miserably. To an extent, that was true, and it was the only thing she could say to her friend without breaking Stone's trust. "His father and mine were best friends. When they were killed together, Stone became my guardian."

"Your *guardian?* How Victorian!" Gretchen's eyes were wide. "And because of that he felt compelled to marry you?" Her eyes narrowed and she gave a snort of disbelief. "Uh-uh. I don't buy it."

"It's true," Faith said glumly. "That's why we haven't—we don't—"

"Give me a break." Gretchen hopped off her stool and paced around the kitchen. "Look me in the eye and tell me that if you were as homely as a mud fence he'd have married you." When Faith's brow wrinkled and she hesitated, Gretchen stabbed her index finger at her. "See? I knew it! No man would sacrifice himself like that. He wants you."

"He doesn't." Faith stopped, remembering the

passionate kisses they'd shared, and her expression reflected her lack of conviction.

"Ha! I knew it." Gretchen was grinning at the look on her friend's face. "He *does* want you. He's just trying to be, I don't know, noble or something. I guess he's got some hang-up about that guardian stuff. Still…if he's hot for you, there's hope. You just have to seduce him."

"*Seduce him?* You are insane."

"No, no, I'm serious." And her freckled face did look surprisingly sober. "I might have been kidding before, but I am so totally not joking about this. Faith, you were meant to be with this guy. And he was meant to love you back. He's just too dumb to know it. You're going to have to go after him big time."

"No way." She shook her head, remembering the way he'd rejected her before, and the way he'd reacted two days ago when she'd tried to encourage him to mend his fences with his mother. "He's made it clear what his position is."

"Oh, come on. Aren't you the girl who came to town without a job *or* a place to live, and found both the very first day? If you really want him, he's toast. You just have to go for it."

"This is a ridiculous conversation." Faith rose and began stacking dishes. "Come on, I'll take you in to meet my mother and her companion before you have to get back."

But Gretchen's words lingered in her mind long after her old roommate had left. *If he's hot for you, there's hope.*

Seven

The trip to China lasted three days longer than he'd planned. By the time Stone left LaGuardia behind and slipped his key into the lock of his town house, he was exhausted. The meetings had been long and ultimately fairly successful from a business standpoint. But the strain inherent in communicating his ideas effectively to people of another culture had worn him down. But it wasn't only that. For the first time in his life, he'd been impatient to conclude his business and get home. Not so that he could get back to work, but so he could get *home*.

Impatient. Right. How about so nervous he couldn't even spit? He checked his watch. It was nearly ten in the evening. He'd been away for twelve days and they'd seemed like twelve hundred.

He'd hated traveling. No, he thought, trying to be honest. He'd hated traveling alone. God, he'd never imagined feeling lonely simply because a certain woman wasn't at his side. He'd never expected to be seized with a barely controllable urge to hop a flight and fly home simply because that's where she was. He'd never, *ever* thought about a woman so much that it shattered his concentration and turned his brain to mush in the middle of important meetings.

But thoughts of Faith had done all that to him and more. He'd lain awake aching for her, knowing that even if he were in New York he'd still be aching for her...and wishing he were there, anyway, because then at least he'd be close to her.

He must have been crazy when he'd married her, he decided as he took the stairs two at a time. How could any man be expected to ignore the temptation of her lithe young body day after day after day? It was natural for him to want her, to ache for her. It was just a physical reaction.

He walked through the house, noting the lamp that was always lit now in the hallway that led to the kitchen. Faith had begun leaving it on for Clarice, in case she came to get something from the kitchen at night. He'd gotten used to seeing the small glow.

He walked down the hallway to his bedroom door, noting that Faith's was firmly closed. Would she come to greet him when she heard him moving around? Probably not. He'd have to wait until morning.

Morning. He realized he'd actually missed mornings at home. On the days he hadn't run from the house at dawn, he'd shared breakfast with Faith and sometimes her mother and Clarice. He'd always imagined he'd find having other people around first thing in the morning annoying, but it was surprisingly pleasant.

It might not be so pleasant now, after the way he'd left things with Faith. But even then, knowing that she was likely to be cool and formal with him, something eased in his chest because at long last he was home again, and she was sleeping right in the next room. He hoped he could make things right with her. He missed her smile, and the habit she had of humming beneath her breath as she moved around the house.

She hadn't done much humming the past few days before he'd gone to China. Their parting had been strained, stiff, the way things had been between them since the day of her mother's accident. He should have apologized for the things he'd said to her about her interference with his mother. Faith had a good heart and a wonderful relationship with her own mother; it probably was beyond her capabilities to understand the way he felt.

He stepped into his bedroom and dropped his suitcase inside the door. A startled squeak made him jerk his head around to locate the source—and there she stood.

She must have just finished in the shower because she had a towel wrapped around her torso and her hair was pinned atop her head. He could see droplets of water gleaming on her shoulders.

Immediately he felt a rush of desire begin to radiate through his body, making him take a short, tense breath as every inch of his skin seemed to sizzle with an electric charge. He'd been thinking of her, wanting her for so long that it only took moments to make him worry that she'd notice the burgeoning arousal pushing at the front of his pants.

"Hello," he said, and his voice was husky. "I didn't mean to scare you."

"It's all right." She smiled at him, and the radiance of her expression tightened every muscle in his body. "I'm glad you're home. I missed you."

"I, uh, missed you, too." He couldn't look away from her. She was smiling, her gray eyes shining, so beautiful that he ached with the need to cross to her and crush her to him. She apparently had forgiven him. Or forgotten their argument. Hah. He doubted Faith would forget something like that.

Then she put her hands up to the top of the tucked-in fabric and his whole body tightened. She took a deep breath, uncertainty flashing in her eyes so fast he wasn't sure he'd seen it to begin with. And before he could say a word, she dropped the towel.

As it fell away from her, he made a strangled sound in his throat. She was as beautiful as all his fevered imaginings, long, slim, sleekly muscled. Her breasts were high and round with deep rosy nipples that puckered beneath his gaze. Her bare feet curled into the carpet and he couldn't prevent his gaze from sliding up her long elegant legs, over the splendid curve of her hip. At the junction of her thighs, a thatch of blond curls protected her deepest secrets.

As he devoured her with his gaze, she fought an obvious battle with shyness and modesty. Her hands came halfway up her body in a defensive posture before she deliberately let them relax at her side again. A rosy blush suffused her neck and climbed into her cheeks, but she held out her arms to him, still smiling into his eyes. "Make love to me."

His blood surged heavily, nearly propelling him into her arms. He wanted her, and he hated himself for it. She was too young.

She's not too young. She's legal.

Well, she was too young for him.

Ten years isn't a huge age gap.

"Stone?" She came through the dividing door into his bedroom and began to walk across the room toward him, her eyes flickering with nerves even though her voice was steady and warm. "This is the part where you're supposed to respond."

She obviously hadn't noticed just how *responsive* he was. He felt himself beginning to sweat. "Dammit, Faith, just stay over there." He backed around the other side of the bed, putting some space between them, appalled at the panicked note in his voice. "You don't want this."

"I do." Her voice was as soft as ever but there was a note of determination in it that shook him. "I thought about it the whole time you were gone. I've been thinking about it since the day you asked me to marry you." She took a deep breath and he couldn't prevent his gaze from dropping to her breasts as the firm mounds rose and fell "I want my first…first time to be with someone I trust and care for. I want it to be with *you.*"

"No, you don't." But her words sent unpleasant images bolting into his mind, images of Faith with another man, and he had to bite back the snarl that wanted to escape.

"I do," she said again. She reached up and took the clip from her hair, tossing it onto his dresser as the silky blond tresses fell down her back and framed her body. She came around the end of the bed and walked to him.

He put out a hand like a traffic cop to hold her off but she slipped inside it and pressed herself against him, her hands sliding up to curl around his neck as her lips grazed the sensitive skin where his shirt collar exposed his throat.

He groaned at the feel of her slim young frame pressed against him. She smelled fresh and sweet, and despite his good intentions, his extended hand dropped to her back, sliding slowly up and down her sleek spine, testing the naked, resilient flesh, moving dangerously down to trace the cleft in her buttocks. His hand clenched spasmodically on her soft flesh, pressing her hips hard against his aching arousal. "We won't be able to get an annulment." His voice sounded hoarse and unfamiliar to his ears.

"I don't care." She kissed his throat again. "How can this be so bad when we both want it so much?"

"I haven't changed my mind about this being a mistake." But he had. The words she'd said, that she wanted *him* to be the one, danced through his head. If he refused...he couldn't even complete the thought. Instead he ran his hands over her silky skin everywhere he could reach, savoring the soft, sweet feel of her as common sense warred with pure carnal need. Finally need won. He dropped his head and sought her mouth, wrapping his arms around her. His kisses were hard and wild, his tongue plunging deep. She gasped and he remembered how innocent she was, so he reined himself in with gargantuan effort, gentling his kisses, stroking the inside surfaces of her mouth with his tongue and teasing her until she followed his lead, her tongue hesitantly joining his, exploring his mouth as fully as he explored hers. Finally he tore his lips from hers, breathing heavily. He kissed her cheek, slid his mouth along her jaw and down the side of her neck. She smelled of scented bath soap and the unique flavor of her silken skin.

He raised his head, capturing her gaze, and his face was rigid with the control he was exerting to rein in the need he felt. "No," he gritted. "I can't do this anymore. I can't fight myself and you both. I can't pretend I don't want to make love to you when every hour of every day, I'm thinking about doing *this*." He slid one hand boldly around to cup her breast and his thumb found the tip of her nipple, rubbing gently back and forth. Her eyes closed as he watched her face, and her lips parted as her breath rushed in and out. Then he bent his head and replaced his thumb with his mouth, suckling her strongly, and her eyes flew wide. Wildly she arched against him as she cried out.

"And this," he muttered against her breast, sliding the same hand down over her rib cage and the softness of her belly, stroking gently before plunging firmly down between her legs to her most intimate feminine secrets. She was moist and slick, surprisingly ready for him. He cupped her, sliding his fingers between her legs as he used his thumb on the small bud hidden beneath the sweet curls. Her body arched again at the new sensation and she gasped. Then she set her hands against his shoulders, trying to push him away, instinctively wary and nervous of such implacable male determination.

"Ah, no, baby, don't fight me." He lifted his head and took her lips again, understanding her momen-

tary panic. Despite her brave invitations, she was still
an innocent. The act of giving herself to a man made
a woman intensely vulnerable. And so he simply let
his hand lay against her as he resumed kissing her
until she felt secure with him, permitting him access
to her mouth without restraint as her legs relaxed.
Then slowly he resumed the intimate caresses. He
slid one finger inside her, groaning at the tight, wet
feel of her clinging flesh and his hips surged forward
as he tried to ease the harsh need driving him.
''That's it,'' he growled. ''I want to make you feel
good. We're going to be so good together.''

Withdrawing his hand from its nest, he slid both
arms beneath her and lifted her into his arms, moving
the short distance to his bed. She put her arms around
his neck and lifted her face to his and he sat down
on the side of the bed, kissing her and stroking her,
torn between the need to bury himself deeply within
her and find release, and the desire to explore her
hidden treasures for hours. But then she shifted
against him, her hip pressing hard against his full
flesh, and he knew he wasn't going to be able to wait
hours.

She lifted her hands and inexpertly began to un-
button his shirt. He rose, laying her on the bed, then
quickly shed his shirt and jacket in one movement,
removing his shoes and socks, taking off his belt, all
without taking his eyes from the bounty of her bared
body.

She was watching him, too, and he saw her pupils
contract as he tore off his shirt. She lifted one hand
from the bed and laid it over the rigid, throbbing
flesh that distended his pants and he nearly jumped
out of his skin. He tore at the fastenings, pushing his

trousers down and off along with his briefs. Her eyes widened again as his need for her came fully free, and her gaze flashed to his. "Can I...touch you?" she whispered.

He gritted his teeth at the unconscious sensuality of her request as her body turned toward him. "Sorry, baby." He caught her wrist and linked his fingers with hers. "That would be a really bad idea right now. This would be over before it ever really got started."

She smiled and her voice was nearly a purr when she said, "Then I'll wait."

He came down on the bed beside her, sighing as his naked flesh met hers for the first time. His erection pressed against her hip and he could feel the moisture he couldn't hold back dampening her flesh. He shuddered, hoping he could wait long enough to make it good for her.

Quickly he smoothed his hand down over her downy belly and feathered his fingers over the sweet folds between her legs again. Her gaze was fastened on his and he caught a hint of apprehension in her beautiful eyes. Leaning forward, he kissed each of her eyelids as they fluttered shut. "Relax," he whispered. "I'll take care of you." He leaned over her and took her breast, suckling firmly until she moaned and tried to arch toward him. His fingers grew bolder, parting her and opening her for him, and he shifted his weight onto her, his arms shaking with the effort it took not to simply shove himself into her and ride her until he exploded. But Faith was a virgin. And she was...special. He wanted it to be as good for her as it was going to be for him. He pulled his hips back and let his shaft rub her, then reached down and opened her further until the slightest surge forward caught the head of his aroused flesh within her.

She gasped.

He groaned.

She raised a hand, and wiped away a drop of sweat that trickled down his temple. "Is this hard for you?" she whispered.

He chuckled deep in his throat. "No, it's hard for *you.*" Her eyes widened as he probed her, alert to the barrier that signaled her virginity. Just within her, he met resistance. "I'm going to try not to hurt you," he warned her, "but the first time might not be much fun." She watched him wide-eyed as he moved his hand between them and found again the pouting bud he'd exposed. As he began to lightly press and circle, her eyes closed and her back arched, pushing him a little deeper.

"That's—too much," she panted. "I can't...I can't..."

"You can," he breathed. "Let it build, baby." He kept his tone soft, his voice low, watching the flush that spread over her fair skin as she gave herself to her passion, to him. In a moment, her hips began to respond to his encouraging touch, rising and falling, and he had to steel himself to withstand the seductive lure of her body caressing the tip of him.

"Stone," she cried, "hold me!"

"I've got you, baby," he crooned. "Let go, let go, let go..."

And she did. He saw the shock in her eyes as her body convulsed, shuddering beneath him, and as she arched wildly up to meet him, he plunged forward, burying himself deep within her responsive body.

"Oh!" Her legs came up to wrap around his hips,

possibly the most erotic feeling he'd ever known, and as her sweet channel continued to rhythmically caress him, he began to move, stroking heavily in and out, teeth clenched, body shaking. He was so ready that it took only moments until he erupted, falling over the edge into her soft arms as he emptied himself deep, deep within her. Pleasure shattered his senses as it spread throughout every cell in his body, rendering him momentarily deaf and blind.

As he began to regain his senses, he looked down at her. "Are you all right?"

"I'm fine."

"I didn't hurt you?"

"Only a tiny bit." She smiled at him, her fingers rubbing the back of his neck. "You were wrong. The first time *was* fun."

He chuckled as he slowly lowered his weight onto her, conscious of her slight frame. But she kept her legs and arms around him when he would have shifted himself to one side, holding him close until he let himself go boneless in her embrace. He rested his forehead on the pillow next to her and moaned as her fingers lightly kneaded up and down his back.

"Stone?"

"Hmm?" He was so relaxed it was an effort to move enough to reply.

"How long before we can do it again?"

His eyes flew open. He started to laugh, lifting himself on his elbows to inspect her face, then dropping his head to kiss her. "A little while, at least," he told her. "I'm pretty tired. But on second thought—" he moved his hips experimentally "—I'm feeling much more rested already."

She smiled, her gaze warm and contented and he

kissed her again, lingering for a moment before he levered himself up and began to withdraw—

And froze. He swore vividly, and Faith's eyes widened in shock.

"What?" she demanded.

He pulled himself back to his knees, then stood and cursed again, his hands on his hips, his still-erect flesh cooling unpleasantly. "No protection," he said grimly. "How the hell could I have been that stupid?" he asked the ceiling. But he knew exactly how stupid he'd been. He'd been so focused on completing the act of making her young, virgin body his that protection had been the last thing on his mind.

Faith went very still, probably as horrified as he was. After a moment, she sat up and eased herself to the side of the bed. Her brow wrinkled momentarily and she winced; he realized she was feeling some discomfort. But she stood, and stepped forward to slide her arms around his waist and press herself against him.

"It's all right," she said. She kissed his collarbone and then looked up at him. "I love you. I wouldn't mind if I got pregnant."

His body had reacted automatically to the soft feel of her curves but her words were a shock of ice water on his rising passion. "Faith," he said grimly, taking her by the shoulders and holding her gently but firmly away from him, focusing on the only part of her statement he could allow himself to believe. "*I'd* mind. This marriage is only going to last a year, remember?"

She simply gazed at him. And he was the first to look away.

"I know you think you love me," he said, desperate to convince her. "It's natural when two people make love for feelings to get mixed up with basic human needs. But trust me, you won't love me in a year."

Still, she regarded him silently. Finally she opened her mouth. "You're wrong. I'll still love you in a year. I'll still love you in ten years, and in twenty."

"Look," he said, frantic to erase the echo of those seductive words, "let's not get into a fight about this."

She smiled at that, and he stared at her, mystified. What the hell was so funny? "I wasn't planning to fight with you," she said. "I want to make love again." She stepped forward, pressing herself against him, burying her face in his neck. Her warm breath stirred the curls on his chest and he shuddered, knowing that she surely could feel the arousal he couldn't prevent.

"This isn't lovemaking," he said above her head. "This is sex."

"Okay." She nuzzled his chest and he leaped a foot in the air when her lips grazed his nipple. "You call it what you want and I'll call it what I want."

If he was smart, he'd walk away from this right now, and not compound one error by making another. But his arms came around her without his permission, and his head lowered and sought her lips all on its own. His body knew what it wanted even though his mind knew better. "And we use protection," he decreed, trying to retain some control of the situation. She was a twenty-year-old recently deflowered virgin. How could she be so unshakably certain of herself?

"If that's what you want," she said agreeably. Her

small hand slipped slowly down his body and his stomach muscles contracted sharply. "Is it okay to touch you now?" she asked.

He closed his eyes and exhaled in surrender. "Yeah," he said, giving himself to this night and this moment. He'd worry about tomorrow later. "But only if I get to touch you, too."

She awoke before dawn, aware of her body in a way she'd never been before. She lay on her side, her back cuddled into the living furnace of her husband. Stone's left arm was draped over her hip, the other was beneath the pillow on which both their heads lay.

With dreamy satisfaction, she relived the hours just past. He'd scared her silly when he'd walked into his bedroom without warning. Even though he'd told her his flight would be in that night, she hadn't really expected to see him. He'd warned her that he'd probably get home in the wee hours.

It was probably just as well that he'd surprised her. If she'd been prepared, she'd never, ever have had the nerve to approach and seduce him the way she had! She took a deep breath, remembering the moment of sheer terror she'd felt when she'd decided to drop her towel and take Gretchen's advice. At first, she'd thought he really was going to refuse. But then she'd seen his hands clenched in fists. She'd felt the barely contained desire he kept on a tight leash and she'd pushed a little more until the volcano had erupted and he'd swept over her with the force of a hot lava flow, incinerating her modesty and her virginity with his sheer delight in her body and his blatant encouragement of her sexuality. She might know another lover someday, but she knew without question that she'd never meet another man who pleased her like Stone did, who anticipated her every need before she even realized what she wanted.

She loved him so much. He still couldn't let himself see that they were perfect for each other. He'd led her to believe it was because of their age difference but the truth was, Stone was terrified of intimacy. Not physical intimacy, but emotional closeness. She knew he'd had scores of lovers in the past, but she was certain none of them knew him the way she did, knew his secret need for a stable home, the sorrow and resentment that threatened to permanently damage his relationship with his mother, the unacknowledged wish for a family of his own.

A family. A baby. How amazing that she hadn't even been thinking much about that kind of future until he'd introduced the possibility. She'd always thought of herself as a good girl. Going to her marriage bed a virgin was simply a given. But it shook her a little to realize that it wouldn't have mattered if she'd been married to Stone or not. If he'd ever tried to seduce her, he would have had her anytime he'd wanted. And it scared her more than a little that she hadn't even thought about protection once she was in his arms.

His grim panic from the night before shot into her mind. The very fact that he hadn't even thought of birth control had shocked him beyond belief. She hadn't thought of it, either, but then again, she wasn't worried about a pregnancy. Had she subconsciously expected him to take care of it? Or had she simply not cared because she knew she wanted his child? Regardless of the reasons for her memory's short-circuits, she'd known the moment he'd said it that very little could make her happier than to bear Stone's baby.

She was married to the man she loved and she knew instinctively that a child would change their lives forever. Stone would never let his child grow up in a broken home. If she did become pregnant, they'd stay married.

And then she'd have much more than a year to show him that he loved her, too.

But she had no desire to trap him in any way. She'd never imagined a man could be so scared by a few little words, she thought tenderly. Though she hadn't expected him to respond in kind, it had still hurt a little that he had so easily dismissed her feelings. Obviously he had never considered love to be a part of their relationship. She could only be patient now, and hope that her confession would get him thinking about love, about her, about making their marriage a forever one.

A surge of love so strong it shook her moved through her. Slowly she reached back with her left hand and let it rest on his hip, gently running her thumb back and forth across his warm flesh, simply needing to touch him. After a moment, his even breathing changed. So did something else, she discovered with pleasure, wriggling her bottom back against him a little more.

"Good morning." His voice in her ear was deep and sleep-roughened. The hand at her hip slid up to cup her breast, plucking lightly at her nipple until it contracted into a small, hardened point that sent streamers of arousal down into her abdomen.

"Good morning," she returned. "Welcome home."

"I thought you already did that."

She giggled. Then all coherent thought fled as he leaned over her and caught her mouth in a deep, sweet kiss. When she had to breathe or die, he lay back again behind her. For an instant he rolled away, and she heard the sound of a foil packet tearing, then heard him quickly fitting himself with protection. He'd insisted on using protection the second time last night, too, though she'd told him he didn't have to. He'd gone still for a moment, then simply sighed, shaken his head and kissed her.

In a moment, he was back. His hand slid down over her body to her thighs and he urged her top leg up, draping it over his as he angled himself into the hot, tight crevice he'd made. She felt the column of blunt male flesh prodding at her and he lifted her leg a little higher, until suddenly, he flexed his hips and slid smoothly into her. She moaned, impaled on pleasure, and slipped her hand back to his taut, lean buttocks to pull him even closer, even deeper.

"Are you sore?" He stopped abruptly. "I didn't even think—"

"I'm fine," she said, shifting her hips and stroking the smooth, hot length of him, "now."

Stone nuzzled her hair aside and kissed the joining of her shoulder and her neck. He flattened his hand on her lower stomach, holding her steady as he moved against her. And again, she welcomed him home.

Afterward, he rolled to his back. She pulled the sheet over her, not comfortable enough with nudity yet to ignore her own modesty, watching as he disposed of their protection.

"I meant it, you know," she said quietly as his gaze met hers.

"Which 'it' are you referring to?" he asked cautiously.

"Everything," she said honestly. "I do love you. And if a baby is a result of this—" she indicated them "—I would be thrilled."

"What about school?" His voice was challenging. "Starting your own business? Or is that all just so much talk?"

"Of course not." She refused to let him pick a fight over this, though she suspected he would feel better if he were able to make her angry. "Having a family and a career don't have to be mutually exclusive." The moment the words left her mouth, she realized that to Stone, who had been the victim of a marriage in which that very thing had indeed been an issue, the two goals were in direct conflict with one another.

"Are you kidding?" He sat up abruptly and swung his feet over the side of the bed. "Women can comfort themselves with that 'I can do it all' mantra as much as they want. But the reality is that something suffers when they try to juggle too many balls." He slapped an angry hand down on the bed between them. "I have no intention of bringing children into this world to be tossed to whichever parent isn't as busy at the moment. In fact, I never plan to have children at all!"

Faith stared at him, shocked by the declaration. She understood that he felt he'd been the casualty of his mother's determination to have a career but she'd never imagined he would let it affect him to such an extent. If only she could get him to walk in his mother's shoes long enough to realize it hadn't been the simple, power-hungry decision he assumed it had been. Her heart ached for him as she understood exactly what his parents' differing points of view could cost him.

Could cost them both.

Slowly, seeing that insistence would only make him more intractable, she said, "I apologize for not understanding how you feel. We have plenty of time to think about children—" unless he threw her out when her year was up "—and I certainly would never try to talk you into doing something you don't want."

There was a long, tense silence.

Finally Stone heaved a huge sigh. He turned toward her, not away, and she knew an overwhelming relief as he took her in his arms. "I'm sorry, too," he said. "I shouldn't have gotten angry with you. We never talked about children because I didn't think it would ever be an issue. Hopefully it still won't be." He pressed a gentle kiss to her forehead. "Can we just enjoy this for now?"

"Of course," she murmured. She tilted her face up to his and kissed him sweetly, deeply, without reserve. With any luck at all, each day that passed would bring them a little closer, and he would see what a long life together could be like. And how very special it would be to add a child born of their love to their family.

After a final kiss, he rose from the bed and went into the bathroom. She rolled over to watch him walk away, admiring the way his wide shoulders tapered down to a lean waist, the way the muscles in his buttocks flexed as he walked, the strong, well-shaped columns of his legs. As he disappeared, her gaze fell on the clock beside the bed.

"Oh, no!" She suddenly realized it was Thursday, one of the days she'd set up to work for Smythe Corp. And she was going to be late if she didn't hurry. She bolted from the bed and headed for the door that connected their bedrooms.

Stone came out of the bathroom and followed her, unselfconsciously naked. She wrapped her robe around her then rushed to her dresser for fresh undergarments and panty hose, wishing she could be as blasé about her nudity.

"What's the rush?" He rested a shoulder against the doorway of her closet as she picked out a sedate gray-charcoal suit. "Do you have plans this morning?"

"I, um, yes." She skirted him and started for her bathroom, but he caught her by the waist and dragged her back against him.

"Can they wait?" He dropped his head and trailed a line of kisses down her neck, and she shivered as his hot breath blasted her sensitive nerve endings. "I thought we could take a bath together and then have breakfast."

She swallowed, tempted by his words, and her body heated at the image of the two of them in the big Jacuzzi tub in his bathroom. "I—can I take a rain check?" She cleared her throat. "I really do have some place I need to be. And don't you want to get back to your office?" Instinct warned her that explaining she was working for his mother probably wasn't the wisest course of action she could take.

"I've been in touch by phone, fax and e-mail," he said. "I hadn't planned on going in early today after traveling for all those hours. Where are you going?"

There was no help for it. She took a deep breath. "I have a temporary job."

His brows snapped together. After a moment, he said, "I thought you wanted to be able to spend time with your mother?"

"It's only a part-time thing," she said. "And it hasn't interfered with my time with Mama. She rests a lot."

"Where are you working? I'm surprised you were able to find anything suitable."

He meant that didn't expose her to the public, she knew. She took a deep breath. The thought of lying to him flitted across her mind and was rejected in the same instant. "Your mother offered me a position straightening out some records that were left in a mess by a departing employee."

"My *mother?*" His expression grew even more forbidding.

She swallowed. "The day we had lunch she asked me to consider it..."

"Why the hell didn't you say no?"

She squared her shoulders and lifted her chin. "Because I was bored. I wanted something to do, some kind of work and you wouldn't even consider it."

"You *have* things to do," he roared.

She'd never thought of herself as a temperamental person but the unfairness of his expectations refused to let her quail before his displeasure. "No," she said stonily. "I don't. The den is redecorated, the thank-yous are written and sent. I still have time to take on any other little projects you throw my way, but two days a week, I will be working at Smythe Corp.''

Stone eyed her expression, apparently deciding he was going nowhere fast. ''Fine,'' he said angrily. ''Have a great time.'' He stalked back to his own room, closing the door between them with a definite snap and she winced, holding back tears.

She'd known he was going to be unhappy about her new job but she hadn't really thought he'd react quite so…strongly. Did it bother him because she would be in steady contact with his mother or because he simply didn't like not being able to control her every move?

Eight

He'd been an ass.

A horse's ass. A *big* horse's ass. Stone stared moodily out the window of his office at the gray Manhattan day. It was raining. He'd really been looking forward to some sunshine this morning, but when he'd stepped out the door to start the jogging that he tried to fit in four or five times a week, he'd been soaked to the skin in less than a minute. The only good thing about it was that Central Park had been nearly deserted, except for a few other hardy exercising idiots like himself.

God, what had he been thinking, to lay into Faith like that?

He hadn't been, he supposed. He was still jet-lagged from the unbearably long flights home. And he certainly hadn't gotten what he could call a full night's sleep last night.

He pinched the bridge of his nose between his thumb and forefinger. Last night.

The mere thought of it was enough to make him start to sweat. He'd woken with her in his arms and as his body had reacted to the sweet, soft lure of hers, he'd acknowledged what he'd been avoiding for days: he enjoyed having Faith in his life. He wanted to make this a real marriage, at least for the time they had left. He'd tried to stay away from her, but fate and Faith had tempted him until he couldn't resist anymore.

He couldn't quite remember why he'd thought it was such a bad idea. There was no reason they couldn't have a physical relationship while they were married. Unless, perhaps, he counted the fact that she might never speak to him again after the way he'd stormed off.

One thing that was certain—perhaps the only thing—was that he owed Faith an apology. He might not like her working for his mother, he might even—if he admitted the truth—feel betrayed in a small way, but he didn't own her. They had an agreement to which she was living up and anything she did that didn't jeopardize that was none of his business.

He didn't like the way that thought made him feel. *He wanted it to be his business, dammit!* He wanted her to be his wife in every way there was. He didn't just want her hostess skills or even her wonderfully responsive young body. He wanted her mind, her emotions, her commitment.

He shoved himself from his chair with an explosive curse. Oh, hell. Oh, no. Oh, hell, no. He was not going to fall into her trap.

Faith had made sure he knew how she felt—that

she wanted to make their marriage a reality in every way. And the knowing was powerfully seductive, the future calling to him with almost irresistible force. But long-term commitments were for other people. He wasn't dumb enough to believe he'd feel like this about Faith forever. Sure, he had friends who appeared to have happy marriages. But he also had friends whose marriages had wrecked them emotionally and financially, and even, in the case of one buddy whose wife had shot him for sleeping around on her, physically. His own parents, with all their money and resources, hadn't made it work.

He knew better than to believe in happy endings.

Still, she had said she loved him. And maybe she did. But his cynical side, the side that was doing its level best to preserve him from stupid, ill-conceived ideas born of passion, that side of him said, *Gee, the timing surely is convenient.*

Her mother was getting worse. He'd given Naomi Harrell a home, kept her companion, offered to provide her with more care. Faith cared deeply for her mother and would naturally appreciate his support. But would she tell him she loved him simply because of that?

She might if she were worried about what was going to happen once you cut her loose. She might if she wanted to ensure that you kept the funds flowing.

No way. His mind rejected the ugly notion. Faith had integrity and honor enough for two people. She'd been determined to secure care for her mother through other efforts before they'd married. She wouldn't stoop to the easy solution.

Would she?

Of course not. She was as aware of the terms of their marriage as he was. But damned if he was happy with them. When he tried to imagine what would happen next March, he failed utterly. He couldn't see himself without Faith. He couldn't see his home without her quiet influence or even, ridiculous as it seemed, her relatives. Before Faith had come, his elegant, upscale town house had been little more than an address to identify him. Sure, it had come to him from his father. But frankly, his memories of growing up in this house were less than stellar. It was a mausoleum. Or at least, it had been.

Now it was a home. When he came to breakfast, Clarice had brought the paper in for him already. Faith almost always saw him off, holding his coat and waving him out the door. When he came home in the evening, Faith and Naomi often were in the den, ensconced by the fireplace playing a board game. Sometimes Faith read to her mother, since Naomi's eyesight was deteriorating to the point that she was becoming unable to read. He had a wonderful new chair in the den, too, one that Faith had picked out herself.

And last night, he'd had just about the best night of his life.

So why was he still planning on getting rid of his wife at the end of a year?

He didn't know. And thinking about it was giving him a royal headache. What he really ought to be thinking about was how to get back in Faith's good graces. And if he were smart, he'd be thinking about what he could do to keep her so busy she wouldn't have time to go hunting for work, for his mother or anyone.

And then he had an idea.

* * *

She hadn't had the best day of her life. Though the assignment Eliza had given her was indeed a challenge, Faith's mind had drifted continually, rehashing the angry exchange with Stone that morning.

It just wasn't fair. Last night, he'd made her happier than she'd ever thought she could be. Then this morning, her happiness was ripped away with the angry words he'd thrown at her.

Faith sighed as she walked briskly from the subway station to the town house. Love was supposed to make people happy, not miserable.

When she came through the door, she was struck by the same feeling she always got when she entered her home…it was cozy, despite its size, and welcoming, despite her husband's anger. It had truly become home. Leaving it was going to be one of the hardest things she'd—

An odd scrabbling sound behind her startled her as she hung her coat over a hook on the coat rack. She whirled. A small furry creature was barreling toward her, skidding and slipping on the smooth polished hardwood floor.

A puppy!

"It's for you," said a deep male voice, and she looked up to see Stone lounging against the door frame at the end of the hall.

She dropped to her knees and gathered up the puppy, talking nonsense to the wriggly little black-and-tan bundle, giving herself time to collect her thoughts. He didn't sound angry anymore. Cautiously she said, "What kind is it?" as she held the puppy up to her cheek. She laughed as the little tongue lapped at her cheek.

"She's a German Shepherd," he said. "Do you like her?"

"She's adorable! She's so tiny."

"She won't be that size for long. I thought she would be a good companion when you're walking around the park alone." He walked forward as she got to her feet with the puppy in her arms and to her shock and pleasure, he drew her close. "I'm sorry about this morning." He dropped his head and sought her mouth before she could speak, masterfully teasing her into a response that flared wildly between them. Then he tore his mouth away from hers. "Will you forgive me? It's none of my business what you do with your time."

She was stunned. What had produced this sea change? "Of course," she said, resting her head against his shoulder. "I'm sorry I didn't tell you before."

"Well," he said in a teasing tone, "I seem to recall that we were somewhat preoccupied...before." Then he set her away from him. "What should we name her?" he asked, nodding at the puppy.

"I don't know! Have Mama and Clarice seen her yet?"

He laughed. "Yes. They were bitten by the love bug at first sight. Or should I say first lick?"

She giggled. Then she snapped her fingers. "That's perfect. How about Lovebug?"

"Lovebug?" He looked dubious. "You'd really make me stand on the streets of New York with a German Shepherd named Lovebug?"

When he put it that way…"Oh, well," she said. "Back to the drawing board."

"It's got a certain cachet, though," he said. "Lovebug." He bent his knees so that he was eye level with the dog in her arms. "Are you a love-bug?"

She smiled at him. "You sound just like a doting daddy."

"That's what I was afraid of."

There was an instant of awkward silence as they both remembered the night before.

"We'd better take her out," he said at the same time that she said, "What will we do with her at night?"

They both laughed, and the moment passed. He put a hand at her back and guided her to the back of the house, where they took Lovebug outside. Then he showed her a crate in the kitchen. "The breeder told me it would be a good idea to get her used to being crated," he said. "For trips to the vet, or if we're away, or if we have parties and we want to protect or confine her. Apparently a lot of dogs like them so much they voluntarily sleep in them if the door is left open." He pointed to the table, where several books and a variety of leashes and toys lay. "I got a few things the breeder recommended."

She shook her head, amused. "You don't do anything halfway, do you?"

"Why don't you let me show you?" His voice dropped intimately.

A thrill of arousal shot through her. "What will we do with Lovebug?"

"Try out the crate?" he suggested. So they did, and to her amazement, the puppy sniffed around her new domain, wrestled once or twice with a large stuffed parrot, and then circled three times and fell asleep on the fleecy dog bed Stone had purchased.

"Hot damn!" he said. "Shall we try out the tub?" He took her hand and pulled her up the stairs into his room.

"We haven't even eaten dinner yet," she protested.

"Later." His voice was a rough growl. He tugged her into his arms and wrapped them around her tightly, so that every inch of her was locked against every inch of him. "I want you," he said. "I didn't get a damn thing done today because all I could think about was you."

She was stunned. And so happy she thought she might just burst. He'd brought her a puppy. A puppy that wasn't going to be anywhere near full-grown in less than a year, meaning…? She couldn't even let herself hope.

But now, now he was telling her things that she'd longed to hear, that she'd never imagined she would. He wanted her. He'd thought of her all day. "I thought of you, too," she said. "I—" But she didn't get a chance to tell him she loved him.

His mouth closed over hers as he bent and lifted her into his arms. He carried her up the steps and into the bathroom, where she discovered that he hadn't been kidding about trying out the tub.

Later, they ordered a pizza and ate it in front of the fire. Stone propped his back against the couch afterward and pulled her against his side, stretching his long legs out and sighing. "I'm still acclimating to the time change. I'm beat."

"Was your trip fruitful?" she asked, curling against him and laying her head on his shoulder. She kept her voice light, trying for an easy conversational tone as she stroked the puppy that lay in his lap.

He rolled his head, stretching the taut muscles in his neck. ''Yes. We're going to begin the application process to open a plant in Beijing. With a little luck and a lot of greasing of official palms, we might be up and running in twelve more months or so.''

He was talking about his work! She hid her elation and said, ''Isn't there an awful lot of corruption in China? How are you going to control your costs?''

''I've factored in a certain amount of overhead simply because of that. And I'm using American managers, at least for the setup, until we get a true cost picture. Once things stabilize, we might hire local managers.''

''But by then you'll know the costs and if things changed drastically you'd know something funny was going on.''

''Exactly.'' He hesitated. ''I'm going to have to go away again next week.''

''Oh.'' She let her disappointment show in her tone. ''Where to this time?''

''Dallas.''

''I'll miss you.''

''And I'll miss you.'' He turned his head and kissed her temple, and her heart doubled its beat. Stone wasn't just acting like a man who had the hots for a woman. He was acting as if he really cared for her. Then he spoke again. ''I thought about asking you to go along, but I'll be so busy you probably would see very little of me. I've managed to schedule five days of work into three, though, so it won't be a long trip.''

''Good.'' She traced a pattern in the thick mat of

hair that covered his chest, exposed by the shirt he'd thrown on and hadn't bothered to button. "I can see I'm going to develop an aversion to your absences."

"Then I'll just have to devote extra time to you while I'm here." He lifted the puppy and surged to his feet, starting for the kitchen. "Let's put her in her crate and go to bed."

"That would be nice," she said demurely.

He looked back as he straightened from the crate, catching the gleam in her eye, and laughed as he started toward her. "It'll be a whole lot more than 'nice,' and you know it."

The following week raced by at the speed of light. He made love to Faith every chance he got, and if she could be more radiant, he couldn't imagine how. She lit up whenever he came into the room, her pleasure in his presence clearly apparent. Stone decided that if all marriages were like his, no one would ever get divorced.

The thought sobered him slightly. When they'd married, he'd planned a quiet annulment at the end of twelve months. Now there was no chance of that. He and Faith would have to divorce. The very word left a bad taste in his mouth.

He was scheduled to leave for Dallas on an afternoon flight. That morning, he went in to the office for a few hours, then came home to pack. Faith sat on the bed and watched as he efficiently gathered his clothing and folded it into the suit bag he was taking.

"You're awfully good at that," she said. "I guess you get a lot of practice."

"Practice makes perfect," he parroted. He looked at her, seated cross-legged on his bed—and suddenly, he knew he was going to have to have her one more time before he left. Her lovely face was woebegone at the prospect of separation; he knew just how she felt. The thought of sleeping without her was making him more than a little desperate.

Setting aside the briefs he was stuffing into corners, he stepped toward her, his hands going to his belt, swiftly opening his pants.

"Stone!" she said. "You've already had your send-off."

"Ah, but that was goodbye." He put his hands on her thighs and slid them up beneath the skirt she wore, dragging down her pantyhose and the thong he'd watched her shimmy into that morning, throwing them across the room. "This," he said, positioning himself and bracing his body over hers as he slowly pushed into the hot, welcoming depths of her body, "is my incentive to hurry home."

Her eyes were dazed, her expression so sensually intent that it set fire to his already raging need for her. He lifted her thighs and draped them over his shoulders, beginning a quick, hard rhythm. She bit down on her lip and moaned, then her eyes flared wide and she arched up to meet him. It was a fast, frantic coupling. He was driven by a need he didn't fully understand, some primitive urge to stamp her as his, and he hammered himself into her receptive body until she convulsed in his arms. Immediately he followed her, feeling himself spilling forcefully into her until he lay over her, panting.

Faith lifted her arms, which had fallen limp to her sides, and clasped his head in her palms. She gave him her mouth in a sweet, deep kiss that he returned in full measure. When she tore her lips from his, she gasped, "I hate it when you're gone."

"I know, baby." He grinned at the pouty expression on her face, kissing her again. Faith wasn't generally moody; she must really be minding this. "I'm sorry. I'll try to cut down on my traveling from now on."

"I'd like that," she said. "I had visions of spending the next couple of decades watching you pack a couple of times a month."

"Faith—" Her words were entirely too seductive, slipping into his mind and twining around the need for her that he couldn't admit, even to himself. With an effort, he recalled his original proposition. One year. That was all he'd ever promised her.

"I love you," she said. He closed his eyes against the stark emotion pooling in hers, defensive anger rippling through him. Hadn't she understood anything he'd said that first night they'd made love? But she continued. "I know you think you don't want children now, but you might change your mind one of these days, and I'd hate for our child to grow up wondering where Daddy is half the time. As it is, Lovebug is going to be devastated. She worships you. I thought in a couple of years maybe we could get her a companion—"

"Faith!"

She finally stopped, and her shock at his tone was evident.

Fighting himself as well as her, he said, "I told you before that I don't want children. And does the phrase 'temporary marriage' ring any bells with you?" The words were harsh with frustration.

Immediately he regretted the question. She recoiled from the words as if he'd struck her. Slowly, she said, "We've been talking—sharing—everything, which I assumed meant we were growing closer. You got the dog, which I assumed meant we'd be sharing her in our future. You've made love to me every chance we got, which I assumed meant more than simply sex. Did I assume wrong?"

He was sweating. Pure fear took over. What if he let himself believe her? He wasn't sure he'd survive if she left him one day. "You knew from the very beginning that this arrangement had a definite end in sight." Forget the fact that he'd been wondering if there was any need to end it. Ever.

Her whole body stiffened. She immediately pushed at his shoulders, trying to free herself. He held her down with implacable force, their bodies still joined, but she turned her head to the side, shutting him out. Tears trickled from beneath her eyelids and ran across the bridge of her nose to disappear into the hair at her temple. He swore, dragging himself back away from her and shoving his clothing roughly into place.

Faith scrambled backward away from him, off the far side of the bed, where she bent her head and ignored him while she pulled her skirt into place, ignoring the fact that she was wearing nothing beneath it. Finally she took an audible breath and raised her head. Her gaze was so tortured and filled with pain that it struck him like a blow.

"I asked you a question earlier. You haven't answered it." Her voice was steady but her eyes were swimming with tears. "I assumed our lovemaking was more than sex. Was I wrong?"

No! Admitting anything would make him vulnerable. He hesitated.

And in that fatal second, he saw that whatever he said wasn't going to be enough.

"Never mind," she said. She turned toward the door.

"I told you before that it was easy to confuse love and lust," he threw at her back, furious at her for forcing this confrontation. "You're too young to know the difference."

She stopped. Turned. And shot him a look of such fury that he was shocked. Then the fury drained away, right before his eyes, leaving her face a stark study in anguish. "You're wrong," she said, her voice breaking. "But if all this is to you is a case of lust, don't expect sex when you come home again. Because I'll be looking for someone to *love*."

"Wait," he said, but she was already gone, the slam of the door echoing around his bedroom. He sank onto the bed, putting his head in his hands. What in hell had just happened? Guilt tore through him. He'd broken her heart. Deliberately. Using words like weapons to hurt her.

And he was afraid she was never going to forgive him.

Why? *Why* had he done that? He could have made his point in a gentler way. But she'd rattled him so badly that he hadn't been able to think for the panic clouding his brain.

He rose, intending to find her and demand that they talk this out, to apologize and grovel if it would keep her from looking at him as if he were lower than an earthworm. She would forgive him. She'd been the epitome of patience and understanding since they'd married; it was only to be expected that she would get frustrated and lose it occasionally. But she'd forgiven him before, each time he'd hurt her by reminding her that the marriage was temporary, that her feelings were transient. Once she calmed down, she'd forgive him again. *She had to.*

Why? asked the smug little voice in his head. *You didn't want her emotions.*

But he did. He took a breath so deep that his shirt seams strained. Oh, God, he did. He wanted her love, her understanding, her happiness, every emotion she felt.

Then the unmistakable sound of the back door closing caught his attention. He rushed to the window in time to see her slide into the smaller of his two cars and disappear down the street.

He was astounded. His gaze shot to the intimate apparel she'd left discarded on the floor. Unless she had underwear stashed in her purse or something, Faith had just left without even bothering to get fresh underwear.

Knowing her as he did, that realization alarmed him more than anything. Faith was the most ladylike of ladies outside their bedroom door. She would never do something so risqué without extreme provocation.

And that seemingly small action told him far more effectively than any words that *she considered their marriage to be over.*

The panic he'd been trying to subdue punched him full in the chest. Too late, he saw what had been within his reach all this time: a long happy life with the woman he loved at his side. But he'd driven her away with his selfish, self-protective actions...

And now he had nothing.

* * *

He canceled the Dallas trip, clinging to a dwindling hope that she would come home and forgive him.

But Faith never came home that night. He called her former roommates, the only friends he knew she had, but they professed not to have seen her.

He went to work the next day because the alternative was answering unanswerable questions from Clarice and Naomi. He had a lot of time to think while he sat in his office trying unsuccessfully to work. He'd tried to call Faith at home several times, but every time the machine had picked up. He'd known, in his heart, that she wouldn't answer even if she were there, but he'd had to try.

More than once, he picked up the phone to call a private investigator to track her down. But each time, he'd set the phone back in its cradle unused. Lunch was as unappealing as breakfast had been and he barely touched his meal.

That night, he explained to Naomi and Clarice that he and Faith had had a misunderstanding and that she'd gone away for a few days. Her mother was clearly alarmed, saying over and over again that Faith would never just go off without telling her. Stone spent an hour reassuring her, telling her that he was the messenger Faith had chosen, that she would be back.

And he'd see that she did return. Even if it meant him moving out.

Five days passed, with the weekend sandwiched in between. On the morning of the fifth day, Faith finally acknowledged that Stone wasn't coming after her. She knew what kind of determination and drive he had. If he'd wanted to find her, he'd have made it happen within hours of her leaving.

He didn't want her.

She lay in the spare bedroom of the apartment that Eliza Smythe's receptionist had offered to share with her when she'd learned of Faith's dilemma and sobbed silently into her pillow. She should be dealing with this better. Hadn't she already cried enough to fill a bathtub?

It was time to contact him, she decided. To let him know she would return and honor her commitment. The very thought brought fresh tears. But she'd made a promise and she intended to keep it. The only change would be that she planned to move into the set of rooms her mother and Clarice shared. That way, she could avoid Stone altogether, except for times when they had to appear publicly.

She couldn't imagine how she was going to get through the rest of the year.

Still, people didn't die from broken hearts. She'd be starting school in another month, and since she had nothing else to think of, she could double the class load she'd intended to take. That would keep her from simply giving up. She hoped.

She couldn't give up! She had responsibilities that were bigger than her own problems. Once she had her degree and a full-time job she could cover the cost of her mother's care herself. And maybe if she worked hard enough and long enough, she'd be able to forget the man she loved.

The man who didn't love her.

* * *

He headed for his mother's office, praying that Faith still was coming to work there twice a week. The shock on the face of the young receptionist at the front desk would have amused him at any other time. Today, all his concentration was focused on meeting with his mother.

He was directed to Eliza Smythe's office, but as he strode down the hallway on the third floor, his mother came to meet him. "Stone! Welcome to Smythe Corp."

"Thank you." He realized abruptly how small she was. She had looked tiny and defenseless as she came toward him.

"I presume this isn't a social call," Eliza said briskly. "Come into my office and we'll talk."

Defenseless. Hah.

He followed her through a quietly elegant outer office to her own, a feminine mirror-image of his, with all the necessary bells and whistles softened by quiet colors and soft fabrics.

"Have a seat," his mother invited. She seated herself in one of the wing chairs flanking a small glass table rather than behind her desk.

He took the other seat and inhaled deeply. He'd spent his life rejecting his mother. It wasn't easy to ask for her help. "Faith has left me," he said abruptly.

Eliza's expression became guarded. "I'm sorry to hear that. I like your wife."

"So do I. I want her back."

His mother studied him for long enough to make him repress the urge to squirm in his seat like a schoolboy. "We don't always get what we want. Why do you want her back?"

"Because." He floundered, unable to force himself to say the words that would leave him vulnerable. "She's my wife."

"Well, that's sure to sway her," Eliza said. She leaned forward. "Why did she leave?"

"We had a...disagreement," he said. "I came here to find out if she's still working for you. I need your help to get her to talk to me."

"Why should I help you?"

"You're my mother!"

"Interesting that you should remember that now." She was unmerciful. "Look, Stone, I made no secret of the fact that I thought your marriage was just a ruse to get your hands on Smythe Corp. But once I saw you two together...I was pleased. And as I've gotten to know Faith better, I think she's perfect for you."

"She *is* perfect," he said. "I just didn't figure that out until too late."

"You wouldn't just be trying to convince me of this because of our agreement regarding your inheritance?"

"There's nothing I want less at the moment than this company." And he meant it. "If it would bring Faith back, you could give it to the first stranger on the street."

His mother's eyebrows rose. "You're serious," she said, and there was pleased wonder in her tone.

"Very." He sighed. "You weren't wrong. Faith and I had a bargain. I married her to satisfy your conditions. She married me because in return I agreed to take care of her mother."

"Which you were doing, anyway."

He was startled. "Says who?"

"I did a little checking into your life before I made my offer," she said coolly. "Imagine my surprise when I found out you were supporting the Harrell ladies lock, stock and barrel."

"Faith was equally surprised," he confessed. "She just found out a few months ago."

"Ah. She confronted you, did she?"

Was his mother a mind reader? "All that's history now," he said. "I just want her back."

"Maybe she doesn't want to come back. What did you do to make her leave?" Eliza hadn't gotten to be a success by dancing around the issues.

"I, um, let her think I didn't love her," he said. It was hard to admit it, much less say it aloud.

"I see." She steepled her fingers. "And you want me to do what? Convince her that you do? Tell you when she's working?"

"All I want," he said, desperate and not caring anymore if he sounded it, "is a chance to talk to her. Then, if she still wants to leave, she can."

"You would lose Smythe Corp." Eliza reminded him, probing the depth of his sincerity.

"I don't give a damn!" he shouted, finally losing patience with explanations. "Hell, I'd even sell Lachlan if it would bring Faith back."

There was a moment of profound silence in the room. He glared defiantly at his mother. Eliza rose and walked around her desk. His heart sank. She wasn't going to help him. It was poetic justice for all the times when she'd tried to be a part of his life and he'd shut her out.

Well, he'd sit in the street and wait for Faith to come out if that was what it took to track her down.

Eliza hit a button on her speakerphone. "Hallie, would you send Faith in here, please?"

"Yes, ma'am."

A moment later, the door opened and Faith started through. His gaze was riveted to her. In the part of him that wasn't absorbed in steeping himself in his wife's presence, he was astonished. His mother must have sent for her when he'd arrived!

But then Faith saw him. She stopped in her tracks and her face was weary and wan, her eyelids puffy. She looked ill. After one quick glance, she ignored him and spoke to Eliza. "You sent for me?"

"There's a visitor to see you," Eliza said.

"There's no one that I want to see." Her voice shook and she bent her head, studying the carpet. He restrained himself from going to her and forcing her to acknowledge his presence, to grab her and hold her so she could never get away from him again. It was obvious that Faith was going to turn right around and walk out the door if he didn't let his mother handle this. The irony didn't escape him. How could it be that his mother, who had been absent for so many years when he'd have given anything for her attention, was the only person who could make his world right now?

"Faith." The president and CEO of Smythe Corp. waited until Faith looked up again. "My son is a very smart man in many ways. But in others, he's…a little dim." She smiled fondly at him. "And since I contributed to his desire to protect himself and avoid commitment, I feel bound to try to repair the damage. Will you listen to him?"

"That's all I want," Stone said quickly. "Just listen. And then, if you still want to leave, I won't stop you.''

She had swung her gaze to him when he began to speak, and he saw doubt, sorrow, hope, and myriad other emotions tumbling in her eyes before she made her face blank again. She shrugged. ''All right,'' she said in a barely audible voice.

Nine

"**W**hy didn't you just hire someone to find me?" she asked. She looked at the floor because she was afraid if she looked at him, the love she couldn't banish would be written all over her face. She didn't have any intention of letting him trample her heart more than he already had.

He shook his head. "It was my mistake. It was mine to fix."

"You could have sent me flowers, or jewels, to ask me to come home."

"Baby, I'll shower you with both if that's what you want," he said huskily. "But those are things. Anyone could send gifts. I didn't think that was the way to your heart."

"I didn't think my heart had anything to do with our marriage." She couldn't hide the note of anguish and her voice wobbled as she fought back tears.

He winced. "I didn't, either, in the beginning," he said quietly. "But I've found that your heart is essential, not just to our marriage but to my survival." He started across the room toward her. "And I've also found that I have to give you mine in return, because it's withering away without you."

She lifted her head and stared at him, rejecting the words. The moment she moved, he stopped immediately, as if he were afraid of startling her into flight. "You don't have to tell me that," she said wearily. "I'd already decided I have to come back and stay for the rest of the year."

"How can I convince you that I love you?" he asked her. "How can I convince you that I need you to love me?"

"You don't have to say that!" she cried. "I just told you I'll keep my end of our bargain."

"There is no bargain," he told her, his gaze steady and warm with an emotion she couldn't let herself believe in. "I told my mother she could give her company to someone else. I don't want it if it means I can't have you."

Her heart skipped a beat, then settled into a mad rhythm that threatened to burst out of her chest. "You can't do that. This company has always been in your family." *And part of your dream is to put your family back together.*

"Watch me." He rose and walked to the door, opening it. "Mother, would you please come in here?"

Eliza appeared in the doorway, her gaze questioning first one of them and then the other. "Yes?"

"What did I tell you before you brought Faith in here?"

His mother looked perplexed. "You mean about loving her or about giving up the company?" She turned to Faith. "Actually I believe his words were, 'I'd even sell Lachlan if it would bring Faith back.'"

Faith's face drained of color. Stone leaped forward, afraid she was going to faint as she groped for a chair. His mother went out again, closing the door behind her but he barely noticed. He gathered his wife into his arms, turning to sit in the wing chair and pulling her into his lap.

She didn't even struggle, just lay passively with her face buried in his shoulder.

She was warm, smelling of the indefinable essence of her, a scent he would recognize anywhere, and he nuzzled his nose into her hair. "God, I've missed you." His voice shook, surprising him as he savored the weight of her body pressed against him. She still didn't move, didn't respond, and he started to worry. "Faith?"

Slowly, she pushed away from him and sat up. "You think I'm too young to know the difference between love and sex."

"No." He shook his head slowly, holding her gaze, trying to communicate the depth of his feeling to her. "The truth is, I was *afraid* you were too young. I felt like I was taking advantage of you— you hadn't known enough men to know whether you loved me or not. And whether or not I wanted to admit it, I was falling for you. I was afraid. Afraid you'd grow up and fall out of love with me, afraid to believe in forever." He ran his palms slowly up and down her arms. "Now," he said, "now I don't give one flying damn if you're too young or not, because *I* know the difference." He swallowed, his throat closing up. "And what we have is love."

He saw her face change, just a slight relaxation of the tense muscles. She believed him! "I love you," he said again. "Forever."

"Forever." Her voice wobbled. "I love you, too."

He sought her mouth, relief almost a painful sensation as she kissed him back. God, he'd been afraid he'd never know her kiss again. He lifted his head a fraction. "As long as we live."

She gazed earnestly into his eyes. "It's all right if you don't want children. We'll have each other."

He considered her offer. "Thank you, but I've changed my mind about so many things I think I'll change it about that, too." He took her face in his hands. "I want to give you babies. I want to be there when they're born, and every day of our lives after that. I want to see your mother's face the first time we put her grandchild in her arms."

"And your mother's." Tears glimmered in her eyes but she was smiling.

"And my mother's," he repeated. He glanced around the room. "I guess she's going to be smug about this for the rest of my life." But his tone was fond. Somewhere inside him, he'd discovered that he could accept his past. He knew he and his mother would have to talk, because she felt obliged to explain. But he also knew it wasn't going to matter. She would be a part of his future.

Faith laughed. "How did she know to call for me?"

"If I had to guess, I'd say that little receptionist out front probably gave her the headsup. She looked like she'd seen a ghost when I walked in."

"'That little receptionist' happens to have become a friend of mine," Faith told him. "I've been staying with her."

Another mystery solved. "I guess I have to thank her, then, for taking care of you."

"We might have to buy her new pillows," she said. "I've sobbed into all of hers so much they're permanently soaked."

He stroked her cheek, sobered by her words. "No more sobbing. Promise?"

She smiled tenderly, her hand coming up to stroke the back of his neck. "Promise."

He kissed her again, pulling her close and the caress quickly turned to a searing passion as he stroked her body, unable to get enough of her after the days of worry. "I want you," he said in a low voice. "I want to get started on making a baby right away."

"Not here!" She straightened immediately, looking shocked.

"It is going to be my office some day," he reminded her, loving the prim and proper streak that was as much a part of her as her love for him.

"Well, it isn't yet!"

He laughed, intoxicated by the feel of her in his arms again. "Then let's go home, wife, so I can show you how much I love you and need you."

* * * * *

Billionaire Bachelors: Garrett

ANNE MARIE WINSTON

For Lucie and Missy,
the original roadkill kitties, and for the staff of
the Waynesboro Veterinary Clinic. For many
years of excellent care and for services above
and beyond the call of sanity!

One

Garrett Holden strode up the cracking sidewalk and stepped onto the low front porch of the dilapidated half-house. He shook his head in disgust as he looked around the tiny dwelling. This was what he got for insisting that he be the one to notify the woman mentioned in his stepfather Robin Underwood's will of Robin's death.

This wasn't an area of Baltimore he usually frequented, with its tiny, narrow duplexes all crammed together on the streets across from the far reaches of the Johns Hopkins University campus. The front yards were minuscule. The backs, as he'd discovered when he'd driven down the alley behind the house on his initial pass, consisted largely of concrete slabs, not a blade of grass in sight. He'd been relieved to find a parking space within sight of the address where he

could keep an eye on his imported sports car. Though
he hadn't seen anyone suspicious, the area looked like
a prime target for crime. He couldn't imagine how on
earth Robin had gotten involved with anyone from
this locale.

The lady apparently had a green thumb, he thought
as he surveyed her small square of earth. Late summer
flowers were everywhere, blooming in great untidy
bursts of color all around the border of the little yard,
growing through the sagging picket fence. A pink
rambler rose completely blotted out the sunlight from
a full half of the rickety board porch that stretched
across the front of the place. There were a few rotted
boards on the porch floor that had broken through and
he stayed close to her front door, hoping that the
owner had had the sense to keep the main entry where
people walked in better repair than the rest.

He put his finger on the bell and pressed hard. No
answering sound alerted the occupants of a visitor.
Pulling open the torn screen door, he rapped sharply
at the wooden door. A surprisingly clean white lacy
curtain blocked his view through the window in the
upper part of the door. Still hearing no sound of anyone walking toward the door, he rapped again.
''Hello? Anyone home?''

''Just a moment.'' The voice was feminine, faraway and distinctly frustrated.

He waited impatiently, glancing twice at his watch
before a rustling at the curtain preceded the opening
of the inner door. A face stared out at him.

Garrett stared back. She wasn't what he'd expected.
At all. Actually, he hadn't known what to expect, but

this—this *wood nymph* wasn't it. It was a fanciful thought for a man who dealt largely in numbers, but it was strangely appropriate.

For one thing, she wasn't nearly as old as he'd expected any acquaintance of Robin's to be. For another, she was one of the most strikingly beautiful women he'd ever seen. Even with her red-gold tangle of tresses jammed into a messy pile atop her head and corkscrew curls escaping to bob wildly around her small, heart-shaped face, she was beautiful. Her eyes were an arresting vivid blue-green, large and lushly lashed, with brows that rose above them on her high forehead like perfect crescents. Her cheekbones were slanted, her little chin almost too pointy. But her mouth was full and pink in contrast to the rest of her creamy satin complexion.

And for yet a third thing, she was, well, *stacked* was the only word that sprang to mind. Beneath a soft jade T-shirt that brought out the color in her eyes and the casual jean shorts was a lithe, curvaceous figure that even the baggiest of shirts couldn't hide.

And hers wasn't baggy. If anything, it had been washed once too often and had shrunk a size or two. The shirt was ripped across one shoulder, baring an expanse of silky-looking skin that made him want to reach through the torn screen and touch. In her hands she carried a handful of multicolored ribbon that fluttered and clung to her body as she moved. One silky strand had flipped upward to curl around her left breast, outlining the full, rounded mound and his gaze followed the path of the ribbon as he tried to fathom her connection to his stepfather.

Abruptly he faced the truth he'd been hoping hadn't been true at all: this woman must have been Robin's lover. Why else would he have been seeing someone so young and…unsuitable for him?

Belatedly he realized that he was staring at her. He flushed, annoyed with himself.

"May I help you?" Her gaze was direct and unsmiling, her words clearly enunciated in a prim British accent.

"I'm looking for Ana Birch."

"You've found her." Her voice was deliberate. "I'm on a bit of a schedule—" schedule came out "shedule," in the British fashion "—and I'm really not interested in whatever it is you're selling." She began to turn away.

"Oh, I think you'll be interested in this," Garrett said in a grim tone, remembering why he had come to this dreary little neighborhood in search of her. "My name is Garrett Holden. Are you acquainted with Robin Underwood?"

"Garrett!" She held out a hand and her face altered immediately, breaking into a blinding smile that completely transformed her serious, intense expression into one of beauty and warmth. Lively intelligence and a hopeful light shone from her eyes as she opened the door and stepped onto the porch, looking past him. "Robin's spoken of you often. Is he with you?"

Garrett stared at her for a moment, ignoring her offered hand as her smile faltered. She didn't know. *She didn't know.* A fierce wave of anger and grief roared through him like a wind-fueled fire. "Robin's dead," he said shortly.

"Wha...?" She put a hand to her throat as ribbons slithered to the floor. She shook her head slowly, speaking carefully. "I'm sorry. I believe I must have misunderstood."

He stared at her coldly, not bothering to hide the contempt he felt. "You didn't misunderstand."

Her eyes widened, the pupils going black with shock. Every ounce of pink drained from her face, and he was absently surprised at just how much color she'd really had before. Now she was white as paper. She groped for the porch rail, then carefully lowered herself onto it in a seated position. The whole time, her gaze never left his. "Please tell me this is a very bad joke," she whispered.

He shook his head. He suppressed the feelings of guilt and sympathy that rose within him, reminding himself that this woman didn't need his sympathy. Unless it was to console her on the loss of the wealthy catch she'd been hoping to land.

"What happened?" Her voice was nearly soundless.

"Heart attack," he said succinctly. "He just didn't wake up. The doctor says he doubted he even felt anything." He didn't know why he'd added that last, except that he was human, after all, and the woman in front of him, whatever her motives, looked genuinely stricken by the news. Then again, maybe she was saying goodbye to the loss of the fortune she'd probably been expecting to harvest once she'd talked the old man around to marriage.

She was shaking her head as if she could deny the reality of his words. Straightening, she crossed her arms, hugging herself and appearing to shrink into a smaller presence. "When is the funeral?"

Nonplussed, it took him a moment to respond. Surely she hadn't expected to be invited to attend. "It was yesterday."

If it were possible for her to lose any more color, she did. She turned away from him and he could see her shoulders begin to shake. Then her knees slowly gave way and she sagged to the floor.

Garrett reacted instinctively. Leaping forward, he caught her as she crumpled. The essential male animal beneath the civility of centuries momentarily clouded his mind as his brain registered the close press of yielding female flesh, the rising scent of warm woman—

She squeaked and yanked herself away from him. She hadn't fainted, as he'd first assumed. And now her face wasn't white, it was a bright, unbecoming red as she flushed with embarrassment.

He only noted it with half his brain, because the other half was still processing the moment before.

Then sanity returned. God, he was disgusting. This woman had been his stepfather's...plaything. His seventy-three-year-old stepfather and this...how old was she? Twenty? Twenty-one? And here he was, enthralled by her body as well. He was truly disgusting. And so was she. No way could she have been sexually aroused by, or satisfied by Robin. Yuck. It didn't even bear thinking about.

She was backing away from him as his thoughts ran wild. "Excuse me, please. I have to...have to go inside."

"Wait—"

But he was too late. She'd fled, yanking open the rickety screen and the door behind it with incredible speed and slamming both behind her. He was left staring at the undulating lace curtain that covered the door's window. Ribbon still lay strewn across the porch.

He swore. "Miss Birch? I have to talk to you." He raised his voice. "Miss Birch?"

No answer.

Then he heard the faint sound of weeping. Deep, harsh, stuttering sobs underscored with unmistakable grief. The kind of sounds it would have been unmanly for him to have made, though he'd felt like it a time or two since Robin's manservant had come to him four days ago and reported that the master appeared to have passed away during the night.

Well, that killed any hope that she'd return. No woman with swollen eyes and a runny nose would willingly be seen in public. Dammit!

He pulled a business card and his gold pen from his pocket and scrawled a note across the back of it: *You are mentioned in the will. Call me.*

That ought to get results, he thought cynically as he strode back to his car, glad to be leaving the dingy, depressing area with its faint air of menace. In fact, he'd lay odds that he heard from her before the end of the day. If she thought there was money involved, the grief-stricken act would fly out the window in a hurry.

He unlocked his sleek bronze foreign car and drove back toward the beltway.

Thirty minutes later, he pulled into the quiet green oasis of the peaceful, shaded cemetery near Silver Spring where Robin had been buried the day before. Parking his car along the verge, he walked over the spongy earth to the fresh gravesite.

"Well, you've managed to surprise me, old man," he said aloud, thrusting his hands into the pockets of his suit pants. "How the hell you managed to keep up with something as young as that, I'll never know. No wonder you had a heart attack."

The flowers had wilted considerably just since yesterday in the humid July weather and he made himself a note to call the groundskeeper of the cemetery and ask him to remove them soon. He'd rather see bare earth than these pitiful reminders of mortality.

"I wasn't ready," he said gruffly. "I wasn't ready for you to go yet." It was the first time he'd allowed himself to think about what he'd lost. Dealing with the medical examiner, the funeral arrangements, and the never-ending calls from sympathetic well-wishers had helped him to avoid thinking about the loss of the man who had taken a rebellious teenage stepson in hand and given him self-respect and love. Now, the grief rose up and squeezed his chest until he could barely breathe, and he leaned heavily on the gravestone that had yet to have Robin's date of death inscribed beside his first wife's.

"Why?" he said. "What was so important about this woman that you put her in the will? Were you that lonely?"

It was possible, he supposed. Legions of aging men had been taken in by the solicitous attentions of glow-

ing young beauties who professed devotion. He
should know. Hadn't it happened to his very own father? Of course, there was one significant difference
between the current situation and the past. Robin
hadn't left a wife and a small child for the sake of a
younger woman. Another was, of course, the age difference. Robin must have been nearly fifty years older
than his paramour, a fact Garrett simply couldn't
seem to wrap his mind around.

Sighing, he laid a hand on the marble of the stone,
still cool even in the heat of the summer. "I don't
begrudge you any happiness you might have found
with someone who cared for you. But the thought of
a woman taking deliberate advantage of your loneli-
ness makes me damn mad." He paused, wondering
why he felt so guilty. "If I neglected you, I am
sorry," he said. True, he'd been busy in the past few
years, but he'd always made time for Robin. Hadn't
he?

Yes. He had, he confirmed as he searched his soul,
and he shouldn't have regrets on that score. If anything, Robin had been the one who had been too busy
recently for the several-times-weekly dinners they'd
often shared. Robin had been the one who had had
plans and had taken a rain check on a number of
occasions. He'd been happier in the last year before
his death than he'd been since Garrett's mother had
died, his step more youthful, his still-handsome features smiling even more than usual. Garrett even had
teased him about having a woman on several occasions, but Robin simply had smiled and lifted his eyebrows mysteriously…until last week.

Last Tuesday, just days before his death, Robin had responded in a different way to Garrett's teasing.

"I'll introduce you to her soon," he'd promised. "I believe you'll like her." The use of the feminine pronoun had confirmed Garrett's hunch. But he'd envisioned someone, well, someone older, more mature, a dignified, pleasant matron. *Not* the very young woman with the cover girl measurements and flawless complexion who looked young enough to be his daughter. Or even more likely, his granddaughter. True, Robin had been good-looking and modestly wealthy, in great physical shape for his age, or so everyone had thought. And it also was true that any number of lonely widows had let him know his attentions would be welcome. But it was a little too much to believe that a fresh-faced girl in her twenties would find him irresistibly attractive.

Unless she had her eye on Robin's fortune. *That* was a far more likely scenario. Robin's assets might have been modest in comparison to the huge financial coffers he, Garrett, had amassed, but Robin was definitely a wealthier man than most. It was more than possible that a young woman would look at that money and consider a few years with an older man worth the price.

He supposed he should be glad Robin hadn't married her. After Garrett's mother, Barbara, his second wife, passed away two years ago, Robin had said he would never marry again. But still…a man in his early seventies might have physical needs to fulfill. Considering he hoped to reach that age someday, he surely hoped so.

He stirred and stood, straightening his shoulders and a deep shudder of revulsion worked through him. *Don't go there.* He'd have to talk to Miss Ana Birch again, despite the deep disgust he felt at the mere thought of Robin with that nubile seductress. The lawyer who served as Robin's executor had been very clear in his instructions. There would be no discussion of the terms of Robin's will unless Miss Birch and Garrett both were present.

When he returned to the house he'd shared with his stepfather, he went straight to his study and reached for the telephone. "Miss Birch, this is Garrett Holden, Robin's stepson," he said when she answered the phone. "You are required to attend the reading of the will—"

"No." Her voice was final. "You can have anything he left me. Send whatever you need me to sign and I'll do it."

And before he could even begin another sentence, she hung up. She was giving up an inheritance?

He stared at the phone he still held, torn between wishing that he wouldn't have to see her again and annoyance at her attitude. He didn't get it. Impatiently he punched the redial button. When she said, "Hello?" he said, "You don't understand. You have to be there."

"I do not." She sounded belligerent now. "Please don't call again." And to his utter astonishment, she hung up on him a second time.

Once he'd gotten past the shock, he thoughtfully replaced the handset in its cradle. Fine. He'd go and see her again. He'd figured her out now. She must want money, and she was being coy and devious in an effort to disguise her greediness. Despite her protestations, he suspected that she already knew the provisions of the will, at least as they concerned her. Which meant she knew more than he did. He'd just have to promise her more than whatever sum Robin had already promised her and she'd get more agreeable.

He rested his elbows on his desk and speared his hands through his dark hair, massaging his scalp. He'd had a nagging headache for the past few days and it didn't seem to be getting any better. It was probably all the stress.

Once the will was settled and he didn't have so many urgent things to attend to, he promised himself a week at the cottage in Maine. The small cabin that looked out over Snowflake Lake in southern Maine had been a special place for Robin and his stepson. Garrett knew he'd built it about a quarter-century ago. He'd long suspected it had been Robin's only indulgence, the single respite he had allowed himself from the burden his first marriage had become as his wife's mental illness had progressed until she'd finally passed away.

Garrett's own mother had had little interest in spending her vacations in a rustic cottage where the principal entertainment consisted of fishing and watching the sunsets. She'd always refused to come to Maine. So the cabin had become a place where Garrett and Robin went at least once a year for what Robin laughingly had called, "Boys' Week." They swam in the frigid lake, fished and canoed around its perimeter looking for wildlife, settled on the deck with drinks and plenty of insect repellent each evening, and gone for the occasional jaunt to the surrounding tourist locations.

Yes, a week at the cottage was just what he needed. It would be difficult without Robin, but in some ways, he felt he'd be closer to his stepfather than he was here in Baltimore where they'd spent the bulk of their lives together.

He drove back into the city in early evening, thanking the long hours of daylight that kept him from making the journey in the dark. This time when he knocked, the inner door opened almost immediately.

"Miss Birch," he said before she could speak, infusing his tone with more warmth than he felt, "I apologize for the insensitive way I broke the news of Robin's passing. It's been a difficult time. May I come in and talk to you for a few moments?"

She hesitated. He couldn't see her clearly through the screen, but she'd obviously changed clothes. Now she wore a sleeveless denim jumper with a short-sleeved top beneath. Her hair was still pulled up, but now it was in a tidier, thick ponytail that bounced behind her head. To his great relief, she pushed open the door. Wordlessly she turned and retreated into the house, leaving him to catch the door and follow her.

The room he entered was a living room, furnished with comfortably overstuffed furniture in a faded flower pattern, threadbare but clean. The small space somehow managed to look uncluttered and on the one

sizable wall there was an unusual collection of hats.
Old hats. Elegant, vintage hats.

She shut the door behind him and he heard the hum
of an air-conditioner cooling the small half-house.

He raised one eyebrow and turned to her, forcing
himself to ignore the leap of his pulse at the porcelain
beauty of her features. Indicating the headgear displayed on the wall, he said, "You like hats, I take
it?"

She nodded. "I went through a stage where I collected them. Those were a few of my favorites that I
decided to keep when I sold the rest." She waved a
hand toward the sofa. "Please, have a seat. May I get
you a drink?"

If this were any other occasion, he'd have been
amused by her scrupulous manners. He shook his
head. "No, thank you." He took a seat on the far end
of the couch, expecting her to join him, but she went
across the room and sat in a rocking chair.

"Thank you for seeing me," he said, though it
grated that he had to be so civil. "Have you given
any more thought to what I said about listening to the
reading of the will?"

"I don't care about the will," she said tonelessly.
"But I'd like to know where he's buried so I can visit
the—the grave."

Right. And he was a little green man. "I care about
the will," he said, watching her closely, "since it
involves me, too."

"You can have everything." Her accent was even
more obvious as she clipped off the syllables, and she
met his eyes without even a hint of guile. She was

good; he'd have to give her that. "I'll sign anything you wish."

"Believe me, I'd like nothing better," he told her curtly, abandoning his attempts to mollify her. What an act. "Unfortunately it's not that simple. We both have to be present for the reading of the will."

"Why?" she demanded.

He opened his mouth to answer her, but a hissing sound and a movement from his peripheral vision distracted him. Glancing over, he caught sight of a striped blur streaking up the stairs. "What's that?" he said, startled, though he was pretty sure the animal had been a cat.

"It's my cat. She's not very friendly yet."

"Yet?"

"I found her lying on the road. Someone hit her and drove away. She was still alive when I finally got to a veterinary clinic. So when she was well enough to come home, I brought her here. She's good company."

"She doesn't seem overly tame."

"She was wild, I think." Ana Birch's face had lost its impassive mask; her eyes brightened and she became more animated as she spoke of the animal. He felt an unwilling tug of attraction; she really was a beautiful woman. "But she's getting used to me."

"Why didn't you just let her go where you found her if she's so wild?"

"She needs seizure medication. She was struck in the head and the vet thinks the damage may be permanent. Besides, she's missing half her teeth on one side and she can't eat anything but very soft foods with any ease. She probably wouldn't survive out-doors.'' Then the soft loveliness faded and her features became set and unreadable once again. ''So why is it so imperative that I attend this will-reading ceremony or whatever one calls it?''

He shrugged. ''That's the way Robin wanted it. He set it up with his lawyer and I've spoken with the man. He refuses to divulge anything unless we're both present.''

She was frowning at him, her light brown eyebrows drawn into a slanting scowl. ''So if I refuse to attend, you get nothing? Is that how it works?''

''Probably,'' he told her, though he was certain of no such thing.

''That old rotter,'' she muttered.

''I beg your pardon?'' he said, startled.

''He knew I wouldn't want anything. He knew I'd refuse, so this way at least I have to hear what he wanted me to hear or you'll lose your inheritance, too. And he knew I wouldn't let that happen.''

An unexpected pang of pure green-eyed jealousy squeezed his heart. There was no doubt in his mind now that whatever their relationship, she'd known—and understood—Robin quite well. Masking his thoughts behind an impassive expression, he focused on the only thing that mattered. ''So you'll come?''

She sighed. ''I suppose. When and where?''

When Ana arrived the next morning, Robin's step-son was already in the lawyer's waiting area. He stood with his back to her, looking out the far window as Ana came down the hall, and she observed him through the plate glass of the office front before she entered.

The set of his shoulders looked as rigid as the man's attitude. A lump rose in her throat as she thought of how certain Robin had been that Garrett would welcome her to the family. It was the only time in the short few years she'd known Robin that he'd been so completely wrong about something.

Robin. She tilted her face up to contain the tears that wanted to escape.

She couldn't believe her father was gone. They'd had so little time together. Oh, she'd known he was older than he looked. In fact, she'd been shocked when he'd told her his age on his last birthday. He had been seventeen years older than her mother. She knew her mother had been more than thirty when they met, which would have made him in his late forties. A large disparity, but at those ages, still quite plausible.

Perhaps they had finally found each other again, her father and her mother. And that thought, strangely, calmed her as nothing else had.

She glanced again at Robin's stepson, technically her own stepbrother, she supposed and as she did, he turned and saw her. When their eyes met, a small *zing* of awareness exploded along her nerve endings. She'd felt it the first time he'd come around, and the second. But now, as then, she'd brushed it away. So what if the man was attractive? He'd proven his beauty to be no more than skin-deep with his nasty attitude. Still, she couldn't help wishing they'd met under different circumstances.

The sense of loss she'd felt since he'd told her of her father's death intensified as she thought of the day he'd come to her house. For months, she'd imagined the day that Robin introduced her to Garrett. She'd built comfortable, civilized little images of a brotherly type, of the three of them sharing holiday dinners and warm, informal get-togethers.

She had never imagined that the first time they'd meet would be under these circumstances. She still couldn't accept that she'd missed Robin's funeral.

And Garrett couldn't be less brotherly if he tried. He'd been so curt and obnoxious yesterday that she'd wanted only to ignore him and hope he'd go away. And to top it all off, she'd nearly fainted like a ninny and when he'd tried to help she'd acted like a skittish virgin. Could this get any worse?

That was probably spitting in the eye of fate, she decided. For the sake of Robin's memory, she was going to try her very best to get along with Garrett.

Though they hadn't been related, he actually looked more like her father than she did. And her father had been a handsome man. Garrett's hair was dark, cut short and severe, and his face was long and leanly molded. He was dressed in an expensive-looking black suit and she suddenly realized that he strongly resembled the most recent actor to portray James Bond in the movies. Unfortunately the resemblance didn't carry over to personality. Garrett's stormy blue eyes regarded her with distinct animosity, and she wondered again what on earth she could have done to make him dislike her. As far as she knew,

Robin hadn't told him about her yet at the time of his death.

She wasn't going to let his attitude cow her, though. He'd insisted she attend this ridiculous will-reading—how archaic was that, anyhow? Why couldn't the lawyer simply have called her and told her whatever was so important? Garrett didn't appear even to have considered the fact that she might have to work, or have plans of her *own*.

In fact, both were true. She had the day off from her job as a teller at a local bank, although she did have to work this evening at the restaurant where she was a waitress. But she had planned to work today anyhow, in another sense.

Two days ago, she'd received a call from the agent who had approached her about doing a book on the history of hats after she'd given a lecture at a local college's textiles fair. The man had an editor at a New York publishing house who was very interested in seeing her ideas for the book.

The phone call had left her buoyant and giddy, although frustrated and apprehensive at the same time. She'd been thinking about the project ever since—and that's about as far as she'd gotten.

It drove her crazy that she had so little time for anything other than simply making ends meet. Since her mother's death three years ago shortly after Ana's twentieth birthday, there had been more bills to pay and less time for designing the line of hats and handbags she'd started. Almost none, in fact.

Her accessories currently were sold at two exclusive boutiques in the Baltimore area and both retailers had told her they could sell anything she could give them. Some days her fingers itched for a pencil and a sketchpad when she was struck by yet another idea or theme for her unique creations. Invariably she was in the car on the way to work, or counting money, or carrying plates of food to a table when it happened. She didn't know how she was going to do it, but she was determined to find more time to design and sew. If she had the smallest hope of becoming a serious artisan, even making a living from her work, she *had* to produce more. Acquire wider recognition.

Publishing a book would certainly help with that goal if she could find the time to fit it in.

She could have worked this morning. And yet, here she was, stuck in an office with a man who couldn't stand her. The feeling was rapidly becoming mutual.

He strode toward the door before she moved to open it, yanking it wide. "Come in. We've been waiting for you."

Irked by his inference, she made a show of checking her watch. "Goodness. You're early, too. Here I thought I'd be the one cooling my heels."

If she'd managed to irritate him, he didn't show it. "Follow me. They've reserved a conference room for us." Without waiting for her answer, he turned and swiftly moved off through the suite of offices, leaving her to follow or be hopelessly lost in the rabbit warren of corridors through which they passed. Feeling rebellious, Ana stuck out her tongue at his broad back as she hurried along behind him. Immediately she felt the urge to giggle. She'd been mocking Garrett Holden!

She would have known his name even if he hadn't been her father's stepson. He was extraordinarily wealthy, reputed to have parlayed a small stock market windfall into the immense assets he held today. In accordance with Americans' vulgar fascination with piles of money, he often made the pages of both gossipy newsmagazines as well as more serious financial tomes. His name had been linked to some very high-profile ladies from the entertainment world as well as the young women whose families inhabited the raritied world in which he lived, but there had never been one who lasted more than a few months, according to Robin.

"He's never confided in me," Robin had said to her once, "but he wasn't always so cynical about relationships. I suspect the change might have stemmed from a bad experience with a woman who wanted his money. It's amazing what a whiff of wealth will do to supposedly decent people."

Now that she'd met him, she couldn't imagine a woman actually *wanting* to spend time with Grumpy Garrett on a regular basis. She'd rather be boiled in oil.

Two

They settled into two stately leather chairs before Mr. Marrow's desk. The lawyer peered over the top of reading glasses at them after examining Ana's driver's license and being satisfied that she really was who she'd said she was.

"Robin's wishes were a bit...unusual," the man began.

"In what way?" Garrett clearly was used to being the one to direct things.

"Perhaps Mr. Marrow will tell us if you don't interrupt him," she said sweetly. When Garrett sent her a seething glance, she smiled at him, determined to show him his antagonism didn't unsettle her in the least.

The lawyer cleared his throat. "I'll dispense with the legalese and explain this in plain English. The disposition of Mr. Robin Underwood's assets is as follows: To Garrett Wilbur Holden, Robin gives all his worldly goods, possessions and monies with the exception of those specifically designated in this will.''

Wilbur? His middle name was *Wilbur?* She smothered a bubble of hysterical laughter that threatened to pop right out of her. At her side, Garrett's elegantly clad foot stopped the ceaseless tapping motion it had been making since he'd sat down. She supposed what he'd just heard had reassured him that she wasn't going to get any breathtaking bequest that would threaten his inheritance. Although why Garrett Holden needed to worry about inheriting money was beyond her. Though she was a pragmatic person who accepted the way fate had shaped her life, she couldn't help but think of the difference that even a small amount of money could have made to her.

Her attention returned to Marrow as he plowed on with his explanations. ''To Ana Janette Birch, Robin gives one half of the property known as Eden Cottage on Snowflake Lake in the state of Maine, in the county of—''

''What?'' Garrett sprang to his feet, his tone outraged. ''What kind of crazy bequest is that? It makes no sense. Why would Robin give her half the cottage?''

She sat up straighter in her chair, equally astonished at the gift. A *cottage?*

Mr. Marrow held up one finger for silence. ''Additionally, Ana is to receive a sum commensurate with the total of her rent and utility bills for the Bal-

timore home as well as a living allowance for the
thirty-one-day period immediately after her residence
in Snowflake Cottage is established.''

''What?'' Now it was her turn to interrupt the man.
She lived in Baltimore!

''To Garrett, Robin bequeaths the other half of
Eden Cottage. There is, however, a condition attached
to the transfer of ownership to each of you. If each
person named herein is unmarried, for a thirty-one-
day period beginning no later than one week from the
reading of this will, Ana Birch and Garrett Holden
are to cohabitate at the cottage.'' The man's prim
voice and stuffy language gave the word ''cohabitate'' overtones that echoed uncomfortably through
the spacious office.

There was a dead silence in its wake. A *tense* silence.

''I hope this is Robin's idea of a joke,'' Garrett
finally said, and there was a restrained fury in his tone
that made Ana want to move her chair to the far side
of the room. ''He can't have been serious. Why in
God's name would he want Ana and me to live together?'' He turned to face her. ''It's unenforceable.
This can't be legal.''

''I'm afraid he was deadly serious and it is fully
legal, unless you married previous to the reading of
this document,'' Marrow said. ''You did not. Nor did
Miss Birch. My job was to ensure that. If either of
you should refuse to comply with the requests contained in the document, you both will lose the property and it will be sold, proceeds to benefit a charity
also specified herein.'' The lawyer clearly was grow-

ing more nervous, his speech reverting to the no doubt comforting dry obfuscation of the legal language in which he dealt. "If you don't wish to accept the conditions, I'll start proceedings to liquidate the cottage and property and arrange to donate—"

"Don't start anything," Garrett said. "We need time to think about this." He paused. "Robin specifically said that she and I are to share the cottage for an entire month? And then each of us will own half of it?"

Marrow nodded.

"May I have a copy?" It wasn't a request, but a royal command.

"Of course." The older man rose. "I'll have one made for each of you right now. Excuse me." And he left the room.

Ana wished *she* could leave the room. When she glanced up, Garrett was staring at her with narrowed eyes. She bit her lip, not knowing what to say. She honestly couldn't blame him for being angry and she felt a surprising spurt of annoyance penetrate the sense of loss she felt for her father. Robin had put them both in an untenable position.

Garrett cleared his throat. "I'm taking this to another legal expert. It can't be as ironclad as that old fool wants us to think. I'm assuming you don't want to be saddled with half a cottage in Maine?"

She shook her head. "Of course not. But—"

"Good. I'll buy you out. Pay you a fair market value for your half."

"You're familiar with this place?"

It was amazing. The moment her words registered,

his face changed. There wasn't a great difference but something…softened. His eyes warmed to a glowing blue. She was astonished. The small shift in his expression made him dangerously compelling and even more seductively attractive than he already was—and he hadn't even smiled. If she were a smart woman, she'd keep him angry, because if he ever directed a look like that at her, she'd probably be his slave for life.

"Robin and I went there together every summer," he said, his eyes unfocused, his face gentler than she'd have thought a man as hard as he appeared to be could manage. "We'd fish and canoe around the lake looking for loons and eagles' nests." Then his gaze cooled as he focused on the present—on her—again. "It means a hell of a lot more to me than it ever will to you."

She wasn't so sure about that. Robin had left her half of the cottage; it must have been very special to him. What was there that he'd wanted her to see badly enough to insist that she share it with her stepbrother for a whole month? And then it struck her. The odd phrasing: "…if each person…is unmarried…"

"I think," she said hesitantly, "I think he might have been trying to set us up."

"Set us up?" Garrett repeated. "As in romantically? You and me?" There was a wealth of disbelief and disgust in his tone. "That's an extraordinarily self-serving bit of wishful thinking. Robin never would have done anything so…so…distasteful."

She flinched, sliced to the bone by his cruelty, not understanding it. "What have I ever done—"

"Or maybe," he said, "it's hopefulness. Did you really think you could hook me after Robin died?"

She sucked in a quick gasp of shock, both at the crude question and the hateful tone in which it was delivered. "I didn't think enough about you to consider the idea." Her voice was shaking and she hated the tears that sprang to her eyes. "And even if I had, you can rest assured that meeting you would have changed my mind instantly."

"Good." He was infuriatingly unfazed by her verbal arrows. "I'll buy out your half of the cottage and as soon as we sign the papers, neither one of us will ever have to see the other again."

"Fine." She stood and marched to the door, not waiting for the lawyer's return. "I can't think of anything I'd like more than signing you out of my life."

It wasn't until she got home that she calmed down enough to think about the ugly scene again. And when she did, her hand flew to her mouth in stunned shock at the implications of his behavior. He didn't know who she was. Or, to put it more accurately, he didn't know *what* she was.

Did you really think you could hook me after Robin died? Emphasis on the *me*.

He thought she was Robin's…his…his lover!

Word by word, expression by expression, she reviewed each moment of the three times they'd met. And as she did, her anger grew. And grew, and *grew*.

How dare he jump to a conclusion like that? Oh, she could admit that it might not be such an illogical one to make, but she knew he'd known Robin for years, ever since Robin had married his mother. How

could he not have trusted Robin's integrity? How
could he even imagine Robin would take up with a
girl of her age? She was *furious* with Garrett for
Robin's sake as much as for her own.

Nasty, bloody-minded pervert. There wasn't a word
bad enough to describe him, with his sewage-for-
brains stupid assumptions. If only she had some way
to make him sorry. How she wished she were a man.
How she wished she could—

She could! She had in her hands a wonderfully
wicked way to pay him back for his rude, callous
actions.

She actually rubbed her hands together, cackling
with glee as she decided how best to flummox Mr.
Gutter-mind Garret Holden. Obviously that property
meant quite a bit to him. He'd shared special moments there with her father. She suffered a pang of
conscience for a moment. Her father had loved Garrett. God knew why, but he had. Still…Garrett apparently hadn't loved or understood Robin as he
should have or he never would have believed for a
minute that his stepfather would have an affair with
her.

And that reminder solidified her desire to pay him
back. She nearly leaped for the phone and called him,
but thank the Lord she came to her senses before she
did. She could wait. She would wait, until *he* was
forced to come to *her*.

He called her the next day, full of unctuous courtesy. It was amusing. She wondered what he *really*
wanted to say, but when he asked if he could come

by that evening, she merely agreed. "It'll have to be after ten, though," she said. "I'm working tonight and I won't be home until then."

"I didn't realize you had a job." His tone was stiff.

Oh, this was too good a chance to miss. "Of course. My schedule changes from week to week, so I never know whether I'm going to be working days or nights or both."

There had been an ominous silence on the other end of the line and she'd had to bite her lip to keep from laughing at his expense. Oh, she couldn't *wait* to tell him who she was. He was going to feel so foolish and she would make certain she was there to see the moment.

But aloud, all she said was, "So I'll see you around ten, then?"

"Ten it is." And he hung up without even a farewell.

That evening, luck was with her and she didn't have any late tables, so she was home shortly before ten. She took a quick shower to rid herself of the food odors, dried her hair enough to scrunch wild curls around her face, and sprayed herself liberally with her favorite scent, an expensive one she wore rarely but figured was appropriate for this evening. Then she dressed in a white silk blouse cut in a discreet vee, a slim, short black skirt, and a pair of high-heeled pumps that made her legs look a mile long. Battle gear. She supposed she might look like an expensive hooker, if that's what one was predisposed to think. The doorbell rang just as she was walking down her narrow staircase.

"Good evening," she said as she opened the door. "Please come in."

"Your home needs some work," Garrett said without even greeting her.

"Yes. It's getting rather shabby," she agreed.

"The porch needs to be repaired," he pointed out, "and the whole place could stand to be painted."

"I'm sure it could." She smiled brightly at him. "Would you like to sit down?"

He came in and took the exact same seat he'd taken before on her couch. "You could do a lot to this place with the money I'll pay you for the cabin."

"I'm sure I could," she agreed. "If I owned it."

She'd managed to surprise him and it showed. "You don't? I just assumed…"

"You're quite good at that," she said pleasantly.

She watched with gleeful eyes as he fought back a snarl. Finally he said, "If you don't own it, who does?"

"The landlord." She waited a moment until he looked ready to explode. Then she smiled innocently. "We moved here from England when I was ten and my mother bought the place. It was a reasonably nice little neighborhood then." Her smile faded. "Mother died three years ago and I needed money. I didn't care to stay here permanently. The area's getting seedier and seedier. So I sold it with a provision that I be able to rent it for up to five years." But she didn't tell him about her mother and Robin. She might never. He didn't deserve to know.

"All right," he said impatiently. "So you don't have to take care of a property. That should make the money even more appealing. You can bank it. Travel.''

"Go back to school," she suggested.

His eyebrows rose. "If that interests you." He paused. "Does it?"

"No," she said serenely. "I don't need additional education to further my life plan."

"I just bet you don't," he murmured.

Now that she knew what he was thinking, cryptic comments like that made sense. He'd been insulting her steadily and until recently, she hadn't even known it. She felt her blood begin to boil again and she pushed the anger away, concentrating instead on this chance to rattle him. "So when do we leave?" she asked.

"What?"

"When do we leave?" she repeated as if he were a bit slow. "For Eden Cottage. What a pretty name. I can't wait to see it. It must have been a very special place for Robin to consider it Eden."

"*We* aren't going anywhere," he said. "I've already dropped off the will at another legal firm. I expect them to be able to get us out of that insane clause. Then I'll buy you out and we'll be done with it."

"Buy me out?" She widened her eyes. "Oh, did I forget to mention my change of plans?"

He regarded her with distrust. "Apparently. What change?"

She cleared her throat, enjoying the moment. "I've decided not to sell my half. It was special to Robin so I've decided to keep it."

"I thought you needed money." His voice was tight, as if someone were squeezing his neck hard enough to affect his vocal cords.

"I do, but not that desperately," she said. "If we go to Maine for a month, it's essentially an all-expenses-paid vacation for me. We can chat at the end of that time if I've changed my mind." She stood. "I hate to throw you out, but I've had an exhausting day."

He stood, too, but instead of heading for the door he stalked across the room in her direction. "If I can get that clause changed, you'll have half a cabin and *no* free ride. And I'll expect you to pay half of all taxes and expenses related to the cabin's upkeep."

"Even if you get that clause changed," she said blithely, "I probably still will go. Maybe I'll even move there permanently. Owning half a cabin in Maine has to be less expensive than renting in Baltimore."

He practically was foaming at the mouth, he was that angry. She watched his hands clench and unclench at his sides, fascinated by his battle for control. "We're not done discussing this," he warned her before he stomped out.

He heard from the other lawyer late the next afternoon and when he ended the conversation, it was all he could do not to throw the phone across the room. His temper was short these days and he knew at least part of the reason why. He hadn't slept well since Robin had died. Though he'd managed not to wallow in grief during the day, he'd had vivid dreams of his

stepfather every night, dreams that always ended with
Robin closing a door in his face or disappearing
around a corner.

It didn't take a psychologist to figure out that he
was trying to work through his sense of loss at
Robin's unexpected death. Still, between the lack of
rest and this business with that stupid will Robin had
made... Once again he went back over the will's specific provisions. Every lawyer who had seen the language of the will had been of the same opinion: unless
there was some clear question about Robin's sanity
at the time he had it drawn up, it was perfectly legal,
perfectly enforceable.

Since Robin unquestionably had been quite sane, it
looked as if there was no way to win a challenge to
his wishes.

He sighed, the anger draining from him. How in
hell was he going to stand thirty-one days in Maine
with her? He couldn't imagine being cooped up in the
small cottage with Ana Birch for more than four
weeks. Still, he supposed there was no use in pro-
longing the inevitable. He'd survive it.

When he called, Ana answered her phone.
"Hello?"

"I've had an answer from the other lawyer about
Robin's will." He didn't bother to identify himself or
to wait for her to speak. He hated eating crow but he
supposed he'd had it coming. "It can't be changed.
So we're going to be stuck with each other."

"When do we leave?" She didn't sound smug or
superior, just interested.

"*I'm* leaving tomorrow morning. I can't speak for

you.'' Surely she didn't think he'd spend sixteen hours in a car with her. ''But the sooner you get up there, the faster this farce will be over.''

He hung up and immediately called his house-keeper to instruct her to start packing. Now that he'd made up his mind, he wanted to get to the cottage as fast as possible. Before Ana, that was for sure. He had a sneaking suspicion that if she arrived first, she might just take his favorite bedroom out of spite.

The following evening, he pulled off the small country road and took the long central lane back to the smaller, rougher track that wound another half-mile along the lakeshore to Eden Cottage. There was a porch light on, waiting to greet him through the dusk, and he reminded himself to give the caretakers a bonus next month. The old man and his wife who looked after the place had cleaned it and brought in a few groceries earlier as he'd asked when he'd called to tell them he was coming.

He'd left at dawn and driven with only the most necessary stops the whole day. He was glad it was summertime, still light outside. He got out of the car and stretched, looking down the steep hillside at the flashes of silvery water revealed through the white-trunked birches. He'd pushed himself for a reason. Much later and he'd have had to wait until morning to see this view.

The cottage was perched above the lake with decks on three sides. It was surrounded by towering trees and from the back, looked quite unprepossessing. It had been built into the hill so that the second-floor section that jutted out to the back had a wide garage-style door at what was ground level there, so that the boats and outside furniture and supplies could be stored there through the winter.

He walked down the hill a little way and stepped out onto a rocky outcrop above a small pebble-beached cove. *Ahhh.* He took a deep, cleansing breath of the fresh, pine-scented air. "It's good to be here," he said aloud. As he stood motionless, absorbing the utter peace that was one of the hallmarks of the little lake, the eerie laugh of a loon floated out over the water.

Garrett chuckled in response. This wouldn't be so bad. Even though he'd arranged to have an office's worth of equipment, including fax and computer, delivered tomorrow, he'd still feel like he was on an extended vacation. But the momentary buoyancy faded as he envisioned himself sharing the small rooms with Robin's little fling.

The stutter of a poorly tuned engine could be heard in the distance, and he looked around, distracted from his annoyance. The sound was rare enough to make him scan the lake with a frown. Usually, back this far, there was little to suggest other humans were around. Only canoes and rowboats were allowed on the lake and there was a bare handful of other homes scattered along the shores. When summer ended, nearly all of those would empty out as summer residents returned to their real lives again.

The engine grew louder instead of fading, and he turned. It almost sounded as if someone were heading toward his cottage. But unless the caretaker had forgotten something, he couldn't imagine why anyone would be back here. There were clear No Trespassing signs posted both at the end of his small lane and at the larger one that led to the road.

He surged up the bank, reaching his own sturdy four-wheel-drive vehicle just as headlights played across the cottage and red brake lights flared. A door opened and a figure straightened from the driver's seat of a small, battered-looking car.

"This is absolutely beautiful!" Ana Birch said.

Garrett just stared at her. How in the hell had she managed to get organized fast enough to arrive here at practically the same time he had? He'd never known a woman who could pack and travel in less than a day's time. His mother would have needed at least a week to get ready. And that would have been pushing it.

"Have you been here long?" She bent and touched her toes in one lithe motion, drawing his eyes to the long, smooth line of her back beneath the T-shirt she wore. As she placed her palms flat on the ground and swayed from side to side to stretch out her back, her bottom stuck up in the air in an incredibly provocative manner. He caught himself in the middle of wondering just how limber she really was and banished the thought. She might have bewitched Robin but he, Garrett, knew what she was.

"I—ah, just arrived." His voice sounded rough and uneven to his own ears. "How did you get here so fast?"

She shrugged, straightening and flipping her hair back over her shoulders, drawing his gaze to the shining, curly mass. "I didn't really have much to worry about," she told him. "I packed everything I thought we'd need, stuffed the cat in a box—"

"The cat! I never said anything about sharing my cabin with a cat."

She shrugged. "I'll just have to keep her in my half, then. As I was saying, I hopped in my car late last night and started driving. When I stopped for breakfast, I called the bank and the restaurant and quit, effective immediately. I can get another job or two like that easily enough when I get back if I need it."

"Jobs? You worked for a bank *and* a restaurant?"

"Some of us don't have a fortune at our disposal," she told him tartly. "What on earth did you think I did for money?"

The question fell into the space between them like a hand grenade with the pin ready to fall out. He bit his tongue, knowing that if he said what he'd thought, there would be open warfare in the cabin for the next month. It was going to be bad enough as it was without picking a fight with her.

"Never mind." She turned away and walked around to the trunk of her car. "I already know the answer to that."

There was an odd, wistful tone in her voice that made him, for one strange moment, feel guilty for the way he'd treated her. Then he reminded himself that she was nothing more than a gold digger, snagging an old man and talking him into putting her in his will. Two jobs...no wonder she was looking for an easier way to make a living. She hadn't really loved

Robin, he was sure. He'd had his own experience with the fickle nature of a woman's love for anything but money, and nothing could convince him otherwise.

"Why do you have two jobs?" He opened his car door as he spoke and lifted out the suitcases.

"Employers don't want to pay benefits so they get around it by hiring part-time help," she said succinctly. She shrugged, and lifted out a large box. "The flexibility works just as well for me."

He started down the path. "Follow me and I'll give you the nickel tour of the cottage. I had the caretakers clean and open it earlier today." But he couldn't keep himself from wondering why she worked two low-paying jobs. She seemed bright enough. Surely she could find something more suitable. *She did,* answered his cynical side. *Bewitching an old man.*

Unaware of his thoughts, she said, "Good idea." She hefted her box with both hands. "I'll have to go and meet them. Did you tell them I'd be arriving?"

"No," he said shortly.

There was silence behind him as they came to the porch. He set down the bags and unlocked the door, then picked them up and shouldered his way through the door, leaving her to follow with her unwieldy box. She wasn't there by his choice, he told himself fiercely, and he wasn't going to spend thirty-one days being courteous, holding doors and carrying everything in sight. In fact, it was probably better if they established ground rules first thing.

He headed straight for the stairs, ignoring her, and took his bags to his bedroom. When he came down again, she was still standing in the living room, looking out through the plate glass at the lake. It was nearly dark now so he knew she couldn't see much.

He said, "The bedroom to the left at the top of the stairs is mine. You can have the other one that has a lake view. The one to the back is—" he caught himself "—was Robin's den."

She nodded.

"This is the living room and back there is the dining area. Those doors lead to the deck. The kitchen's through here and—" he moved through the house "—this is my office. There's a half bathroom in the hall and a full one upstairs. Laundry room is opposite the downstairs bath." He paused as he realized just how intimate this enforced cohabitation was going to be. "Tomorrow we'll make up a schedule of who gets the bathroom and the kitchen at what times. You'll have to help chop and stack wood, too."

Her eyebrows rose. "You don't buy it by the cord?"

He shook his head. "Nope. A lot of it's broken limbs we salvage from the previous winter's storms. If you want to share this place fifty-fifty, you'll have to share half the work." He doubted she was used to lifting a finger to do much more than some light cleaning. After all, she'd sold her own home rather than deal with maintenance and upkeep. Cleaning. "The caretaker's wife comes in once a week to clean," he told her, "but you'll have to do your own laundry, dishes and pick up any messes you make."

She simply nodded.

There was an awkward silence.

"Well," he said. "I guess I'll finish unloading."

Ana awoke to the sound of a bird trilling insistently right outside her window the next morning. The quality of the light coming through her window told her it still was very early. She'd been exhausted after the long drive and unloading her car last night, and she hadn't expected to wake at dawn, but she knew she wouldn't be able to go back to sleep now.

She threw back the light blanket and sheet with which she'd made her bed last night. Roadkill, the cat, leaped off the foot of the mattress where she'd been sleeping with a startled hiss and disappeared beneath the bed. She chuckled. "Relax, girl. I bet you'll come out of there fast enough when I return bearing food." She sat up and put her feet on the floor. *Brrr!* Even in midsummer, the night was cool.

Sliding her feet into sandals, she went to the window. Her bedroom looked out over the lake, and from this floor, she could see the earliest of the sun's rays making the water sparkle and dance, casting outsize shadows from anything in its path. The cabin was situated on the west side of the little lake, facing the sun, and its warmth was just beginning to steal over the horizon. She'd stopped at the little general store for directions and soda last night, and the clerk had told her the lake was small. But looking north and south, she couldn't see either end. Across the lake, there was a wooded shore. Farther down, just one other house peeked from between the trees, its dock floating out from the shore into the water.

A dock. She looked down and saw that Eden Cottage had a dock as well. The sight automatically brought a lump to her throat as childhood memories came flooding back. When she was young, her mother had rented a cabin along the Choptank River each summer for an entire week. It was their one annual splurge. Her mother, Janette, had loved the water and had taught Ana to swim as a very small child. They'd rowed on the river, swam and dived, held weenie roasts on their small stretch of pebbled beach and laid on the dock stargazing after dark.

Those times had been among the best of her life. They'd been anonymous vacationers, not a weird artist from England and her illegitimate child.

She dashed the tears away, annoyed with herself. Those had been good times. There was no reason to cry over them.

But oh, how she missed her mother sometimes.

That thought brought back another memory, and she almost laughed aloud in the quiet morning silence of her new house. Her new *half* a house, she corrected herself. Which half of the dock was hers? The boat? The lake? As she grabbed a towel and went down the stairs on tiptoe so as not to wake her grumpy step-brother—who probably would be even grouchier if she woke him at dawn—she had the whimsical thought that they ought to buy a huge roll of fluorescent orange tape so that they could mark off their boundaries. Because she was fairly sure she was going to have trouble remembering where she was and wasn't allowed to tread.

Except on Garrett's toes. There would be no avoiding that.

She stole out of the house, cussing the squeaking screen door. *Oil for you later, buddy,* she promised. The path from the cottage down to the lakeshore was steep and stony, covered with a slippery layer of pine needles.

Once on the tiny crescent of water-worn rocks that served as a beach, she stood for a moment, inhaling deeply and enjoying the first warmth of the sun on her face. It was going to be a beautiful day. Despite Garrett's unfriendliness, she knew she could be happy here.

She crossed the rocks and walked out onto the dock. Looking up and down the lake, she could see no one. Perfect! She slid her feet out of her sandals, then quickly removed the oversize T-shirt in which she'd slept. Beneath it, she wore nothing. The air was warm and fresh on her body and the sensation brought back more memories from her childhood. Since she didn't know how deep the water was, she used the ladder at the end of the dock to lower herself into the lake, shivering with cold at first.

It was invigorating, though, and she began to swim strongly, energetic strokes up and down past the dock, until she had warmed up again. Garrett hadn't said anything about the lake, whether there were strong currents or hidden rocks, so she stayed fairly close to the dock, although she was an excellent swimmer and probably could have swum to the far shore and back again. At least, she could after a little training. It had been a long time since she'd done any regular swimming.

Finally she was ready to get out of the water. The sky was growing lighter and she was afraid someone might come by if she lingered any longer. As she put her hands on the ladder rungs, she cast an intent, nervous glance up at the house, but nothing stirred. She was pretty sure Garrett was still sleeping. Quickly she climbed the ladder and reached for her towel, drying herself as best she could, then pulling her T-shirt over her head and pushing her arms into the sleeves before wrapping the towel around her. Her body was still wet and the fabric clung to her. Tomorrow, she'd have to wear a robe.

Oh, it was so wonderful here! The moment she'd walked into the cottage, she'd known she couldn't simply sell her half. She'd said that the other day solely to get under Garrett's hide, because it served him right for being so judgmental and hateful. But now…she didn't think she'd ever want to sell it. Not even to Robin's beloved stepson. Robin had left half of this beautiful retreat to her, his daughter, for a reason.

Her good mood was dampened as she thought of her father. She'd gone to the cemetery three times before this abrupt change of address, and though the fresh grave was mute testimony to the reality of her loss, she still couldn't believe he was gone. She was certain that if he'd lived longer, he'd have brought her up here. Thinking of him, trying to imagine him in this place made her eyes burn with the tears she didn't want to start shedding again. She'd barely met him and already she'd lost him. For a heart that had craved the love of a father throughout her whole life, it was a terrible blow. As she hurried up the path to the house, the lump that so quickly rose to her throat these days made it hard to swallow.

Three

Garrett stood at the large plate glass window in the living room, his body quickening with elemental male interest. He still wasn't sure what had awakened him, but he was damn glad he hadn't succumbed to the urge to go back to sleep. He set his coffee cup down on the windowsill, shaking his head in disbelief and pure sensual appreciation.

There were some experiences every man ought to have before he died and a moment like this was one of them. It was no wonder Robin had been taken in by this temptress, he thought as he watched Ana prepare to emerge from the water. If he didn't know what women like her really were after, he might have been hoodwinked himself in similar circumstances.

The water receded as she steadily climbed the ladder down at the dock. She had an absolutely beautiful body, with high, plump breasts and a tiny, nipped-in waist that flared to smoothly rounded hips and long, slender thighs and legs. Everything, however, was scaled down to perfect proportion for a woman as petite as she was. She probably wasn't more than five foot two, if that. He really ought to look away. He felt uncomfortably like a voyeur…but there was no power in the world that could have torn his gaze away from her just then.

Besides, he reasoned, she'd gone swimming in the nude, right out in plain view in the lake. There could be a dozen people watching her right now, for all she knew. If she hadn't been splashing so much as she swam back and forth, he might never have noticed her in the first place. And if she'd worn a bathing suit like any normal woman, he'd never have stayed glued to the window like this.

He completely disregarded the fact that he'd swum nude in the very same place more times than he could count. He was a man.

He hastily moved away from the window as she came up the path in the clinging, wet T-shirt and large towel. She already thought he was pond scum; what would she think if she realized he'd been watching her?

Why should you care?

He didn't. Of course not. But he headed for the kitchen and began getting himself a bowl of cereal. She was nothing but an interloper, a minor inconvenience, a blip on the radar screen of his life. He knew what she'd said about not selling the place but he also knew she'd get tired of being hidden away up here in the woods real quick once the novelty wore off. And then, when he made her a handsome offer for her half as soon as the time was up, she'd take the money and get out of his life for good.

Sort of the way Kammy had vanished, except that he wasn't stupid enough to be in love with this woman and he wouldn't be devastated when she left. He snorted in disgust. He hadn't thought of Kammy in…well, one hell of a long time. She'd been nothing but another blip on the radar screen, he assured himself. Only difference was, he'd learned a lesson from her: some women would do anything for money.

The squeak of the door warned him that Ana was coming into the house, and he made a point of pouring milk onto his cereal and replacing the container in the refrigerator as she came into the kitchen.

"Good morning." Her voice sounded distinctly wary. "Have you been awake long?"

"Long enough." He deliberately didn't look at her. He already knew she was wearing the wet T-shirt with a large towel wrapped around her sarong-style over top of it, and that her wet hair was clipped atop her head. And he wasn't going to ask her any additional questions that would necessitate further conversation, like how the water was. The less contact he had with her, the better.

There was a short silence, as if she were trying to decipher his meaning. Then she said, "That cereal looks good." She turned to the cupboard and began looking through the dishes. "Where are the bowls?"

"Third cabinet on the left from the sink." He kept his voice cool and casual. "Did you pick up any groceries last night? I left the right side of the refrigerator for your food. Same with the shelves in the pantry. We won't be able to split up the dishes easily— there's only one of most of the cooking utensils—but if we each clean up as soon as we're done using them, we should be able to keep out of each other's way.''

She set down a bowl and turned slowly to face him, her face a porcelain study in disbelief and something that looked suspiciously like…hurt? ''Are you telling me not to eat your food?''

''Of course not,'' he said smoothly. ''If you haven't laid in supplies yet, feel free to use some of mine. The store opens at ten, I believe.''

''I assumed,'' she said in her precise little accent, ''that we would share meals and food expenses. Wouldn't that be easier than cooking for one all the time?''

''Not for me,'' he said promptly. ''I don't want to have to worry about stopping work to make dinner or coming to the table at a certain time. My hours aren't particularly regular.''

She was still staring at him and there was a clear look of doubt mixed in with the shock. She knew he was lying, knew he simply didn't want to have anything to do with her. As he watched, her gaze dropped and she bit down on her lower lip. Turning back to the cupboard, she slowly replaced the bowl she'd removed and started out of the room.

''Hey,'' he said. ''I told you to feel free to use my stuff until the store opens.''

''Don't be silly.'' She didn't even stop. ''I wouldn't dream of imposing like that.''

He was not going to let the pathetic droop of those shoulders or the quaver in her rich, round tones arouse his sympathy, he lectured himself. She was a hell of an actress. She must have been, to fool Robin so completely. Still, he couldn't quiet the guilty feeling that made him sorry he'd chased her away. She hadn't even eaten any breakfast—no! That was no concern of his. "I'll make up a tentative schedule today," he called after her, "for us to share the common rooms and the light cleaning. You can look over it and we can make changes if something doesn't work for you."

She was through the living room and halfway up the stairs now and he heard her mutter something beneath her breath, though he couldn't make out the words. Somehow he doubted it was a compliment on his efficiency.

He barely saw her for the rest of the day. He took the canoe out of storage and maneuvered it down to the beach. It was a good thing he was the size he was. Someone as petite and delicate as his new housemate could never have done this alone. He felt rather magnanimous. Even though she hadn't helped him, he wasn't going to begrudge her the use of the small craft.

He caught a glimpse of Ana while he was supervising the deliverymen who were bringing his computer equipment through the main entry into the hall and right around the corner into his office. She was staggering down the hill from her car with two huge suitcases. To his surprise, she didn't come through the open door, but disappeared through the other entry that led directly into the kitchen. He saw her repeating the action and several times, heard her footsteps moving up and down the stairs. Shortly after that, she came out and got into her compact car and chugged off out the lane. To the store, he presumed.

After the delivery guys left, he got everything set up the way he liked it, and then sat down to deal with e-mail. His assistant had gotten him set up with the local service provider and so he was able to connect immediately. By then, it was well past lunchtime, so he went downstairs and made himself a couple of sandwiches and some instant lemonade, then carried them back up to his office. The refrigerator was still bare except for the few things he'd bought. He'd have to drive into town later for a full load of groceries. While he ate, he roughed out a tentative schedule for using the kitchen, the laundry and the bathroom. He figured Ana could schedule herself around him, or if she had some real problem with one of the times he'd appropriated, they could discuss it. He was a reasonable guy.

Ana still hadn't come back by the time he left to drive into town. He was only aware of it because she shared his home. Maybe she'd gotten lost. She'd never been up here before. A lot of the little winding roads looked alike. If she'd lost her way or had an accident, he would be the logical one for her to call.

Then he remembered the way her lower lip had quivered before she'd bitten fiercely on it in the kitchen earlier. No, she wouldn't call him. Once again the guilt rose and this time he couldn't ignore the little voice that asked: *How would Robin feel about the way you've been treating Ana? He raised you to be a gentleman.*

All right. He could admit that he'd been a real bastard. He'd try harder to be more tolerant, if not outright kind, to her. After all, Robin had cared for her. And as he thought of the spring in the old man's step and his good spirits in the last year of his life, he had to admit that she'd made Robin happier than he'd been since Garrett's mother had died over two years ago.

Whoever, *whatever,* she was, Ana must have been good to Robin. He supposed that was something to be grateful for.

Ana was delighted all out of proportion over the simple discovery of an exceptionally well-stocked fabric and craft store in town. She hadn't needed much, but how wonderful to know it was close enough that if she ran out of something, she wouldn't have to drive halfway through New England to find a store that stocked it. And she'd made her first new friends in Maine.

The proprietor of the store was delighted to meet her and quickly introduced himself. Teddy Wilkens was a young man who didn't look much older than she was. When he found out she was going to be living in the area for a while, he quickly pressed a little buzzer that she could hear faintly, echoing in some other part of the two-story shop.

"We live upstairs. We just bought this place at the beginning of the season from a couple who wanted to retire to Florida. It's a thriving business and we're excited about the possibilities,'' Teddy told her as he carefully wrapped and tied her purchases into a large bundle. "Unfortunately my wife is having a difficult pregnancy and doesn't see many people. She'll love it if you can stay and visit for a few minutes.''

"That would be lovely.'' And she meant it. Just then, a hugely pregnant young woman came into the shop through a door in the back. "Nola, this is Ana Birch, who's living out on Snowflake Lake.''

"Pleased to meet you.'' Nola Wilkens smiled warmly.

"You, also,'' Ana said, "but please, don't stand on my account.'' She pointed to a pair of rocking chairs set in a corner of the store. "Why don't we go over there and visit?''

Nola waddled ahead of her and carefully lowered herself into a chair. Ana learned that they were from Virginia originally, and that this was Nola's first child but that they'd just learned she was expecting twins, though they had chosen not to learn the sex of the babies. She was due in the early part of September.

"And that's if I go to term,'' Nola said. "The doctor thinks I'll probably deliver early. So I could have three weeks of this left, or seven, depending on what happens.''

"Please let me know when they arrive,'' Ana told her. "If I'm still here, I'll bring you some meals in exchange for a chance to cuddle a baby.''

Nola laughed. "I have a feeling we'll be so glad for an extra pair of hands that *we'll* want to feed *you*.''

The young woman was cheerful but obviously tired and uncomfortable. As she took her leave, Ana decided she wouldn't wait for the babies to arrive. She'd take Teddy and Nola a meal the next time she came into town.

The cottage was dark and Garrett's truck was gone when she pulled to a halt at the top of the hillside above the cottage. *Good.* She already was sick to death of his hostility. Before she'd come into the kitchen earlier, she'd been so stupidly optimistic that they could live together amicably for the next four weeks. He'd wasted no time in bursting that little fantasy bubble. She'd bet he didn't even know the word amicable existed. Fuming, as angry as she'd been when she left, she slammed canned goods down on the counter as she unloaded grocery bags. Then she saw the schedule he'd left on the kitchen table. It was a neat grid of the days of the week with each hour in a separate space. He'd written in the times he wanted the kitchen and bathroom. Across the bottom was a note in a strong, masculine hand: *If any of these are a problem, we'll negotiate.*

Negotiate? Negotiate, her fanny. He wanted war, he'd get war. She hunted a pencil out of a drawer and began to scribble on the schedule, muttering to herself.

She was a reasonable person. Generally kind, inoffensive, thoughtful. Teddy and Nola Wilkens certainly hadn't found anything objectionable about her. But Garrett had gone out of his way to be as hateful as anything she could have imagined. Why? Why was he so sure she'd been Robin's lover? *That* made her madder than anything. It was insulting to her, but even worse, it was insulting to Robin. Garrett had known the man for years; how could he imagine Robin would engage in an affair with a woman decades younger than himself, much less include her in his will?

She finished bringing in her groceries and put everything away in her designated spaces. Just like a parking lot at an office. Park here, stay out of that space. Yes, she surely was going to make the man sorry he'd started this, she thought as she went to her room for the recipe box she'd brought. Crab dip would be the first salvo. Tomorrow, she'd make that fabulous chicken-broccoli casserole that filled an entire house with aroma. She could make an extra one for Teddy and Nola. It was a good thing she'd gotten that big package of chicken on sale. And she'd make pies with the Michigan cherries she'd found at that produce stand. Ha! Take that.

She really, really hoped that Garrett's cooking skills were limited to grilling and fixing things out of a box.

Then the guilt struck and her angry thoughts drained away. She was mourning Robin. How must Garrett feel? He'd lived with him, had loved him since he was a young teenager. He was grieving, too, and it wasn't unbelievable to think that his boorish behavior was born of his grief. Everyone dealt with losing a loved one differently. Garrett had been the one to find him, the one to deal with all the funeral arrangements, the one left holding all the responsibilities. He'd moved through denial, the stage she figured she still was clinging to, and perhaps now he was angry.

And who better to take it out on than her? She might not like the conclusion he'd jumped to about her character, but she could forgive it. And she would. Tomorrow she would tell him that she was Robin's daughter and set this whole mess straight.

Feeling a lot better, she went back out to her car and brought in the things she'd bought from Teddy. She took them upstairs and into the room that had been Robin's den, where she'd stored her other supplies earlier in the day. It was an ideal workspace, with enormous windows on three sides to offer plenty of light as well as to give adequate ventilation when she was working with toxic-smelling substances like glue. In addition, there was an extraordinarily good overhead lighting system. She knew Robin hadn't an artistic bone in his body or she'd have thought this space was designed to be a craft or hobby room of some kind.

The room contained a large television, a top-notch stereo and a few pieces of comfortable furniture, but there also was a lot of unused open space. At the far end, beneath the wide window, a large table stood— perfect for her to cut fabric and lay out design ideas. And there was room enough beside it for the sewing machine in its portable cabinet that she'd brought along. A sizable wet bar was built into a countertop beneath which there was a plethora of cabinets that stretched across the whole wall beneath the window. It was perfect for her supplies and for cleaning up.

And an oversize closet with louvered doors along one wall was completely empty.

She set up her workspace, unpacking her sewing machine and arranging her fabrics and decorative accessories. A surge of pleasure ran through her as she fondled a piece of satiny burgundy felt and she had a sudden image of a subtly elegant clutch purse. Pair it with a petite pillbox with that black feather wrapped around the brim… It was a welcome relief from the blank lack of creative energy she'd been experiencing since Garrett had hurled the news of Robin's death at her four days ago.

Four days! It felt as if it had been much longer than that. She felt the tears welling again. For most of her life, she'd thought her father was dead. Her mother had spoken of him rarely, and Ana hadn't had the courage to ask of him often. On the few occasions when she had, Janette's eyes invariably would fill with such a desolate sadness that Ana knew, without a doubt, that her mother still loved the man who had fathered her. Ana herself had known only that he had been an American, that they had met a little more than a year before her birth, that they had never married but that they had loved each other deeply. The beautifully tragic landscapes for which her mother had become famous were a reflection of her feelings.

Early in her career, Janette had been a portrait artist. Ana had four pieces of her mother's portraiture: one done in soft, lovely oils of herself as a child asleep in a pram, the other two quick sketches of subjects for whom she'd later painted formal family portraits. The fourth piece was the one she cherished most: a charcoal self-portrait her mother had done of herself with Ana peeking around the edges of Janette's long, flowing skirt as she sat at an easel. Ana had been less than two when the sketch had been done. They had moved back to England, where Ana's grandparents had lived, shortly afterward. Ana had other pictures, photographs, of her mother, but this one, done by Janette's own hand, was the dearest possession she owned.

She had nothing so personal by which to remember Robin.

She shook her head as the tears fell, blinded by her scalding grief.

And jumped a mile in the air when the door banged open a moment later.

Garrett loomed in the door of her new workroom, narrowing his eyes against the bright lights. "Where were you all day?" he demanded. Then he paused, clearly unsettled when he saw her struggling for composure.

"Out," she said shortly, annoyed that he'd caught her in tears. She turned her back on him.

His footsteps advanced into the room. "What is all this?" His voice didn't sound pleased.

"My work," she said, still keeping her back to him as she used the hem of her T-shirt to wipe her face.

"I thought you quit work."

She turned, beginning to get angry all over again at his accusatory tone. "I quit my jobs," she corrected. *He's grieving. Remember that.* "Millinery is my work."

"Hats." He sounded dubious. Picking up a piece

of black netting, he arched an eyebrow. "You add frills and feathers?"

"I make one-of-a-kind hats and matching hand-bags." She picked up a framed citation from the Smithsonian thanking her for her work in assisting with a Confederate headgear restoration. "I also con-tract to work on special projects and I've been asked to put together a book, an overview of hats through the ages."

"Wow. I'm impressed." He sounded sincere, but she'd been taken in before by his seeming civility before he'd shredded her with unkind words again, so all she did was eye him dubiously.

"I am," he said. "How did you get so knowl-edgeable about hats?"

"I told you before that I was fascinated by hats when I was young."

He nodded.

"My mother encouraged my interest and helped me acquire a sizable collection, which I donated to the Smithsonian last year. I also studied the history of fashion and millinery at college."

"Very impressive." Again he sounded as if he meant it. He fingered another stack of silk in various shades of blue. "Did Robin know you did this?"

She looked at him as if he were crazy, though the two simple words had made her pulse jump in a ri-diculous way. "Of course. He was very encourag-ing."

"And you've never been here before? You didn't know he had this place in Maine?" His eyes were intent.

She shook her head, baffled by the apparent change of subject. "No. Why?"

"I think Robin remodeled this room for you," he said.

Garrett watched Ana's face. He hadn't really planned to blurt that out, but he'd just realized it and before he'd known it, the words were hanging in the air between them.

"What?" Her face was stricken, her voice incredulous.

"This room and the storage area next door were one big unfinished area until a year ago. When we were here last summer, Robin decided to put in a wall and divide the storage in two. He turned this one into a room he was calling his den. But he never used it. We always shared the downstairs office, and by the time this was finished, it was time to go back to Baltimore."

He looked at Ana closely. Her eyes were shiny and her nose was pink; she'd been crying when he came in. Crying over Robin? The thought annoyed him immensely, erasing the relaxed atmosphere.

He wasn't sure why the thought of her grieving for Robin got to him; it wasn't as if he had had a monopoly on his stepfather's attentions. But...the context in which he believed the woman had known Robin was still so offensive it made him want to throw up. How could she have let an old man's age-spotted hands run over that smooth alabaster flesh? How could Robin have let himself be blinded by her fresh, glowing face and stunning figure? God, he'd asked himself that question at least a million times in the past couple of days. Shouldn't the very thought that she was interested in a man so much older have been a red flag to his stepfather?

"Anyhow," he said, "I was planning to move my office up here."

Ana stood up, placing her hands on well-shaped hips. The action pulled her shirt taut against her breasts, flattening them slightly, and he could clearly see the outline of her nipples. It was hard to drag his gaze back to her face.

"This is a marvelous space for my work. I'm not switching. Especially if Robin created this with me in mind."

"We're sharing this place," he reminded her. He didn't really want the room so much as he wanted to let her know she was only there on sufferance. It was clear she was quite talented at the unusual career she'd chosen, although it didn't sound as if it brought in much income.

"That's exactly right," Ana said. "You have a bedroom, I have a bedroom. You have a workroom, I have a workroom. You chose yours first, I just took what was still vacant. I plan to work in here and if you want it, we can fight for it." She paused for breath and looked around the room, and when she spoke again, her voice was less strident. "Robin would be thrilled that I'm using it."

"Oh, and you're the expert on what Robin would have wanted."

"No." She seemed to deflate before his eyes. "You had him for nearly two decades. I'm sure you know many, many things about him that I don't.'' She turned away and began to fiddle with small boxes of gems and sequins, aimlessly arranging and rearranging them.

"So you're pretty good at this," he said, letting it drop. He eyed the Smithsonian citation. She must be better than good; she must be *excellent.*

She didn't answer him.

"Are you?"

Ana stopped. "Robin thought I was," she said in a small voice. "I'm sure that's why he made this provision for me. He wanted me to have the time to work without having to worry about making ends meet."

"Well, you've certainly managed that," he said, anger rising again. "And when I buy out your share of this place, I have no doubt that I'll be paying three times the market share."

"I told you before that I'm not selling." Her eyes had narrowed and the hesitancy he'd sensed had fled.

"We'll see." He sneered. "I've met women like you before." As he turned and strode out the door, all he could see was a woman who had wanted a man for his money. And unlike his dear, departed fiancée Kammy, Ana had managed to get what she wanted.

She started her campaign to take him down a few pegs the next day at lunchtime. So what if he was grieving? He'd been a perfect ogre last night and he deserved everything he got, she thought, still smarting from his last comments.

She'd had breakfast at seven-thirty, despite the fact

that waiting so long after rising at six and swimming made her feel faintly nauseous, because Garrett the Grinch had the kitchen from six-thirty until seven-thirty.

Then she had to turn around and have her lunch hour beginning at eleven-thirty because he got the kitchen at twelve-thirty. She was quietly steaming and ready for action when she stopped for the morning.

The first thing she did was boil the chicken while she assembled the ingredients and mixed together the rest of her casserole ingredients. Next she mixed up a generous amount of crab dip with the meat she'd bought when she ran to town a few hours ago. Living along the coast had its advantages, she decided as she popped a bite of the succulent Dungeness crab into her mouth.

Ordinarily she would have let the chicken cool before picking and chopping it into small chunks, but because of the time constraint, she had to do it as soon as it was done cooking.

The fact that she burned her fingertips was another black mark against Garrett's name.

It was 12:25 when she finally got the chicken mixed into the casserole with the broccoli, cream sauce, mushrooms and herbs. She liberally topped it with cheese and crumbled breadcrumbs then popped it into the preheated oven just as Garrett walked in the door.

He made a production of checking his watch. "Am I early? I don't want to rush you out of the kitchen."

She smiled as graciously as she could manage, buoyed by the thought of what was going to happen in the next hour. "No, I was just finishing. I hope you don't mind—I left a casserole in the oven to bake."

He shrugged. "I wasn't planning on using the oven. Feel free."

"Thank you." She shaded her voice with just a touch too much gratitude. "I'll be back to get it out but you'll be almost done in the kitchen by then." She turned to the counter and picked up the plate of crab and crackers she'd set out.

"What's that?" he asked.

"A little crab dip I mixed up," she said airily. "I have a fabulous recipe."

As he watched, she turned away and headed for the door. "Since it's your kitchen time, I'll take myself out onto the deck. After that, I'm going to take the canoe out for a little while." She smiled to herself, imagining him drooling.

To her surprise, Garrett trailed after her. "Do you wear a life vest when you go out alone?"

She shook her head. "No. I'm quite a strong swimmer." Then she smiled. "Don't worry. I won't drown before the month is up and we own the cottage."

He shot her a look of annoyance. "Water safety is nothing to be flippant about. You should be wearing a vest." He paused. "Actually, you shouldn't be going out alone at all."

That surprised her. No, that *shocked* her. Anger began to simmer. "You do."

He frowned. "That's different."

"Oh?" She made her voice mocking. "Because

you're a big, strong man and I'm just a silly little woman who needs taking care of?''

"No." His eyes were growing dark and stormy. "Because I've been coming here for years and I'm familiar with the lake and you're not. There are some dangerous rocky areas out there. And unlike most of the lakes, this one isn't so heavily populated that you'd be rescued anytime soon. Even if you didn't hurt yourself and drown, you might have to wait there until I missed you."

"Goodness, that *could* take a while," she said acidly. "Since we both know how likely it is that you'd miss me for anything other than a convenient target for your rotten temper."

His face was growing red; he looked furious. "Are you going to be sensible or not?"

She smiled and waggled her fingers at him as she stepped out onto the deck. "Not."

Four

He woke up in a bad mood.

As Garrett swung his feet over the edge of the bed and stood, he heard a raucous squeak, then the quieter *snick* of the kitchen screen door latching. He stopped in mid-stretch and glanced at the clock. Six-thirty. That meant that the sound he heard must be Ana coming in from her swim. He told himself he wasn't disappointed that he hadn't risen early enough to see her emerge from the lake. But a part of him could still visualize the perfect, slender limbs, the full breasts and rounded hips and his body called him a liar.

What was the matter with him, lusting after a woman who had probably slept with his stepfather? He was afraid he knew exactly what was wrong with him. The luscious Miss Birch was intensely attractive, immensely sexually compelling. The same thing that had worked on Robin was working on him, as well.

The thought made him want to snarl as he shrugged into a T-shirt, shorts and dockside shoes before heading downstairs. Why had men been made this way? It wasn't that he liked *her*, he assured himself. It was just that she was so incredibly well put together. As he entered the kitchen, he wondered where she had gone—but his question was answered when he saw her standing at the counter spreading butter and jelly on two slices of toast.

"Good morning." He forced himself to be civil.

"Good morning." She sent him a beaming smile. She wore a long beach wrap that clung to her wet body and her hair was wrapped turban-style in a towel. She wasn't wearing a scrap of makeup but his gut clenched as the potent impact of her shining beauty hit him. Life just wasn't fair.

"It's past six-thirty," he said abruptly. "My time in the kitchen."

Ana gave a gusty sigh and the smile faded. "Oh, heavens, please excuse me. God forbid I should be in the kitchen during *your time*." Her voice dripped with sarcasm.

It fed his general discontented feeling and he shot her a glare. "We made a deal. The deal is you're out of the kitchen when it's my turn. You can eat before or after, whichever you choose."

"Before or after doesn't work well for me." She picked up her toast and placed it on a plate, then poured herself a glass of orange juice. "I'm starving.

I can't wait until seven-thirty to put something in my stomach or I feel ill."

"Six-thirty to seven-thirty is my kitchen time," he said stubbornly. "You get up at six. Eat before you swim."

"I can't. It's not good to exercise on a full stomach."

"So swim later in the day."

"I don't *want* to! I like to exercise first thing in the morning. If I get caught up in a project I'll forget if I leave it until later." She unwrapped the towel from her hair and began to comb her fingers through the wild tangle of irrepressible curls. "Who in the world needs an hour to eat breakfast, anyway? It's not like you make a gourmet meal. You eat *cereal*."

"I read the paper. Drink my coffee."

"And you couldn't do that in the living room?" She sniffed as she picked up her dishes and started out of the kitchen. "Admit it. You're still mad about me inheriting half of this cottage and you're taking it out on me. *Robin's* the one you should blame."

"Robin's not the one who wormed his way into an old man's will." The moment the words left his mouth, he regretted them. Not because they weren't true, but because he really hadn't wanted to push Ana into a state of war. Life in the little house was difficult enough.

Ana whirled. Her exercise-pinkened face had grown pale, except for two spots of color high on her cheekbones, and she was practically shaking with anger. "For your information, Robin is the one who sought me out. After we met, I never asked him for anything except the pleasure of his company.''

She stomped out of the kitchen. Her cat, Roadkill—what kind of a name was that to stick an animal with?—darted after her, pausing in the doorway to whirl and hiss at him with a sobering display of fangs. He'd heard cat bites were extremely painful and often got infected. That animal was dangerous. He should demand that she keep it penned up or get rid of it.

He took every minute of the rest of his hour to read every inch of the paper that the caretakers delivered just after dawn. When he got his milk and orange juice out of the refrigerator, he couldn't help but notice the casserole she'd made yesterday afternoon. It didn't look like much, just a baking dish with a crumb-covered cheese crust inside. But the smell of the thing while it was baking had practically had him drooling. He wondered if he could get her to give him the recipe to take home to his cook. Then, remembering the harsh words they'd just exchanged, he decided he'd be a fool to ask. She'd probably give him a recipe for something poisonous.

He went down to the lake and took a good swim as Ana had earlier. But when he came back to the house and settled in his office, the mood of restless discontent still rode him. He checked his watch. Eight-forty. His New York office didn't open until nine and L.A. was three hours behind that. While he knew he paid his staff generously enough that he could call one of them at home, he refrained. He tried never to infringe on his employees' downtime except when truly necessary. Today it wasn't.

Rising from his desk, he wandered through the kitchen into the living room.

Ana was standing on tiptoe at the door with a small bottle of oil in one hand, stretching up to reach the top hinge. Guilt struck immediately. He'd been inexcusably rude. And worse than that, just plain mean. He shifted uncomfortably as another truth struck home: *Robin would have been ashamed of him.*

A bolt of sorrow shot through him as, once again, he faced the fact that never again would he hear that voice, that laugh. And he remembered what Ana had said in the kitchen earlier. She'd never wanted anything but his company. Even as the cynic inside him said *right,* he realized that she also must be feeling a tremendous sense of loss. It made his voice less antagonistic, gentler, as he asked, "What are you doing?"

"Oiling these hinges," she said in a distinctly defensive tone. "Every door in this place squeaks. It was driving me crazy. I really want to be working, but I know I couldn't concentrate until I got this done."

He couldn't blame her, he decided as he walked over to stand beside her. He was the one who had started this. "How many have you done?"

"This is the last one downstairs except for the far door in the kitchen." She turned to look at him with lifted brows, and her green eyes were wary. "Why?"

He reached out and took the bottle from her. "I have a few minutes to kill until my offices open. Go ahead and work. I'll finish these."

Her face was so suspicious he would have been

insulted if he hadn't known full well he deserved her skepticism. "Really?"

Strangely, the seething anger with which he'd awoken seemed to melt away in that moment and he smiled. "Really."

Her whole face lit up. "Thank you!" And she dashed up the stairs without another word.

He oiled the remaining hinges downstairs, then went upstairs and methodically worked his way through the rooms. The last door he tackled was the door of her workroom. Just as he opened it to work the oil into one of the hinges, she pulled it open from the other side and barreled through.

She crashed straight into him, and they both staggered. Automatically he reached out and caught her by the shoulders, feeling the press of her soft skin beneath his palms. He let go of her instantly and stepped back. "Whoa. You all right?"

Ana stared up at him. She licked her lips. "Um, fine. Thank you," she added belatedly.

"No problem." He smiled at her, trying not to stare at her mouth as she nervously moistened her lips again, then felt the smile fade. "I, ah, owe you an apology for what I said earlier."

Her eyebrows lifted in that silent-but-oh-so-eloquent manner he'd come to recognize, but she didn't say anything.

"I...cared for Robin." He looked at the floor. "It's been difficult to adjust to the thought of sharing him with anyone, even in memory."

"I'm sure." She shifted beneath the weight of the backpack he'd just noticed she was wearing. "He talked about you all the time, you know. He was so proud of you. I don't think he ever thought about you not being his biological son. He—he loved you.''

Garrett stared at her. *Men don't cry,* he reminded himself fiercely. But he couldn't prevent the tight knot that rose in his throat and constricted his breathing, nor could he banish the tears that welled. He blinked them away, smiling crookedly. ''I loved him, too. He married my mother when I was a fourteen-year-old hell-raiser, and he took me in hand. I learned rules, and I learned manners. And somewhere along the way, I forgot that I didn't want to like this guy who'd invaded my life.''

Ana smiled. ''He was pretty irresistible.''

An awkward silence hung in the air as their eyes met and held. And held, and…held. Her green gaze was filled with sadness, warm fond memories and something more. Something that told him she was very aware of him as a man.

His pulse quickened. It was the first time he'd had any inkling that she was feeling the attraction he'd been fighting. And even though he told himself to ignore it, he wondered what she would do if he pulled her against him.

Then she broke the moment, giving him a wide berth as she stepped past him. ''I'm going to take a walk. I seem to think creatively when I'm walking. See you later.'' She paused. ''Thanks again for oiling the doors.'' The last was tossed over her shoulder as she rushed down the stairs.

Just as the door closed behind her, a movement from the corner of his eye distracted him. Turning his head, he was surprised to see that the cat had leaped up onto an end table and was peering out the window.

"I thought you were shut in her room," Garrett said softly.

The cat jerked its head and gave him what looked like a less-than-friendly feline stare.

"You fell into it. and came up smelling like a rose," Garrett informed the animal. "I hope you know how lucky you are to have found a sucker like her." He took a step closer. Immediately the cat sprang to its feet. Though it didn't leap away, it was clear that he wasn't to be trusted.

"All right. I'll fix you," he murmured. Moving as slowly as he could, he backed away from the cat and went downstairs. In the pantry, on Ana's side, were stacks of canned cat food. He popped the top on one and forked half of the contents into a small bowl. After covering and refrigerating the other half, he carried the food back upstairs. The cat was still perched on the end table.

"Hey, cat, I'm back. And do I have a treat for you." He eased as close as he dared, watching the cat's muscles tense. He kept talking in a soft, soothing tone as he extended the bowl and set it on the floor not far from the animal. The cat's nose was twitching. "Go ahead, dig in," Garrett invited. "See what a good guy I am?"

The cat continued to eye him mistrustfully as he backed away. Then, once the animal judged him to be less of a threat, it leaped down from the table and attacked the food with gusto, glancing up occasionally to make sure Garrett hadn't invaded its personal space.

''Good stuff, huh?'' He watched as the cat cleaned the bowl with vigorous strokes of its tongue until it appeared as clean as it had been before he'd put food in it. Only the fishy smell still lingered.

When the cat finished eating, it sat and began to clean itself with delicate swipes of one striped paw. ''You really are a beauty,'' Garrett murmured. And it was. It was, as he'd deduced the first night he'd glimpsed it, a pretty tiger-striped tabby. But instead of plain stripes, the bands of contrasting color whorled into a perfectly round bull's-eye pattern on each side.

He took a step closer, and then another when the cat ignored him. He crouched and snagged the bowl, and the cat looked up. He extended his hand. ''Hi.'' The cat sniffed his hand, finger by finger, for a very long time. Then, just as he knew he was going to have to get up before he lost all feeling in his legs, the animal stretched forward and butted its head against his hand. He turned his hand over slowly and gently scratched behind its ears. A loud rumble filled the room as the cat began to purr, the noise sounding like a poorly-tuned outboard motor.

''Well, I'll be damned,'' Garrett murmured. ''You big faker.'' He moved his hand away and began to rise. The cat shot him one wild-eyed look, laid its ears back and hissed, then vanished into Ana's room.

Garrett chuckled. He shrugged as he picked up the bowl and carried it downstairs. ''Oh, well. Small steps are better than none.''

It was past time for his offices to be open, so he headed for his study and worked for the rest of the morning. Around eleven he smelled something delicious, something like...cherry pie? It was a good thing Ana didn't know what the smell of her cooking was doing to him or she'd have a good laugh at his expense, he thought as he forced himself to ignore the odor. At twelve-thirty, his watch alarm reminded him that it was lunchtime, a fact his stomach already knew, and he finished his last conference call and went into the kitchen.

Ana stood by the counter, lifting the casserole she'd made out of the refrigerator and setting it into an oversize picnic basket he'd seen in the pantry. Her curly hair was caught in a loose ponytail at her nape and wild quirky strands formed a halo around her head. She wore an ivory sundress, a gauzy thing with a fitted bodice and gathers down the front that gave the skirt additional fullness.

"Hello," she said, placing a wooden thing that looked like a miniature table into the basket with its legs on either sides of the casserole dish.

"Hello." He eyed the basket. "Going on a picnic?"

She shook her head. "No. Taking a few little things to a friend in town." She turned from him and lifted a pie from the counter, setting it on the second shelf she'd made of the little wooden thing.

He couldn't help himself. "Is that cherry pie?" He sniffed appreciatively. Hopefully.

"Yes." She snapped shut the basket lid and swung the basket down from the counter, and he could see the play of smooth muscle in her arms as she absorbed the weight. "I'm having dinner in town so you won't have to worry about me infringing on your kitchen time tonight. See you later."

"See you later," he echoed stupidly as she whisked around him and out the back door. As she started up the hill, he had to restrain himself from charging after her and demanding, "Dinner with who?"

It's none of your business, he admonished himself. As if he didn't know what she'd say if he were to do something so stupid.

She still hadn't returned by the time he'd cleaned up the dishes from his solitary meal that evening. The peace and quiet was kind of nice, he told himself stoutly. He'd never been up here without Robin, never had to eat his every meal alone. There was absolutely nothing wrong with it. Absolutely nothing.

He decided to do a little fishing, so he cut up some bait and took the canoe to the far southern end of the lake where he knew there was a good small-mouth bass hole. After an hour and a half, he'd caught three fish—more than enough for dinner the next evening— and dark was falling. It was peaceful and pretty on the lake as the light dimmed and the sky moved through pinks and lavenders to indigo and finally black. The loons hooted insanely as they prepared to settle in for the night.

As he paddled leisurely back toward the cottage, he realized there was a light on in the living room. He'd turned it off, he was sure, because the only light he'd intentionally left on, the one by the door, was still shining, a beacon beckoning to him.

Ana must be home. His pulse sped up and there was a surprising sense of anticipation churning in his belly. He hauled the canoe out of the water and stowed the paddles and life vests, then lifted his string of fish and strode up the steep trail through the pines and the birches to the light.

The moment he stepped through the door he smelled popcorn. He inhaled deeply, reflexively, as he took the fish to the kitchen.

"Hello," Ana called as he flipped on the light above the sink.

"Hi." Then he remembered she'd had dinner with someone, somewhere. "Have a nice evening?"

"Marvelous," she said in a cheery, breezy tone, and he wondered who she'd been with to put that note of happiness into her voice. He couldn't think of any way to ask her without risking another angry exchange. And though he'd started the hostilities, he found he didn't really want to fight with her anymore. It took too much energy, all negative.

The sound of the television show she was watching penetrated his consciousness as he was washing his hands after finishing cleaning the fish. "Hey," he said, moving into the living room. "I didn't think about the television. We're going to have to set up a viewing schedule, I guess."

Ana glanced at him, and he saw her shake her head in resignation, smiling wryly. "All right," she said. "I get tonight. And Monday. Anything else is negotiable."

"But tonight's Thursday." He shook his head. "I

like the Thursday night lineup on NBC. And there are a couple of shows I enjoy on Monday night, too.''

"So do I." Her eyebrows rose and there was a challenging look in her eyes. "And I was here first."

He thought for a moment. "We could flip for it."

"Not a chance." She dismissed him and turned back to the television. "But I'm willing to share with you. Think we could spend time in the same room without coming to blows?''

He snorted, well aware that he'd been the unreasonable one right from the start. "I guess we could try it and see." He dropped down on the sofa at an angle to the easy chair in which she sat. "I'll even let you sit in my chair."

"Gee, thanks," she said dryly. "You're too kind." Then she uncurled her legs from where she'd tucked them up beneath her. "I'm going to make some more popcorn. Want some?''

He looked up at her. She'd lit the fire and at the moment, she was standing directly between him and it. Her thin, gauzy dress was sheer enough that with the light behind her, he could see the soft curves of her body. "Oh, yeah," he said. "I want some."

Ana blinked. Two vertical lines appeared between her brows as she processed the response, as if she thought he might have meant something more than simply popcorn. Then she shrugged. "Okay. I'll be right back." She turned and whirled out of the room, the dress flowing around her, and he was reminded suddenly of a fairy, or a sprite. Not a typical thought for him, but then again, there was little typical about the way Ana had affected his life.

She was as good as her word and in a minute she returned, bearing not just a bowl of freshly buttered popcorn, but a drink for him. "I assume the beer in the refrigerator is yours," she said, smiling as she handed him the can, "since it isn't mine."

"You assume correctly. Thank you." He popped the top on the beer and took a long, cold drink, then stretched out his hand in her direction. "May I have the remote, please?"

Ana made no move to hand it over. "This remote?" She held it up. "You mean the one that controls the channels?"

"That's the one."

"How do I know you aren't planning a devious channel-changing operation the minute I hand it over?"

He had to chuckle. "A devious channel-changing operation? Nothing so impressive. It's just a guy thing—I feel incomplete without that remote in my possession."

Ana's gaze met his, and then she laughed aloud. "Now *that* explanation I believe. You know," she said and he noticed she still didn't hand over the little box, "I truly can't believe that a man with as much money as you have—or Robin, for that matter— wouldn't have more than one television in this place."

"It's called a cottage for a reason." He tossed a piece of popcorn into the air and caught it neatly in his mouth.

"I suppose you're right." Her eyes lit up, a glowing sea-green in the flickering light of the fire. She smiled warmly at him.

He felt his own lips pulling into a smile as he gazed into her eyes. There was a pleasant stirring of arousal lightly flirting with his senses. He forced himself to look away from the lure of her smooth skin. "May I please have that?" He gestured for the television remote control she was holding.

She was still laughing at him. "Going into withdrawal?"

"Yeah. Am I looking peaked?"

"Good try." But she handed it to him. "Here. I just hope you're not one of those frantic button-pushers who has to check ten other channels on every commercial break."

He held his tongue.

She groaned. "Oh, no. You *are*."

He had to chuckle again. "Relax. I'll be a perfect remote handler, I promise. So what other shows do you watch in the evening?"

Comparing their tastes, they found that they both watched a few select shows on Monday, Wednesday and Thursday. The rest of the week, neither really cared whether or not they even turned it on.

"Except for the financial news," he amended. "I like to keep track of the stock market."

She wrinkled her nose. "Be my guest. I check out the headlines and the weather channel and that's it."

He finished his beer and emptied the popcorn bowl after she said she was full. Her cat wandered in a short time later and licked the butter off the bowl, then hopped up into Ana's lap. It gave him one beady-eyed glare, apparently forgetting that he'd been the bearer of food just that morning, then completely ignored him.

"She's getting a lot friendlier," Ana commented. "When I first brought her home I couldn't even touch her. She hid under the bed all day and came out at night to eat."

"So how did you get her to come to you?"

She grinned, and the mischievous expression tightened his gut in a manner that had nothing to do with amusement. "I withheld her food until she came out after it. After about two weeks of that, she let me touch her."

"And you've had her how long?"

"Four months."

He was impressed with himself. He'd touched the cat practically the first time he'd made any effort. Then again, Ana had already done the hardest work of socializing the animal.

They shared laughter during two particularly funny sitcoms. The one-hour drama from ten to eleven was as intense as it ever had been, and he caught her wiping tears when a young boy died. She had a tender heart, he thought, watching the way the cat had curled up against her, its paws over her forearm as it purred loud enough for him to hear.

He'd probably purr, too, if she touched him like that, he thought, watching as her hand stroked steadily from the cat's head to its rump. The small action mesmerized him, and it wasn't until Ana said, "Would you like to hold her?" that he realized she had stopped watching the television and was watching him. The news had come on but he'd have been hard-pressed to tell anyone what the hot story of the day was.

"Uh, no." He could feel a dull flush sliding up his cheeks and he stood abruptly, grabbing the popcorn bowl and his beer and taking them out to the kitchen.

What the hell was wrong with him? He was *not* interested in Ana Birch. Well, okay, he wasn't going to lie to himself. The woman had a killer body, hair that made a man want to plunge his fingers into it and rub it against his skin, and the sweetest smile he'd seen in a long time. And she was nice. Really nice, unless she was a far better actress than he was giving her credit for. It was all too easy to see why Robin had fallen for her. And he must have, to have included her in his will.

The thought of Robin sobered him quickly. He couldn't reconcile the woman he was growing to know as warm, funny, and sunny-tempered when he wasn't provoking her, with the cold-blooded seductress that she would have to be to have seduced Robin for his money.

The two images simply wouldn't fit together and as she came into the kitchen with the cat weaving around her ankles to put her glass in the dishwasher, he muttered a good-night and escaped to his room.

Which one was the real Ana?

She was not going to fall for Garrett Holden.

She was *not* going to fall for Garrett Holden. A week later, Ana scrubbed the plate glass of the large living-room window that overlooked the lake with far more force than necessary. He was a bully and a brute and a mean, hateful person…but that hadn't been true for the five days since what she'd come to think of as The Television Truce. And if he smiled at her one more time and spoke to her in that deep, dark, honey-over-whiskey voice, she might just grab him by the hair and kiss him until this ridiculous fascination was slaked.

He wasn't playing fair, suddenly turning into an approachable, charming man.

She was *not* going to fall for him. At twenty-three, she'd had a number of relationships, though she couldn't say any of them had matured into love. The last one had been the longest: nine months. But she'd ended it a year ago when he'd made it clear he considered her millinery aspirations a little hobby that she probably wouldn't have time for once marriage and children came along. She sniffed, recalling the stupefaction on Bradley's face when she'd given him his walking papers. He truly hadn't understood.

But she had. Her mother had loved only one man in her whole life: Robin Underwood. And though Janette had been the one to leave and had never gone back, Ana had grown up knowing that such an all-consuming love was both powerful and possible. Maybe that was why she'd never had her heart broken. She was, perhaps subconsciously, looking for that kind of feeling.

But she'd never imagined that one person could feel such a love without the other reciprocating. She didn't love Garrett that way. *Yet.* Instinctively she sensed that he could break her heart without even trying. He—

"Good morning."

She jumped at least a foot in the air and the hand holding the wet rag sloshed a long, dripping streak across the newly cleaned window. Turning, she saw the object of her thoughts standing in the door to the kitchen.

His chest was heaving and he wore nothing but brief jogging shorts and footwear. His big body was as hard and sculpted as anything she'd imagined, and he glistened with sweat.

It took every ounce of willpower she had not to go to him and trace her hands over all that bare, tanned flesh. "Good morning," she said, hoping her voice didn't betray her state of nerves. "You scared me."

"Sorry. I was out running." He paused. "What are you doing?"

"Washing the windows." Wasn't it obvious? "I took down the drapes and threw them in the washer. When they're done I'll hang them out back and we'll have a nice, fresh-smelling room tonight."

Garrett was frowning. Good. She was used to his frowns. "We can hire someone to do more heavy-duty cleaning, if you like. You shouldn't be doing that."

She stood and stretched her back. "Why not?" Then she realized that the position she'd taken, with her palms behind her massaging the base of her spine, thrust her breasts forward in a way that probably seemed like an invitation. Garrett had noticed; his gaze had strayed from her face to her body and she saw him swallow. The betraying motion sent a shiver of sensual heat through her and she had to catch her breath. She was *not* falling for him, she reminded herself as she quickly lowered her hands and crossed her arms.

She could almost see him forcing himself back to the conversation. He spread his hands, clearly searching for an answer. "I, uh, I don't know. If you think the place isn't clean I can have a word with the Davenports—"

"Don't you dare!" She let her exasperation show. "They've done a wonderful job with routine maintenance and housekeeping. But every so often a house needs a thorough top-to-bottom cleaning. Like these windows, for instance. And the refrigerator and freezer should be defrosted and cleaned. The cushion covers on the furniture should be washed or dry-cleaned and the traps in the sinks should be—"

"Okay. I get it," he said. "We can hire someone younger and more energetic to do something like that."

She shook her head, smiling at him to soften her refusal. "No, 'we' can't. I can't begin to afford half of what that would cost. Don't worry, I don't expect you to do half the work. This is entirely voluntary."

"I thought you came up here to work on your hats and your book." He didn't sound angry; he was merely stating a fact.

"I can't work every minute," she told him. "Creativity just doesn't work like that. This kind of mindless work gives me a chance to recharge my battery."

"Does cooking serve the same function?"

"I guess so." She hadn't really thought about it before. "Yes. I sort of put my mind on automatic pilot when I'm cooking, too."

"Maybe we can make a deal," he said, and his eyes took on a crafty gleam. She could see his mind leaping ahead and she suddenly realized just how he'd parlayed an initial stock market windfall into a billion-dollar empire. "I'll pay for someone to do the housecleaning you want if you'll spend your creative downtime in the kitchen...*and* if you'll agree to let me share some of the product of your labor."

She stared at him, wanting to howl with laughter and knowing she'd better not. If Garrett thought she was pulling a fast one on him, they'd be back to armed warfare again. But still...men were so *easy* when it came to their stomachs. She'd hoped her cooking would get to him. Apparently she'd succeeded. "I suppose that would be okay," she said, drawing it out so that she sounded appropriately reluctant. Then she held up her hands, red and wrinkled from the morning's work. "My fingers will thank you."

Garrett smiled at her. Not a polite you-made-a-funny smile, but a warm, easy flash of teeth that scrambled every brain cell she had. Before she could regroup, he crossed the room, clasped her hands in his and drew her to her feet. "And my stomach will thank *you*." He didn't move away, simply held her hands between them in a loose clasp, looking down into her face.

His hands were hard and warm and she felt breathless, as if his proximity had stolen all the oxygen from the atmosphere around them. She was so close to his chest she could see the individual hairs that formed the curly mat across his breastbone, and he seemed to radiate an irresistible heat that enveloped her.

She felt tongue-tied, and abruptly flustered. Pulling her fingers free, she turned back to pick up the bucket and rags she'd been using. "I, uh, I guess I'll put these away and get to work now." She didn't glance at him as she carefully moved around him toward the kitchen door, but she was aware of the suspended quality of his stillness.

She emptied the bucket into the sink and rinsed it, then took the rags outside and draped them over the deck railing to dry. When she came back into the kitchen, Garrett stood beside the kitchen table, where she'd set a pile of old magazines she'd gathered up and set aside to throw out.

"Where did you find this?" His voice was sharp enough to make her jump. She turned in time to see him thump a finger on the top-most cover. It was a woman's issue, featuring exclusive makeup and hair-styles, thousand-dollar handbags and advice on how to make your mark at a society function.

"It was in the bathroom in that basket, I think. Who did this one belong to? It doesn't seem quite your style." She'd meant the comment to make him smile again, to be humorous since the other maga-zines all dealt with sports, finance or world news, but the moment he'd seen the magazine, the light had drained from his eyes, leaving a cool, expressionless mask that didn't reveal his thoughts.

"Toss it."

There was an awkward silence.

After a moment, she picked up the stack of magazines and started for the door. "All right."

"It belonged to my old girlfriend." His tone was almost grudging and with a flash of intuition she realized this was an uncomfortable topic for him.

She stopped in her tracks, turning slowly around though she didn't speak. His gaze met hers, and she was shocked to see raw pain in his face.

"She only came up here one time. It wasn't her thing," he said in a low voice.

He'd been hurt. Odd. She'd never thought of him as being vulnerable. Sympathy welled within her. "I'm sorry," she said, though he hadn't indicated there was anything wrong.

He shrugged. "Life happens. We move on."

They stared at each other across the space of the kitchen as his words echoed between them.

They did, indeed, move on. Guilt struck her. She needed to tell him who she was and why Robin had mentioned her in his will. Now she regretted that she hadn't done so sooner, regardless of his attitude.

But before she could speak, he said, "Would you eat dinner with me tonight? I hate eating alone." His voice was plaintive and she smiled.

"I thought you wanted it that way."

His answering smile was wry. "So did I. But it's lonely. Robin wanted us to share this place and I haven't done a very good job of honoring his wishes."

Tell him! urged the voice in her head.

But as she gazed into the sapphire depths of his

eyes, she simply couldn't open her mouth. The room was full of new, fragile feelings, feelings such as she'd never experienced before, and she couldn't bring herself to ruin the moment.

Soon, she promised herself. *I'll tell him soon.*

Five

Four more days passed. In a little over a week, the month would be over.

Nine days, and he would never have to see Ana again. The knowledge didn't delight Garrett as it might have a few weeks earlier. Tonight they'd had grilled steaks that she'd marinated all day and he'd done on the grill. They'd worked together chopping up a salad with an ease that he found far too appealing.

He stepped through the sliding door and walked down the steps from the deck to the path that led to the beach. As he picked up his fishing gear and eyed the setting sun, his gaze automatically swept the area.

Ana was in the same spot she often was at this time of day, relaxing on a chair she'd dragged down from the deck, her sketch pad in her lap.

"Hi," he said, pausing as he passed her. "Any requests for tomorrow night's dinner?"

She tilted her head as if considering her answer, and he was distracted by the heavy fall of curls that swung across one shoulder. Without thinking, he reached out and pushed it back. His fingers slipped over the smooth, warm skin of her shoulder, bared by the sleeveless tank top she wore, and he couldn't prevent his index finger from extending itself and stroking a small pattern back and forth on the creamy flesh. God, she felt good!

"How about a few small-mouth bass?" Her voice sounded breathless, but it effectively broke into his most inappropriate thoughts about what he'd like to be doing to that skin.

Reluctantly he dragged his hand away. It was becoming all too easy to touch Ana. Bodies brushed in the kitchen, hands met over the remote control, and once or twice she'd asked for his help navigating the computer. He'd leaned over the chair behind her, trying desperately to resist the urge to bury his face in the wild, sweet-smelling curls of her hair and trying even more desperately to hang on to his common sense. Getting involved with her would be a huge mistake. Capital *H*, capital *M*. *Huge* Mistake.

"Would you like to come fishing with me?" Even as the question left his mouth, he was kicking himself. He didn't need to spend any more time around Ana. If anything, he should be spending less.

She'd set down her pencil and twisted around to look up at him, and her eyes were a vivid aqua in the late-day golden light. "I'll come if I don't have to touch the worms," she said.

The distaste in her elegant tones made him laugh. "I think I can save you from that. I'm using minnows for bait."

"Dead fish?" She shuddered and he chuckled again.

"I promise you won't have to deal with them." He paused. "Unless you want to."

She snorted and smiled. "Fat chance." She rose and he stepped back, waiting while she put away her things. Then they walked down the path to the little cove. He offered her his hand as she stepped into the canoe, trying not to notice how small and delicate her palm had felt in his, then untied the canoe, climbed into his end and settled down with a single paddle.

It was a beautiful evening. The last rays of the sun skipped across the lake and an eagle soared over their heads to its nest in the top of a tall tree. The craft cut easily through the smooth, calm waters toward the point where, years ago, he'd learned that the bass congregated.

"Robin taught me to fish," he said before he thought about the risks of introducing the older man into their easy silence.

But Ana only widened her eyes with an incredulous smile. "Really? I can't quite picture a man who seemed as suave and debonair as Robin in a sleeveless T-shirt working worms onto a hook."

He grinned at her reference to his attire. "There are those in the corporate world who couldn't imagine it of me, either. I guess we all have our little secrets.'' He looked over at her. ''What's your secret, Ana?''

She was trailing a hand through the water while he paddled. When she looked across the length of the canoe at him, he got the impression that she'd gone somewhere far away in her head, and the smile faded from her face. ''I'm illegitimate,'' she said.

She was what? He didn't know what he'd expected, but a bald confession like that definitely hadn't been it. He didn't know what to say. ''I'm sorry,'' didn't seem adequate. ''You were raised by your mother in England, weren't you?'' he said carefully. He'd suddenly discovered that he wanted to know about her. All about her.

Ana nodded. ''But I was born here. My father was American. My mother always told me he'd died before they could marry, but not long ago I found out he was still alive.''

''That must have been a shock. How did your mother explain that?''

''She didn't. Couldn't,'' she amended. ''She passed away when I was twenty.''

He was surprised. ''My mother died of a blood clot when she was sixty-six but your mother must have been a good bit younger than that. What happened?''

''Breast cancer.'' She drew out the words in her distinctive accent. ''She was only fifty-one. Far too young to die,'' she added quietly.

He nodded, letting the silence soothe them for a moment. Then he said, ''Did she really believe your father had died?''

''No.'' Her voice was quiet. ''It turns out he was

already married. Apparently she knew that from the beginning, but when she found out she was pregnant, she left him."

"*She* left *him?*" he repeated. "That's not usually the way it happens."

Ana smiled slightly. "My mother wasn't a usual sort of woman. I imagine that she didn't want my father to feel pressured and she didn't want him to marry her simply because of me."

Some women in that situation, he reflected, would have been only too happy to use a pregnancy as a lever for marriage. It spoke highly of her mother's character that she'd made the difficult choice she had. "She must have wanted you very much, to have raised you alone," he offered.

She smiled and he could see the memories in her eyes. "She was my best friend."

"You were lucky." He cleared his throat. "My father met another woman and left when I was nine. It was an ugly, messy divorce."

"And then your mother met Robin?"

"Not until I was fourteen." He smiled, thinking back to those days. "By then, I'd turned into a seriously obnoxious little hoodlum. I bet Robin's heart sank the first time we met, although he was too nice ever to tell me."

"But you got along well with him, obviously," she said.

"Not at first." It wasn't something he liked to admit, but he felt the need to answer her honestly. "I was on the verge of becoming a true delinquent. Running with the wrong crowd, smoking, defying my mother, you name it. Robin stepped in and laid down the law as soon as we moved in with him. He insisted on meeting my friends' parents. He imposed curfews. He cut off my allowance until I started helping with chores and being polite to my mother. God, I hated him!'' he said with a laugh. ''But he made me settle down. I started paying attention to my grades because he paid me for each *A* I got. Robin was quite wealthy by most standards, and I liked the lifestyle, so I decided I'd better learn what I could from the old man.''

She looked startled. ''Did you call him that?''

''No, but that's how I thought of him. He was fifteen years older than my mother.''

''My father was seventeen years older than Mother,'' she said.

''Well, I didn't think of Robin as old for very long.'' He shook his head. ''He took me skiing and beat me down the damn hill every time. He taught me to fish, and to golf—''

''And to make money, apparently,'' she broke in with a mischievous smile.

''Well, yes,'' he admitted. ''He was pretty thrilled with my success.''

They were gliding into the grassy shallows along the point by now, and he slowly set down the anchor, then baited a hook and tossed it in. Ana didn't speak again, and he let the silence lie comfortably between them, amazingly content simply to be sitting there in a lazily rocking boat with her.

He caught three fish in less than half an hour, plenty for tomorrow's dinner for the two of them, and after retrieving the anchor, he began to pull for their cove. They were traveling against the current now and though it was calm, he had to put more effort into it than he had gliding along with the flow of water earlier.

"Brrr." Ana rubbed her bare arms. "It's getting brisk out here. I should know by now that I need a sweater in the evening."

"You can have mine," he said. He liked the mental image of her in his sweater, sleeves flopping well down over the ends of her arms, the soft fabric draping over her breasts—

"That's all right. We'll be back in a minute."

But he rose to his knees anyway and began to strip the sweater over his head. The boat drifted for a moment as he did so, and just as he pulled his arms out of the sleeves, he heard Ana say, "Oh, no!"

And that fast, they were in the water.

It was *cold.* He sank beneath the surface and came up kicking. "Ana!" he yelled as soon as he could drag air into his lungs.

"I'm right here," she said immediately. "I'm fine." He relaxed as he heard the laughter in her voice. "But this water is *freezing.*"

"What the hell happened?" he asked. They were treading water, and he looked around, grabbing the boat before it could get away. Ana swam around and collected life preservers and the blue-and-white cooler in which they'd stashed the fish.

"Well," she said in a surprised tone that made him start to laugh. "I do believe it was my fault. You were taking off your sweater and I turned around to get the cooler from the front since we were getting close to the dock. I must have leaned a little too far over on the same side you had most of your weight on—your *considerable* weight on—and the next thing I knew, we went bottom up.''

He was still laughing. ''There's no point in trying to get back into the canoe. It would take us longer than it will just to swim in.''

She agreed, and they set off, side by side, herding their respective items in front of them until they reached the dock. In the shallower water, he was able to stand, and he flipped the canoe upright again, then tied it at the end of the dock. She was already up the ladder when he hauled himself onto the dock and they stood there looking at each other, grinning like idiots.

''If Robin could see us now…'' she said.

''I think he can.'' He wanted to believe it. ''He's probably rolling around on what passes for the floor of Heaven, laughing at us.''

She smiled at him, shaking her head and lifting her hands to wring the water from the mass of her hair.

How could she be so beautiful, soaking wet? The sun was almost gone now but he could still see her clearly. There was something ineffably feminine in her movements, the graceful bow of her back as she bent at the waist, her vulnerable nape as her lifted arms pulled her hair forward and wrung out the excess water. He wanted to kiss her there, right on that exposed spot. He wanted to nuzzle beneath her hair and nibble on her neck, to take her face in his hands and lift it for his kiss.

He took a deep, unsteady breath, conscious of his racing pulse. This wasn't right. And then Ana straightened. The dripping tank shirt clung to every curve, and though she wore a bra, he could see that her nipples had drawn into tight little points. God, he thought, it wasn't fair. How could he be expected to resist her?

He dragged his gaze up to her face. Her mouth was slightly open, her color high. Then their eyes met—

And he was lost.

"Ana." He breathed her name as he took a step forward and pulled her into his arms. She made a startled sound, and her palms came up against his chest, but she didn't pull away.

They stared at each other for a long, suspended moment. Her gaze didn't move from his and he could see in her eyes the exact instant when she accepted the inevitable. Her pupils dilated and her shallow breathing echoed his as he said her name again.

"Ana."

Then he slowly lowered his head.

She sucked in a sharp breath, almost a gasp, as his lips settled over hers, and a sound like a small moan came from her throat. Her fingers dug into the pads of muscle on his chest but he barely noticed the small pain. All he noticed was her.

Beneath his mouth, her lips were soft. So soft. They moved willingly beneath his, clinging as he changed the angle of the kiss.

His hands were on her back, and he slowly rubbed one palm up to her nape and settled it beneath the wet mass of her hair, directly on that tender, sweet skin he'd been fantasizing about only a moment ago. Her hands and arms relaxed and she slid them up around his neck, her small fingers caressing his skin as she pulled his head more firmly down to hers. The motion left a cold, empty space between them and without thinking he tightened his grip on her and slid one hand down her back, drawing her against his hard, aching body.

The feel of her firm, gentle curves made his breath shudder out in a ragged cadence. Her gently rounded breasts flattened against his chest and her soft thighs cradled his. He felt arousal rush through him, felt her body firmly pillow his rapidly hardening flesh, felt the involuntary shiver that arched her silently against him, increasing the pressure in his loins and tantalizing him with the sweet shift of her hips moving over his. It was such an exquisite sensation that a deep growl of frustrated delight rose in his throat—

And in an instant, she wrenched herself out of his embrace. Her hands flew to her cheeks. "Oh, heavens!" she said. "This was a mistake!" And before he could form even the beginnings of a coherent thought, she spun and raced up the path to the cottage as fast as she dared to move over the uneven path.

He stood where he was, looking after her until she vanished inside the door. *What had he been thinking?* As he trudged up the slope with the fish cooler, he decided it wasn't a question of what he'd been thinking, but one of why he *hadn't* been.

He could hear the water running in the shower when he got inside. After he gutted and cleaned the fish and refrigerated them for tomorrow, he changed into dry clothes. He built up the fire while he waited for her to come out, all the while trying to decide what he was going to say to her. But before he was ready, before he'd figured it out, he heard her coming down the stairs.

He popped up from the couch where he'd been sitting and rushed into speech before she'd even reached the bottom of the steps. "You were right when you said it was a mistake. Please accept my apology." He shrugged, trying to lighten the tension. "It seemed like the thing to do at the time."

Something changed in her eyes, as if a door closed in his face. "Apology accepted." She never even broke her stride, merely continued through the room and on into the kitchen, effectively dismissing him.

He opened his mouth, about to go after her and protest, about to tell her…tell her what?

That he wanted to make love to her more than he'd wanted anything in years?

That he couldn't keep his eyes off her beautiful body, couldn't keep his mind off the intriguing puzzle that she was?

What he needed wasn't her so much as it was a woman. Any woman. He'd never been big on short-term indiscriminate sex, so he tended to go without while he was between relationships. Which he was now, and had been for too long to bear thinking about.

He reviewed the few women whose acquaintance he'd made over the years he and Robin had been coming up here. He'd gone out with one woman last summer a few times, and found her a pleasant enough companion, quite pretty, and though they'd never been intimate…he was pretty sure she wouldn't say no if he opened that particular door.

Good. He'd call her tomorrow. What was her name, anyway? Ellen? Elaine? No, Eileen. That was it.

He was almost positive.

Ana took a stuffed chicken and apple dumplings in to share with Teddy and Nola the next evening. As she took the meal from the oven, she wondered if Garrett was eating his bass. He'd been quiet and polite—and noticeably distant—all day. When she'd told him she was having dinner in town, he had grown very still for a long moment. Then he'd said, "I guess you'll miss the fish. Sorry."

While the meal baked, she and Nola had played Scrabble. She'd also talked Nola into letting her wash two loads of infant sheets, blankets and clothing and getting it all folded and put away while Nola supervised from a rocking chair. The young woman was growing larger by the day and it was becoming increasingly difficult for her to get around. Ana knew Teddy was worried. Nola's blood pressure had been higher than the doctor liked, he'd confided, and they were hoping the twins did come a little early. Sonograms showed both babies were a good size and appeared to be doing well.

She stayed to clean up after the meal and didn't get home until nearly eight. Garrett's car was gone when she pulled into their lane, and she told herself it didn't matter. She hadn't expected to see him.

Even if it was a Thursday and they always watched their shows together.

Immediately after that thought came an image out of nowhere. She sat on the couch with Garrett, cuddled into the curve of his arm. As the television show took a commercial break, he turned to her and sought her lips as she wrapped her arms around his strong back and pulled him down.... *Stop it, Ana Janette!*

Oh, how she wished she could. All day long she'd been trying not to think about The Kiss. All day long she'd had her brain invaded by the breathless, tingly sensation that accompanied any thought of the way he'd gently tugged her against him. His hand had played in her hair, his lips had been warm and firm and far too enticing. And when she'd stopped thinking and let herself go with the moment, sliding her arms up around his neck, he'd pulled her against him—against every muscled, hard, hot inch of him— and she'd nearly swooned in his arms with an overwhelming urge to drag him down to the dock and give herself to him.

It had been a shocking self-revelation, and she'd torn herself from his arms, angry with her yearning body and even more upset that her heart ached at least as much.

Too agitated to sit down and watch the television, she decided to take a run. She hadn't exercised today, other than swimming, so it would do her good. But as she established a steady pace, watching the rutted lane carefully for spots that might twist an ankle, her thoughts went right back to the evening before.

The time they'd shared on the lake had been lovely. Garrett had been friendlier and more open than ever. In fact, he'd been getting gradually more approachable all week. When he'd brought up Robin, she'd thought there might be an opportunity to tell him about her relationship, but he'd seemed to need to talk and she hadn't wanted to distract him...and she hadn't been able to bring herself to ruin the evening. She was a coward. It was as simple as that. If she'd confessed, she would have spoiled the perfect evening they'd been sharing, and lost the chance to learn more about Garrett.

And he'd never have kissed her.

Oh, that kiss. Thinking about it made her toes curl inside her sneakers.

Earlier, when he'd paused to talk and invited her to go out on the lake with him, he'd pushed her hair back and his hand had grazed her shoulder. He'd brushed his finger lightly but quite deliberately over her skin for a moment, and she'd had to catch herself before she reached up and laid her hand over his to hold the contact. Then he'd taken his hand away and she'd been sure he was sorry for letting himself touch her like that.

She'd been even more aware of him than ever out on the lake. She'd tried not to stare at the ripple of muscle in his bare arms as he rowed, tried not to notice the way the last rays of the sun had picked copper highlights out of his dark brown hair and turned them to fire, tried to keep her gaze from returning to the fascinating flex of his strong thighs as he braced for each stroke. She'd tried.

What a moment that had been on the dock, when she'd straightened up after wringing out her hair and caught him...wanting her. That was the only way to describe the look on his face as his gaze had traced a path down over her body, pausing at her breasts.

She had figured she probably looked like a candidate for a wet T-shirt contest and from the expression on his face, she'd been right. His naked need had shot out and enveloped her, making it impossible to move, to protest, to do anything but wait breathlessly as he pulled her into his arms.

And then he'd kissed her. She'd wanted it to last forever. Contrary to what she'd said, it hadn't *felt* like a mistake. It had felt like Heaven. It had felt *right*.

So why had she stopped him?

Because, she thought miserably, she hadn't been honest with him. And she knew him well enough to know that when she explained who she really was, there were going to be fireworks between them. And they wouldn't be the kind she'd welcome.

"Hello, dear!"

She shook her head as she waved at Mrs. Davenport, who was seated on her front porch. The older woman had a bowl in her lap and another on the floor, either shelling peas or snapping beans. Without even realizing what she was doing Ana had run all the way to the end of the lane. "Hello, Mrs. D," she called, slowing to a walk. "How are you this evening?

The caretaker's wife nodded. "Good," she said with the spare economy of a native of Maine. "You?"

Ana nodded. "I'm good. How could I be otherwise, up here in this lovely spot?"

"And with a handsome man like Mr. Garrett," the older woman said, a sly twinkle in her eye.

She hoped Mrs. Davenport wasn't a mind reader, Ana thought. The last thing she needed was for anyone to know how she was growing to feel about Garrett. "Having a handsome man around is always a bonus," she said lightly.

To her surprise, the woman's smile faded. "Don't you hurt that boy," she said. "That Kammy girl was bad enough."

"Kammy?" echoed Ana. "Do you mean the other woman Garrett brought up here? Because he and I aren't—"

But her words were lost on Mrs. Davenport. "Sneaky one, she was," the old lady muttered. She rocked faster, as if the chair were as agitated as she was. "Running around behind his back, all the while planning to marry him. I saw her meet her fella at the end of the lane. Kissing and carrying on something awful." She shook her head and repeated, "Sneaky one."

Running around behind his back...? Ana's sensitive heart shrank with pain. "But why...what kind of woman wouldn't want Garrett?" She stopped, conscious of the impropriety of discussing him with his employee, yet too shocked to hide her reaction.

Mrs. Davenport positively glowered, her normally pleasant countenance drawn into a fierce scowl. "After his money, she was. That's the story I heard from Mr. Robin." The rocking chair slowed its pace a fraction. "Burned him bad. You're the only one he's brought here since." She shook a finger at Ana. "So don't you hurt him now."

"No, ma'am." Desperate for a change of subject, Ana pointed at the bowl, which she could see was full of peas. "You got a good crop this year."

"It's been a good summer." Mrs. Davenport smiled, apparently dismissing the topic now that she'd said her piece.

After a few more moments of conversation, Ana said, "Well, I'd better get back."

Mrs. Davenport nodded. "I'm going in soon. The skeeters'll make a meal of you if you don't." She shot an odd, challenging glance at Ana. "Your mama always said those skeeters were big enough to carry her away."

"My...mother?" Ana felt like she'd been dumped into the lake. Icy fingers of shock dribbled down her spine. "You knew my mother?"

"I did." The elder woman's eyes assessed Ana's face. "Knew you were hers the minute I laid eyes on you."

"How...?" She stopped. The "how" was obvious. Robin had brought her mother here. "Robin brought my mother here," she said quietly.

Mrs. Davenport nodded. "The first time they came, 'tweren't nothin' but woods back there. They hiked back and looked around, and when they came out, Mr. Underwood bought it from us on the spot. Got the whole place built by the end of the summer, and the next summer, they spent the whole season up here. He had to go back down south a few times on business and she stayed here, but other than that, they hardly left." She smiled. "Never saw a couple so happy." Her smile faded. "But the next year, he came alone. I thought they'd get married, but she left him. Haven't ever seen her since."

Apparently the Davenports didn't know Robin already had been married when he'd brought Janette Birch to Maine. They'd adored him; telling them now would serve no purpose, so she merely said, "My mother's gone."

Mrs. Davenport's eyebrows rose. "I'm sorry for your loss." She hesitated, then set her peas aside and rose from the chair slowly. "Let me get a bag and you can take some of these peas along. We'll never eat 'em all."

Ana left to run back the lane a few moments later, a bag of green peas bouncing along in her hand. A peace offering of sorts, she imagined. And with every step, the shock of the caretaker's words vibrated through her anew.

Robin and her mother had come here together. Picked out the land and built the house. Together. And according to Mrs. Davenport, had spent the whole of the following summer here.

A fresh frisson shivered through her as the implications of that revelation struck her fully. She'd been born in early April...and very probably conceived right here in Eden Cottage the summer before.

Back at the house, she decided to wait until she had cooled down from the run before she showered. As she stowed the peas in the refrigerator, she bumped a container of lentil soup. It teetered on the edge of the shelf, then crashed to the floor, spilling soup across the kitchen. Muttering, she filled a bucket and began to scrub the kitchen floor. She was really going to need that shower, she thought ruefully. It was just as well Garrett wasn't home.

Garrett. She sat back on her heels, the scrub brush

motionless in her hand. She still found it hard to believe that any woman could prefer another man to him. Garrett was everything a woman could possibly want. Handsome, unquestionably. If she'd ever met a more attractive man, she couldn't remember when. Wealthy, yes, but in her book, wealth was definitely optional. Far more important, he had a sense of humor. He was intelligent and enjoyed a good argument. He definitely wasn't a man who thought women were a lesser species. And he was kind. A weird thing for her to think, given the way he'd treated her earlier in their…relationship. But though he didn't know it, she'd seen him with Roadkill, patiently talking to the skittish cat, slipping her treats, trying to win her affection.

Then that pesky *R* word surfaced again. Relationship. She and Garrett were not in a relationship, she reminded herself. Except one born of necessity and of the family connection about which he didn't even know yet.

Her heart sank, and she picked up the brush and dipped it in her bucket, then slopped a patch of soapy water over the floor and redoubled her scrubbing. She *had* to tell him about her father. Tomorrow. She would definitely tell him tomorrow, though she dreaded the thought. No man liked to look foolish, and she was very much afraid that's how Garrett would feel when he learned the truth. He might even think she'd kept it from him deliberately, that she'd been laughing at him for the past three weeks.

She hoped not. If nothing else, she hoped they could salvage the friendship from their relationship once he got over his anger. There was no one else who had known Robin like he did, and her lonely heart craved those shared memories almost as much as it did the other things Garrett could make her feel.

"Hello."

She bobbled her brush as someone behind her spoke. She wasn't sure whether it was fright or delight for a second, but the feeling of utter pleasure that hearing his voice provoked washed through her. She relaxed and her heart began to beat heavily, her reaction to him beyond her control. Garrett was back. And she knew what she had to do. She had to tell him. Right now, tonight.

She sat back on her heels, turning with a smile on her face. It froze in place when she realized he wasn't alone.

"Hello," she said uncertainly, looking from Garrett to the woman beside him.

The newcomer was blond. Very blond, and though it would have been nice to know it was a dye job, Ana suspected the color was real. It certainly highlighted her pale, porcelain skin and wide blue eyes well.

"Ana, this is Eileen." Garrett performed a perfunctory introduction. His gaze met hers and her heart contracted at the aloof expression on his face. As if he didn't care one bit what she thought.

And then she realized that he didn't. Why should he? She was the only one who was letting her heart get mixed into this mess Robin had forced on them. Unable to bear the distance between them, she transferred her gaze to his date.

"Welcome to Eden Cottage." Ana forced herself to smile at the other woman, though she could feel her cheeks burning.

"Thank you." The blonde's voice was clear and sweet.

Steadfastly, Ana kept her eyes on the other woman, refusing to look at Garrett again. The hurt rushing up inside her made her voice tight as she said, "I'm just finishing up here. I'll be out of your way in a minute."

"No rush," Garrett said. "We're going out on the deck." He took a bottle of wine from the counter, slipped a corkscrew into his pocket and pulled two fluted goblets from the cupboard.

He ushered his little blond beauty out of the room and she heard them pulling open the sliding glass door and stepping onto the deck.

Ana stood and carried the bucket to the sink to be emptied, then quickly mopped the floor with clean water. He was so *obvious.* Just like a man. Couldn't he have simply left things alone? After all, she was the one who had called a halt last night and pronounced their kiss a mistake. So why had he felt compelled to rub her nose in another woman's presence the very next evening? Did he think she was stupid? If he wanted to be sure they never got caught up in a moment like that again, all he had to do was say so.

A burning knot rose in her throat, and her chest felt as if it were being squeezed in a vise. She would *not* cry over him. She placed both hands on the edge of the sink and dropped her head, trying to control the feelings that wanted to burst out of her.

Oh, God, how had she come to this in three short weeks? The truth was, she didn't dislike or despise Garrett anymore.

She loved him.

Six

"I'll be back in a minute," Garrett said to his date.

"I'll be waiting," Eileen said coyly. She tossed him a smoldering look from her blue eyes and Garrett realized belatedly he was supposed to respond. But all he could manage to do was send her an abstracted smile as he stepped back into the house.

She hadn't been bad company. In fact, they'd had a very pleasant evening. He'd taken her to a restaurant high on a cliff overlooking Penobscot Bay and they'd enjoyed a bottle of local wine while they'd chatted. He'd found her as likable and pretty as he remembered. She also was a mathematics whiz, and she knew far more about the stock market than anyone would ever suspect. Still, he hadn't been attracted to her in any but the most generic way. When he'd invited her back to the cottage, he'd done so with the

express purpose of letting Ana see that he had other
fish on the line, that he didn't need her. Didn't want
her.

But the moment he'd walked into the kitchen earlier,
he'd known he'd made a mistake. One of monumental,
only-a-man-would-do-something-so-dumb import.

Ana had been wearing a brief pair of yellow jogging shorts that showed her magnificent legs to advantage, and she must have gone running because she
was still wearing her sneakers. The T-shirt she wore
was liberally splashed with the water she was using
to scrub the floor.

God. The last thing he needed was to be confronted
with the sight of Ana in a wet T-shirt again.

Her hair had been carelessly twisted atop her head
and stray curls fell down to wave around her face.
She was working at a hot, messy job and her fine skin
glowed with exertion. She should have looked like
hell. Instead she looked as desirable as any woman in
a sleek cocktail dress ever had looked to him.

She hadn't heard them come in, and for the barest
moment before she'd registered Eileen's presence,
there had been something warm and welcoming in the
private smile she'd begun to send him. Possibly even
something intimate. He hadn't imagined it, of that he
was absolutely positive.

But then she'd seen his date. The smile froze, then
disappeared. The expressions that rushed across her
mobile features—shock, humiliation, and worst of all,
unmistakable hurt—had been easy for him to read.
The shock he'd expected. The humiliation he hadn't

intended, but any woman caught scrubbing a floor when guests arrived would have felt the same. The hurt…how could he have known? he asked himself rather desperately. She'd made a point of rejecting him last night. She hadn't even stuck around to discuss what had happened, had simply dismissed it out of hand as a mistake, which had stuck in his side like a burr beneath a saddle. And so he'd decided to get a date, had taken a petty, juvenile action just because he wanted to show her that her words hadn't bothered him. A mistake, she'd said.

But the moment he'd seen her face tonight he knew she'd lied. For whatever reason, Ana hadn't wanted him to know how that kiss had affected her.

If it affected her anything like it affected me, we're in big trouble. If he had any sense, the last thing he'd be doing was going back inside to confront Ana. If he had any sense, he'd pretend he hadn't seen the raw emotion that had slipped out beneath her facade a few moments ago. If he had any sense, he'd lock himself in his room for the next few days and get the hell out of here on the thirty-second day without looking back.

But as he walked across the living room to the kitchen doorway, he knew he didn't have a single grain of common sense where Ana was concerned.

And then he saw her.

She stood in front of the sink, head down, with her elbows locked and her hands gripping the counter, as if she needed the support of her arms to hold her upright. There was defeat in her slumped posture, the way her weight rested on one leg. Even her curls seemed to have lost their spring.

"Ana," he said softly.

Her head jerked up and she whipped away, putting her back to him. But the one wild-eyed glance she'd shot in his direction had shown him clearly the tears brimming in her beautiful sea-green eyes. "Go away." Her voice was muffled; she hugged herself tightly with crossed arms.

"We have to talk," he said, as quietly as before. The urge to cross the room and take her in his arms was nearly irresistible but he forced himself to wait, sensing that she'd reject comfort—or anything else— right now. "Let me take Eileen home and then—"

"No," she said sharply. "I do *not* want to talk to you." Her voice was thick with distress and her back was rigid as she moved down the short hallway to the door. Before he could figure out what to say, how to handle this whole awful situation, she'd slipped through the door into the night beyond.

The *snicking* sound of the screen door latching galvanized him into action. Striding down the hall, he stepped out onto the porch, expecting that she'd be huddling there in the dark. It took a moment for his eyes to adjust, an especially long one because there was just the barest sliver of a new moon in the sky, but when they did, he realized the porch was empty.

Then he heard her footsteps on the path that led to their little beach. "Ana? Ana, wait."

The footsteps didn't slow. If anything, her pace increased. Garrett started to move as fast as he dared down the pebbled path, instinctively knowing what she intended. "Ana!" he shouted. "Don't go out on the lake. It's not safe."

Her footsteps thudding across the dock were the only answer he got, and he cursed vividly as he skidded on pine needles and nearly missed one of the rough rocks that served as steps. By the time he burst onto the dock, she was nothing but a dim blur moving rapidly away from the shore. Dammit! She knew he hated her going out alone. Now she was alone, on the lake, in the dark. His worst nightmare.

"At least wear a life jacket," he shouted after her.

"Garrett?" It was Eileen calling down from the deck where he'd left her. "I hate to break up the evening, but I need to get home soon." God, he'd forgotten all about her. Hell. Now he was stuck with her until Ana decided to come back in. No way was he leaving until he saw with his own eyes that she hadn't come to grief out there alone on the dark water.

"I can't leave," he said grimly. "It would be dangerous to leave while Ana's out on the lake alone."

Silence. He wondered if he sensed her surprise and rising suspicion, or if it were merely his conscience creating it in his head. Finally Eileen said, "She's a big girl," and there was the first touch of annoyance in her tone. "I suspect she's gone canoeing before without you to baby-sit."

He didn't bother to answer that, simply turned and stood at the edge of the deck, wishing to hell there was at least a little moonlight so that he could see where Ana had gone.

"I have to get going." Eileen tried again. "I have to work in the morning."

"I'm sure she'll be back soon," he said.

But Ana didn't come back soon. Half an hour

passed. He started to get concerned. What if something had happened to her out there on the pitch-dark water? Concern escalated into near-panic, and when Eileen said, "Calm down, Garrett. I'm sure she's fine," he realized he was pacing back and forth from one end of the deck to the other.

"Probably," he conceded. "But I still don't want to leave until she's out of the water."

His date cleared her throat. This time, when she spoke, there was a definite note of unhappiness. "Garrett, I really need to go home. Your roommate, or whatever she is, is being awfully inconsiderate, if you ask me." It was a blatant fishing expedition for an explanation.

"I didn't," he said between his teeth.

Eileen drew back with an affronted look on her face. "I beg your pardon?" she said in a frosty tone.

He dug his hand into his shorts' pocket and fished out his car keys. "Here," he said, tossing them at her. "Why don't you take my car? I'll get it tomorrow."

Eileen missed the keys. She bent to retrieve them, and as he watched her, he suddenly realized that when Ana made those same motions, it elicited a very different reaction. The sight of Ana's hair sweeping down, the bared, tender flesh of her nape, and the sweet curve of her bottom all turned him on. Totally, completely turned him on. As undeniably shapely as she was, when Eileen did it, it wasn't memorable in any way. At least not to him.

"Well, thank you," Eileen said in a voice that implied he deserved no thanks at all.

"I'm sorry this didn't turn out to be such a great evening." He knew he ought to at least go through the motions if he wanted to get this woman out of his hair without a scene.

"I'm sorry, too." From her tone, he surmised that he'd just been forgiven. She crossed to him and raised her arms to give him a brief hug. "If your... roommate moves out one of these days, give me a call again." She moved away then, a pretty woman sure of her appeal as her high heels tapped across the deck and around to the porch. "I'll leave your keys under the mat."

"Thanks," he said.

Thirty minutes later, Ana still hadn't returned. He was sitting on the deck nursing a beer, moodily reflecting on the past three weeks, when he heard the cat meow behind him. Actually it wasn't so much a meow as it was a squeak, and he wondered if its vocal cords had been damaged when it was hit.

Not it. She. It figured that Ana would have a female cat. Contrary critter. He turned and saw Roadkill sitting at the sliding door. "What's the matter, cat? Do you hate your name that much?"

The cat meowed again.

"I don't blame you," Garrett said. "I'd hate it, too. You deserve something prettier."

He'd slid shut the screen but had left the glass open and as he spoke, the cat raised one delicate paw and patted at the screen door.

"I can't let you out," he told her. "Ana would kill me if something happened to you." He looked down into his beer. "She probably wants to kill me, anyhow."

The cat meowed a third time and patted the screen harder, and he heaved himself to his feet. "I'll feed you," he offered. "Maybe that'll take your mind off the great outdoors." The cat ran a few steps away when he went to the door, but to his surprise, she stayed close, meowing around his legs as he went to the kitchen and got out her food. The moment he set it down, she attacked it, and in minutes the bowl was licked clean.

"Good stuff, huh?" he asked her as she finally walked away from the bowl. She kept a wary eye on him as she sat and began to wash herself.

He might as well get his book, he decided, and read until Ana decided to come home. Ignoring the images of the canoe, overturned and empty, floating on the lake that assailed his imagination, he walked up the stairs. To his surprise, the cat came with him. He went into his bedroom and picked up the book he'd been reading from his bedside table, and she jumped up on his bed and daintily pranced across the quilt until she was close enough to touch.

"Tease," he told her. He slowly reached out his hand and her ears went back. He didn't move back but he stopped moving. They eyed each other. After a moment, she arched her head up beneath his hand, and he heard the ragged sound of her purring as he tentatively stroked her back. A ridiculous satisfaction leached through his tension. It was pretty pathetic when all it took to make him happier was one dopey cat.

She jumped down then, and went to the doorway, looking back over her shoulder as if she wanted him to follow her. He was going back downstairs anyway, so he snapped off the light and obliged. But she didn't go downstairs. The minute she saw him coming, she began to walk down the hallway, her tail held regally high, still purring like a poorly-tuned motorcycle. She went straight to the door of Ana's studio and disappeared inside—

Ana's studio! The door stood wide open. He knew she usually kept it closed because she didn't want the cat to get into any of the ribbon or lace that was all over the room. He knew because he'd checked a million times to see if the door was open and he could casually stroll by, maybe catch a glimpse of what she was working on. He'd seen very little of her work.

The door was open. The cat had gone in. He was going to have to go into her studio and get that cat. It wasn't snoopy; it was the act of a good… housemate? Roommate? Eileen had called her that, and her tone of voice had given the term a decidedly sexual meaning. His whole body tightened with a different kind of tension at the thought of sharing a room with Ana, of stripping away her clothing and baring that magnificent body, of laying her beneath him on his bed, of letting her masses of hair fall across his pillow.

He stood in the upstairs hallway and faced what he'd been avoiding for all these days, since the very first time he'd laid eyes on Ana. He wanted her. Not just the general wouldn't-it-be-nice kind of wanting, but a very specific I-have-to-have-*this*-woman kind of wanting. Even more than that, he was determined to have her. The kiss they'd shared could have started a fire in the kitchen and he knew instinctively that sex with her would be better than anything he'd ever known.

Had it been that way for Robin? The thought still pricked at him—at his pride?—but he was rapidly growing past caring that she'd been his stepfather's lover first.

If, indeed, she ever had been. Deep down, he couldn't reconcile the two images of Ana. The woman he was coming to know had integrity, honesty. She wouldn't have slept with an old man for his money. And though she'd undeniably known and loved Robin, he didn't get the sense that she was grieving for a lover.

But how else could she have known Robin? He knew for a fact that the only child Robin and his first wife had ever conceived had been stillborn. A son. The lack of children had been one of Robin's deepest regrets, and it spoke volumes about his integrity that he'd refused to divorce his first wife despite her obvious mental illness. No one would have blamed him, Garrett was sure. And after her death, he'd married Garrett's own mother Barbara, who at forty-nine was well past considering a pregnancy. Robin himself had been in his mid-sixties then, and his dream of children had died a quiet death years before.

No, Robin had no children. Otherwise, Garrett might have thought she was a grandchild. He tried to superimpose Ana's wild strawberry-blond ringlets and green eyes over the blue eyes and dark hair his stepfather had had in pictures he'd seen of Robin at a younger age, but he failed. The two looked nothing alike. Besides, he was sure Robin had had no other living relatives. They'd discussed it several years ago when Robin was drawing up his will naming Garrett his heir.

Nice try, he told himself. He was barking up the wrong tree, trying to come up with reasons, excuses, that would allow him to consummate this raging lust he felt for Ana without feeling too weird about the whole thing. Even he could see that.

Disgusted, he shook his head started down the hall. At the door of the studio, he stopped to flip on the lights, then blinked for a moment before moving forward. The light was bright. Very bright. He supposed that made sense for someone trying to work with color.

There were seven completed sets of hats and matching handbags laid out on the long counter along the wall. He studied each one, standing before them for long moments. He didn't know squat about women's fashions, but he did know that women wanted to look chic and expensive. And these accessories certainly looked to be both of those. They were good. *She* was good.

He'd known Robin must have thought she had talent, but discovering it for himself was another matter. No wonder Robin had wanted her to have time to pursue her craft!

The cat meowed, and he started for the door. But as he passed her big worktable, strewn with felts and fabrics, ribbons, feathers and other decorative items, he paused and stared.

The sketchbook she used to draw up rough drafts of her ideas lay open on the table. But there was no headgear displayed on the page. Instead a sophisticated sketch of a man's figure caught his eye. It was him! Himself? He? Whatever. The drawing showed him in profile, standing on the dock with his hands in his back pockets, eyes squinted as he looked out over the lake. He'd stood that way many times. And she'd noticed.

Curious, he flipped through a few of the other pages—and was struck dumb.

She'd drawn at least a dozen images of him. Standing, sitting. Sleeping, laughing. Close-ups and full-length views. It was extraordinarily odd to see himself drawn, though the sketches were so cleverly done that she'd made him look as if he were ready to step off the page.

Was there any significance to the fact that she'd drawn him? Or was it simply that he was the only person who was around on any regular basis? Why was she spending her time drawing a person at all?

The sound of the deck door sliding open and shut made him jump. Ana was finally back. Relief deeper than anything he'd ever experienced rushed through him; then he realized where he was. The last thing he wanted was for her to catch him snooping around in her studio, so he looked around for the cat. She was sitting atop a counter, washing herself again. He strode across the room and picked her up. "Come on, trouble. You don't belong in here."

Just as he stepped out of the room and turned back to close the door, Ana appeared on the stairs. Her eyes were huge, dark pools that looked bruised and weary in the harsh hall light and she hesitated when she saw him. He had the distinct impression she was about to flee again, but then she saw the cat in his arms. "You're holding Roadkill!"

Abruptly he realized that in his agitation he hadn't even thought about the cat's skittish nature.

Hastily he set her on the floor. "The door to your studio was wide open and she went in. I figured you probably didn't want her in there."

"Thank you." She was looking at the cat rather than at him, and she didn't appear to even have thought about the fact that he'd been in her workspace. "I could tell she was getting used to you but I can't believe she let you touch her."

He shrugged. It seemed silly to tell her he'd been courting her cat. Instead he said, "Why did you go out on the lake alone? You know how dangerous it could be at night."

It was her turn to shrug. "I figured you and your date would appreciate the privacy." There was no mockery in her tone, only a quiet resignation, and he shifted uncomfortably.

"You figured wrong. Tomorrow you're going to have to take me to town to pick up my car."

"Your car?" He'd startled her into looking at him and as her eyes met his, he felt an increase in the tension.

"She needed to get home and I didn't want to leave while you were out on the lake," he said. A flash of incredulity lit her gaze and she opened her mouth. Knowing that she was about to argue with him, he forestalled her by saying, ''I need to talk to you.'' He didn't try to move closer; she was radiating distress signals that he knew he'd caused and at his words, she tensed as if she might flee and her gaze slid away from his.

''I—not now.'' She was looking at a spot somewhere around his shoulders rather than into his eyes, and he felt his frustration rise at the small gesture of avoidance.

''When, then?''

She moved to the door of her bedroom, making way for the cat who scampered in ahead of her. ''We only have to be here for four more days and we'll have fulfilled the terms of the will. I'm sure we'll be called to the lawyer's office again when we return to Baltimore. You can say whatever needs to be said then.''

She shut her bedroom door in his face almost before she'd uttered the last syllable, leaving him no opportunity to reply.

He stood perfectly still as he counted slowly to twenty. Even then, it took every ounce of self-persuasion he owned to make him turn and walk back to his own room. She'd never know how close he'd come to breaking down her door and demanding she listen to him.

She deliberately rose later than usual and took her time about getting down to the kitchen. As she'd hoped, he was already in his office. The last thing in the world she wanted to do was talk to him, so she grabbed a pastry and an orange and closeted herself in her workroom for the morning.

Images from the night before continued to flash through her brain until she felt like screaming. She didn't know what to feel, what to say, what to believe. He'd brought home a date, that much was unassailable. And even worse, he'd seen the warm welcome she had been prepared to offer him—until she realized he wasn't alone.

"Humiliated" didn't come close to describing how she'd felt. She'd bolted for the lake without even thinking about the inadvisability of paddling a canoe through the water in the dark.

But why had he pursued her? Was it really simply that he thought it wasn't safe to be out there alone at night? Giving the keys to his SUV to his date and letting her drive herself home seemed a little extreme, considering that he knew Ana was both a good boatsman and an excellent swimmer. She chose a pleasing shade of forest-green and began to form the felt on the wooden block, but when she realized she was still thinking about Garrett rather than the placement of the pert little brim she'd envisioned, she laid down the scissors and sighed through a mouthful of pins.

We have to talk. She could swear his eyes had been telegraphing an apology, but she wasn't sure what he would feel the need to apologize for. Unless it was to tell her he was sorry for asking someone else out, to tell her he only wanted her, Ana.

Fat chance of that happening in this lifetime. The animosity he'd shown early in their relationship might have faded, but she wasn't going to be stupid enough to let herself dream of happily-ever-after with him. What could—

"Ana?" Garrett's voice sounded as if it were just outside her studio door. "May I come in?"

"I—yes," she said, though her heart sank. "Come in." The last thing she wanted to do was conduct a postmortem on the events of last night. But he seemed determined. She might as well get it over with.

The door had been slightly ajar. He pushed it open and slowly came into the room, smiling tentatively at her. "I, uh, just wondered how your work is going. Are you getting as much accomplished as you'd hoped?"

She shrugged, trying for nonchalance when she met his eyes. "I didn't really have any quantifiable amount of work that I wanted to produce. But I've been working steadily every day, and I've got more designs in my head than I'll get finished in the next year, so I'd have to say it's going well."

"Good." He prowled the edges of the room. "What do you do with your finished pieces?"

"Pack them up and ship them to one of the two boutiques that've been selling me."

"No," he said with surprising patience. "What do you do with them here?"

"Oh." She waved a hand at the large closet along the wall. "They're in there."

Garrett walked to the closet. He had his hand on the doorknob when he stopped and looked over his shoulder at her. "May I?"

With the laser intensity of his blue eyes trained on her, she could barely think. "Sure," she managed.

He opened the closet doors wide so that the long rack she'd installed was completely visible, then stepped back a few paces and took it all in. He stepped closer, examining each set, picking up a hat here or a small clutch purse there.

Ana found she was holding her breath. She was attaching far too much importance to his opinion, she told herself sternly.

Then he turned to face her, shaking his head and smiling. "These are amazing. I bet women fight over them."

She stared at him. "You like my work?"

He grinned, and her heart skipped a beat at the flash of white teeth as his eyes warmed. "Don't sound so surprised."

She exhaled a shaky chuckle. "Artists are notoriously insecure about their efforts, no matter the medium. I'm no exception."

"When someone tells you they like something you look for the hidden criticism?"

"Something like that." She smiled back, glad for the easy banter.

Then he lifted his head and found her eyes again. "No wonder Robin thought you should be doing this full-time. These—" he indicated the completed pieces with a sweep of his hand "—are extraordinary."

"Thank you." She turned back to the pattern she'd been tracing.

"You know," he said, "you ought to be looking

for an investor. With enough capital, you could set yourself up to produce these things on a scale large enough to make it profitable.''

She shook her head. ''Right now it's just a labor of love. I don't want to share it with anyone else. I guess it's silly, but I feel very protective about my work.''

He was silent as he looked again at one or two of the pieces on the rack. Then he swiveled back toward her. ''Ana, if it's a question of money, I could—''

''No, thank you.'' She kept her voice calm. ''I wouldn't be comfortable accepting money from you, even in the form of a loan.''

He nodded. But in that instant, she saw something flicker in his eyes—and her heart contracted painfully. As if he'd said it aloud, she realized he was thinking that when he bought out her half of the cottage, she'd have more than enough money to start a small business. Despite what she'd told him, he still expected her to succumb to the lure of the eternal dollar.

And despite the physical pull between them, he clearly didn't trust her, or even like her very much.

At that moment, a sound that had been buzzing at the edges of her consciousness penetrated and she frowned. ''Is that a car coming back here?''

''Maybe Eileen's bringing my truck back,'' Garrett said. He went to the big window that overlooked the lane and the grassy meadow beyond the birches. ''Nope. It's an older-model black Jeep, I think.''

''A black Jeep...?'' She rose and walked to the window as the vehicle ground to a halt behind her old compact. The driver's door opened, and she recognized the occupant instantly. "Teddy!" Fear lent wings to her feet as she bolted down the stairs and through the house in record time. Her friend was still walking down the wide, shallow steps on the path when she met him.

"What happened?" she called as she neared him. "Is Nola all right? Do you need help—"

"Whoa!" Teddy was laughing. He grabbed her elbows and shook her lightly. "Everything's fine. In fact, everything's fantastic. We have identical twin daughters."

"Nola had the babies? Congratulations!" She was genuinely thrilled. She flung her arms around him and hugged him exuberantly. "When? Where are they? How can I help?"

Teddy was laughing as they drew apart. "Nola went into labor around nine-thirty and we went straight to the hospital. They were born at six forty-two and six forty-nine. They're a few weeks early but the doctor says they're in very good shape and as soon as they begin to gain a little weight we can bring them home."

"Six forty-two?" she cried. "They're only—" she checked her watch "—four hours old! Why are you out here?"

"Nola insisted," he told her. "We didn't want to tell you over the phone. She and the babies are sleeping right now so I was just twiddling my thumbs and drooling over their incubators." Then he fished in the pocket of his light jacket. "I brought pictures."

Ana squealed. She pored over the instant shots, exclaiming over the tiny, wrinkled faces in the pink knit caps. "They're beautiful! Do they have hair? What are you naming them?"

"They both have curly blond hair," he said, "though who knows if it will stay that way? And I think we're going to name them Jenna and Danielle."

"Jenna and Danielle," she repeated, still looking at the photos. "Oh, Teddy, thank you so much for coming all the way out here and bringing these." But when she tried to hand them back to him, he shook his head.

"These are yours to keep. Just promise you'll come in soon and meet them."

"I'll be there this afternoon," she promised him. They beamed at each other for a moment, then she took his face between her hands and kissed him noisily. "Congratulations again!"

He wrapped his arms around her in a bear hug and lifted her clear off the path for a moment. "Thanks."

"You'd better get back. One of your little girls might wake up and need her daddy." Ana turned him and tucked her elbow into his and they walked companionably back toward his Jeep.

He laughed. "I doubt that. Nola's breastfeeding so there's not a lot I can do for them right now."

"Except love them and cuddle them constantly." As he folded his lanky frame into the vehicle and the engine turned over, she waved energetically. "See you this afternoon!"

Seven

Garrett stood in the window where Ana had left him, frozen in place as he stared rigidly out the window. When Ana threw herself into the arms of the slender blond man, he made a guttural sound deep in his throat, a primitive growl of warning though there was no one to hear.

Was this the man she'd been sneaking off to meet? Teddy, she'd called him. He conveniently ignored the fact that she'd hardly been sneaking, that she'd even left him notes on several occasions telling him she'd taken a meal to friends in town. He watched as the guy gave her something—pictures, perhaps?—and they laughed and chatted together. When she took his face between her palms, kissing him as he reached out to enfold her in a hug, Garrett had seen enough.

Turning from the window, he stalked down the

stairs, intending to break up the little reunion. But as he came toward the cottage door, it opened and Ana strolled in. She was beaming. "Guess what?"

"Is that who you've been taking all the meals to for the past couple of weeks?" he demanded. "You told me you didn't know anyone up here, but the first damned time I turn around, you're cooking for some guy every couple of days."

All the happy light drained from her expression. She stopped just inside the door, staring at him as if he were crazy. Maybe he was. If so, it was her fault. But a little voice inside him cautioned: *Just because you want her doesn't mean you own her.*

In a tone cool enough to lower the room temperature by ten degrees, she said, "Yes. That's who I've been taking meals to. I met him the first time I went to town." Then her eyes changed and he could see the growing fury behind the searing glance she shot his way. "How dare you?"

"I—"

"How dare you?" she repeated. "You've been jumping to conclusions—*wrong* conclusions—since the first day we met. You think I met some guy and promptly jumped into bed with him, don't you?"

"Not exactly." He knew he'd overstepped the boundaries they'd drawn in recent days. Hell, he'd overstepped the bounds of common courtesy a long time ago. What was it about her that brought out the caveman in him?

"Ha." She stepped toward him and raised a hand and he instinctively caught her wrist.

"Wait a minute. Just wait a minute."

"I will not." It was a snarl. She shook her hair back from where it had worked its way free of the loose braid she'd worn while she worked. "Let go of me. I want to show you something."

He glanced at the hand he still held then, and realized that she had photographs clutched between her fingers. Feeling a little foolish, he released her. "Look, I'm sorry—"

"At least you got that part right," she hurled at him. She raised the photographs and shoved them beneath his nose, practically vibrating with anger. Her hand was shaking so badly he couldn't see the images so he plucked them from her fingers and looked at…babies?

"Those," she said pointedly, "are my friends Teddy and Nola's twin baby girls who were just born this morning. Nola's had a difficult pregnancy and appreciated the meals and the help I offered. They're both lovely people and I've enjoyed making friends in the area." She stopped. "Why am I explaining myself to you?" she demanded. She snatched the photos from him and turned toward the steps.

He grabbed her arm and spun her around. "Wait."

"No!" She wrenched away and stormed toward the stairs. "I am sick and tired of being judged by you. I cannot *wait* for the next four days to be over so that I never have to set eyes on you again."

Garrett stood in the middle of the living room as she vanished up the steps. Her door slammed with a resounding thud and he winced. He'd never seen her in a real temper before but he should have guessed that with that hair there was the potential for fireworks.

He heaved a sigh and rubbed the back of his neck. Dammit. She was right. He had been judging her, jumping to conclusions again, and he felt like a fool. Slowly he mounted the steps. Ana's door was shut and Roadkill sat just outside it, a tentative paw raised and planted against the wood.

"What's the matter, girl?" he asked. "Did she lock you out?" Stepping forward, he knocked on the door. "Ana?"

"Go away."

Oh, hell. Her voice sounded thick and he knew she was crying. And it was his fault. Again. "Your cat wants in," he told the door.

There was a soft scuffling sound and the door swung open just wide enough for the cat to enter. But as it closed again, Garrett stuck out his foot and held it open. There was a pause as she realized what he was doing, then the pressure on the door eased and he pushed it open.

Ana stood in the center of the room, her back to him.

"I was jealous." The bald admission hung in the air between them.

He saw her slowly shake her head, as if the words made no sense. "What?"

Crossing to stand directly behind her, he repeated the words with more conviction. "I was jealous."

She turned to face him, eyes wide and shocked. "But...but why?"

He cleared his throat, raising one hand to cradle

her cheek, sweeping his thumb along the smooth skin of her throat and jaw as he wiped away her tears. "Can you honestly tell me you don't feel it? There's something between us, Ana, something that gets stronger every minute we're together. I know it's wrong to want you," he said hoarsely, "but I'm tired of fighting myself." Beneath his cupped hand, the bones of her jaw felt fragile, the skin silky smooth. He stroked the pad of his thumb across her lips.

"It's not wrong," she said against his thumb. "I've been wanting to explain for the longest time—"

"No. No explanations." He was seized by a sudden, irrational fear. He could sense the intimacy in the moment; words would destroy it. With slow deliberation, he bent his head and replaced his thumb with his lips. "Just this," he said. He slid his arms around her and pulled her to him, growling with deep satisfaction as his hungry body was cushioned by her soft, yielding female form.

For a moment, she stood docilely in his embrace, neither rejecting nor accepting his caresses. But as he slanted his lips more fully over hers and teased the tender bowed line of her upper lip with his tongue, her carefully neutral posture softened and she melted against him as she made a small sound. Her mouth opened to admit him to the hot, sweet depths, and her arms came up, first to rest tentatively on his shoulders, and then to twine more securely around his neck as the kiss deepened and the undeniable sparks between them caught and blazed high.

He'd felt himself getting hard the moment she'd turned to face him in the intimate confines of her bedroom. As she stood on tiptoe and pressed herself to him, he slid one hand down the elegant line of her back and palmed one of the sweet, rounded globes of her bottom, hauling her higher against him, pushing his eager flesh more firmly into the heated notch of her thighs. The fit was so satisfying that he groaned aloud.

Then Ana raised one leg and hooked it high around his hip, opening herself to him completely and suddenly he knew there was only one way for this embrace to end. Though he hadn't woken up planning it, he was going to make love to Ana Birch today.

Pivoting, he took the few strides to the side of the bed with her still clinging to him. He set her on her feet on the braided rug beside it, then used his tongue to dip and circle, to slip into and explore every hidden corner of her mouth as he pulled handfuls of T-shirt free of her shorts.

He'd wanted her for so long. He'd fantasized about her silky body, the full curves of her breasts, the gold-brushed curls between her legs…and she was going to be his. Finding the hem of her shirt, he drew it up and off, then resumed kissing her while she fumbled with his shirt. When she had it off, he drew her close again, unhooking her bra and dragging it away, then pressing her satiny flesh to his. The feel of her bared breasts against his naked torso was a staggering delight, but he drew her away so that he could look down at the beauty he'd uncovered. Her skin was a creamy ivory, the pale rosy shade of her nipples a stunning contrast, and he brought both hands up to cup the sweet weighted mounds in his palms, brushing his thumbs over her nipples until her eyes went blind with pleasure and she clutched his shoulders, pleading, "Please…"

"Please what?"

Her hands slipped to the fastening of his shorts, wordlessly indicating her needs. But when she got there, instead of dealing with the button, her small fingers slipped lower to press and explore him through his pants. He nearly leaped out of his skin at the hesitant, intimate touch and he couldn't prevent the shudder of desire that danced down his spine as he rolled his hips heavily into her hand. Reluctantly leaving her breasts, he dealt with his shorts, shoving them and his briefs down and off in the same motion. In another moment he had hers off as well.

Then he urged her backward onto the bed, coming down beside her. He bent over her and claimed her mouth again, giving all his attention to her sweet, responsive mouth until they were both breathing in ragged gulps. When he finally lifted his head, she buried her face in his throat. He explored her body with his free hand, stroking and petting every inch of her yielding feminine treasures until finally he swept his fingers down to tangle in the silky thatch of curls at the vee of her legs.

Ana gasped beneath his mouth when he extended one long finger, slipping it slowly, inexorably down through the damp folds of skin to the slick warmth inside. He pressed and circled her there, dragging his mouth down her body to suckle strongly at her breast as her back arched off the bed and she held his head to her with trembling fingers. Her hips were rising and falling in rhythm with his finger, steadily caressing his hot, hard length where he pressed against her thigh. At one such rise he slipped the single digit deeply into her body, pressing upward. She uttered one short, sharp scream and her body convulsed in his arms.

His own body was screaming for attention as he drank in her response. As she shook and trembled beneath him, he quickly withdrew his finger and rose over her, kneeing her thighs apart and guiding himself to her. She was hot, very wet, and though he knew he should go slowly, at the first yielding of her tender flesh, his hips flexed and thrust forward in one great spasm that propelled him deep inside her as she still quivered in the grip of her own ecstasy.

She screamed again and arched up against him, her hands sliding to his buttocks and pulling him sharply to her, deeper and deeper as her inner muscles flexed and squeezed. He was caught in the grip of an irresistible force, snared in a hot, silky net of need. He could feel himself losing control, abandoning all attempts to hold back and make it last, and in the next moment, he was seized by his own finish, hips thudding against her, back arched, neck straining as he delivered his seed deep inside her.

Inside her! Instantly he tried to pull out but her hands still held him to her and his own body resisted his commands. Unable to resist, he gave himself to the shivering, delicious sensations and let his body take over.

When the last spasm had ended and they both lay

limp and drained, Garrett raised his head from the pillow where his face was buried.

"Are you on the pill?"

Ana froze. The shock in her face told him before she even opened her mouth. "No." She closed her eyes. "I'm so sorry. I wasn't thinking."

He propped himself on his elbows and kissed each of her eyelids. "I'm the one who should have been thinking." He grinned crookedly. "But I was busy." Then he sobered. "Don't worry. We'll deal with it if there's a consequence."

Her eyes opened and she stared solemnly up at him. "I can't believe you don't keep anything with you."

He shrugged one shoulder. "I think I hoped that if I didn't have any protection I'd have the sense not to give in to...this."

She stiffened, and he realized immediately how he had sounded. "Ana," he said. She wouldn't look at him. "Ana." He dropped his head and kissed her until she responded, then lifted his head and looked deep into her eyes. "I didn't mean I don't find you desirable. I was trying to...I don't know, keep to the high road, I guess. Right now I can't remember why that seemed so important."

She relaxed again and he bent to capture her lips once more until he realized she was shifting uncomfortably. He needed to move; she was far too small to support his weight. Withdrawing and sliding to one side, he pulled her into his arms. Tucking her head beneath his chin, he lay silently, watching the patterns of dancing leaves in the sunlight on the far wall. If he'd ever felt so content before, he couldn't recall it.

Ana's warm body snuggled bonelessly against him, the wild curls of her hair drifted over his shoulder and turned to fire in a ray of light that lay across their bodies. He felt...protective, he decided, cuddling her closer. And possessive. She was his now.

"Garrett?" Ana ran a lethargic hand through the dense mat of silky dark hair across his breastbone, following its path as it arrowed into a thin line down past his navel, then bloomed again beneath.

"Hmm?"

"What did you mean, we'd deal with it if I were to get pregnant?"

He went still beside her, alert to an odd tone in her musical voice. "I don't know," he said. "I just wanted you to know I wouldn't walk away and leave you to handle something like that alone."

"Because I would never—I couldn't—"

"I would want a child if it were to happen." He turned his head and kissed her temple, soothing her agitation as he realized what was troubling her. "Is it likely?"

She thought for a moment. "Likely? I suppose it's possible." She sighed. "I always promised myself that a child of mine wouldn't grow up without its father like I did."

It was his turn to still. "Why would it?" he asked carefully. "Unlike the guy that fathered you, I'm not married to someone else and I'm not about to run from my responsibilities." A child...with Ana. A vague shiver of anticipation tightened the muscles of his stomach. He could think of worse fates. In fact, he wasn't sure he could think of anything he'd like better.

Then he realized that Ana hadn't answered him.

Tightening his arm, he drew her up onto his chest and put his other arm about her as well. "Let's not get ourselves bent out of shape for no reason, all right?"

The curtain of her hair shut out the sunlight as she looked down at him and her eyes were dark and mysterious. "All right," she finally said.

He ran one hand up the silky expanse of her back and threaded his fingers through her hair, cradling her skull and pulling her head down until their lips met. Though he'd intended it as a kiss of comfort, her instant, wholehearted response brought his body leaping alive again, and he finally had to set her from him with a grimace. "No more sex until I have a chance to get to a store."

He felt her body move in silent laughter. "Not…anything?"

"You little tease." He rolled, pinning her beneath him. "I'm not taking any more chances on forgetting. Come on. Let's go to the store." As he tugged her out of bed behind him, he acknowledged that condoms were a necessity. Now. Making love to Ana was addictive; already he wanted her again. But he didn't simply want to play games, as she'd intimated. No. When he made love to her, something within him demanded the basic, primitive need to be buried deep inside her.

But as he tossed her clothes at her, she shook her head. "I need a shower."

He grinned. "Why? We're just going right back to bed as soon as we get home."

"But I promised to visit Nola and the twins, remember?" She brushed past him, lithe and lovely in her nakedness, but he put out a hand and caught her wrist. Turning her to him, he took a long survey, drinking in all the fine details he'd missed in the frantic rush to completion earlier. Her hips were slender; her legs long. He already knew that, as he'd known her breasts were full and her arms lightly muscled. What he hadn't known, however, was the lovely pale rose of the crests of her breasts, the glint of gold in the thatch of hair between her legs, the way her torso nipped in to her waist and flared so gently out to her hips again.

Ana was staring at him. "What?"

He smiled at her. "You're beautiful."

Her face softened. Then, to his dismay, her eyes filled with tears. "Thank you." She tugged her hand free. "I'll make it fast in the shower."

The trip to town was quiet, though not awkward. Garrett didn't talk much on the way but when she'd climbed into the passenger seat he threaded his fingers through hers and leaned across the console to give her a lingering kiss. Ana didn't talk, either, half-afraid to damage the new, fragile relationship they shared.

She had to tell him about her father. Today. She'd tried earlier, honestly tried, but he'd cut her off and once he'd begun to kiss her she'd forgotten all about it. But she knew she needed to get it out into the open. This evening, she would tell him.

Thinking about her father led to thoughts of her mother. A wave of nostalgia swept over her. What would her mother think of Garrett? She slid a sideways glance across the seat toward him.

He was watching her.

Flustered, she looked away again, and he gave a low chuckle. "What are you thinking?"

"Not the same thing you're thinking," she said tartly, and he laughed again. "If you really want to know, I was wondering what my mother would have thought of you."

"She would have thought I was handsome and charming," he said promptly.

It was her turn to laugh. "And modest."

There was a small, comfortable silence between them. Then he said, "Tell me about her."

She was warmed by the interest in his voice. "She was a painter. A very, very good one. Her name is well-known in international art circles." Her voice caught and Garrett squeezed her fingers. When the lump in her throat had eased, she said, "Tell me how your mother met Robin."

She saw the smile that lifted the corner of his mouth. "It was a setup."

"A setup?"

He flashed her a grin. "My mother was a bit on the helpless side. Her skills were limited to being a good hostess and keeping a perfect house. After my father died she was completely over her head. Her friends started introducing her to their friends, hoping that a man would come along to take care of her again."

"Did she love Robin?"

"She adored him." His voice grew reflective. "I think she was far more in love with him than he ever was with her."

"What makes you say that?" Every small snippet of information she could add to her meager store of details about her father were precious, even those regarding his life with the family of which she hadn't been a part.

Garrett shrugged. "For a long time, it was just a sense that I had. He was always wonderful to Mother, but there was something...something a little sad in his eyes sometimes."

He raised her hand to his lips and kissed her fingers. "He was such a great guy. Getting him for a stepfather was the best thing that could have happened to me."

She was sure that was true and she stroked the back of his hand with her thumb as his voice thickened.

"I still can't believe he's gone," he confessed. "At least once a day I reach for the phone to call him before I remember that he won't be there."

Her own throat was too tight to speak. All she could do was stroke his hand in wordless sympathy.

They didn't talk again after that until they reached town, and she was content to sit beside him with his hand enclosing hers. It felt *right* with him, and she supposed that Robin's plan to throw them together had worked in that regard. Living in the same small space had accustomed them to each other's quirks and routines and given them a level of comfort they'd never have known under other circumstances.

At home again after picking up his truck and stopping by the hospital, Garrett hurried her through the door, then tossed their purchases on the kitchen counter and turned to take her in his arms. She snuggled against him, loving the solid feel of his big body, the warmth of his arms around her, the perfect fit of her head in the crook of his neck.

"Want to go for a canoe ride?" he said against her ear.

She shivered as his lips found the delicate shell and he bit down gently on her earlobe. "Th-that would be nice."

"Yeah." But he made no move to release her. Against her belly, she could feel the rising length of his desire and her breath grew short as her body softened and tingled. She slowly rubbed herself back and forth over him the slightest bit, brushing her sensitive nipples across the hard planes of his chest.

Garrett lifted a hand and circled her throat, tipping her chin up with his thumb. He bent, covering her mouth with his in a long, languid kiss as his hand slipped down to shape and stroke her breast, tugging at the tender peak until she was writhing in his arms.

"I think," he murmured against her mouth, "that the lake will have to wait."

She fumbled blindly along the edge of the counter with one hand until she found the bag from the store. Withdrawing the box of protection he'd purchased, she held it as he lifted her into his arms and carried her up the stairs and into her room, where he lay her on the bed. It took him only moments to methodically strip away her garments and then his.

She opened her arms to welcome him, sighing with relief when his full weight came down atop her. "Oh, Garrett," she whispered, "I lo—" Then she stopped, shocked by the words that had nearly escaped. *I love you.*

"Hmm?" He was kissing a path down her neck and across her collarbone and she shivered as his beard-roughened skin dragged over her.

"I like the way you do that," she mumbled, but her brain was still reeling at the near-slip. Although she wasn't sure, she suspected that Garrett still wasn't ready to admit to anything deeper than a physical attraction. But once he knew about her father...then, she hoped, he would be able to see that what they shared could be permanent.

The next three days were idyllic, if he didn't think about the fact that they were about to end. On the afternoon before they were to leave, they'd spent the day packing up everything nonessential and putting dustcovers over the furniture in preparation for the long winter when the cottage would stand alone in the snow.

But after they'd cleaned and put away the deck furniture, Garrett reached out and tossed her up over his shoulder as he headed inside.

"Garrett!" Laughing, Ana pounded her small fists on his back. "What are you doing?"

"Taking my woman to bed."

"Your woman? Feeling a little primitive today, are we?" She gasped as he let her bounce onto the mattress, then followed her down before she could wriggle away.

"Feeling a little primitive *every* day," he corrected, fastening his teeth lightly on her earlobe and flicking his tongue along the tender rim. "You belong to me and I intend to make sure you don't forget it." Then, as if he'd realized just how he sounded, he dropped his head and kissed her, a slow, lingering mating of lips and tongues that roused her sluggish pulse even as his words roused the love hidden in her heart. She wrapped her arms around his muscled shoulders and pressed herself to him, offering her love in the only way she would allow herself, and within moments, they were naked and rolling together across the wide bed.

More than an hour later, a rumble of thunder disturbed their lethargic contentment.

Garrett turned his head and looked toward the window that faced out over the lake. "Looks like we're in for a storm."

"Mmm-hmm." Ana pressed an openmouthed kiss to his bare chest. "The weather service called for thunderstorms all along the coast this evening."

He sighed. "I'd better go down and bring the canoe onto the beach. If the lake gets rough, it's too fragile to be slammed against the dock."

She made a small moue of discontent but obediently sat up and reached for the closest garment at hand, which happened to be his T-shirt. "I'll close all the windows and stack the deck chairs."

Together they walked down the stairs. Ana went out onto the deck while he moved on through the kitchen. A moment later, he appeared again, heading down the path toward the dock. As he walked, he turned and called to her, "The back door was open. I must not have closed it firmly when we came in."

She couldn't prevent the smug smile that spread across her face as she surveyed him. All he wore were his pants and the muscles in his chest and arms rippled as he gestured. "Guess you had other things on your mind."

He grinned in return. "Guess I did." Then his grin faded. "You'd better check on the cat. I doubt she got out, but just in case…"

Roadkill. She felt her own good mood flee. The cat needed medication twice a day to ward off the seizures she suffered. Without it, her brain would succumb to the frightening fits more and more frequently. Roadkill would probably die if she were left on her own now.

She checked every room, every corner, every nook and cranny where she thought the cat might be likely to hide. She liked small spaces, and had been known to squeeze under low chairs and into the picnic basket in the pantry. But she wasn't anywhere.

Garrett came in the door just as she was out of ideas, and she turned to him fearfully. "I can't find her anywhere. I think she might have gotten out."

"Are you sure she isn't here?" He moved past her to the counter and took out a couple of tins of cat food. "Let's open this and wave it around. If she hears the top pop or smells it, she'll come running."

Ana nodded, reassured by his calm confidence.

"Okay." She took a deep, steadying breath. "If she comes, she's getting both cans at once."

He smiled, placing one large hand on her shoulder and massaging briefly. "You take the upstairs. I'll check down here."

She moved quickly to obey, but after a few minutes of futile calling and letting the noxious odor of canned cat food waft through the house, she slowly came down the stairs, feeling tears rising despite her best efforts. "She isn't here, is she?" she asked, biting down hard on her lip to keep it from quavering.

He hesitated for a moment, then shook his head. "It doesn't look like it. She must have sneaked out that door." He set down the cat food on the counter in the kitchen. "I'm sorry. I should have made sure that door was closed."

"It wasn't your fault." She tried to smile. "Neither one of us was thinking about the door."

His expression softened. "No," he said. "We weren't."

The sudden sound of rain hissing against the windows interrupted him as the storm unleashed a deluge that pounded down on the cottage and the pines and birches surrounding it. Lightning flashed and thunder clapped almost simultaneously, making her jump. Garrett gathered her close.

"Look," he said. "If she is out there, she's probably scared silly and will be thrilled to see you. Get your keys. You can drive down the lane in the car and call her from the window."

"What will you be doing?" She was already moving toward the hook that held the car keys.

"I'll check around the outside of the cabin." As she shrugged into a rain slicker and prepared to make the dash to her car, he took her by the elbow and held her back for a moment. "Promise me," he said intensely, "that you won't get out of the car. These storms can be dangerous."

"You're going out in it," she said.

"One of us has to. There's no sense in both of us taking unnecessary chances."

She hesitated. "I'm afraid I'll see her and she won't come."

He shoved one of the open cans of cat food into her free hand. "She'll come. Stay in the car."

Reluctantly she nodded. "All right." Then she went into his arms and kissed him quickly. "Please be careful."

Eight

Garrett waited until the driving rain obscured her taillights as Ana drove out the lane. Then he took the other can of food, grabbed a flashlight and stepped out onto the porch, taking a deep breath. The rain was still drumming down with stinging force. There was another flash of lightning, but this time the thunder was delayed by several seconds, indicating that the storm was no longer directly overhead.

Where would the cat have gone? He looked around. It hadn't been raining when she'd gone out, so she might have moved some distance away from the cottage, but he'd bet she'd found cover once the full force of the storm hit.

He plunged off the porch into the pouring rain. First he circled the cabin, calling the cat as he checked all the spaces around the foundation and under the porches where a small animal might hide. As he knelt to shine the light into the recesses of the lean-to where he stored split logs, he hoped that skunks didn't like cat food. Unfortunately—or fortunately, he thought wryly—nothing of any species appeared to be hiding there.

As he approached the cove, he crunched over the gravel, heading for the far end of the beach. But as he drew abreast of the canoe he'd overturned above the waterline only minutes before the storm started, he thought he heard a sound. A cat sound.

He stopped in his tracks. Pivoting, he shone the beam of the flashlight beneath the canoe. It reflected eerie light from a pair of close-set eyes. Cat eyes.

Garrett closed his own eyes in relief. "Roadkill? Come here, you ungrateful cat."

A plaintive meow answered him clearly through the diminishing patter of the rain, but the eyes didn't move.

He sighed. Kneeling, he shoved the tin of cat food right to the edge of the canoe. "Come here, you moronic critter," he said in what he hoped was a loving tone. "You're worrying your pretty mistress to death."

Roadkill meowed again, and then the eyes moved. He moved just as fast, pulling the food out of reach, out into the open. His other hand hovered just above the opening where the cat would have to emerge.

And he waited.

The eyes blinked, then moved again, slowly. Inch by incremental inch, the small tiger cat came slinking out from beneath the canoe on her belly. She looked completely spooked, her eyes wild and dark, and he could see it wouldn't take much to send her running into the unfamiliar terrain again. He kept a firm hand on the can, unmoving, and eventually she decided she wanted the food more than she feared his presence. As she settled down to her feast, he put a large, firm hand on the back of her neck and took a fistful of cat scruff.

Roadkill froze. Quickly he pulled her up against his chest and shoved the cat food beneath her nose as she began to struggle. "Here—ouch! Dammit, cat—eat!"

Apparently realizing that her days of freedom were at an end, she relaxed in his arms and buried her face in the can of food he offered.

He looked down. Two furrows of cat scratches oozed blood just below his left collarbone. "I should have let you go," he grumbled to the little animal as he climbed the path. "You're a—"

"You found her!" Ana was coming down the wide steps above the house. "Oh, Garrett, where was she? I can't believe she came to you!"

"She didn't exactly come to *me,*" he said ruefully as she reached them and lifted the cat from his arms. "She was a lot more excited about the food."

Ana preceded him into the house, cooing and cuddling the little ingrate, who streaked out of the room and up the steps to the second floor the moment Ana set her down. They both laughed, and Ana turned to him with a shining face and launched herself into his arms. "Thank you, thank you, thank you!"

He still held the cat food and the flashlight, but she

wound her arms around his neck and pressed herself against him, fervently raining kisses across his chest and up his chin. Unable to resist the invitation, he reached behind her to set down the items, then put both hands on her bottom and hauled her up against him as she found his mouth and began to kiss him.

She was a wild thing in his embrace, burning him alive with her mouth and her tongue as he let her take the lead. Slowly she slipped down his body, pausing a moment when her mouth brushed over the cat scratches. "We should clean those," she purred. "They can be nasty." But she already was moving on, finding his flat male nipple with her swirling tongue, nipping at him until the sweet sensation plucked a strong answering chord in his groin and he threaded his fingers through her hair and pressed her to him.

"Later," he said hoarsely. "We'll clean them later."

Ana slid farther down his body, her mouth following the line of hair that arrowed down his torso, her tongue probing his navel as her hands worked at the soaking fabric of his trousers.

He closed his eyes and leaned back against the wall, groaning as he felt the fabric give way. Cool air washed over his erect flesh, then Ana's warm hand closed around him, easing him free of the clinging material. "Lord," he said in a guttural tone that he barely recognized as his own, "Ana, stop. No, don't stop." He bared his teeth in a feral smile as she sat back on her heels and looked up the length of his body with triumphant eyes.

Her hand moved slowly over him as she returned the smile with a slow, confident feminine expression that tightened his body in another wild rush of sensation. He saw her intent in her eyes moments before she leaned forward, bathing him with her sweet breath for an instant before her mouth closed over him.

His breath wheezed out in an agonizing sound of pleasure too great to be borne and his hands clenched in her hair as her questing fingers brushed between his legs and clasped his thighs. She loved him with hot, wild strokes of mouth and hand, using her tongue to bring him quickly to the point of no return. As he gave himself to her sweet ministrations, the storm broke over his head, driving him to a harsh, breathtaking climax that left his knees shaking as he stared blindly at the ceiling, gasping for breath.

Ana rose fluidly to her feet and took his hand while he was still trying to regulate his breathing, saying softly, "Let's go upstairs."

But as she turned away, he used the handclasp to drag her back against him. To his shock, he realized that all she wore was the T-shirt she'd pulled on earlier. He yanked up the fabric in handfuls and pressed her smooth bare curves hard against him, seeking her mouth as her warm female form ignited a desire he'd have sworn he couldn't possibly feel again so quickly.

"Ana," he muttered against her mouth as his hands streaked over her body possessively. "Do you know what you do to me?" Cradling her skull, he held her head against his shoulder as he kissed her long and deeply, loving her mouth as thoroughly as she'd loved him minutes before.

When he lifted his head, she raised a hand to his lean jaw, and her eyes were dazed with soft pleasure. "Garrett," she murmured. "I love you."

The husky words confirmed something he had barely allowed himself to consider, and he was shocked by the fierce masculine satisfaction rushing through him. Although he couldn't pinpoint the moment when his life had changed, he knew it had. Forever. He could no longer imagine his future without Ana in it, could no longer imagine his life without her.

But at the same time, a desperate voice in his head shouted for caution. Very deliberately, he shut off the thoughts clamoring for his attention. He could think later. Right now...right now it was enough simply to feel.

Ana stirred in his arms and he realized her words still hung between them. Touching his mouth lightly to her forehead, he said, "Let's go upstairs." He set his mouth on her again and lifted her into his arms at the same time. Her arms went around his neck as he carried her through the living room and up the stairs to the bed they'd shared through the hours of the morning.

I love you.

The scary thing, Garrett decided as he lay sleepless several hours later, was that he'd wanted to say the words back to her...*had* nearly blurted out those three small, single-syllable words that could irrevocably change a person's life. His life.

And though everything in him had urged him to

throw caution to the winds, he'd held his tongue. He cared for her, cared for her in a way that he had to acknowledge he'd never felt before about any woman. Even Kammy. Especially Kammy. He'd thought she was special, had thought he'd loved her. But now…now he knew better. And the knowledge made it even more difficult not to respond to Ana's declaration.

But he couldn't. Wouldn't, because he knew these feelings weren't real. Thank God his last attempt at intimacy had ended as it had; he was a lot smarter because of it. Though he'd hated Kammy at the time, now he realized he was lucky to have learned the truth about her before the wedding.

So what was the truth about Ana? He desperately wanted to believe she wanted to spend the rest of her life with him, as well. But he couldn't believe it was that easy. The facts gave him pause.

He had money. Ana needed money. Even if he did buy out her half of the cabin, it wouldn't be a sum that would last her any length of time. Realistically it would barely be enough to allow her to properly set up the kind of small business she had in mind.

The logical extension of their new involvement would be for her to move in with him. Was that what she'd been angling for all along?

Ana mumbled something and shifted in his arms, and he realized his embrace had tightened around her. Carefully he relaxed the tense muscles of his shoulders. She snuggled more closely against him again and a pleasant sexual shiver ran down his spine as her warm breath feathered across his throat. Her body was soft and pliant, her sleep deep and peaceful. He liked the way she felt in his arms, the way she fit so perfectly against his body, the way she moaned and arched up to him when he took her. He probably could spend the rest of his life in bed with her and never mind it for a minute.

No, she didn't really love him, he decided, though she even might believe she did. A few weeks ago, he'd have thought she was using those words as Kammy had, in order to wrap him around her finger for money or security or whatever her particular needs happened to be. Now he knew that wasn't the case, at least, not the *whole* case. If Ana said she loved him, she thought she was telling the truth.

I love you. It was the sex talking. It had to be. And that, of course, was why he'd nearly responded. It was easy to confuse the two. Great sex produced strong emotion, and a lot of people believed that was the same as love.

He knew better, he reminded himself again, though perhaps *she* didn't realize there was a difference. Ultimately it didn't matter. If she wanted to fool herself, it was fine by him. The bottom line was that he'd sworn never to let himself be manipulated by a woman who might be after his money ever again. Ana wasn't like his former fiancée in most ways, true, but…there was a niggling corner of dark doubt in his mind. She needed money. He had money. He was merely being realistic. The bottom line…if he'd been penniless, would Ana still tell him she loved him?

He didn't know. He honestly didn't. But as long as he accepted the real bottom line, there was no reason he couldn't enjoy her for as long as they were together.

And they were going to be together for a while, of that he was positive. Whatever her relationship with Robin had been, he no longer cared. She'd made his stepfather's last years of life happy, had given him joy and pleasure that he clearly hadn't known before. How could he resent that?

She woke when Garrett eased his arm from beneath her neck and slid from the warm nest of the bed. Slitting her eyes against the early-morning sunlight that flowed in the large window, she watched as he padded naked across the floor to the bathroom. God, he was beautiful. His legs were long and straight, and the lean hollows of his buttocks made her palms tingle with the need to trace the smooth skin. His shoulders, in contrast to his narrow waist and hips, looked as wide as a house.

As he disappeared into the bathroom, she inched over into the warm depression he'd left. She didn't want to wake up, didn't want the day to begin.

Things would be different between them now, she feared. He hadn't responded to her declaration of love last night. She hadn't really expected him to, hadn't really even intended to say the words herself, but they'd burst out without warning. She wasn't sorry…exactly. But she was a little nervous. Would it change things between them? Would he step back from the warmth and intimacy they shared? Yesterday, she'd assumed that when they returned to Baltimore they'd be returning together, making plans together.

His silence last night had erased all her assumptions.

He came back out of the bathroom without warning, and before she could close her eyes and play possum, his startlingly blue, stunningly beautiful eyes had snared her gaze. His held a warm intimacy. "Good morning," he said as he crossed to the bed.

"Good morning." She cleared her throat. He perched on the edge of the bed, cupping the ball of her shoulder where it was uncovered by the sheets. His thumb gently stroked her sensitive skin.

"Want to go for a swim, sweetheart?" he asked.

"That would be great." Her heart lurched at the endearment even as she told herself it meant nothing. Then she screeched as he tossed back the blanket and scooped her into his arms. She clung to his neck as he strode down the stairs, balancing her on his knee while he unlocked the door. Then he carried her out of the cottage and down the path to the lake.

"Garrett! Put me down! We can't just run around naked."

He paused and looked down at her, laughing. "Why not? You've done it before." Negotiating the steps to the dock, he walked all the way to the end. And before she realized what he intended, he shifted sideways, lifted her higher and swung her out over the water, releasing her at the last second and she splashed into the cold water with a shocked exclamation.

When she surfaced, pushing handfuls of wet corkscrew curls back from her face, he was treading water beside her, still chuckling. She couldn't hide the bubble of amusement that rose as she turned over onto her back and floated beside him. "Very funny. You know what they say about paybacks."

He gave a mock-shiver. "I'm shaking in my shoes." Then he reached out and pulled her to him, moving around the side of the dock into water where he could touch bottom, though Ana still couldn't. The water made their bodies slippery and silky and as his thigh slid between hers and his mouth descended, she forgot to laugh. Against her lips, he whispered, "There's something I've always wanted to try in the water. Want to share a first with me?"

He was hard against her belly as she wrapped her legs around his hips and offered herself to him. "I'd love to."

"There's something I've been wanting to talk to you about," she said an hour later, industriously buttering two slices of toast.

"I know." He was busy flipping over the eggs.

"You do?"

"Yeah," he said. "Today's the day. As of today we are officially the owners of Eden Cottage. And my original offer still stands. I'll be happy to pay you full market value for your half."

She was stunned. "That wasn't…it's not…" She'd supposed they had gotten beyond that. It was a shock to realize that the time they'd spent here together had done nothing to alter Garrett's thinking. "I still don't want to sell it," she said carefully.

There was a moment of silence. She could sense the tension growing between them. "You need the money," he said, "don't you? I thought you wanted to get your business off the ground."

"I do." She could barely speak around the lump in her throat that threatened to choke her. "But this place has become very special to me. Robin wanted me to have it. To share it with you."

He didn't say anything.

And suddenly she realized that this was the moment, though she hadn't planned it as carefully as she'd intended. The time she'd been avoiding for weeks. She took a deep breath. "The reason it's so special," she said, "is that Robin was very special to me. He was my father."

Garrett went still. "Ana—"

"Robin was my father." She rushed on when he only stared at her in silence, his gaze dark and unfathomable. "He and my mother fell in love but he wouldn't leave his first wife because she was already mentally ill. When my mother found out she was pregnant, she decided to go away."

Garrett's eyes narrowed and he spoke for the first time. "Why? Seems like that would have given her more leverage to press for marriage."

His words hurtled against her like hailstones and she felt a defensive retort rise. "You didn't know my mother," she said in clipped tones, lifting her chin. "She wouldn't have wanted to put Robin in the position of having to make a choice that would have haunted him forever. And at that point in time, no one had any idea how long Maggie would live."

"And you know this because…?" There was little inflection in his cool tone.

"When my mother realized she was terminally ill, she wrote Robin and me each a letter to be delivered by her attorney…afterward." She had to stop and swallow the grief that rose. "When Robin learned that he had a daughter, he was on my doorstep the very next day. My letter, as you can imagine, was quite a shock, since I thought my father had died years ago."

"I'm sure it was," Garrett murmured.

Encouraged, she said, "Mrs. Davenport told me that Robin and my mother built this place together. They only spent one summer here together before she left."

Garrett dropped his face into his hands and pressed hard against his forehead. "Ana…" He hesitated.

She looked at him expectantly. Surely now he understood why she didn't want to sell. And he also must realize that his assumptions about her had been completely off-base from the very beginning. "No apologies are necessary," she said. "I intended to tell you long ago, but you made me so mad I decided to let you think whatever you wanted. And then I meant to, several times, but it just was never right, and then last night—"

"Ana." His voice was firmer, and she stopped in midsentence. "You don't have to do this," he said quietly. "If you want to keep half the cottage that badly, you can have it." He patted his knee. "Come here."

Confused, she allowed him to take her hand and

pull her down. What did he mean, she didn't have to do this? Do what?

"I want you," he said, looking deep into her eyes. "Your past isn't important to me. I'd like you to come to live with me."

At first the words made no sense. But then her paralyzed brain began to sort out sounds and meanings again and she nearly cried aloud as the ugly truth pierced her heart. He didn't believe her! Dear heaven, in all the ways she'd envisioned this scene playing out, that he wouldn't believe her hadn't even been on her mental movie screen.

"Ana?" His beautiful eyes were studying her, waiting for her answer.

She was dying inside, her heart shriveling into a dried-up, unusable state, and the cold calm of utter shock took over. *You can't break down,* she told herself. *Not in front of Garrett.* "For how long?" It was the only response that came into her head, not a question to which the answer particularly mattered. Not now.

He shrugged. "Do we have to put a time limit on it? Why don't we just see how it goes?" His hard arm was warm around her back and his fingers caressed her waist and the curve of her hip. "Just think how good it will be for you. You won't have to find a new place to rent. You won't have to work extra jobs. You can build up your millinery business while we're together." When she would have risen, he held her in place. "If it's capital you're worrying about, I'll give you the money. How much do you estimate you'd need?"

She recoiled. Pain punched a hole through her heart. "I don't want your money."

"All right, if you won't accept a gift, I'll make it a low-interest loan. You can pay me back—we'll set up a monthly schedule."

"No." Quietly, but with steely resolve, she disentangled herself from his arms and rose, putting a safe distance between them. Her chest ached and the lump in her throat made it hard to speak. She swallowed. "Why are you so determined always to think the worst of me? Millions of people have had a bad experience with love and they don't use it as a shield to hide behind."

"I'm not hiding behind anything," he retorted, his eyes narrowing as the set expression on her face finally registered. "But I'm realistic. We enjoy each other's company. We like some of the same things. We're one hell of a match in bed." He stopped and looked away, his features hardening. "Love has nothing to do with what's between you and me."

The shattered shards of her heart were crushed to dust beneath the flat pronouncement. She studied him silently for a long moment, long enough that his gaze met hers again. He began to look distinctly uncomfortable under her uncompromising gaze. "If you truly believe that," she told him, "I feel sorry for you, Garrett. Sorry that you let your father's behavior and one woman's deceit dictate your entire future. Sorry that because of those bad breaks you're willing to throw away what we could have had together." She paused and walked to the doorway. "You're giving the past far too much power."

"I'm not—" His voice was tight, strident.

"I loved you," she said quietly. Tears were rolling down her cheeks but when he made an involuntary movement toward her she threw out a hand to stop him. If he touched her again, she'd break down completely. "My mother and father lost their chance at happiness but I was sure I'd found mine." She closed her eyes. "What a blind fool I was."

Silently she turned away then, walking down the hall and to the door. She didn't know where she was going but she knew she needed distance between them.

Garrett stood where she left him, his whole body rigid with denial. He heard the screen door open and close and her footsteps crossed the porch. Then he couldn't hear her anymore.

Finally he couldn't take the silence. He slammed the kitchen door behind him with a satisfying bang but the harsh sound did little to assuage the rage that boiled and churned inside him. His stomach hurt and his hands shook. His chest felt like it was banded with a restricting bar of iron. His thoughts whirled like a tornado, fragments rushing by too quickly for him to hang on to, torn away by the force of the gale.

Why would she lie to him like that? Surely she wasn't crazy enough to think he'd buy such an outrageous story. He swallowed repeatedly, but the lump in his throat wouldn't budge. Disappointment mushroomed, filling every corner of his being.

How could he have been so wrong about her? She'd seemed so different. But in the end, she wanted him for her personal gain, just as Kammy had. The only question now was how long she'd keep up the pretense of being wounded before she tried to get him to support her as he'd offered.

And she was wrong about him, he assured himself. The past didn't enter into this equation, except for its role in making him smarter and less gullible. His father had been a jerk, but that had nothing to do with today. *Nothing.*

He walked out onto the deck, noting that Ana was sitting on the edge of the dock, her feet dangling in the water. Abruptly he turned away, heading for the hiking trail that led around the lake. Angrily he kicked at sticks and pebbles as he strode along the path, then he veered away from the trail and began to hike through less accessible terrain. The physical challenge as he hiked over and around boulders and downed trees expended the worst of his first furious reaction, and a bone-deep sadness seeped in, chilling him despite his exertion.

Why? Why had she told him that?

Robin's heir would be entitled to a sizable portion of his estate, whispered an insidious little voice in his head.

Exactly. When she'd begun to speak, he'd felt his heart sink to his toes, leaving a leaden heaviness behind. Hadn't he told her he'd take care of her needs? Apparently that wasn't enough. She'd wanted more. A lot more.

Then an equally insistent thought intruded. *You could be wrong. Maybe she was telling the truth.*

Nah. He rejected it immediately. Of course she

wasn't Robin's daughter. Robin would have told him about that.

Wouldn't he?

For the first time in years, a tremor of insecurity rocked the stable world his stepfather had given him. *I'll introduce you to her soon. I believe you'll like her.* There hadn't been any hint of a leer, though Robin was too much of a gentleman for that anyway. But the quiet happiness that had shone from his still-vivid blue eyes had been unmistakable. He'd cared deeply for her. And back when Garrett assumed that Robin's ladylove was a dignified widow, he'd had no problem with it.

The problem had occurred when he'd met her and wanted her for himself.

Garrett stopped dead in the path. Slowly he lowered himself onto a rotting log and sat with his elbows on his knees, hands dangling between his knees while his breathing leveled out.

Good God. Was this all about jealousy? He was uncomfortably afraid that was exactly what had transpired.

How would he have felt if the older woman of his imaginings had inherited half the cottage? He forced himself to examine the scenario honestly. He would have been annoyed. More than annoyed. But would he have treated her as he'd treated Ana?

Absolutely, positively not.

An older woman, though, wouldn't be claiming to be Robin's biological daughter, he reminded himself.

He sat for a long, long time, watching the sun-dappled patterns of light and shadows play over the path and the edge of the lake where the trees grew right down to the rocks. Finally, as the shadows lengthened, he rose and started back toward the cottage.

It was a good thing the month had come to an end, he told himself firmly. He and Ana would only have one more uncomfortable night to get through before they headed back to Baltimore in the morning. He lifted a hand and pressed two fingers to his chest to relieve the pressure that centered there. Indigestion. That's all it was.

They wouldn't be spending that last night together.

He plodded on. As the cottage came into view between the trees, regret rose too large to suppress. The thing was, he could have been happy with Ana. She was comfortable to be with. He'd known enough women to know how rare it was to find someone with whom a shared silence wasn't a strain. In bed, he'd never known a woman so generous with herself, so able to rouse him to passion, so desirable. They both enjoyed the leisurely pace of life at the cottage, and he was certain she'd prefer a quiet lifestyle to a whirlwind trip to a high-rolling place like Las Vegas, as he did. She was a good cook, a quick wit, so tenderhearted that he longed to make the world perfect so that her heart would never be broken—

His feet stilled again. An inexorable tide of dread rose within him as he finally stopped lying to himself and faced the truth. He'd done exactly that—broken Ana's heart.

And his own, as well. The truth slapped him in the face.

Yes, he'd been jealous of Robin's relationship with her...because he'd wanted her for himself from the very first time he'd seen her. But even more, he'd begun to fall in love with her as he'd come to know her. *He loved Ana.*

In a single white-hot instant of clarity, he realized how little meaning his life would have without her. He could imagine waking to the sight of her glowing face each morning. He could imagine sharing the ups and downs of business and daily life with her. He could even, he realized with a sense of amazement, imagine adding a couple of kids to their lives: little girls with their mother's wild curls.

But the images froze as he recalled the devastation in her face before she'd walked away from him. He'd hurt her deeply, for reasons that now seemed petty and invalid. How could he make her understand that no matter how they'd first come together, he wanted to be with her forever?

A hint of panic touched his heart and he began to run up the path toward the cottage. He had a strong prescience of disaster, foreboding. He had to talk to Ana right away.

Inside he rushed up the stairs but she wasn't in her room. The door stood open, the room was empty. Not empty as in without a body, but unoccupied. Everything of any personal meaning gone.

A tiny demon of fear danced inside his gut as he forced himself to enter her studio. Also deserted. The counters were pristine and uncluttered again, the big worktable untouched. His gaze shot to the window beneath which she'd set her sewing machine, but the spot was as blank as it had been the day they'd arrived.

His lungs burned, and he realized he'd been holding his breath. Releasing it, he took a burning gasp of air. Ana was gone.

Nine

Ana was gone.

Her little car was no longer parked beneath the birches. Slowly Garrett moved down the stairs, confirming her flight with each step. Her beach towels no longer fluttered from the rail of the deck in the gentle breeze. The cat's bowl no longer occupied its place in the corner.

He stood in the middle of the kitchen, big hands lax at his sides. She'd left, and he really couldn't blame her. He'd been brutal. Moving into his office, he sat down in front of his computer, dashing off a quick request to his office manager in Baltimore to let him know when Ana Birch returned home, no matter how late it was, or how early tomorrow. He'd have to go after her and apologize.

He glanced up from the computer at the sketch of

Robin that had hung on the wall for years, since the office had originally been Robin's. It was one of his favorite images of Robin, clad in a casual sweater and pants. He sat on a rock by the lake in three-quarter view, a coffee cup cradled in both hands. A slight smile curved his lips, his eyes gazed into the distance. Garrett had seen him sit in that very pose more times than he could count.

"Well, old man, what do I do now?" he asked rhetorically, feeling the weight of hopelessness descend upon his soul. "You were right when you said I'd like her."

He stood and moved restlessly to the window. Something was bothering him, though he couldn't put his finger on it. Something...

Suddenly he snapped his fingers. Turning, he looked again at the picture of his stepfather. He'd never realized it before, but the picture had to have been drawn here, by a skilled artist who knew Robin well enough to capture that sweetly absorbed expression he often wore.

The hair on the back of his neck rose in automatic reflex as the truth kicked him in the face. *Ana's mother had drawn this.*

Walking across the room, his eyes scanned the bottom portion of the sketch—there. There, in the bottom left-hand corner: *JB*. And the date, all in a miniscule, elaborate cursive that looked as if she'd been drilled in the Palmer Method as a young girl.

Slowly he groped his way back to his desk without taking his eyes from the sketch. Sagging into his chair, he tilted his face toward the ceiling, closing his

eyes as he exhaled heavily. An unyielding fist
squeezed his chest, making it hard to breathe. He
hadn't wanted to believe her but deep down, he'd
known she wasn't lying.

And the proof hung right over there on the wall.
Ana had told him her mother had gone through a brief
pen and pencil phase before moving on to oils early
in her career. Robin and Janette Birch had come here
together, indeed, had created the cottage with their
mutual needs in mind. And Ana's mother had
sketched her lover in the setting where they'd been
happy. No wonder Robin seemed to leap off the paper—Janette Birch had known him so well she probably could have drawn it without even having him in
front of her. Just as Ana had drawn *him*.

Ana should have told him right away—but as he
remembered his behavior in Baltimore, he knew he'd
brought this on himself. No wonder she hadn't told
him. He'd barely given her a chance. And she'd probably realized early on that he'd call her a liar when
she tried to explain.

He dropped his head into his hands and speared his
fingers through his hair, tugging hard enough to make
himself wince. He'd been utterly, completely despicable to her. Smug, condescending, superior. God,
how would he ever get her to forgive him?

Abruptly he spun on his heel and headed for the
stairs to pack. He needed to get back to Baltimore.
But halfway there, he stopped abruptly. Her friends!

Ana wouldn't leave Maine without saying goodbye
to her friends. He might have made some monumental
misjudgments where Ana was concerned, but he knew

how she felt about friendship. She'd never take off without talking to Teddy and his wife first.

Grabbing his car keys, he made one brief stop in the study before racing up the path to his truck.

It was a good thing cops in rural Maine were few and far between, he decided, or he'd have been nailed for exceeding the speed limit ten times over in his rush to get to town. When he pulled onto Main Street and saw the familiar little car parked in front of the art supply store, a wave of intense relief swamped him. He pulled into a parking space and simply sat for a moment, dropping his head forward to rest against his hands atop the steering wheel.

Thank God he'd caught her.

He straightened and began to climb out of the car. The momentary rush had faded and his steps felt leaden and hesitant. What could he say to her to fix the mess he'd made of things between them?

He was almost at the front door of the art supply shop when he saw Ana walking toward the door. His gaze met hers through the glass and she stopped for an instant, then slowly began to exit the store.

She forestalled him by asking, "Did I forget something?"

"No." How was he going to change her mind?

They stood there awkwardly for a long moment. Finally she took a wide step that would allow her to pass him.

"Ana, I don't want you to leave." He turned as she moved past him and walked with her toward the cars.

She shook her head without looking at him. "I

have to,'' she whispered. "Please don't, Garrett.'' Her car was parked in front of his larger vehicle and she wrenched the door open, fumbling for her keys. "You can have the cottage," she said. "When I get back, I'll go to Mr. Marrow's office and sign anything he needs to make you the sole owner."

"I don't want it," he said. "I want you. If you won't share it with me, I'll sell it."

Shock snapped her head up. "You wouldn't do that. Robin wanted you to have it."

"Your father wanted *us* to have it," he said.

"He—" Then his words sank in. "My father…?"

"I didn't want to believe you," he said. "I was jealous. Robin was *my* father in all the ways that mattered, and I couldn't stand the thought of someone else meaning more to him."

"Robin loved you so much," she said quietly. "No one could ever have taken your place in his life."

"I know that now," he said. "I'm sorry for all the things I said to you." His voice lowered. "The things I believed."

"Thank you." She appeared to have trouble getting the words out and she made a show of looking at her watch. "I have to go now."

But as she moved to slide into her car, Garrett caught her wrist. "I love you."

She stopped. "What?"

He slid to one knee, still holding her wrist, and he brought it to his mouth as he spoke again. "Ana, I love you. I want to marry you."

"Stand up," she said in a low voice, "and stop it. We're on Main Street!"

"I don't care." He didn't move.

Wildly she glanced around. Down the street, he could see a few tourists turning and staring. A man came out of the post office, glanced their way, and then stopped for a second look.

She tried to tug her hand free. "Garrett—"

"Marry me," he said again.

A bell trilled and he saw that Teddy had come out of his shop. "Everything okay?" her friend asked.

"Yes—"

"No," Garrett said. "I love her and I want to marry her. She hasn't said yes yet."

"Maybe that's because she doesn't feel the same way," Teddy said in a cool voice.

A sudden spear of uncertainty shot through him. "You said you loved me." But there was a hint of vulnerability in his tone and his grip on her wrist lessened.

A tear rolled down her cheek and she swiped at it with her free hand. "I do," she managed to say.

He stood and pulled her into his arms, folding her small body against him with all the tenderness he was feeling. "I don't want to wake up without you beside me," he said. "I don't want to spend a day wondering where you might be or if you've thought of me. I don't want to be like Robin, missing the only woman I'll ever love until the day I die." He ran his hands up and down her back. "I love you," he said again.

She swallowed. "It's not just sex?"

A chuckle from Teddy made them both stop and look his way. "A man doesn't chase a woman down Main Street and declare his love in front of half the town just for sex,'' he said, grinning. ''I think he means it.''

''I'll shout it loud enough for every one of them to hear if you want me to,'' he told her.

''No,'' she said hastily.

''Then say yes.'' He pressed a kiss to her forehead, overcome with the need to make her see how much he needed her.

''Yes.'' Her voice was a whisper.

Relief nearly made his knees buckle. ''You'll marry me?''

''Yes,'' she said again. She pulled back enough to see his face, and a dawning radiance broke through the sadness that had shrouded her features. ''Yes!''

''All right!'' said Teddy.

Garrett barely heard him. All his attention was focused on Ana as he hauled her off her feet and swung her in a wide circle on the sidewalk. Clapping and laughter erupted from the people along the street. Her arms wound around his neck and he held her closely against him as he halted, searching for her mouth and kissing her deeply.

''I love you,'' he said. ''And you're marrying me. Anything else is negotiable.''

''Children?'' she asked in a hopeful tone.

''As long as they don't come in pairs like his.'' He jerked his head in Teddy's direction. Then the import of their words hit him. ''Grandchildren,'' he murmured. ''Our children will be Robin's grandchildren.''

Ana's eyes were bright with tears, but she was

smiling. "Nothing would have made him happier."
Then she shook her head. "That old matchmaker."

"Matchmaker? More like manipulator," Garrett
said, chuckling. "He knew I wouldn't be able to resist
you any more than he could have your mother." He
drew her close for another kiss. "Let's go home and
make wedding plans."

"All right." She trailed a finger over his lips and
his blood heated at the look in her eyes. "Let's go
home."

*   *   *   *   *

Celebrate 100 years of pure reading pleasure with Mills & Boon®

To mark our centenary, each month we're publishing a special 100th Birthday Edition. These celebratory editions are packed with extra features and include a FREE bonus story.

Plus, starting in February you'll have the chance to enter a fabulous monthly prize draw. See 100th Birthday Edition books for details.

Now that's worth celebrating!

15th February 2008

Raintree: Inferno by Linda Howard
Includes FREE bonus story Loving Evangeline
A double dose of Linda Howard's heady mix of passion and adventure

4th April 2008

The Guardian's Forbidden Mistress by Miranda Lee
Includes FREE bonus story The Magnate's Mistress
Two glamorous and sensual reads from favourite author Miranda Lee!

2nd May 2008

The Last Rake in London by Nicola Cornick
Includes FREE bonus story The Notorious Lord
Lose yourself in two tales of high society and rakish seduction!

Look for Mills & Boon 100th Birthday Editions at your favourite bookseller or visit
www.millsandboon.co.uk

0108/CENTENARY_2-IN-1

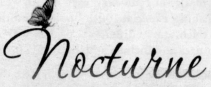